Unlikely Twins

by
Thomas L. Eckert

Order this book online at www.trafford.com
or email orders@trafford.com

Most Trafford titles are also available at major online book retailers.

Note for Librarians: A cataloguing record for this book is available from Library and Archives Canada at www.collectionscanada.ca/amicus/index-e.html

Printed in Victoria, BC, Canada.

ISBN: 9781-4269-0952-8

We at Trafford believe that it is the responsibility of us all, as both individuals and corporations, to make choices that are environmentally and socially sound. You, in turn, are supporting this responsible conduct each time you purchase a Trafford book, or make use of our publishing services. To find out how you are helping, please visit www.trafford.com/responsiblepublishing.html

Our mission is to efficiently provide the world's finest, most comprehensive book publishing service, enabling every author to experience success. To find out how to publish your book, your way, and have it available worldwide, visit us online at www.trafford.com

www.trafford.com

North America & international
toll-free: 1 888 232 4444 (USA & Canada)
phone: 250 383 6864 ♦ fax: 250 383 6804 ♦ email: info@trafford.com

10 9 8 7 6 5 4 3 2 1

**UNLIKELY TWINS is a sequel to Thomas L. Eckert's
LETHAL TWINS, published in 2004 by Xlibris Corp, with ISBN Nos.
1-4134-5517-4 (hardcover) and 4134-5516-6 (paperback).**

1

It was déjà vu that brought Tom Mueller back to his hometown of Toledo, Ohio. At least this time there wasn't snow and ice to contend with – yet. The late fall chill was in the air, and most of the leaves had already fallen, causing homeowners fits as they tried to rake them to the curbs.

This visit was a crusher. Tom had returned for the funeral of his mother, his muse and great friend. Her death came on the heels of two other funerals, those of his father and his beloved Sheila Bond, a fellow agent at the Central Intelligence Agency. But his mother's passing was especially poignant, more so considering that she had longed for a grandchild and had hoped in vain that either Tom or his late twin brother Fred would father one before her death.

Coming back to Toledo also tweaked other emotions, most especially concerning Fred. Growing up, they were as unlike as identical twins could be. Tom forged a career with the U.S. Government, first as a sniper with the Marines during the Korean War and later as a CIA agent in Langley, Va., on the trail of drug smugglers. Fred, meanwhile, had taken an opposite path, and one that also led to lethal consequences: He became involved in the lucrative life of a drug lord, falling under the spell of a well-connected mobster in Manhattan. Tragically for Tom, his twin brother's life on the other side of the law ended horribly: He died in an explosion and fire aboard a yacht carrying a major cargo of marijuana.

Needless to say, the twins' paths up until then crossed in ways neither of them could have anticipated, and the intersection of their fates was much on Tom's mind as he prepared for his mother's funeral. For one thing, he was having trouble reconciling the guilt he felt over what role he may have played in Fred's demise. During many long, sleepless nights, Tom was tormented by thoughts such as, "Should I have looked after him more, offered protection, taken him under my wing?"

After Korean combat with the Marines and a CIA sniper mission in Colombia, Tom found himself still with the CIA as a recruiter and trainer of new agents, most of them fresh from college. But others were cherry-picked from different branches of the service, including helicopter pilots and those with experience flying smaller fixed-wing aircraft. He also trained applicants on the firing range before they were shipped off to parts unknown.

With such a grueling schedule, Tom Mueller's best friends pretty much could be counted on two fingers. One of them was Leo, a 260-pound mastiff whose loyalty, demeanor, and canine instincts seemed to suggest some sort of innate human intelligence. The other was Felix Santana, Tom's partner in many dangerous intrigues over the years. With the CIA's permission, Tom was allowed to take Leo as an escort wherever he went as he performed his recruiting and training duties. As coincidence would have it, Felix himself, a little guy with a big laugh and a lusty taste for beer, showed up out of the blue, footloose and ready to give Tom a hand wherever his work at the CIA took him. In the company of these two great friends, one human and one almost so, Tom was as happy as could be expected considering the deaths that besieged his family. It was Felix who witnessed the explosion and raging fire on the yacht in which Tom's twin brother died, and it was Felix who also knew about the strange box that Fred had sent to his mother's house in Toledo before his fiery demise.

The solid wood box, which came wrapped in shipping paper, sported an intricate locking mechanism and a note of instructions to Tom taped to the top.

"This is but a sample of what awaits you at the enclosed New York City address," Fred's note read. "Tom, you and Mom are co-beneficiaries of the $25,000 insurance policy contained herein if I have passed on. You will also notice that its value doubles in case of accidental death. The policy is paid-up and is part of my estate you and Mom will share as a small atonement for my insufficiencies as a brother and son. Bro, when you go to the building I lease in New York, follow the enclosed instructions carefully."

The note continued: "The ring of keys in this box will give you entrance to my place, as well as to property I own in Key Largo, Florida. Do with that what you please, for I have considerable equity in that property. Also enclosed are names and telephone numbers of 'specialists' who will assist you."

Tom shuddered, trying but failing to conceal his nervousness. Questions raced through his mind: What telepathy had prompted Fred to ship this package to Toledo at this time? What preconceived thoughts of personal disaster might he have had? Why exactly would he have made it a point to double the value of his insurance policy in case of accidental death? What "specialists" was he referring to?

The questions only made things more muddled, but one thing seemed certain: Big trouble, with possibly lethal consequences, lay ahead for Tom and Felix and Leo.

2

When Tom opened the lid of the box, holding his breath, he could hardly believe his eyes. Under another package of instructions , the insurance policy, and other papers which he sat aside for later study, were row upon row of neatly aligned plastic envelopes containing every variety of gemstone imaginable. Each was labeled. diamond, emerald, sapphire, ruby etc. Inside each envelope under the gem was approximate carat weight and grade of the stone.

Tom was only familiar with emeralds, and his find on the mission to Colombia of the gigantic emerald that was still at the jewelry store in New Orleans was his only experience in the lapidary field. How in God's name had Fred accumulated this treasure trove?

Tom carefully passed the box to Felix then picked up the papers he'd set aside. The deed to the Key Largo property, the insurance policy with double indemnity for accidental death, and a further directive on the New York computer-sales business that his twin was operating. This sheaf of papers he now studied while Felix was sputtering in English and Spanish over the contents of the box.

Tom had always been a quick study, yet he had to read through Fred's neat handwritten missive twice before he could come to grips with the extraordinary lengths Fred had gone to conceal his find, and the exceptional sleuthing he'd done in discovering the combination of the hidden wall safe. In some ways Tom hardly recognized his own sibling, at least he never realized to what depths Fred would go in pursuing his goals – legal or not. Tom looked over at Felix.

"I think it would benefit me to rearrange my schedule for a trip to New York City," he said. "My brother also briefly mentioned a girl named Lila Colozzi who was employed during the shop's makeover and also assisted in the remodeling of the Key Largo property."

Felix retrieved two more beers from the refrigerator, handing Tom one along with the box of jewels. "Sounds ta' me like she might have been more than just an employee, amigo. How often do ya' hear of bosses takin' the hired help ta' the sunny south on business trips to remodel a private residence? Ya' probably oughta talk with her if an' when ya' go ta' NYC, heh, heh, heh."

Tom knew he had some vacation time on the books. He'd only taken the few days for his mother's funeral and although the trip up to New York City was necessary he was loathe to take time away from the range until this particular group of trainees finished. Something was stirring in his mind concerning Rocky Newbole, one of the trainees, a fellow large enough to wear size 16EEEE shoes. It was slow in coming yet Tom knew from past experience if he didn't dwell on it , the idea or thought would surface by itself.

"One more beer, Felix, then it's sack time for me. You know where your room is so you can stay up or whatever – suit yourself."

Leo was getting antsy, and Tom knew what that indicated so he let him out to the back yard for his nightly constitutional, which the mastiff accomplished without any nonsense. He returned to the door within two minutes ready to settle in for the night, always alert for any uncommon contingency that could upset the norm. Tom quickly dropped off from the mental exertions of the long day, aware that Leo on the floor next to the bed would warn him of any possible threat during the night.

The answer to the thoughts on Newbole struck Tom with such clarity he was instantly awake sitting up in the bed. Tom's sudden movement caused Leo to rise to his feet instantly, his large head even with Tom's elbow and swiveling to all quandrants of the room as though fearful he had missed something which had caused his master's anxiety. Tom absentmindedly scratched behind the dog's ears to calm his fears. "It's nothing, Leo, just a thought that woke me. A possible solution to tie up what has been on my mind since earlier today." He was rewarded for scratching behind Leo's ears by the usual sloppy kiss from the dog's large tongue.

Tom turned on the bedside lamp to notice the time was 4:45 A.M. Might as well get up and put on some coffee, he thought. The mastiff padded softly behind as Tom entered the kitchen and sat waiting patiently for his meal. The ritual never varied. Then Tom would let Leo out for his morning constitutional. He knew the dog needed some alone time to pursue his doggy business, preserving his personal territory from any intruding critters. He would spend up to a half hour every morning following through with that procedure, returning to the back door when he was satisfied.

"Isn't it about time ya' find a swingin' door for him amigo? It would save ya' from wearin' out yer' knees gettin' up for him every time he wanted ta' go out, heh, heh, heh."

"Didn't know you were up Felix. Did he make too much noise out here?"

"Naw, I smelled the coffee. I've had enough sleep anyway. What kind of wood and hardware have ya' got stashed around here?"

"Why? Don't tell me you're a carpenter too among all your other accomplishments."

"Fair ta' middlin' heh, heh, heh. Tell ya' what, let me look around after I have my coffee and whatever I can't find we can buy after the stores are open or do ya' have ta' work Saturdays too."

"It just so happens I'm off this weekend. I have alternate weekends. So if you think you can do this, it will save me a call to an outside contractor."

"Lemme look around an see what ya' got. Ta' begin with have ya' got a tape measure?"

"I think the only measuring thing around here is a yardstick and I'll have to hunt for that."

"Any kind of tools at all?"

"You're talking me right out of this, Felix. What do you think this is a hardware store?"

"Don't get up tight amigo, I'll make do with what I can find. Ya' just keep Leo out of the way until I have a template made." Felix disappeared on his search for materials.

"What do you think Leo, can he do it or should we just forget the whole thing? It's not like we can't afford a contractor for the job you know. Leo lumbered over putting his massive head in Toms lap. Tom scratched behind his ears and received his usual reward. "Don't know how I could cope without you big fellow, you make my entire existence worthwhile. Let's go outside out of his way." Leo knew the word 'outside' well enough and made a beeline for the door but looked over his shoulder as he went to see if Tom was following.

Once outside they broke into their usual exercise trot, Tom leading. Man and dog made one circuit of their usual route when for some unknown reason Leo pulled to a sudden stop staring fixedly at a sedan parked where nothing had been earlier. Tom led by five yards when he heard that low growl, Leo's warning sound. He quickly turned back toward the dog who was head down, tail rigid, his most threatening posture. Tom moved back beside him. Leo was now silent but quivering. "What is it boy?" Tom whispered. "What has drawn your attention?"

Tom knew danger lurked close by and that Leo somehow sensed, a situation not to be taken lightly. He reached for his ever-present snub-nose .38 revolver holding it at the ready, safety off. It was then he noticed the dark sedan parked at an unusual angle on the other side of the road. He had been so deep in thought he would have jogged right by it not paying it anymore than a cursory glance. Because of his position, Tom couldn't tell if the car held any occupants yet it had to in order to warrant Leo's reaction.

Tom saw the muzzle flash before he heard the weapons report and immediately dropped to the ground beside Leo. It didn't help that he was wearing his old light Ohio State jacket. He stood out like a beacon for the shooter to aim at. The second shot kicked up dirt not a foot from his head. Tom rolled to his left and motioned Leo to crawl back the way they'd come with hand signals. He certainly didn't want his valuable dog to get hit, but Leo ignored the signals – he had his own agenda planned and it didn't include leaving his good friend in danger even to save his on hide.

There was no mistaking who the shooter was targeting, the only questions were who and why? Tom didn't take any longer to mull the problem over. He snapped off a shot at the car door below the window being used to give the shooter something to worry about. He didn't expect to hit anyone, just wanted to let the party know he wasn't defenseless.

The shots alerted a couple of residents who turned on their porch lights adding further illumination to the scene. Tom hoped they stayed inside but called the police.

Tom looked around for Leo, he'd lost track of him in the last minute or so. The mastiff had crawled or scampered forward to where he was almost beyond the sedan, apparently unnoticed. For the life of him Tom couldn't understand what his disobedient dog had in mind.

He didn't have time to consider it further as another round hissed over his head smacking something metallic to his rear. Tom was ready to return fire when the sedan's engine started. The shooter was ready to flee. But Leo had a different idea. At full speed he raced toward the car, the last ten feet he was airborne. He hit the now closed driver's side window with the velocity of a cannon round going through it, back to his rear haunches. A God-awful scream shattered the now quiet street so that Tom could hear the approach of wailing police car sirens. Flashing red lights bounced off homes and trees.

Tom could see Leo's rear legs scrambling on the outside of the now-stationary car as he ran toward it. He could also hear high garbled screams coming from the car's interior. Obviously Leo had the shooter. He pulled up beside Leo just as the first squad car pulled into the street behind him, rolling to a stop. Tom wasn't concerned by their presence, his main worry was that Leo might be cut or otherwise injured from his leap through the window. There was no possibility of extracting Leo by himself, the dog weighed too much for Tom to handle alone.

Tom looked back to two policemen standing by their squad car with guns drawn.

"How about some help here? I can't manage my dog alone."

"Who are you? We received a call for shots fired."

"I'm a federal agent. I'll show you my picture identification after you assist me."

The two patrolmen exchanged glances like they didn't believe Tom for a minute. "Step away from the car please and raise your hands where we can see them." They advanced on Tom cautiously when a voice behind them said, "You guys don't listen so good do ya' ". And there appeared Felix who had been alerted by the sirens and his amigo's' prolonged absence. "You guys step aside. This man is a federal agent like me so if you're not gonna' help him, get outta' the way so I can." You'd have thought their station commander had ordered them to cease and desist. When Felix took command with his authoritative voice interspersed with Spanish slang and split infinities he could not only demand and get obedience but utterly confuse those he was talking to. He got between Tom and the patrolmen and took the situation in with one glance.

"Hold on to his rear legs while I try ta' ease him out."

"I don't know if he's cut or not, but the way he dove through that window he's undoubtedly hurt in some way."

"Who is that guy and why was he firin' at ya'?"

"I don't know that either – yet. I'll find that out next. C'mon Leo, let go of him and help us a little or do you want to sleep here the rest of the night?" The mastiff let out one last growl to the groveling person who was blubbering he needed medical attention for his shoulder. Felix yelled at the policemen, "Bring me a blanket, right now." He was immediately accommodated. "An' call an ambulance while yer' at it."

Felix handed Tom the blanket. "Put this under his stomach so we can slide him out when I lever him up." Felix stooped and slid under Leo's hind quarters using some tricky maneuver to fast to follow raised Leo off the window ledge. "Now amigo", he grunted. Slicker than snot, Leo began sliding out. When he was lowered to the ground he rewarded Felix with a sloppy kiss and sat by his side. "Don't give me that, ya' overgrown cocker spaniel", and he grinned while wiping a combination of blood and saliva from his face and scratched behind Leo's ears.

Tom had the door opened now and for the first time had a look at the shooter. "What the hell do you think you're doing, Hoogeman? You are in trouble."

Hoogeman, a recruit who had given Tom some disciplinary problems at the firing range, looked over at Tom and in a belligerent tone said, "You're the reason I was cashiered from the training group at the range when you and that beast that attacked me."

"From your exhibition of marksmanship here tonight, if your attempt at picking me off was any demonstration of your prowess with a rifle, it's quite evident you hadn't learned much in your courses," Tom said. "Not only is it against the law to use a firearm in such a manner, endangering innocent citizens, but you will be charged with attempted murder. As far as Leo attacking you, that can be proven as self defense in protecting me, and you're damn lucky he didn't rip your head off instead of just nipping your shoulder. Now get out of that car before I drag you out. I've had about enough of your insolence."

As an ambulance roared up, Felix led the now-docile patrolmen to the car where they heard the last of Mueller's statement. They promptly placed the perpetrator under arrest, confiscated his rifle, and escorted him to the ambulance, where one officer climbed in with him for the trip to a hospital. His partner called a tow for the car, then started his vehicle and went the way of the ambulance.

Leo sat right where he'd been placed when extracted from the car. He looked at Tom with a steady gaze that asked a question, "Did I do good?" Tom met his gaze and nodded. That's how close the two had become, where they could practically read each others minds. Tom reached down and scratched behind Leo's ears. The long tongue dropped out and Tom could swear the dog was grinning. OK, let's go home boy, we've had enough excitement for one day." Leo swiveled and plodded along at his side. Tom knew he should find some special treat for his protector as a reward when they arrived.

3

Tom notified his boss, Alf McHenry, he was taking a few vacation days to go to New York City on personal business but might be able to produce some Agency business at the same time.

"Keep us apprised of your location at all times, Tom, so if you need backup we can provide it," McHenry reminded him. "You understand vacation or not you are always on call and after that debacle near your home in Franklin Park you are on more than one hit list. You are too valuable to us to be taken out by some Mafia enforcer."

"I'm taking Felix with me to keep me out of trouble."

"Why?"

"Why, what?"

"Don't be obtuse this late in our relationship, Mr. Mueller. It doesn't become you."

Tom realized he was treading on dangerous ground, so he quickly changed tack, not exactly revealing his itinerary but inferring that more of his pursuits were agency related than personal.

"Are you taking the dog, Tom?" The change in names used by McHenry indicated that he was becoming less suspicious of Tom's motives and was really concerned for his safety.

"Where I go, Leo goes, sir. He knows how to behave unless highly provoked or I am threatened with bodily harm. That also goes for Felix, who Leo considers part of the family."

"I've heard he is a very smart dog, and quite large, which brings up my next question. How are the three of you going to get there and where will you stay? I won't ask how Mr. Santana joined up with you."

"When I attended my Mom's funeral in Toledo and made the arrangements for selling the house and her possessions, I discovered an unopened parcel addressed to me among her belongings that were from my deceased twin brother. It included the address of a business he owned, with living quarters above. We'll stay there."

"Just so we know where you are, Tom. Believe me it's important."

"Yes sir, I will."

Felix, silent until Tom finished his conversation with the boss, finally said, "Other than checkin' out your brother's business what exactly are your intentions amigo? I mean how deeply do ya' intend ta' get involved in the New York City underworld with just the three of us?"

"That depends strictly on what I learn from that girl Lila Colozzi who Fred was implicated with. If she turns out to be just another pretty face without any knowledge of the mob's dealings in the drug trade, we'll just shut down Fred's business and turn over any names we run across to the proper authorities. Does that quiet your anxieties?"

"Yeah, just wonderin' how long this is gonna' take is all."

Leo rose from his supine position and after looking at Tom nonchalantly plodded over to where Felix was sitting lying that massive head in his lap.

"What do you want, ya' big galoot? as if I didn't know. Careful ya' don't spill my beer." Leo's big tail started wagging in anticipation of the ear scratching he knew he'd get. Felix looked over at Tom. "What's with your dog ,amigo?"

"Show him a little affection, partner. He just might save your butt someday. He remembers how you extracted him from that broken car window of that Hoogeman character and this is his way of showing his appreciation. Humor him."

Tom returned with a dried beef stick, still chuckling, which he used to lure Leo down from the chair. "That's another word Leo has learned since you've last seen him and it always attains predictable results." He handed Leo the beef stick which the dog began worrying at his feet. "There are always plenty of these beef sticks hidden in the upper kitchen cabinets out of his reach, because if he knew where they were he'd probably figure out some way to get at them while I was otherwise occupied."

"Lemme use your car and I'll go to a hardware and pick out what's needed to fix that door so he can get in and out at will. While I'm gone ya' can explain ta' him it'll be a present from his Uncle Felix, heh,heh."

"Oh, explanations won't be necessary partner. He'll pick up your scent from the construction and automatically understand. Trust me on that."

When Felix finally left on his shopping trip Tom started to pack a suitcase with the clothes he thought would be appropriate for his foray against the New York City underworld, careful to include his dark light-weight suit he purchased at the airport. He also included a box of .38 caliber slugs for the Cobra. He didn't intend to be defenseless while mingling with Mafia enforcers despite having Leo and Felix for back-up. Leo would always be within sight of him he knew, but Felix was another matter entirely. He could get side-tracked at any time and for any number of reasons.

Tom and Leo took an extended walk-trot-walk and were gone almost two hours. By the time they returned to the house they found Felix ensconced in a chair, his feet up on a chair he'd brought from the kitchen, beer in hand. He was reading a week old newspaper, naturally turned to the sports section.

"Where ya' been? I thought maybe ya'd decided to walk to New York City an' leave poor old Felix behind." Leo went out to the kitchen where they could hear him noisily lapping water from his bowl.

"What are you doing, taking a rest break from your undertaking?" "Aw I thought ya' knew me better than that amigo. The job's finished. Go take a look an' bring me another beer when ya' come back. That was thirsty work."

Tom returned with the beer, laughing to himself. "Leo's one smart dog. He figured your trapdoor out by himself. He's outside checking his territory for miscreants already."

4

It was a slow trip to New York City because several pit stops were made to water and let Leo do his duty. They arrived in Manhattan shortly after dawn then went directly to Fred's so-called computer business. Felix slept most of the way and Leo only occasionally put his head over the front seat to have his ears scratched before returning to his blanket. So Tom had plenty of time to think over his plan of action. Before leaving Franklin Park he had put the box containing the gem stones in his safety deposit box only bringing the directions to Fred's shop, the keys to get in, and the directions for finding the hidden wall safe on the third floor and the larger concealed strongbox in the basement. What he wasn't prepared for was the opulence of the second and third floor living quarters. Fred couldn't live in both places. Who occupied the second floor? While Tom and Leo were investigating the third floor, Felix was nosing around below. Following the instructions, Tom found and pushed the camouflaged button. The door slid open revealing the combination lock. Tom dialed the numbers carefully and pressed the handle down. It opened silently showing two compartments. The lower was the larger and it contained about two dozen drawstring pouches of various size. Tom grabbed a handful and carried them over to the neatly made bed. Leo plodded in and sat watching his friend with that quizzical cock to his head he often got when trying to understand something. Tom opened one of the heavier pouches first and swore out loud when he saw the contents. A hand full of emeralds lay sparkling there. Tom knew emeralds after his find in Colombia. The largest, two carats then diminishing to about .750 of a carat. Other pouches held sapphires, rubies, and diamonds. Many diamonds. He had just returned the gems, took out the papers on the top shelf, closed the door, and pushed the concealed button when he heard Felix calling his name. Leo did too. The dog made a beeline for his voice, Tom following. Tom pulled up to a dead stop when he saw Leo turning his head in all directions trying to figure out where Felix had gone – there was no sign of the little man. He had vanished.

Tom called his name. "Felix, where are you?"

His partner answered at once. "You're not gonna' believe this, amigo." His voice sounded like it was emanating from behind the wall of the kitchen. Suddenly to Tom's left a portion of the wall swung out, and there stood Felix holding a double-barreled shotgun at the ready. "This place is like a fortress, with secret passageways from the basement ta' here, with enough weapons stashed throughout to withstand an assault unless they had a tank or bazooka. I'm tellin' ya' amigo, it's unreal. I don't know what your brother had in mind when he constructed all this but I can tell ya' what I think."

As soon as Felix entered the room Leo was all over him. "Lemme' alone, ya' overgrown cocker spaniel, Uncle Felix ain't got nuthin' for ya'."

"Leo, behave yourself. All right, Felix , what in your expert opinion do you think Fred had in mind for this place?"

"Well before I show ya' the proof let me lay this on ya'. Your brother went to an awfully big amount of expense ta' expect a return from simply sellin' computers. There's a huge safe in the basement that I'd bet holds some sort a' drugs and that ain't all. There's an escape hatch connected to the next building that if ya' didn't know was there you'd be hard pressed to locate. I'm tellin' ya' amigo, you're gonna' have ta' see this stuff to believe it."

Tom knew in his mind what Felix was alluding to was in the most part basically the truth. How else could Fred have amassed his wealth?, not only the jewels and Key Largo property, but the stock portfolio, insurance, and yacht. Fred was definitely involved in an illicit undertaking. It would warrant contacting Lila Colozzi forthwith.

"OK, partner, take me on tour of the secret parts of this building. There is little doubt in my mind that you are mostly right in your assumptions, so lead on, McDuff." Again he received the blank stare that Felix used when trying to come up with a suitable reply. "Oh, let's go, Felix."

It truly was amazing. How this inner hidden stairway with its branching passageways was ever built without anyone knowing was a marvel in itself. Not even counting on the cost, the sheer audacity of completing such a feat in a rented building was more than Tom would have attempted. Felix was right. At every twist and turn of the passageway another weapon was planted. Every model of firearm used by the armed forces today from pistols to semi-automatic rifles was present. And the huge safe in the basement, Tom wondered how they ever got it in. It was taller than he was and he couldn't reach both sides with his arms extended. It had a combination lock and Tom wondered if the papers in the wall safe contained the numbers? Surely Fred, as smart as he was , couldn't rely on his memory alone with all the other irons he had in the fire. He'd check when he returned upstairs and fessed up to Felix on the contents of the wall safe.

"I've seen enough, Felix, come on upstairs with me, I want to show you something."

"Don'tcha' want ta' see the slick escape door ta' the next building? It's really somethin'."

"Later, right now there's something more important."

"Muy Dios, Tom, ya' just keep gettin' richer and richer. Ya' didn't have ta' show me these ya' know."

"Yes I did. There was no point of having it on my conscience that I didn't disclose my resources to you. Now maybe you won't raise so much fuss when I decide to give you money or buy you something. That reminds me, I have to find a meat market to get you know who, you know what. Right, Leo?" The mastiff ambled over as he knew he would so he could have his ears scratched. Tom accommodated him with the usual reward given.

"Don't know about you, amigo, but I'm gettin' hungry and I could use a few beers too. Can't remember the last time I had a decent meal, how 'bout you?"

"Sometimes you have the same capabilities for reading my mind as our other friend there, not to mention any names. Meet you down in the showroom after I give him instructions for guarding the place. Make sure you're armed because where we are going anything might happen. I'll explain that in further detail on the way."

"Did Leo give ya' any argument 'bout stayin' behind?"

"He wasn't too thrilled about staying there alone, but I'll guarantee you one thing, nobody will break in while we're gone and get out in one piece. He'll take out his frustration on anyone he doesn't recognize. Now as to this restaurant we are headed for. It's supposedly owned by an uncle of Lila Colozzi, the girl that Fred was seeing. He is reputed to be highly connected in the Mafia, or whatever you want to call the underworld of organized criminals of New York City. Fred didn't disclose whether he was present all the time at Alfredo's Fine Foods or was an absentee owner. I would venture to guess the latter if he's that highly placed in the organization."

The restaurant was below street level where the entrance door was covered with fancy wrought iron. Upon entrance Tom was somewhat surprised that there was no odor of oregano or garlic-spiced tomato sauce which always lingered in Italian restaurants. They either had a great ventilation system or the place was being operated under a false guise despite the Italian name. Tom even detected the smell of fried fish which further discounted the nationality. The main dining room was half filled with mostly businessmen with a smattering of what appeared to be secretaries occupying a few tables. There was no bar along a wall but Tom noticed some variety of mixed drinks present and several pilsner glasses of beer spotted around. They grabbed a table along a wall, both looking over the patrons with suspicious glances. Two waitresses were hustling about refilling coffee cups and drink glasses. One was a tall redhead, the other a petite blonde with a pony tail. The redhead spotted them and brought menus.

"Would you gentlemen like something to drink while looking over our menus?" Felix answered as Tom knew he would. Ya' can bring us each two cans of Bud with cold glasses if ya' can find 'em, Miss." She disappeared through the swinging kitchen doors and was gone less than two minutes before returning with a tray bearing their order. While in the kitchen she mentioned to Lila that newcomers had seated themselves at a table in her section. The smaller man of the two is so ugly he's cute, and he's very suave in an odd sort of way. When I take their drink order to them and you have a spare minute look over to table six and you'll see what I mean."

"Oh, Gennie, you are impressed by every stray male that comes in here. I just don't know about you."

Lila had just finished filling a fresh pot of coffee from the urn and was compiling her food checks for distribution when her Uncle Ferdie, the owner of the establishment, entered from the kitchen proper. he was resplendently attired in a lightweight black suit, white shirt, and a subdued tie.

"You look pretty spiffy, Unc'. You going to an organization meeting or something?"

"Exactly, my dear. Why else would I have a tie on choking me like this? That brings up another point I've been meaning to talk to you about. How long are you going to moon over that Fred fellow you were so enamored with? I hate to see you waste away like a widow when you're still so young."

"Uncle Ferdie, I'm pretty busy right now. Can't we discuss this another time?"

"I'm sorry, my dear. It was rather thoughtless of me. You go about your business and we will talk later, maybe at home."

Lila gave him a quick peck on the cheek then gathered up the food checks in one hand, the coffee pot in the other, and headed out the door, her thoughts still on her lover, Fred Mueller. God, she missed him so. It seemed like he had disappeared into thin air and she didn't know where to go or who to contact to solve the problem. And not just him, his trusted friend Jocko Jordan was missing too. Lila was so distracted by her inner thoughts it would take a shock of electricity to bring her back to reality. She went about her routine of refilling an occasional coffee and distributing checks in her usual pleasant manner, working her way to the inner edge of her table territory where she got the shock that would change her life. Gennie was standing at a table talking to a customer and there – there sat Fred Mueller staring straight into her eyes. The last thing she remembered was the room spinning as she hit the floor, the coffee pot shattering as it fell from her hand.

Tom and Felix were at the girls side like cats pouncing on prey, Tom rubbing her hands and Felix giving orders in his most authoritative manner. The surrounding crowd dispersed and a cold towel appeared as if by magic. Tom placed the towel on her forehead and continued rubbing her hands his thoughts returning to the apartment where he had done the same thing for Sheila when she was found injured. Lila was regaining consciousness and as her lovely eyes fluttered open she was looking directly into Tom's.

"Oh, Fred, I've missed you so much. Don't ever leave me again like that. I'd just die."

"No Lila, I'm Fred's twin brother. Are you feeling well enough to get up and sit here?"

"Where's Fred?"

"I'll explain all of that in good time. C'mon now sit over here at our table and drink some water."

As they guided her to their table Gennie was cleaning up the broken coffee pot mess. Patrons were leaving money on the tables as they left. "An' ya' say I've got a way with women. I've never had one swoon by just lookin' at me, amigo, heh, heh, heh."

By the time Lila had drunk two glasses of water some color was returning to her cheeks. She kept her gaze on Tom as if she was afraid he might disappear like her lover did.

"When are you off work?"

"Actually I'm off now, why?"

"Would you come with us to the computer store? My reasons are threefold. First I'd like to buy three raw T-bone or porterhouse steaks. Second, I'm sure there are personal belongings there you might want to take to your home. Third, we can have a long talk where all your questions will be answered and you might shed some light on a few matters for me. Agreed?"

"I'll get your steaks. Tell Gennie and the chef where I'm going and be back in a few minutes."

When Lila returned to the kitchen Felix piped up, "Not a very trustin' soul is she, amigo?"

It didn't take long to get to the store and there was very little conversation on the way. Tom couldn't imagine what thoughts were coursing through Lila's mind. Tom looked through the shop's front door window before inserting the key. He could just make out Leo toward the rear lying in his crouched position ready to spring forward and attack anyone who was foolish enough to enter. Tom had seen the mastiff assume that position many times.

"Felix, give me the largest steak and wait out here with Lila until you know who calms down enough to be sociable. He's probably a little frustrated by now. Lila had a quizzical expression on her face but held her tongue waiting to see what this was all about. What is this, I mean you two lured me over here on the pretense of picking up personal items and then I'm told to stand in the street while someone gets fed – raw steak yet. If he doesn't come back out in two minutes, I'm leaving, Fred's brother or not." Felix turned on the charm trying to stall her threat of leaving. He didn't know what Tom had in mind for the girl yet whatever the ploy, it wouldn't work if Lila was gone. She was strong-minded and on the verge of splitting when the shop door opened and his amigo reappeared.

"Sorry I took so long, folks, we're ready. It's show time. Lila, stick close to me when we go in and the only advice I'll give you is don't use the word yummie inside." He winked at Felix. It was all Felix could do to suppress his laughter as he followed them in.

Leo was lying on his stomach, his big front feet holding what was left of the large steak. He was gnawing furiously at the remnants, but his huge head came up when he spotted the person with his friend.

"Leo, if you're done gorging yourself come over here and meet this nice lady."

Leo rose effortlessly and slowly plodded his way toward them, his head swinging back and forth to keep them all in view. "Holy Mary mother of God, what is it?" Lila held Tom's arm in a vice grip.

"'It' is a pedigreed mastiff named Leo which was repayment for a favor I did for a client. He is my friend and associate along with Felix here. Besides that he is a free thinker with almost human feelings and invaluable as a protector . He has saved my life more than once."

During Tom's discourse the dog had positioned himself directly in front of Lila, who hadn't slackened her grip on Tom's arm in the least. Leo was staring at Lila , his long tongue hanging like a flag from his mouth, his stare mesmerizing her to the point where she was feeling as she had upon first looking at Tom in the restaurant such a short time ago.

"If you want immediate approval reach over slowly where he can see your hand is not threatening and scratch behind his ears."

"Are you kidding?"

"Not in the least. Try it, he won't bite you , will you big guy?"

Lila had to release her grip on Tom's arm to free both of them and follow his instructions – which she did reluctantly. When she reached his ears she was amazed at how soft his fur felt, almost silken. Lila kept her fingernails fairly short, contrary to the fashion of the times, both for cleanliness and to facilitate her work at the restaurant. Leo's reaction to her attention was immediate and predictable. He almost purred his pleasure and before Lila could step back Leo gave her one of his sloppy kisses much to the delight of Tom and Felix. At first she was horrified but the men's laughter was contagious and she soon joined in.

You have now been officially baptized and have a friend for life, isn't that right Leo?"

His fun over for the moment, Leo returned to what was left of his steak and before too long was stretched out taking a nap. Tom decided now that the frivolity was over it was time to get down to business with Lila under the guise of picking up any of the personal belongs she may have left here. They snapped the lights off and took the inner rear stairs to the third floor being careful to leave doors open to allow Leo free passage when he decided to join them. The dog never left him out of his sight for long.

Tom took Lila into what used to be Fred's office, sat her down across from the desk and began to explain what he knew of Fred's death and who was actually responsible for it. Not far into the tale he saw that Lila had that glassy-eyed stare that preceded shock. Tom told himself to back off. He didn't want her passing out again, here. Felix was out in the kitchen cooking something, Tom could smell the aroma from where he sat. Another one of Felix's hidden talents. Leo must have smelled it too because he wandered in, took a look to see where Tom was, then headed for the kitchen.

"You must be hungry, Lila, and the master chef is cooking something that will certainly be gourmet." Now they could both hear Felix good naturedly scolding Leo for crowding him while he was at work. "Gimme' some room, ya' overgrown cocker spaniel ya'. Ya' might get some when I'm done so move it!

Tom told Lila to gather anything up that was hers and bring it here. This was to keep her mind occupied and a purpose to keep her body in motion. He was no psychologist but he felt deep down inside he should help the troubled girl. While she was thus occupied he joined Felix in the kitchen.

"Leo, quit pestering Uncle Felix and go lay down, you've eaten enough stuff already today to spoil your dinner. Then instead of a walk later I'll take you down to the basement where you can do your duty." As an aside Tom told Felix, "While I'm there I'll check the contents of that big safe, partner. The combination was in among Fred's papers."

"Ya' want me ta' go along?"

"No, you keep an eye on Lila to see what she has collected, then we'll call her a cab to get here home. Does that sound reasonable to you?"

"Whatever ya' say, amigo."

While Tom was attending to the big Mosler, Leo was sniffing around looking for a likely spot to make his deposits. He chose a beam supporting part of the overhead and let fly. Tom was far enough away that he couldn't smell anything because he was concentrating on the recalcitrant combination which was touchy to say the least. On the fifth try it finally let loose and when he pushed the handle down and pulled.

One huge door swung silently open. Felix was right when he assumed the hidden monster held some sort of drugs. There were steel shelves spaced in an irregular pattern, some spaced about a foot apart and others maybe two feet. There were packages of marijuana about two kilos in weight, then he saw a double-wrapped plastic bag of white powder he would bet was cocaine – Felix would know. Tom closed the safe door but didn't spin the combination and started for the stairs. That was when the full stench of Leo's bowel movement hit him like a hammer blow. "It wasn't such a good idea to let you use this closed-in room for your toilet boy. After this is cleaned up, we're going to use some air freshener in here. You can use vacant lots or even the roof from now until we vacate the premises. The way things are shaping up, God only knows how long that will be. So let's go upstairs and join Felix and Lila."

When they reached the third floor, Felix and Lila were just finishing what Felix had put together. They were talking just as if they had known each other for years instead of hours. Felix had that effect on women of any age. Leo sauntered right over to the little table and sat watching their every move. This was his usual procedure because he wouldn't demean himself by begging. The next occurrence surprised both men. Lila hand-fed Leo a morsel off her plate. She daintily put the thumb-sized tidbit in front of his nose where he could smell it, and much to Leo's credit he fastidiously picked it from between her fingers without grazing her skin. "Good boy, Leo", she cooed. Quite a change from the girl who less than two hours ago was deathly afraid to be in the same room with the animal.

Leo must have detected some sound that they were unaware of for he was off like a shot and we could hear him thumping down the stairs. Tom had seen him move that fast many time when he thought someone or something was encroaching his territory. Then Felix was right behind him moving at his own breakneck speed. Tom hand signaled Lila to stay put and followed. He was between the second and first floors when he heard the commotion below. It was unmistakably some sort of confrontation between Felix, Leo, and an unknown party.

When Tom entered the showroom from the rear stairs he saw what caused Leo's quick reaction. He and Felix had a man up against the wall to the left of the front door. The door itself wasn't damaged so he must have used a key to enter. Brilliant deduction, Sherlock, Tom thought to himself, but who is he?

"Ahhh ,Mr. Mueller would you please call off this ruffian and his beast. I'm Mr. Levine from the rental agency. Don't you remember me?"

The man mistook Tom for his twin so Tom didn't correct the misconception. "Of course, Mr. Levine, but what brings you here? Leo, come!" The dog backed away from his quarry and sat by his friend continuing to watch Levine with the scrutiny of a watch dog – which he was.

"I was in the neighborhood so I decided to see if this property was still occupied. You are a year in arrears, you realize, and it's only because there were no offers from anyone to lease the place that the agency hasn't foreclosed before this."

"That was an oversight on my part, sir. There were a pair of deaths in my family separated by a short period, my brother and mother. With the handling of their estates and disposing of their property, the monthly checks were simply forgotten. If you will agree to it, I will write you a check for all the debt due and pay ahead for three months. Will that satisfy your agency?'

Tom thought Felix was going to explode while holding his hand over his mouth to avoid laughing out loud at his outrageous prevarications. Mr. Levine was flabbergasted for a different reason. He was certain Fred was going to default on the contract and was probably anxiously hoping to make a tidy profit from the furnishings – if he only knew. Levine stuttered his reply, "I, I, I'm certain it will be acceptable, Mr. Mueller."

"Then the check, or money order if you prefer will be mailed tomorrow morning."

"Oh, your check will be fine. We have to show a little trust too, hah, hah."

"Then I'll bid you good afternoon, Mr. Levine, and thank you for your understanding." Tom ushered him out the door, locked it and put the closed sign facing outward.

"Let's all go back upstairs and see what Lila is up to, besides we have to get her home pretty soon. When they reached the third floor Lila wasn't where Tom had left her. They looked around for a few minutes before Tom noticed the bathroom door was closed. "Lila are you in there?"

"Yes, but I'll be through in a few minutes. Wait for me in your bedroom. I want to talk with you alone."

Tom told Felix to keep Leo with him for a little while because it seemed Lila was going to give him some of the information he was seeking. He didn't know how long it would take but she had emphasized alone. Tom was sitting on the bed staring at the hidden wall safe, deep in thought about how ingenious its design was, so he didn't notice that Lila had entered the bedroom until that sixth sense that had saved his bacon so many times alerted him of her presence behind him. Tom turned around to find her stark naked. Lila was absolutely gorgeous, and despite himself he felt a stirring in his loins. He could understand why Fred had been so captivated by this beauty, with a body like that. "Tom, please indulge me this once and make love to me." She placed her hands on his shoulders which brought her erect breasts to within inches of his face. Tom was only human after all with the normal sexual drive of any man his age and even though it had lain dormant since Sheila's death, with this sudden invitation he would be hard pressed to decline. His common sense warned him what giving in to this temptation might entail, yet the first contact of her skin to his sent an electric shock through his entire system that overrode his feeble objections. She felt like a cashmere sweater when next to him, warm and soft. So soft yet occupied with a passion that made Tom outdo even his younger escapades with the opposite sex.

"Oh, Tom", she gasped during a lull in the action, you're even better than your brother and I didn't believe anyone could top him. How am I ever going to explain you to my Uncle Ferdie? He didn't particularly like Fred but because your brother was so good to me 'Unc' put up with him. Just earlier today, he asked me how long I was going to stay dateless and that I was too young to act like a grieving widow."

"What makes you think you have to explain me to him?"

"Well he is my guardian and he'll certainly notice the change in my behavior and habits after working hours ... Wait a minute, you're not going to disappear from my life too are you? Not after this last hour. Oh Tom I couldn't stand it, a second time to boot."

5

Tom knew it wouldn't be long before he got a visit from her guardian, so he went about the business of placing weapons throughout the building. Felix had confirmed that indeed the white powder in the Mosler safe was cocaine and according to his testing had yet to be cut. When that process was completed he estimated the street value to be in excess of one hundred thousand dollars. Tom wondered how Fred had come by that lode. Did he use gemstones to purchase such a quantity? and from whom? All these questions to be answered and his only contact at the time was Lila. Really, despite himself , he was reluctant to become too involved with her. She was a gorgeous woman with the body of a goddess, yet her actual personality seemed somewhat fragile. Tom was unsure how far he could push her for information, or how far he could trust her for that matter. With all the weapons spotted around the building she could be a real threat if she was so inclined. The next day after Tom had sent Lila home in a cab after calming her down, sure enough, a representative of her Uncle Ferdie appeared in the showroom. Felix was in the basement cleaning up Leo's mess and trying to get the stink aerated. Tom and Leo were putzing around when the enforcer rapped on the glass. Leo was up and to one side of the door before Tom could open it. A quick appraisal was all Tom needed before opening the door. "Stay, Leo." The man was dressed in a dark suit despite the rising temperature and as soon as he opened his mouth Tom knew who and what he was.

"Da' Boss sent me to invite ya' to the restaurant for a confab."

"And who might the boss be?" Felix used that moment to arrive on scene. He was also a quick study and knew immediately who he was and from where he came." Ask the man in, amigo, so we can reply politely, heh, heh." Tom ignored the sarcasm and replied, "You tell your boss if he wants to discuss anything with me to come here with his entourage, and if I'm available we'll talk." The hood went inside his suit coat as if to draw a weapon but Leo circled around from behind his friend and nudged him aside, staring at the intruder with his mouth open showing his teeth. One look at the beast was enough for the hood and he froze. "What da' hell is this?"

"You don't want to find out the hard way I'm sure, so just return my answer to your boss."

When all three returned to the third floor Tom told Felix he was going to call McHenry for another body to assist them as the situation was heating up. "Nothin' we can't handle that I can see, amigo."

"Trust me a little here, partner, I know what I'm doing."

McHenry understood the predicament right away as Tom related his take on the events of the last thirty-six hours. "But why Mr. Newbole? I can have any number of our men from the New York office there in an hour. By the time we locate, brief, and transport Mr. Newbole it will be sometime late tomorrow before he can join you."

Tom explained his reasoning for wanting Rocky in particular rather than the agents from the local office. Not only would they avoid any leaks from the agents in place who he was certain would be recognized, but a new face among them would not arouse any suspicions despite his tremendous size. McHenry came around to Tom's thinking and understood since he was in charge at the site and they wanted to shut down that family of the Mafia which could also possibly affect the Brooklyn bunch he would be wise to give Tom his desires. Tom Mueller was the key figure to unlock the growing menace in the Big Apple.

Rocky Newbole arrived, via taxi, from the airport the following afternoon just as Tom and Felix were getting ready to leave the store to try another restaurant they knew of which was across the street from Grand Central Terminal. Tom knew about the place because one of his crew in Korea told everyone if they ever got to Manhattan, they should stop in because his father owned it. They would be hard pressed to pay for a beer or anything to eat for that matter. Of course, Tom had left the team earlier than the rest and had forgotten the invite. Now with Rocky there, Tom showed him where to stow his gear on the second floor before he called another cab to convey the three of them to Lexington and 43rd, the entrance to Grand Central Terminal. The restaurant simply named Voelker's was almost directly across the street from the old terminal, a busy thoroughfare full of cabs, buses, and delivery trucks of all sizes jockeying for stopping and turning rights. To further confuse the scene pedestrians were maneuvering for their own space in pursuing their destinations – a totally madhouse panorama. Mounted police were present trying to cite the more flagrant traffic flow violators and control the situation before anyone got hurt.

Tom noticed Rocky had a stoic expression on his face as though he was completely unconcerned with the mass confusion because he had experienced it many times before. Felix would flash one of his smirks whenever he made eye contact, as though he wanted to wade into the melee to control it his own way.

They walked into the place and Tom introduced himself to a counterman, who informed him he was Mr. Voelker. "Did you know my son was killed after you left the team? Tom had another burden to bear, as if he didn't have enough guilt up to this point. "I'm sorry to hear that Mr. Voelker."

Fritz Voelker turned out to be everything his son had bragged about. He worked his counter in a manner which would give credit to three men. There were forty-some stools running the length of the room and the behind counter space was arranged to utilize every inch. Two grills, one at each end, were manned by short-order cooks who were turning out plates of every variety of foods imaginable. Each grill was accompanied by two deep fryers and short counters which contained hooded stainless steel covers over condiments and salad ingredients. Fritz was constantly moving up and down the counter serving the food and keeping a running conversation going with each patron. From what Tom could overhear most of the verbal exchanges concerned the upcoming World Series of baseball with some spirited conversations throughout the room.

Tom's little group had to wait over ten minutes to find three stools empty side by side and as they were placing their orders, Felix, who was on the right side of Tom, half turned toward him and said, "Don't be too obvious, amigo, but check those three characters who just entered."

"I already spotted them, Mr. Santana," was Rocky's aside. "If I'm not mistaken Mr. Voelker is about to be robbed along with every other person in the place. Let them start to make their move and I'll handle the tall one while you choose between the remaining two. That OK with you, Mr. Mueller?"

Tom nodded, while thinking what complete idiots would attempt a daylight robbery in such crowded surroundings. They had to be desperate or first-timers. "There's probably a lookout posted outside to prevent anyone else coming in while the team is at work so when these three are subdued I'll go out and check. Maybe I can whistle up one of those mounted patrolmen while I'm at it. Here they go, Rocky."

The next few minutes were rapidly paced. The three would-be heisters had made no attempt to disguise themselves and they looked like young Chinamen or of some Asian extraction. The taller one was within an arm's length of Rocky and was in the process of drawing a weapon when the big man whirled on his stool and slammed his huge boot into the novice's knee while at the same time delivering an uppercut to the chin, which floored the man like a stone, with his pistol flying into the air. Tom lost track of Rocky's next move since he was occupied with the youngster toward the front of the room who had produced an automatic and was waving it in all directions, not realizing it wasn't cocked. Tom threw a running block reminiscent of some he had used at Page Stadium behind DeVilbiss High School. It still did the trick, as his man was bowled over and breathless laying on the floor. Now total pandemonium had broken out among the patrons most of whom had the good sense to also hit the floor. The few women in attendance were adding screams to the din. Tom dragged his would-be robber over to where Rocky was using a kitchen towel to tie his unconscious target to a stool base. Felix had the third youngster in some sort of wrist lock moving to join Rocky. Tom reversed course, heading for the front door. Outside he quickly found what he had suspected, almost knocking the lookout down as he was trying to enter to help his buddies. While wrestling him to the sidewalk his luck held, a horse-mounted patrolman was heading his way at full gallop dispersing the gawkers who always gathered at any disturbance that broke the monotony of their hum-drum lives. As he reached Tom, Fritz Voelker joined them from inside. He called the policeman by name and added, "You best call a paddy wagon, Mac; there are three more robbers being held inside by Mr. Mueller's two friends."

I'll use your phone inside if its all right, Fritz, that way the correct procedures will be implemented and I can start lining up eye witnesses for the detectives to question. The uniform does have a calming effect for your customers too. I'm sorry they will be detained here for awhile until all their names and addresses are recorded."

"What about your horse?"

"Don't worry about him, Fritz; it would take a tank to move him after I've given him his orders. These animals are highly trained for this type of situation. How was it Mr. Mueller and his two friends happened to be here when this folly was undertaken?"

"It's a long story, Mac, but I'll try to shorten it for you once you have the people settled down."

Tom had remained silent while Fritz and the patrolman were conversing and while the latter made his phone call for assistance he moved away to join Felix and Rocky. After seeing the big man in action he knew he had made the right decision in asking for him here to begin with. He would definitely be an asset for his team. He had an unshakeable demeanor , a rare commodity in someone his age. Like right now, he was sitting on a stool at the rear of the diner talking in a cool and collected manner to Felix who was first to see Tom's approach. "Never a dull moment around ya' amigo, heh, heh, heh. Maybe that Seal, Hullinger, had ya' pegged right after all, heh, heh."

6

The trio cabbed back to the store, after promising Fritz Voelker they would drop by his diner as often as possible. They arrived at dusk.

Leo was in a pout until presented with the two grill-fried steaks. He began working on them when they reached the third floor.

"Felix, why don't you familiarize Rocky with all the hidden passageways, the weapons available, the Mosler and exit to the next building. Leo will stay with me to keep out of your way."

"Right, amigo, and Rocky ya' better watch ya' don't bang yer' head where we're goin', heh, heh, heh." Rocky turned to Tom. "Is he always this jovial?"

"You don't want to be on the opposite side when he gets serious. That little man can pack a powerful punch when he's really riled." Tom winked at Felix.

"Ya' think I'm somethin'. I'll tell ya' who not ta' fool with. It's that overgrown cocker spaniel over there. He can kill ya' in the blink of an eye heh, heh, heh. C'mon, times-a-wastin!"

When they left the room, Tom turned toward Leo. "Did you hear Uncle Felix talking about you, boy?" The mastiff's large head came up from his meal upon hearing his name spoken. It was cocked to one side which indicated he was practically read his friend's mind. This always made Tom laugh. "Which reminds me, fellow, you're getting spoiled by all these steaks. Tomorrow we will have to buy more of your regular food before you turn up your nose at it."

Lila Colozzi was a devious woman, as a good many of them are. She had experienced a taste of the good life and all it cost her was sex, something a young female her age liked and needed. She had no intention of spending the rest of her life waiting tables, even if her Uncle did treat her well. She knew her countenance drew men to her with certainty like a magnetic force. So far she had picked winners – well, only one but she had her sights set on the next and she would go to any lengths to get and keep him. If he needed information about her Uncle Ferdie that she could provide, so be it. After all you were stuck with your relations but you could choose lovers and husbands. Her uncle wasn't going to live forever not with the real business he was in and who knew , he might even will her the brownstone when he passed on. She knew he had plenty of clout in his organization – look at the way he took care of that Brooklyn enforcer from another family who had threatened her. Yet for all her charms and wiliness she was still at a loss for the clinching stratagem. If Tom Mueller was as dedicated to his goals as she was to hers it might prove a stalemate and she had no intention of letting that happen.   Lila was quite vain, and she was certainly devious, too.

———

Tom awoke with a start and looked around the dark room as if trying to remember where he was. His sudden movement brought Leo to his feet. The dog was ever alert to his friend's position and since he never slept so soundly that a change in Tom's posture would escape his notice his huge head swiveled looking for the cause.

"It's all right, Leo, just another one of those recurring dreams of mine. They are more prevalent when I'm in unfamiliar surroundings. The dog went over to the bed and lay his head on the mattress. It seems Sheila spoiled me for sleeping alone. True confessions time, huh, boy? You won't rat on me will you?"

Tom would have sworn Leo shook his head. he was letting his imagination run away with him. Leo was as close to human as a dog could get, granted, but still ... Now that he was almost entirely awake Tom knew it was futile to lie back down so he hand-signaled Leo to follow him out on to the veranda. When they passed through the kitchen, there sat Felix.

"What's the matter, amigo, too hot ta' sleep?"

"No, just one of those recurrent dreams of mine. You'd think enough time had passed since we lost Sheila that sleeping alone wouldn't bother me any longer, but that's not the case. One frantic session with Lila convinced me that sleeping alone for the rest of my life can't be my lot." The more he dwelled on it the more Tom realized he was convincing himself. It was a condition similar to that which prompted him to contact McHenry after the Largo fiasco where Pepe Basquez made up the fable that the invaders of his father's property were actually gunning for Tom. It was that incident more than anything else that opened the breech of their former fellowship. Maybe that wasn't the right comparison but it was the only thought Tom had to work with at the moment.

"I hate to interrupt yer' deep thoughts, amigo, but ya' got that thousand-yard stare again. What sneaky scheme are ya' thinkin' up now or is it too brutal for my gentle ears? heh, heh, heh."

"Just thinking of the girl again, partner."

"Muy Dios, amigo, ya' know her background, how could ya' explain her ta' our superiors? There are many beautiful women all over the place. Why do ya' have to pick that one, or isn't that any of my business?"

"She is going to provide me with inside information about her uncle's organization that will hasten our dismantling of their family. Isn't that what we were sent up here for? Look at the situation through my eyes, Felix. You know without her assistance we wouldn't have a clue on how to penetrate that outfit. She was our contact, remember? What I do after we bring them down would be my private affair."

"Ya' know best amigo, I'd just hate ta' see ya' jeopardize your career is all."

Leo had been napping a few feet away while the two men were talking but suddenly rose to his feet, his massive head cocked to the side, listening to something only he could hear. Tom noticed his sudden movement and put his finger to his lips to silence any further comments from Felix, then pointed his fore finger toward the mastiff. Felix picked up the hand signal immediately and turned his head toward the dog. Leo was a split-second faster to head for the inner stairs then the two men were to rise and follow, Felix heading for the secret passageway picking up an automatic shotgun from its resting place as he passed through the hidden entry. Tom followed Leo's route almost colliding with Rocky at the second floor juncture. Rocky held a .45 automatic in his right hand which was practically hidden by his boxing-glove sized paw. The presence of that weapon attested to the seriousness he regarded from whatever he had heard from his one floor closer nearness to the situation. All Tom had was the five round Cobra for fire power. A street light lit up the forward portion of the showroom, where Tom could see Leo had pinned a thug to the floor. He had him by the arm between wrist and elbow and was shaking his head back and forth while standing on the man's chest. The hood was groveling around, screaming like a stuck pig. "Get this thing off me. Shoot it, for Chrissake."

That's all Tom needed to hear before he swung into action. But before he could reach the two, Rocky came down on the screamer with such suddenness the man didn't see it coming. One quick kick to the head with his 16EEEE boot, and the clown was out cold. Leo looked at his new friend just a second before releasing his grip and aiming for another hood who had a pistol drawn. He never got the chance to shoot. Felix appeared from his blind side, giving him a butt stroke to the head with his shotgun stock. That left one other intruder, but Leo and Rocky converged on him together. The hood dropped his gun and raised his hands in surrender. Tom called to Felix. "Go upstairs and phone for the police to report that we have the perps in custody.

The police took took the burglars away, and an hour later two men arrived who introduced themselves as Detective senior-grade Langlois and his partner, junior-grade McCauley. After producing proper identification they got to work. Langlois getting Tom's team's stories written down in a notebook he took from his suit coat pocket. Meanwhile McCauley, who had produced a Brownie camera with flash attachment, was snapping pictures of the front door damage, inside and out. Leo was well behaved throughout this commotion, laying like a beached whale toward the rear of the showroom. Tom glanced in his direction now and then to make sure the dog wasn't edging toward the detectives with some ulterior motive of his own he might be thinking up. Everyone had ignored him the last hour or so going about their business of cleaning some of the glass, and other debris from the front door that had been scattered on machines, counter tops and the like and Leo couldn't stand to be ignored too long, spoiled as he was. When detective McCauley was done with his picture taking he began nosing around the rest of the showroom. That was when the inevitable happened. Tom was just explaining to Langlois how they happened to subdue the burglars so readily when McCauley almost tripped over Leo. The diminutive detective let out a God-awful screech when the dog rose from his indolent pose, quickly gaining his full height. McCauley back-pedaled in an attempt to distance himself from what he imagined was a lion. Then Leo, thinking he had a new plaything began crowding the detective. Thankfully the man wasn't stupid enough to draw his sidearm because Leo would have immediately switched from his play mode to confrontation and acted accordingly.

Tom intervened. "Leo, come." The mastiff who had not let Tom out of his sight, obeyed the command at once and sat facing his friend which greatly amused Felix. He had a somewhat weird sense of humor anyway but Tom would rather see him laughing than in his hostile tempers. That you're bored you know." Felix piped up, "Yeah, ya' overgrown cocker spaniel, try pickin' on someone your own size for a change, heh, heh, heh. Now ya' better go apoligize to Mr.McCauley.

Scratch him behind his ears detective an' you'll have a friend for life." Leo looked from Tom to Felix and back again. "Go show him you're sorry Leo." Tom knew what Felix was up to but went along with the gag. Leo sauntered slowly to the detective who glanced at his partner for advice. Langlois nodded he should scratch the dog's ears. The smallish detective didn't have far to reach down to accomplish the task and since Leo stood still as a statue the man became bolder and using both hands. The only movement that showed the dog was enjoying his treat was the dropping open of his mouth with the long tongue dropping out. "Nice dog ", McCauley uttered as he started to back away. That was when Leo gave him his reward. The huge tongue lashed upward with force, saliva splattering its target – McCauley's face. Everyone cracked up, even the staid Newbole.

"All right Leo, that's enough entertainment for now. I'm certain Mr. McCauley knows you two are friends." "Heh, heh, heh" from Felix.

"Now if you two gentlemen are finished here we would like to shore up the shop door and get to bed. It's been a long day."

After the detectives were gone the three men cobbled up the door with materials taken from the basement. It wasn't pretty but it would suffice until the next day and proper repairs were undertaken by professionals. "Come on, Leo we'll go out on the roof where you can empty out before we hit the sack." The dog followed his friend obediently to the third floor and when Tom left him out Leo started sniffing around before finally finding a spot that suited him. Tom stood just inside the rear door where his thoughts returned to Lila. He was trying to figure out how he could keep seeing her without the rest of his team knowing. Using this place again was out of the question as was hers. He could certainly afford setting her up in an apartment on neutral ground. Tom decided at that moment he would discuss it with her tomorrow. She had lived here all of her life so she might know of a place now. Leo was sitting just outside the door waiting patiently to be let in. He sensed that his friend was thinking about something, something that might entail a part for himself. The dog was almost human after all comprehending his mortal counterparts with almost extra sensory perception. "All right, Leo, let's go to bed."

7

About nine-thirty the next morning Tom called the closest carpentry company listed in the phone book and made arrangements to have the front door fixed before noon. An estimator would be here within the hour. That done his next call was to Lila. She answered on the third ring. Rather than bring up his thoughts of the previous night he asked if she might accompany him to dinner tonight at any restaurant of her choice.

"I'd love to, Tom, I know just the place. I'll call a cab and pick you up at your place, say eight o'clock."

"No, just tell me where it is and I'll meet you there."

"It's called Broadway Joe's and most taxi drivers will know where it is. I'll meet you there about eight-fifteen. If you get there first ask for a banquette, OK?" "It's a date."

Now, Mr. Mueller, Lila thought, I've got you right where I want you. We'll see if you can withstand my charms any better than your brother could. I doubt it; after all you were twins. Lila called Alfredo's and made excuses for her evening shift then spent the rest of the time readying herself for the evening taking special care with her hair and skin. She put on a sheath dress which revealed almost every one of her attributes. It was a sure thing she'd get what her sights were set on.

Tom with his ulterior motive would be more than her match. He had already decided how he would play her. Yet when she walked into Broadway Joe's she was so alluring he forgot everything he had thought of the night before. Lila sat down next to him and immediately began rubbing his leg.

"I'm glad you got this banquette. This way we can sit closer." Her hand motion on his leg was irritating Tom. He couldn't concentrate on his game plan. Foreplay was fine but not in a public place where waitresses and bus boys could see and pass their gossip on to the rest of the help. Tom gently but firmly removed her hand. "Now is not the time for that, babe, later maybe."

"Oh you're just a spoilsport, Tom."

"Possibly, but there is something we have to discuss which could determine our future together, unless you're not interested in our future."

"I didn't mean to imply that I wasn't, if that's what you're thinking. Go ahead and lay it on me, Mr. Serious."

"Well, if you are as attracted to me as I am to you what would you say about renting a small apartment, say an efficiency type, somewhere between where you live and my shop. After what happened last night at my place it's obvious we can't use it, and you know why your place is out..."

Lila's eyes lit up when she thought what that could lead to.

"You know what I do for a living and why we're here to begin with so we don't have to go into that aspect of the situation. Since you're a native New Yorker you should have a better idea of where to look. What is needed is some form of phone code to contact each other at prescribed times, but that can be worked out between us after we find a place."

The dinner went quickly, the conversation entirely about what they planned to do when they found the suitable flat. The only interruption of that topic was when Lila who was daintily picking at her steak interjected a tidbit of gossip about restaurants. "I read an article in the Times about a place your brother and I had eaten at and liked in Florida. According to the news story the head chef of the Jumping Dolphin a popular, mainly seafood place in Miami Beach, had recently been arrested for causing a serious outbreak of ptomaine poisoning there by buying some tainted shrimp and letting its storage area temperature to rise above the freezing mark through negligence. Lucius Melchior, who would squeeze a nickel until it bled to make a profit had gone too far this time in his avaricious pursuit of profits. He was about to face some hard time where it was certain he would not be allowed to practice his trade among his fellow inmates."

"That's another topic I would prefer you wouldn't delve into Lila. Fred is gone and there is no use of your comparing the two of us. We were exact opposites in personalities even though we were identical in countenance."

"You certainly are laying down multiple rules for me to follow Tom. Are you trying to reshape my personality Because if you are you might be disappointed in the results."

"Not at all babe, you are who you are and nothing I can say or do can change that."

"One last reminiscence Tom then I'll stop. Fred was always calling me that, even when he was scolding me for some misdeed he imagined I'd committed. So don't tell me you weren't somewhat alike in personality."

"You got me there, babe." Tom realized he was treading on dangerous ground so he quickly changed the subject. "In the meantime when you finish your food what say we check into a good hotel where we can order from room service if we want anything to eat or drink before morning."

"Are you sure I meet your higher standards to be seen with you at a posh hotel?"

"Are you simply trying to start an argument or do you have an ulterior motive for this behavior of yours?" "I'm sorry, Tom, I guess I'm behaving like a juvenile. Lead on and I'll try to get my emotions under control, until we're in bed of course."

They entered the spacious lobby of the Waldorf Astoria at ten o'clock without luggage or reservations. They approached the concierge at the front desk, arm in arm like honeymooners. "May I help you sir?" "I hope so, we're in kind of a bind. We are from out of state and my brother was supposed to make reservations for us at the Essex; however when we tried to check in earlier we were informed they had no reservations in my name and were filled up, some convention or other", Tom lied glibly. "The manager there recommended you here. We have no idea where our luggage is and frankly we are both tired and could use a good nights sleep before trying to straighten out these screw-ups tomorrow."

"Where are you from, sir?" The man was eyeing Lila like she was some high-priced call girl not really believing Tom's story of woe. So then Tom played his trump card.

When Tom showed his pictured ID, the mans' demeanor took a complete reversal. "Yes, Mr. Mueller we can accommodate you." He punched the counter top bell and a bellboy appeared out of nowhere. "Show Mr. Mueller to room 1215."

"Not to complain already but do you have anything on a lower floor?"

This time there was no hesitation. He asked if 415 would be better. "That will be fine. Would you prefer I pay in advance?"

"That won't be necessary, sir."

When they entered the room and Tom had over-tipped the bellboy, Lila disappeared into the bathroom telling Tom to get undressed, she would be right out. Tom wasn't quite prepared for bed nor totally undressed yet when Lila returned. Their first tryst at the shop should have alerted Tom to how unorthodox her preliminaries to making love could be yet he was flabbergasted at the sight of her now. Her state of undress was sexier than if she had been completely naked. Tom could only stare at her completely speechless. Her lush breasts were brassiered but she had cut holes in the tips somehow, her distended nipples protruding, making them all the more appetizing. She was otherwise naked from there down to her thighs where she was clad in three-quarter length nylons and her high heels. The effect on Tom was exactly what she had intended. Besides being struck dumb he had an instant erection. "Well, don't just stand there" she said, "Do something!" They came together in a tight clinch and the ensuing kiss left them both breathless. Then they couldn't get to bed fast enough. The bedspread stayed intact, as they used the entire surface rolling from one side to the other. Lila's goal was to wear Tom completely out so he wouldn't have the energy or wherewithal to ask for any information about her Uncle Ferdie this night. Those questions could be asked and answered once they had their own place. Fortunately, she wasn't a screamer when in the throes of passion or they would have to soundproof the new place. Her designs were being achieved, she could feel Tom start to soften inside her and also relax his grip on her hips. She was covered with sweat from their exertions but once he was asleep she could disengage and take a leisurely shower before returning to sleep next to him.

Tom woke up slowly as was his wont, only this time he knew exactly where he was and with whom. He could detect her pleasurable scent next to him. It was the pre-dawn hour which was apparent by the grayness just outside the window and as he remained still thinking over his schedule for today, working on a blueprint of his activities step by step. He realized of course it depended on what information he could get from Lila. Plus he needed a plausible story for Felix and Rocky to swallow for his being absent from the shop overnight without forewarning.

That just happened to be the moment Lila turned toward him, a simple roll-over in her sleep but it was enough to make Tom forget about his schedule – pleasure at hand before future business. Forty-five minutes later they decided on a communal shower which with more play took another twenty minutes.

"Look, Lila, we could continue these games all day but we both have things to do. Call down to the arcade and buy something suitable to wear."

8

Felix telephoned Alfredo's from the store and asked for Gennie. When he told her how he knew her and under what circumstances they had met casually, he asked her when she would get off work. Now she remembered the suave little man with the deep authoritative voice she had been attracted to the first time she had seen him. Felix picked up on her change from reserved to anxious manner at once. "I'll be done in an hour, why?"

"How 'bout my pickin' ya' up out front in a cab an' we can go somewhere for the evening, your choice?"

"Sounds O.K. to me, except it can't be anywhere fancy. I don't have a change of clothes here and I'm in my uniform."

"All right, see ya' in an hour."

Felix had no intention of taking her anywhere "fancy" other than a motel. He'd been without female companionship long enough and he intended to remedy that situation tonight. He yelled for Rocky who answered from the floor below. They met on the stairway and Felix explained he had a date tonight and to take care of Leo while both he and Tom were gone. "Make sure ya' let him out on the roof to do his duty before ya' go ta' bed. I'm tired of cleanin' up his messes."

"You have a date too huh? Looks like I'm odd man out here."

"Naw, you'll find someone your size one of these days. This town is full of good lookin' women, heh, heh, heh."

She was standing out in front when Felix pulled up, promptly getting in when Felix opened the rear door. "Been waitin' long?"

"Less than five minutes and I'm off tomorrow so what do you have in mind?"

"Do ya' live around here?"

"Not too far from here, why?"

"Will ya' quit askin' all these questions. Why don't we go ta' your place an' ya' can change inta' somethin' more comfortable."

"Well one reason that's not a good idea is because I live with my mother." The cabbie turned and asked "Where to now buddy?"

Felix looked Gennie straight in the eye, they were already holding hands, " the nearest hotel, with a decent bar and restaurant." Gennie didn't even blink, just squeezed his hand a little. The cab driver said, "I know just the place. We'll be there in two shakes."

"I take it that's all right with you." Gennie squeezed his hand again, a little harder. "Whatever you decide."

"We're gonna' get along just fine, doll."

"I trust you have an ulterior motive in mind."

"You betcha."

After paying off the cab they entered the Essex Hotel where Felix went directly to the main desk, checking in. "Do ya' have any specialty shops that are still open?"

"Yes, sir, they are on the mezzanine. I trust you will find just about anything you desire there. They are quite complete", handing him his room key.

"All right skip the sales pitch, if they don't have what we're lookin' for you'll be hearin' from me personally."

"C'mon, doll, you have some shoppin' ta' do for somethin' more suitable for this posh joint. Gennie's eyes widened when she saw all the beautiful clothing displayed. "I can't afford these prices, Felix."

"Who said anythin' 'bout you payin'. Just pick out what ya' like, try em' on an' model for me. I'll tell ya' if it suits ya'." She returned from the dressing room all agog and spun around in front of her benefactor. The dress flared then returned to mold to her shapely hips. Matching high heels and her hair let down and combed gave her a sexy look that instantly affected Felix. "That'll work." He paid the clerk and arm in arm they headed for the elevator. Gennie dispensed with her work clothes and excused herself to use the bathroom. She returned with just a touch of eye liner which added to her sexiness. Another dilemma faced Felix. Take her to bed now or eat and drink some beer. She's ready now, he thought but this had been thirsty work and he'd promised her dinner.

They sat in a half-filled dining room and were waited on by a male waiter. Felix picked a table against a wall which was his usual habit, a trick he had learned from Tom, the better to see everyone without having to worry about anyone behind him. Felix was also armed. He wore a leg holster which Gennie hadn't detected so far. The jig would be up once they went to bed.

"What are ya' gonna' have, doll? Ya' want a drink first or just order?"

"Oh a small ribeye with salad and a split of Asti Spumanti to wash it down, I guess. What about you?"

"That sounds good ta' me too, but I'll drink some Bud with mine."

"I can't really put my finger on what attracted me to you that first time I saw you at Alfredo's but I'm glad you called me when you did. I haven't been dating since breaking up with my steady about six months ago. He was turning into a real louse, so overbearing and demanding. I don't know what I saw in him to begin with. Just another good looking Italian I suppose."

"Ya' don't have ta' worry 'bout that with me, I realize what I look like when shavin'."

"I think you're cute."

"Course ya' know what I do for a livin'."

"Lila told me you worked with Mr. Mueller is all."

"Yeah we've been together quite a while, but do ya' know what we do?"

"Oh Felix let's not talk business now; here comes our food anyway."

Felix let the distraction of their food arriving to allow the preceding subject to die on the vine. They would discuss more on it after dinner in the confines of their room. "Bring me two more Buds, one will hardly get me started."

Gennie suddenly looked toward the front door where two men came into the room. The first, a smallish person dressed impeccably in a black pin-stripe suit looked like an insurance salesman, an innocuous get lost in a crowd sort of individual, but he was followed by a giant of such huge proportions he could only be a bodyguard.

Gennie put her hand on Felix's thigh and whispered, "I know those two men. I've seen them come into Alfredo's on occasion. They usually have their heads together with Lila's uncle, never eating. I think they are connected to the mob in some way."

"Ignore them, doll. Concentrate on yer' food an' me." Felix took a glance at the two Italians under the guise of looking for the waiter. Something about the large one rang a bell in his memory.

24

When he'd been in New York a few years ago he'd seen that brute. He just couldn't place where or under what circumstances. It would come to him; it always did.

Their waiter arrived breaking his meditation. "Will there be anything else, sir?"

"No, just bring me the check."

They left the dining room hand in hand as they'd come in and took an elevator to their room floor. Once inside Gennie again excused herself." You might as well get ready for bed, I'll be out in a minute and when I come out you better be ready to perform. My intentions are not quite honorable so we'll see if your expectations can match my enthusiasm." Felix thought finally his abstinence was about to be resolved. His Spanish blood was beginning to boil over in anticipation as he carefully turned back the covers of the bed. Only a bedside lamp was left on, so he undid his leg holster and put the weapon on the floor within easy reach if needed. His only attire was shorts which did little to hide his manhood. His virility was obvious. Gennie came out of the bathroom in the buff except for her high heels which showed off her shapely body backlit by the bathroom light. "Do you thing that underwear is necessary?"

"I'm the modest type, doll, but you're makin' my modesty seem kinda' foolish at the moment", as he wiggled out of the garment. "Won't ya join me and stop all this foolishness?"

Felix would never understand what snapped him awake after all the exertions of the night yet he was fully alert, eyes open, and ready to grab for his weapon. His eyes traversed what he could see of the room without moving his head, which wasn't much because of the way Gennie was clamped to him. It had to have been a sound. They were too high in the hotel for it to have been caused by traffic noises and he was too inured to sirens for them to raise his alert senses. So what was it then?

"Dom, did you see that dame who just left the dining room?"

"Yeah boss she looked kinda familiar."

"If you'll quit feedin' your face a minute and think about it you'd know she's a waitress at Alfredo's."

"Yeah I remember now, so?"

"How about the malignant dwarf with her. Ever see him before?"

Dominic stared at Livio with the blank gaze that denoted he was completely in the dark. His brutish ignorance infuriated his boss, one of the Brooklyn mob big shots in the drug trade. "I'm tellin' you Dominic the older you get the dumber you act. I saw that guy maybe five years ago when I was tipped off the Feds were making raids on suspected wholesalers in and around the City. He was somehow involved, I tell ya'. Now here's what I want you to do. "First after you're done eatin' take a room for the night here and get some sleep. Second, I'm sure that guy isn't livin' here on a permanent basis. He's probably enjoying a one-nighter with that waitress, so I want you ta' follow him early in the morning to wherever he goes. If he splits with her at anytime let her go and stay with him. We know where she works, Also it doesn't matter if he sees you or not, what's that little man going to do against you? Ya' follow me?"

Now Greco not being the brightest of individuals and wanting to please the boss bullied the desk clerk into revealing his quarry's floor and room number. He decided he would get up early and check the exact location before choosing the best spot to lie in wait before starting the chase. Dom's ponderous tread in the hallway and its stopping just outside his door is what woke Felix and alerted him to a possible danger to begin with. Early the next morning, Felix unglued himself from Gennie because his bladder was calling for relief. Finished, he decided a shower was in order.

Thoroughly enjoying the beating hot water that was dousing him, he was unprepared for the embrace of a soft body that pressed against his back. "I'll wash your back if you'll wash mine", Gennie cooed into his ear while holding his manhood. This was a new experience for Felix; he had never made love standing under a waterfall. The participation was heavenly.

"Ya' better get ta' washin' now, doll," helping her to her feet. Change back inta' your work clothes and I'll take ya' for an early breakfast at a place I know nearby."

Felix called a cab from their room rather than waiting for the doorman to whistle one up. He still had the uneasy feeling from earlier that danger lurked close at hand. This was a sensation he knew better than to ignore from previous experiences. He had been to this city in years past and Gennie's whispered comment about seeing those two Italians in Alfredo's had laid abeyant in his mind ever since – especially the hatchet- nosed thug.

The taxi dropped them off in front of Fritz's and they quickly entered. Felix was greeted by most of the help as he headed for a table in the rear. Fritz Voelker alerted by a fellow employee of his entry was at their table almost before they were seated. "Good to see you again, Mr. Santana. Are your two friends joining you soon?"

Felix introduced Gennie and the two were chattering away before he could answer Fritz's question. "You sure can pick them, Mr. Santana. This is a lovely woman. Now what can I get you? I'm sure you didn't come in here just to listen to me!"

"What are ya' gonna' have, doll?

"Oh, just orange juice and coffee for me, Felix.

"Is that how ya' keep your girlish figure doll?"

"And you, Mr. Santana?"

"I'm starved. Steak, medium. Eggs hard over, toast and coffee should do me, Fritz. My figure isn't gonna' get any bigger no matter how much I eat, heh, heh, heh."

"Right away, sir."

"An' Fritz ya know me well enough ta' drop the formalities. Felix will do."

"He seems like a nice man, have you known him for quite awhile?"

"Not really. My partners and I broke up a little skirmish here a while back. He then went on to explain the foiled robbery attempt. Just as he was finishing their breakfast arrived.

Felix hadn't taken more than three bites when he spotted old hatchet-nose filling the front doorway. The man had to weigh close to three hundred pounds. Now twice in less than twelve hours was more than coincidence, Felix thought to himself. "This guy must be stalkin' us", he said to Gennie. Sure enough, the grizzly bear shuffled toward their table, veering to a counter stool not ten feet away at the last moment.

"Ignore him, doll. "If he says anything to ya' let me handle it."

Felix actually saw her shudder as she cast her eyes down to her coffee cup. The woman was obviously frightened. That thug was most likely used to intimidating women and smaller men with his scowling countenance and over-sized bulk. Felix knew that most men of that ilk were not only slow-witted and sadistic but hopelessly limited in reaction or response to anyone with any knowledge of the martial arts. He had studied several forms of the arts and held a black belt in an obscure form taught by Japanese, something that was not common knowledge in his agency.

It didn't take long for the brute to make his move. "Hey sweet piece, don't I know you from Alfredo's restaurant? You in the waitress get-up I'm talkin' to."

"Watch your mouth when ya' talk to or 'bout this lady with me. I don't like it."

"Shaddup, pipsqueak, before I come over there an' cut you down to a size smaller than you already are. That honey needs a man to service her, not a sawed-off runt like you. Right, baby?"

Fritz noticed the beginnings of a fight and hurried to the phone to call the police.

When Felix heard the inflections of the diatribe, he had the thug identified in his memory. How could he ever have forgotten that Brooklyn branch of the mob? Livio Stefino was the head honcho, but this jerk was his underboss and enforcer. The agency hadn't made a case against them because of a leak somewhere, either city police or someone in their own outfit. Regardless, when their combined force raided the warehouse all they discovered was a legitimate olive oil business, no trace of any narcotics. So much for inter-agency-cooperation.

"Let's blow this joint sweet piece, I'm in the mood for some lovin'."

Greco started directly for her chair, arm outstretched to forcibly lift her from her seat. That was what Felix was waiting for. He rose quickly grabbing Greco's arm with both hands and using the thug's forward motion used the leverage to spin him against the wall where he bounced back slowly, stunned. Felix was just getting started. "Move away from the table, Gennie."

Greco was in a blind rage. He took one pace toward Felix reaching inside his jacket for a weapon when Felix struck again. With one hand on a chair back for balance he flung out both legs, his feet aimed at the man's nearest knee. The ensuing snap and bang of the wounded heavyweight falling could be heard throughout the restaurant, accompanied by his roar of pain and rage. Felix had rolled under the table where he retrieved his own pistol from its leg holster. He came out on the other side near Gennie. "Listen, doll, I want ya' ta' stay outta' his range. Cross over to the stools while he's down."

The ensuing snap that was heard was the dislocation of Greco's knee. Greco was attempting to rise but the knee wouldn't hold his weight. He was swearing a blue streak in his native tongue interspersed with enough English to make his ravings understood. He had finally retrieved his weapon from its shoulder holster, a Colt .45 automatic, and was trying to get a bead on his tormentor when Felix struck again from his blind side. In two quick moves he used his own weapon as a bludgeon to crack him across the temple while kicking the automatic out of his unsteady hand. He had no desire to have a round to be fired in the crowded restaurant where some innocent patron could be wounded or worse regardless of the damage done to the man's head. He strode over to where Gennie was hunkered down between two stools. "You OK, doll?" Her face was tear-streaked and pale but she stood and wrapped her arms around her protector.

Fritz approached cautiously. "Are you all right, Felix?" I called the police and they should be here any minute. Man, I've never seen anyone move as fast as you. You sure you're all right?"

"Yeah, but ya' better call an ambulance for that bozo. He won't be usin' that leg for a while." "He hasn't moved an inch since you whacked him that last time and kicked his weapon away. I hope he remains unconscious until the police arrive." "So do I." He looked at Gennie. "I've had enough exercise for today, heh, heh, heh." She actually blushed.

A patrol car pulled up in front and two uniformed officers entered the restaurant. They didn't seem to know Fritz by sight so he introduced himself as the proprietor of the establishment. One of the officers spoke, "Sorry for the delay but this call is off our district. Crime seems rampant this morning for some reason. What happened here?" Fritz proceeded to explain the disturbance in detail, pointing to the perpetrator who was in the same physical attitude as when Felix was done with him. The other officer looked from Greco to Felix and back again. "You were kind of over-matched there weren't you? Do you have some picture identification?" Felix pulled out his agency ID. "Well I guess that would explain it, but why don't you tell me your version of it anyway." While Felix went through his story the other officer went to check Greco's condition. "I called for an ambulance, it should be here shortly." Within minutes two plain clothes detectives entered. They zeroed in on Felix . It took the better part of an hour for an explanation of the events leading up to the confrontation and the ensuing result to be hashed over for the detectives. All of that being corroborated by Gennie and Fritz as they meticulously wrote everything in their notebooks. "One thing I would like to verify here", said one. "What is your address while you're in the city?"

"Ya' have to understand my team is here undercover an' we don't want our location made available ta' just anyone, but I'll give ya' a phone number where I can be reached." The two detectives exchanged glances but held their peace.

Fritz called them a cab after fixing them a sumptuous breakfast to replace the one gone cold. "Don't be strangers now ", he added as they left.

Felix had the cabbie drop Gennie off at the address she gave him after promising her they would be seeing each other again soon. "Do ya' like baseball, doll?" She answered that she was a staunch Yankee fan, listening to their home games on radio whenever they didn't conflict with her working hours.

"I'll get some box seats at their next home stand and let ya' know ahead of time so ya' can make arrangements ta' go. Wouldn't miss a chance to see them while I'm in the city."

9

"Get away from me, ya' overgrown cocker spaniel, Uncle Felix ain't got anything for ya' an' he's kinda' tired so leave him alone." Leo had pounced on Felix when he'd opened the front door of the shop. Since his main friend had left him alone most of the time since Felix had last been here his nose was out of joint and he wanted to play but Felix really was tired and not about to put up with his shenanigans. "Go find Rocky if yer' lookin' for a playmate."

Could it be he was starting to slow down? He didn't think his maneuvers had suffered from lack of practice yet something had caused a shift - but what? He knew he wasn't a great one for self-involvement. His entire existence had been action to action, never allowing self-immolating thoughts to interfere.

Felix understood a confrontation with his amigo, Tom Mueller, was about to come to a head – over women, of all things. They had never had a serious disagreement before in their working relationship. He couldn't ask for a better partner or friend. Their only discord had come from Tom's insistence on giving him money, which all stemmed from his finding the emerald. Felix couldn't imagine having the kind of money his amigo possessed. The stone, in addition to what his twin had willed him, Muy Dios, what a windfall. Felix also realized he'd stirred up a hornet's nest by his fight with Dominic Greco, he only hoped it hadn't fouled things up too much. As his head hit the pillow the last conscious thought Felix had was: If only Sheila Bond hadn't been killed...

The next morning Felix was rudely awakened by of all people, Rocky Newbole. "What have you been up to Felix? I just took a call from the NYPD detective bureau asking me to vouch for your agency credentials and whereabouts. Since Mr. Mueller wasn't here to advise me I had to wing it, and hopefully I didn't mess anything up for us."

Leo was standing just one pace to Rocky's right, his long tongue hanging from his maw watching Felix as Rocky spoke.

"Where is Tom?"

"I have no idea but I hope he gets back soon. I'm the junior member of this team and shouldn't have to make these important decisions."

"There's no such thing as a junior partner, we're all equal ya' know? An' when Tom returns he'll back me up on that statement. Now how 'bout takin' him with ya' in mannin' the phone. Don't wake me unless there's somethin' ya' can't handle."

———

Instead of a walk-up apartment, what Lila had found was a basement four-roomer. Bedroom, kitchen, bathroom, and combination living-dining room. All utilities except telephone were included and it had a front and rear entrance. The latter was beyond an adjoining apartment to their rear and exited into an alley that contained nothing but garbage cans, similar to what some of the same looked like in the older sections of Central and East Toledo, Tom's hometown. When Tom first looked at the place and Lila told him how much the rent was he knew it would be perfect for their clandestine trysts. It was only a short distance from Alfredo's and four blocks from the shop. The signing of a six-month lease didn't bother Tom at all; even if they were transferred to another location for some reason, Lila could probably sublet it. At the moment she was all enthused about redecorating and putting their personal touches into the place. Tom figured he'd let her run with it, if it satisfied her, while he took care of other business.

When he called the shop, Rocky answered and was obviously upset. When he explained what Felix had been involved in and the NYPD detective bureaus' reaction, Tom was somewhat perplexed but when he heard Gennie, the other waitress from Alfredo's, was with Felix, he realized this was some form of oneupsmanship for his involvement with Lila.

"And, Rocky, keep an eye on the little guy. Make sure he doesn't leave the shop before I get there, in about an hour. We have to sit down and parley, which will also include you."

But Felix had his own agenda planned. When Rocky left his room accompanied by Leo he was up and dressed within minutes. He took the inner hidden stairway down to the first floor and was out of the building before Leo could detect his movements. He snickered to himself as he walked away. It wasn't often you could put something over on the dog. He hailed a cab about a block away giving the cabbie instructions to take him to the Yankee stadium ticket office, not that a New York City hack needed them.

"Wait for me will ya', just gonna' pick up some tickets."

"Take your time buddy, the meter's running."

Fortunately there was only one customer ahead of him and he was finished. But when Felix reached the counter he was struck dumb. The clerk waiting for his order was Sheila Bond. "How may I help you, sir.?"

"I, er ah, want box seats for two on the third base side as close ta' the dugout as possible, Sheila."

The woman took a double-take. "Why did you call me that?"

"Cuz I was acquainted with a woman in Washington, D.C., who looked just like ya'. Her name was Sheila Bond." The tickets were forgotten for the moment as Felix continued to stare at the woman. She returned his stare.

"That woman is – was my twin sister", she stammered. How well did you know her?"

"Well enough ta' know who she was gonna' marry. He's my closest amigo, Tom Mueller." Now tears started streaming down her face, while she had a white-knuckled grip on the counter.

"We have to talk Mr...."

"Santana, but ya' can just call me Felix."

While the woman was trying to get a grip on herself, Felix's mind was in high gear. Wait 'til Tom finds out Sheila's twin is right here in the area. He'll drop Lila like a hot potato and probably pursue this one like he did Sheila. "I'm due to be relieved in about fifteen minutes, Felix. Can we go somewhere for a cup of coffee or something while I catch up?"

"Sure, ya' drivin'?"

"Are you kidding, nobody in their right mind drives around here."

"I've got a cab waitin'."

"Let it go, I'll call another when we're ready." Felix did as she ordered but when he returned to the office there were several people lined up waiting for tickets. As he waited, an older woman joined Stella behind the counter, and between the two they made quick work of the remaining patrons. When the place was again empty Stella introduced Felix as a friend of her twin sister. Felix immediately began charming the older woman while Stella called another cab.

As they rode toward Stella's pre-picked destination she said, "You certainly have a way with women, Felix, of any age. Barbara can be a cranky curmudgeon most of the time."

"Must be my Spanish blood, heh, heh, heh. Hope this place we're goin' serves beer."

When they were seated at a table, near the rear of the place – at Felix's insistence, he noted they indeed served beer and wine. He ordered two Buds with a cold glass while Stella had coffee. So far she hadn't said a word about Sheila so Felix thought he'd wait her out.

"Ya' married, Stella?"

"Not yet..." She didn't clarify the statement so he didn't pursue it for the moment. As the silence grew Stella started to fidgit. Felix knew she would open up in her own good time. He waited.

"There must be some way to ease into this but I'm at a loss to understand how. Her agency refused to give me any pertinent details of her death so I didn't know who to go to for further information. How much do you know?"

There it was. Felix took a long drink of beer, stalling while he decided on how much, and what, he could and couldn't disclose. "Look, Stella, I work for the same outfit she did so I can't divulge too much either. It has to do with security, ya' understand, but I'll give ya' a watered down version if you'll accept that."

"Do I have much choice?" "Stell, there are some things it's best ya' don't know for your own safety. Ours is a pretty rough world. Our opponents don't care who they hurt to further their goals. They'd just as soon kill ya' as look at ya' if they thought ya' knew somethin' about their operations. I kid ya' not." Felix began the story from Tom Mueller's attraction and subsequent falling in love with her sister, to what they found on that fatal day. "So ya' see the only stuff I'm not tellin' ya' is the names of suspects. I will say there's an international manhunt going on right now for one of them, an' it's only a matter of time. The guy can't hide forever."

"The team I'm with right now is a multi-agency one pursuin' the New York City and environs' mobs who are dealing heavily in the drug trade an' it's a complicated situation, that's why I'd like ya' ta' meet Tom." Of course Felix had an ulterior motive; once Tom saw Stella and had a chance to talk with her one on one he just might forget about Lila and the threat to his job by seeing her. At least that was what he hoped for. Felix believed the attraction was purely sexual.

"Just for my own information, Stella, did ya' have any other sisters or brothers?"

"A brother but he was killed in combat in Korea."

"What branch of the service was he in?"

"Marine Corps. He was only in-country two months when my parents were notified of his death. That was 1951 and my mother never got over it. I think that loss contributed to her death two years later - a broken heart. Dad followed her less than a year later."

30

"Ya' know, Stella, the more ya' tell me about your family history, the closer the parallel is between yours and Tom Mueller's. An' there's a very good chance he knew your brother in Korea."

"This Mueller person sounds quite intriguing. I don't suppose it would hurt anything to meet and have a talk with him."

"I've got a cab waiting."

"Let it go, I'll call another when we're ready."

10

Tom Mueller finally pulled away from Lila's clutches and returned to the shop only to find an unhappy Leo, a frustrated Rocky, and no sign of Felix who had somehow skipped without being detected.

"How could he have left without alerting Leo?"

"I don't have an answer for that, Mr. Mueller. If the dog couldn't hear him there was no way for me to."

"Did you look all through the place? There's no chance he could be lying somewhere injured I don't suppose." He just received a look of disdain for an answer which made him realize how stupid the question had been. There was no reason to provoke this man like that. Rocky had been put into a no-win position and Tom knew he was grabbing at straws to shift the blame from himself. "Didn't mean to imply you weren't thorough, Rocky? He'll turn up when he's good and ready. In the meantime, why don't you relax? I'll keep Leo up here with me while I make some phone calls."

Rocky nodded and left. When Tom heard his steps grow fainter he headed for the office motioning for Leo to follow. Sitting at the desk he turned to speak to the dog but Leo wasn't there. Tom was just about to order him in when the phone rang distracting him. "Hello".

"Is that you, amigo?" "All right, Felix, what have you been up to, and where are you?"

"Firs' things firs'. I'm with a woman I think ya' should meet." Tom remained silent, he'd wait him out.

"Ya' still there, amigo? I jus' met her today so it's not who you're thinking of. C'mon, amigo, lighten up. There's more to this story. This woman has somethin' ta' do with your past. Ya' won't believe it."

Now Tom was intrigued. Who had his partner discovered, and how? His mind was ticking off all the women he had known over the years that somehow Felix might have known about, surely no one from Toledo. There was only Marie Fowler and she was dead. Who then? Knowing the way Felix was around women, of any age, Tom was bitten by the curiosity bug.

"Got ya' thinkin' huh? Heh, heh, heh. Ya' gonna' be at the shop for an hour or so?" Tom wasn't going to let Felix off that easily. I'll await your arrival, Felix; you've got quite a bit of explaining to do about your escapades of the last couple of days. You put Rocky in a rather precarious position you know. He's a valuable part of our team and didn't deserve that kind of treatment."

"I'll make it up ta' the big guy. See ya' soon."

Leo had finally wandered into the office apparently over his snit because he placed his head in Tom's lap waiting for an ear scratch. When Tom accommodated him and received the usual reward it seemed all was forgiven between them.

"Sorry to have ignored you so much lately, fella, but things kept popping up. What have you and Rocky been doing while I was gone?" Tom turned to use the phone and Leo was off like a shot hitting the inner stairs at full gallop. Tom could hear him pounding down the steps in wild abandon as though his life depended on reaching the first floor of the shop before anyone else. Tom had seen him do that before so he followed, but at a more leisurely pace. When he reached the rear of the showroom he half expected to witness another confrontation like the one where the intruders had broken into the front door yet nothing of the sort was taking place. As he neared the front he was at first startled, then dumbfounded because there petting a stuporous Leo next to Felix was Sheila – his Sheila Bond. What, a mirage, a look-alike or a figment of his imagination? Tom simply stood, staring at the apparition, his thoughts awhirl.

"Amigo, meet Stella, Sheila's twin sister. Surprised? Heh, heh, heh."

"The dog seems to like you Miss, er, Stella", Tom stammered.

"It's a beautiful animal, and so gentle. I'd love to own a dog like this."

No, it wasn't Sheila; she could barely stand the dog , even when he was just a pup. She'd never mentioned a twin sister to him even after he confessed to having a twin brother to her. Maybe that was why she was so set against his marriage plans, afraid she would give birth to twins also. Those and other thoughts coursed through his mind as he stood staring at the gorgeous woman. Any thoughts of Lila were shelved as he continued his gaze. He had to know more about this Stella Bond.

"What's the matter, amigo, cat got yer' tongue?"

"Felix, do me a favor. Let Leo take you for a walk for an hour or so while Stella and I get acquainted. He could stand the exercise and it will get you out from underfoot at the same time."

"Oh sure, I do all the leg work gettin' ya' together then I gotta' take a walk. There's just no justice. C'mon ya' overgrown cocker spaniel, Uncle Felix knows when he's not welcome so we'll go out an' see what kinda' trouble we can stir up in the neighborhood. Ya' never know there might be some great adventure awaitin' us. At least ya' can water some fire plugs, or maybe we can run across one of those teen street gangs an' ya' can get some body parts ta' chew on. Would ya' like that?" Leo just stood motionless while Felix put a body harness on him so he could attach a twenty foot lead to it. "We have ta' obey the leash laws, right?"

For the first few blocks of their walk Leo plodded along, sniffing her and there, like the gentle cocker spaniel Felix often referred to him as, the leash dragging along on the cement. Then the inevitable happened, Leo took off like a shot, the leash now taut and Felix hard-pressed to keep up.

—

"There's no point in our standing down here. Let's go up to my apartment where we can be more comfortable while we talk. Follow me, Stella." Tom hesitated at Rocky's floor and called out. "I'll be upstairs so you don't have to worry about the phone. I'll take any incoming calls."

Tom guided Stella directly to the kitchen. "Take your jacket off while I get some coffee brewing, or would you prefer something else?"

"No, coffee will be fine."

"Isn't it strange that Sheila never mentioned she had a twin sister to me? I mean when I told her about my twin brother that was the obvious time to bring it up, but she didn't. I wonder why. But then again she could be quite secretive at times."

"Sheila and I might have been look-alikes but we had totally different personalities. We loved each other as sisters but we went separate ways after college. She was a gifted pianist, you know, and could have made a career on the classical circuit or even working clubs as a soloist; her voice wasn't bad either. But no, she caught the law enforcement bug letting the more promising careers go by the wayside, an absolute shame."

"What about you, Stella, do you have an artistic talent? I'm certain your goal in life isn't to be a sales clerk in a ticket office."

Stella stirred her black coffee and had what Tom recognized as the thousand-yard stare, a symptom most infantry grunts experienced after a grueling battle under any dire circumstances.

"Sorry, Tom, I was just remembering how my life turned in the direction it did. My artistic gift turned out to be painting, mostly oils, but some water color and charcoal also. When I say gift I mean no formal education in the art was provided. The urge to express my thoughts on paper and canvas simply struck me at a time in my life when I needed some way to share those thoughts with others. My brother had just been killed in the Korean War and Sam was my best friend in the world."

"Now let me get this straight, you also had a brother named Sam. Were there any other siblings?"

"No, just the three of us. Sam was the oldest and joined the Marine Corps in 1950 and was sent to Korea in 1951. He was only there about two months before my parents got the notification that he'd been killed. Mom died less than a year later – Dad said of a broken heart."

"Is your father still alive?" "No, he passed on exactly a year later, to the day, which left Sheila and I alone to face the world. Then she was gone and I found myself without a family."

"You poor kid, to lose everyone in such a short span of time. Any further consolable words were interrupted by the phone ringing in the office. He excused himself and left the kitchen. It was Lila. "I miss you, lover. Why don't you meet me at our apartment in say, about a half hour, I've got some great things to show you." Tom mumbled. He'd have to pass because he was waiting for an important phone call. There was a pregnant pause at the other end of the line. "You're not tired of me already are you, Tom?"

"Look, Lila, I do have work to do, and I just can't drop everything to satisfy your whims. We'll get together again soon. Now I have to clear this line so I'll call you as soon as I can. Business is business, and my time isn't always mine to do as I wish. Bye."

Tom was worried that Lila would become too demanding. He needed her for information about her uncle but maybe Felix was right – bedding her might jeopardize the whole operation, and his career. And then there was Stella. There were so many aspects to consider. Had he not been so dedicated to his cause, the elimination of as many marketable narcotics as possible, it might be reasonable to forget the whole thing, settle down and raise a family and get away from this seamy side of life. God knows, he could afford it, thanks to the emerald and Fred. Enough of these recriminations, he'd better get back to Stella before she got her nose out of joint and left. He wouldn't put it past her. She was a strong-willed woman besides being beautiful and talented. Yet when he returned to the kitchen she was still seated at the table where he'd left her. "More coffee, Stella?"

Stella was looking at Tom over the rim of her raised cup and as the silence between them grew he was becoming mesmerized by her gaze. "I suppose we better be getting you home", he said, breaking the spell. I'll call a cab,"

"I can take the subway."

"Nonsense, you came all this way to meet me because Felix talked you into it so it's the least I can do to recompense. Besides I'd like to see some of your work. I'm no art critic by any means but I know what I like." On the way out Tom gave Rocky Stella's phone number where he could be reached. "I shouldn't be gone for more than a couple of hours, Rocky, and in the meantime Felix should be back from his walk with Leo, so hold the fort, Sport."

The cab ride took over a half hour during which time not more than ten words were exchanged between Tom and Stella. They both had window seats which separated them like total strangers sharing a ride. Tom couldn't tell if she was nervous about allowing him to see her artwork or tense because they would be alone in her apartment. Some women of good breeding, which she obviously was, would hesitate to let a situation like that arise with someone she had only known for a few hours.

When they arrived at her place and Tom paid the cabbie, he followed her up the steps of a four-family brownstone which looked to be in good repair. Her place was a lower left. He trailed her into it with trepidation not really knowing what to expect. "This is it, such as it is."

While Tom looked around she disappeared toward the rear. Her furniture was as good as Sheilas' and all of it was sparkling clean. Of course there was more of it because her place was much larger. "I'm putting coffee on so make yourself comfortable."

No knicknacks or doilies like most women liked to spread around, no frilly curtains or dolls clustered on shelves, just no-nonsense furniture, tables, floor lamps, and drapes for privacy. It looked more like a mans' room than one for a single female. No piano, either, backing up the difference between her and her twin sister. Tom was sitting on a sofa when she returned with the coffee. She had also taken the time to change clothing since she had been in her work clothes and must have felt the need for fresh clothing now that she was home for the evening. A short-sleeve sweater and slacks with slippers, all in matching shades of green actually complimented her figure rather than down-toning it. He'd have to be careful not to let her catch him staring at her breasts.

"I thought you would like to relax for a few minutes before looking at any of my paintings. There is a room in the back that I use as my studio. The light there is fabulous toward sunset. It's quite a mess with all of the makings so I wear a smock when working because most of the paint would ruin everyday clothing. So you be careful not to rub up against anything that's still tacky."

"How will I know what is and what isn't, wet, that is?"

"I'll point out what I have been working on as you enter, Tom. One is on an easel, so that one will be obvious."

When Stella opened the door of her studio the odor of linseed oil, turpentine, and paint was practically overpowering. She flipped a switch and an exhaust fan began pulling the combined smells out of the room. "Since it's been enclosed since yesterday there's an automatic reek of build-up that has to be dispersed before the room is livable again, that's why I had that fan installed." While Tom stood just outside the door Stella was puttering around inside, straightening some items which she had left helter-skelter, not knowing a visitor would be entering her sanctum. An unframed canvas on the far wall drew his attention. It was an oil rendition of Sheila seated at a baby grand piano deep into whatever selection she was playing, a Sheila younger than when he had known her, yet so life-like as to talk to. He could understand why he had fallen so deeply in love with her.

"My God, Stella, that's a beautiful painting of Sheila. You captured her in a way I never knew her."

"You have to understand, Tom, she was my twin and I knew her from puberty."

"Are you only a portraitist? I don't see any landscapes or still-lifes anywhere, or do you keep those stacked in another room?"

"I have a few, mostly of our old homestead where we all grew up, and the surrounding area, but you're right they are in another room. I have to have some space to work. All is not fun and games plus you can't turn creativity on and off. I've gone days just sketching out in the living room without coming in here except to turn the blower on for short periods."

"You really have a talent, Stella; have you ever considered showing some of them in a gallery?"

"Oh I've had those dreams like every starving artist, but they're just that, dreams."

At that moment Tom was standing next to her and could not help but stare at her breasts. She turned toward him and the temptation was too great, he grabbed her face in a moment of utter lust but kissed her gently.

"I wondered how long it would take you to do that", and she put her arms around his neck returning the kiss with ardent fervor, boring those beauties into his chest. When they came up for air, Stella grabbed his hand. "Come with me Tom."

She led him down the hall and into her bedroom. Her sweater was off in a flash, then she was taking his shirt off. They hit the bed in a tangle of arms and legs, both gasping in their efforts to remove each others remaining clothing. For Tom the ensuing period of time passed while he was in both a state of confusion and bliss. Confusion because Stella was so much like Sheila that his mind couldn't comprehend to whom he was making love. Bliss, for the reason it really didn't matter. He couldn't imagine in his wildest dreams to have replaced his true love with an exact duplicate who not only looked, thought, and smelled the same but had the same mental capacities. As they lay spent, arm in arm during a lull of their strenuous activities they were staring into each others eyes without a word being spoken aloud. Were it to be known, they were thinking along similar lines. Stella was imagining how her life would turn out coupled with this man who had loved her sister. He had already proven he was a deep-thinker with all of his responsibilities being juggled without losing any tenderness. His love given to Leo, his mastiff, his loyalty to his team members in a world she could only wonder about, and his devotion to his occupation. Would that interfere with bearing his children and raising a family? Just lying here she could see something approaching adoration emanating from those deep, blue eyes. She wouldn't rush this joining. Let Tom make the decision in his own mind first.

He moved to her shoulder, neck, and ear with tender kisses which had the desired effect. They floated together into oblivion locked together like long-time lovers. Tom was asleep within minutes, totally relaxed for the first time in months, if not years. His usual restless mind which never allowed more than five to six hours of dreamless sleep had unconsciously changed its ways.

11

Leo made an abrupt right turn down an alley where Felix was forced to release the twenty-foot leash or wipe out a row of garbage-laden trash cans waiting pick-up at the entrance. The dog only trooped another thirty feet or so before coming to a screeching halt. There stood what had attracted his pell-mell rush. A gray Irish Wolfhound, obviously a female and in heat, stood quivering while Leo sniffed her from one end to the other. Felix followed until stopping fifteen feet short, where he lowered himself to the pavement. He was panting as hard as Leo but for a different reason. Felix had never seen one of this breed in person, only pictures. It was a majestic looking animal, a good thirty inches high at the shoulder. This was not a stray, for Felix could see a collar with license affixed around her thick neck. The dog had somehow broken away from its owner who was more than likely searching the area frantically. If you're gonna' do anything ya' better get goin', Felix thought. Leo had to realize the animal was of a different breed yet how many mastiffs would you imagine were housed in the city? A union between these two would certainly produce some odd-looking offspring. The deed was consummated forthwith. Felix approached both dogs slowly and copied the license information off the now-docile Wolfhound. He hoped he'd got it right in the ill-lit alley. Leo looked up at his friend with that silly expression he sometimes had, the long tongue drooping from his maw.

"Yeah, ya' did good, ya' overgrown cocker spaniel. Let's go home, and slowly if ya' don't mind. Won't Tom be surprised when I tell him you're gonna' be a father soon, somethin' he's been wantin' ta' do, heh, heh, heh."

Much to his confusion when Felix entered the shop and looked for him, Tom was not there. He yelled for Rocky but he was either gone someplace or sound asleep. He looked at Leo. "Ya' don't suppose my amigo is tryin' ta' do what you just did, do ya'? Wouldn't that be somethin' if he and Stella were ... naw that's too far-fetched. But then again, stranger things have happened. If I thought for one minute he would take advantage of her this quickly I'd have found someway ta' get them together sooner, impossible as that wouldda' been." Lila will have a fit, he thought, I only hope I didn't mess up the whole project since she can be a loose cannon at times which has already been proven.

Felix noticed Leo roaming around the third floor like a lost soul looking for Tom. He'd already been up and down the inner and outer stairs searching for him. It was really something the way those two were attached to each other. Unfortunately he couldn't own a pet and friend like that what with his being constantly transferred from pillar to post.

Felix was rummaging around in the kitchen cupboards looking for something to eat while Leo crapped out on the floor between the kitchen and the office, tired partly from his exertions with the Wolfhound and partly in boredom with not finding Tom. He had to be really pooped, Felix thought, because he was actually snoring. Felix had never heard him do that before. Maybe he was reliving his tryst. Felix heard a door slam on the floor below indicating Rocky was up or had returned from someplace. He was right in the middle of opening some canned goods for a combination of some ungodly type to help fill his growling stomach when Rocky called up the stairs, "Is that you, Mr. Mueller?"

"Naw it's me, Rocky, c'mon up, but be careful of the dog, he's layin' in the doorway. He's kinda' tired."

Rocky looked, then stepped over Leo, ducking slightly as he entered the kitchen.

"I've never seen him just lie motionless when someone entered the room, friend or foe. What's the matter with him, is he sick?"

So Felix related Leo's sexual adventure to explain his drowsiness. "Wait until Mr. Mueller hears about it; he won't be too happy. How do you like my new shoes? I paid a bundle for them but it was worth it. The cashier in the shop and I really hit it off. You were right, Felix, there are a lot of beautiful women in the city. Esther and I are going to an off-Broadway play tonight on our first date. And for a plus she's only four inches shorter." Rocky was wearing a cheshire grin.

"I told ya' that somewhere, sometime, ya'd find a match but I'll be honest with ya' Rocky, I didn't think it'd happen this quick. Aren't we a merry band of men, though, plus one happy dog? Bring her here after one of yer' get togethers, I'll have Gennie with me so the women can get acquainted.

"Ya' never know they might find some common ground. I'm sure Tom will include his Stella.

36

You'll be seein' her around here pretty soon anyway once he figures out some way ta' ditch Lila, heh, heh, heh."

Somehow Lila sensed Tom was seeing another woman. Nothing had been said which made her feel threatened yet she had made several phone calls to the shop leaving messages for him because he was either gone or would contact her a.s.a.p. but he never returned her messages. Felix and Rocky were very evasive, which ever one she talked to, and she intended to get to the bottom line on this matter soon. She really didn't believe he could withstand their sexual bouts for long. She was that sure of her charms. Lila decided to make up a fictional account about her Uncle Ferdie's reaction to events concerning the attempted strong-arm escapade of three of her Uncle's underlings. If she made it realistic enough, Tom would at least have to see her, if for no other reason than to protect that damn dog of his. She couldn't see what the attraction was between those two but at times he seemed more concerned about that beast than her. If he thought he was going to bring Leo into their new apartment, he had another think coming. Just what she would need, that animal watching them make love, or to trip over him while walking naked in high heels to further entice her lover. Enough of these thoughts, they would only lead to trouble for her and her and her uncle. But as she went through the motions at work she couldn't shake the feeling of disaster that floated over her head like a dark rain cloud, ready to let loose. There had to be some way to avoid being struck by lightning.

"Leo did what? Felix how could you let him do something like that? An Irish Wolfhound yet." The three men were sitting in Tom's office catching up with the different events of the past day and a half. "Have ya' ever tried ta' stop Leo when he really wanted ta' do something', amigo? I mean ya' know more than anyone, that dog has a mind of his own. I coulda' got seriously hurt by tryin' ta' stop him. Not by the two dogs, but by tryin' ta' hold on ta' the leash when he turned inta' that alley. You'll have ta' admit those will be some interesting lookin' pups, heh, heh, heh."

"That may be so but how are we ever going to know? You said you got license information from its collar but you weren't certain of its validity."

"Yeah, but it was kinda' dark in that alley but ya' should be able ta' check it through with the licensing bureau. How many female Wolfhounds can there be in the city? They're about as common as Leo's breed."

"I'll call the agency when I get a chance. Now Rocky, what is this I hear about your liaison with the fairer sex? You're not being led down a garden path too are you?" Tom could see by the animated gestures of the usual stoic Newbole that he indeed was smitten by the Goddess of Love.

"Nothing so drastic as that yet, Mr. Mueller, but I have met an interesting woman who I intend to pursue further. Esther and I are going to an off-Broadway play as soon as I can arrange for tickets..

"We'll all have to have a dinner gathering or something to get acquainted, that is if it doesn't interfere with our main objective and there is some respite in the Mob's actions against us. There's not much point dwelling on that, we'll just have to wait and see. But my guess is they may be playing low-key, waiting for us to make the next move. They seem to have limitless henchmen, enforcers, and button men they can use as a vanguard, but none of them have impressed me, so far, with their worth. That doesn't mean we can let our guard down."

"Whadda' ya' gonna' do 'bout Lila, amigo? Even though she is our contact to the bad guys she's gonna' flip when she finds out 'bout Stella."

"I understand that Felix and a solution to that problem hasn't occurred to me yet. I knew by dipping my wick there what chances I was taking yet I went full steam ahead like I've always done.

If my short liaison with her backfires I'll have no one to blame but myself. To err is human but I seem to be overdoing it lately and I'm open to any suggestions." The two other men looked everywhere but at Tom which he interpreted as that they didn't have a clue. So since he was going solo on the problem he'd do it his way, whatever way that should be. How did you separate the wheat from the chaff? Tom remembered how he had handled Shari back when he went to Ohio State. He had joined this agency and left town, the easy way out. It seemed like so long ago, yet it was only just short of four years. But now that he'd met Stella there was no way he was going to cut and run, too much had happened in the interim. If his choices were limited to the Agency and her then by God the Agency would lose his services.

—

When Rocky picked Esther up at the bootery she was dressed to the nines having brought dress-up clothes to work and changing in the employees' lavatory for their evening date. She was somewhat nervous, hoping she hadn't overdone it. After all, what did she know about this man? The store manager had complimented her effusively which only added to her state of unease. Yet when Rocky arrived all her nervousness was forgotten. He was equally decked out in blazer and slacks with a subdued tie. As they left the shop all eyes were turned toward the handsome couple. On the sidewalk outside a path seemed to open ahead of them creating unobstructed passage as the advanced toward the theater arm in arm. Rocky felt proud as a peacock escorting this lovely Amazon. In her high heels she was just two inches shy of his great height and matched his long strides step for step.

"I don't know why, Rocky, but before you got to the shop tonight I was as nervous as a teenager going on her first unescorted date; not that I'm that far from being one", she laughed. Rocky noticed her laughter was full throated, sounding like a belly laugh, the kind a tickled man would emit. He glanced sideways at her. She was far from being a man. Those breasts were leading the way like twin beacons making saliva rise in his throat.

"I know it's improper and impolite to ask a lady her age but I figured you for about twenty-three."

"Thank you, kind sir, don't I wish. I hate to admit it, but I'll never see twenty-seven again. But I figure age in years itself is unimportant if a person maintains reasonably good health and keeps the mind active. Don't let me get started on that subject unless you have no intentions of going home tonight." Esther looked sideways at Rocky and actually winked. It was one of the bawdiest winks he had ever seen a woman make, not only suggestive but promising. He understood right then he might have is hands full with this woman.

The show was a rollicking musical with intricate choreographic routines which were thrilling to watch and the packed house gave the company a standing ovation at the final curtain. Esther was practically as breathless as the dancers when it was over. She had clung to Rocky's arm throughout the performance, and he was as excited by her grip as witnessing a future smash hit. It was well worth the hassle to obtain tickets to see it.

"Would you like to stop at the restaurant where the cast unwinds after their performances?"

"Sure, but how do you know about the place?"

"I've been there before. It's a long story which I'll try to explain later, Rocky."

The so-called restaurant turned out to be a bistro cum sandwich bar. Any resemblance to an actual restaurant had disappeared somewhere after the place purchased a liquor permit. It was intimate to the extent of consisting mostly of booths with a smattering of small tables taking up the space between the booths and six-stooled bar. Since they had walked from the theater the place was already partially filled with some of the troupe still costumed sans makeup. Rocky was hard-pressed not to stare at some of the leggy young women seated around the place, making no bones about exhibiting their half naked bodies.

"You said you had been here before, Esther, why?"

"She isn't here yet but when she arrives I'll point her out, then you'll understand. Patience my good man, patience." Esther ordered a grapefruit juice and vodka concoction not asking what he wanted, so he took it upon himself to ask for coffee. "You're not drinking?"

"No, you go ahead though, enjoy yourself, mystery woman."

Another bunch of mixed couples entered and one girl separated herself from the group heading directly toward them, the puzzle was now solved. The girl was a shorter version of Esther, not a twin exactly, but very close. "Hi sis, were you at the show again tonight?"

Rocky stood when Esther introduced him and he had more than a foot on her.

"Oooh he's a big one isn't he? You've finally found someone your size, honey. I hope you won't let him get away", she winked, the same lecherous wink he'd received from Esther earlier.

"Pull up a chair, Carolyn, unless you're involved already."

"No, just the same old group, no heart throbs there sis."

"You'll have to overlook the way we talk Rocky, it's sisterly. We understand what we're getting at, but to a non-family member it might sound a little strange, know what I mean?"

Rocky was afraid he did and it wasn't to his liking, but he kept his thoughts to himself.

"Now when you're ready to leave Rocky give me an indication and we'll retire to our place, right ,Carolyn?"

"Whatever you say, hon; it'll take me a couple hours to unwind from the high of the show, as usual, and I'd rather it be at home where I can be more comfortable. Rocky wasn't sure if he should let this scenario play itself out and take an active part, or cut and run while the going was good. He couldn't really figure if their meanings were innocent or contained some ulterior motives. At the moment he could use the advice of Felix, the real womanizer of their team. It wasn't that he couldn't physically handle the combination of the two women but what if other people became involved where brute strength alone wasn't enough and he had to resort to the use of his weapon. Another situation like Felix had to contend with at Fritz's.

Rocky made up his mind in his usual calm, collected manner. As much as he enjoyed Esther's company she was definitely a risk he wasn't prepared to take. His dilemma was solved by chance. A taxi pulled to the curb near them, idling, and the voice of Tom Mueller rang out. "Rocky, can you tear yourself away from the girls for a minute?" It was all the excuse Rocky needed. He bent over to look into the rear window. Mr. Mueller, you're a sight for my sore eyes, I was looking for a diversion to disengage myself from these sisters and you're it. I'll make my excuses to them then join you if that's all right with you. You can drop me off a few blocks away."

"No need for that, Rocky, I'm headed back to the shop and unless you have another agenda in mind you can return with me.

Rocky turned to the sisters who had halted just out of earshot, "Sorry to cut our date short, Esther, but duty calls. I'll give you a call when I'm free if that's OK." She had an expression of disappointment on her face that suggested she was losing a particularly favorite plaything that had ruined what would have been an enjoyable pastime for her and Carolyn. "Make sure it's soon, Mr. Newbole, before I lose interest and look further afield for entertaining companionship."

When he got back into the cab Tom didn't ask for any explanation so Rocky remained silent too. They entered the shop to find Felix in exuberant spirits, keeping Leo occupied, thus contented.

Of course the kitchen on the third floor looked like a battlefield after a grueling skirmish. Somewhere Felix had found a king-size dog dish and between the scattering of his regular dog food and saliva from the toy the room was an absolute mess.

"Ya' won't believe who called about an hour ago."

"Why is it anytime you have any new information you have to present it in the form of a guessing game?"

"That's jus' the way I am, heh, heh, heh. Now do ya' want ta' know or not?"

"Spill it, Felix."

"McHenry."

"And?"

"He wants ya' ta' call him in D.C. at yer' earliest convenience which I suppose means ASAP."

"No further information?"

"Nuthin' that he'd tell me. Ya' know how secretive he can be."

"It seems kind of late to be calling Washington. I can't imagine his being at Headquarters this time of night, it's after midnight."

"Sorry, amigo, I forgot. There's another number written down on yer' desk. If you'll take ya' know who with ya' I'll start cleanin' up in here."

Mr. McHenry answered on the second ring as though he had been sitting right next to the instrument waiting.

"Is that you Tom?" he said before Tom could identify himself.

"Yes sir."

"How are things progressing for you and your team?"

Tom was very careful how he summarized their latest activities, remembering the dangerous ground he had treaded on in a previous conversation with his mentor. No mention of Stella or of any other of their misadventures.

"Maybe this information will sweeten your pot. The fugitive responsible for Sheila Bond's death has surfaced. We knew if he was still alive he wouldn't be able to hide forever, and he hasn't. He was spotted near his father's compound but remains as illusive as ever. We'll get him though, it's only a matter of time."

"I have a personal score to settle with Pepe Basquez."

"We realize that, Tom. Your present job is too important to us to pull your team off, so you can even a personal vendetta. It's not like you to think in those terms. We have no reason to think he'll show up in the New York City area but if he should then you can have a legitimate. Any further data which concerns you will be forwarded." Click, and he was gone in his usual abrupt manner.

12

While there was a lull in the action, Felix kept pestering Tom to get some box seats along the third baseline at Yankee stadium. "It don't matter who they play, amigo, it's jus' that your Stella is able ta' get good ones an' she can arrange ta' get a night off ta' join us."

"What's this us stuff?"

"I been promisin' Gennie I'd take her ta' a game. She's a rabid Yankee fan an' when she's not workin' listens ta' every game on her radio. Hey it's only two or so hours an' I've been itchin' ta' see some good baseball since we got here. After the game ya' and Stella can go yer' way and Gennie an'

I can go ours. Whadda' ya' say?" "I suppose if I don't agree I'll never hear the end of it. I know what kind of a nag you can be."

"Good, ya' set it up an' it'll be my treat. An we can drink some beer while we're rootin' for the home team, heh, heh, heh."

"You think of all the angles don't you, partner?"

"I try ta' amigo. There's some great young players I want ta' watch. That outfielder Tom Tresh is bein' touted as a real comer. He's got an arm like a rifle an' he can hit too. An' if we're lucky, Whitey Ford might be pitchin'."

"OK, OK, nag. I'll set it up. Will that satisfy you enough to quiet you down? To change the subject, that phone call from Mr. McHenry was very informative. Your old pal Pepe Basquez has surfaced again. He was seen near his fathers' compound but remains at large. His luck seems to continue. According to Mr. McHenry there is every reason to believe he's back in business, but where and in what capacity is virtually unknown."

"My ol' pal. Where da' ya' get that stuff. If I remember right, ya' were the one who made friends with him."

"That was before Colombia, partner."

"Don't be so touchy; I was pulling your leg . Now Mr. McHenry also stated there is a possibility, slim but a chance he could show up in New York City or Brooklyn and if that should happen, to quote him – 'you may carry out your vendetta against him'."

"He said that?"

"In almost those same words."

'Well then let's hope he has ta' visit here for some reason so we can let Leo have a crack at him. He'd enjoy that. Other than makin' puppies he hasn't had much ta' do lately heh, heh, heh."

Tom had Stella get tickets for four in box seats almost next to the Yankee dugout for a game with the Boston Red Sox. She also made arrangements to get that day off so she could accompany Felix, Gennie, and Tom to the game. It was August 29th. Now as all New Yorkers' knew, the two teams had never got along and battle royals had broken out at both home ballparks. Therefore attendance was always high whenever they played. Many a fine was levied against participating players of both clubs by the commissioner, which only seemed to cause more hard feelings and in turn further skirmishes. A few players, mostly Yankees, seemed to lie in wait for the slightest miscue of a Bosoxer. It didn't take much, two high and inside pitches to the same batter or an unnecessarily hard-handed tag on a base runner could set off a dugout clearing brouhaha. Felix, a connoisseur of the game and excitable vocally, could get very upset at these shenanigans which he thought took the purely intrinsic values out of the sport. Tom would soon learn of another aspect of his partner and friend, a side which could be both embarrassing and provoking. Woe be to the nearby ballplayer or spectator who took exception to his remarks and tried to physically dissuade any further comments from him. Tom hoped that would never happen while they had any girls with them because he knew he would automatically get involved if the situation so warranted, the odds against Felix got too high. Some of those ballplayers were real bruisers and they kept in good physical condition, especially during the season and they were in a league pennant drive. Tom had always wondered what p-laying a sport on the major league level would be like. Had he chosen to pursue that goal after his football days at DeVilbiss High School instead of enlisting in the Marine Corps he might have tried the next rung up the ladder. He had the ability before going to Korea but unfortunately his war wounds interrupted that pursuit. He couldn't really complain though: While at Ohio State, he was recruited by the CIA.

—

The 14th precinct in the Bronx was an old converted fire station at Prospect and 161st St. The two story building had housed the fire station in the late 1800s when horses were still used. When motorized fire trucks came into being the station was no longer large enough to house them so the Borough Fathers, in their all-seeing wisdom, decided it would be the perfect location for the police station which had outgrown its former quarters not two miles away. City workers from all departments were assembled for the cleanup and renovation.

Captain Ian Fuller, a burly old-timer of Gaelic descent and former head of the detective bureau was made Station Commander and was responsible for some sixty-six to seventy men, a number that fluctuated constantly because of injuries on and off duty, the inevitable sicknesses, and transfers in and out of the Station. This nightmare of personnel changing was handled by the shift lieutenants who reported changes daily to Captain Fuller. Even with his subordinates' diligence the Commander had a difficult time keeping track of his people, along with all his other responsibilities, which aggravated him immensely. He had his eyes on a few patrolmen, including his nephew and godson, who should be promoted as soon as possible. They had the right stuff for advancement, command-dedication, perseverance, and the bodily presence to command respect. Adding to his concerns, the Yankees were in another pennant race under the management of the old double-talker Yogi Berra himself. He had a knack of handling the stars of the team who most of the time couldn't understand what in the hell he was talking about. The upshot of all this was the remainder of the season's home games would bring an influx of some 50,000 additional people to the Bronx, added to the usual tourists and conventions – total traffic chaos. Commander Fuller only had one day off a week, though on call for any serious problems. If his free time coincided with a home game it was a given he would be in attendance, although in mufti.

"Going to the game against the Red Sox tomorrow, Cap?" asked the shift lieutenant, who was bringing more paperwork for him to sign. "Wouldn't miss it, Stash. It seems to be my only entertainment and relaxation from this rat race around here."

"What does your wife say when you go to a ballgame on your only day off?"

"She would find fault if I had every weekend off and puttered around at home. 'When are you going to retire so we can go to Florida during these terrible winters?' "But she likes the money which we wouldn't have if I mustered out on two-thirds of my highest pay scale of the last five years. How about you, Stach, what are your plans for the future? I've heard rumors you've been offered a promotion if you would take over the 10th Precinct when old man Gebhardt retires next month. There would be your next step up the ladder."

"I've talked to my wife about it. It's a continuing subject at our house yet as you say, Cap, between the additional hours and responsibilities, there's the travel time to and from Brooklyn. Marge would never consider selling the house to move there, that would entail yanking my son and daughter out of high school to transfer but we don't need a revolt in the household now too. Then there's the probationary period of six months to consider, so I just don't know."

"Sounds to me like you've given it a lot of thought, Stach. My wife and I went through the same situation, so don't feel alone. Of course my kids were grown and gone, but I'm considerably older than you. My only advice to you is: Decide how much farther up you want to go and as long as your health is good make any sacrifice you have to now to get there. Life is too short to be an also ran."

There discussion was interrupted by the ringing of the phone. It was Inspector Beseske, Fuller's friend and mentor. He waved Stach out while he waited for Art to get to the point. "How are things going for you out there, Ian? Having any major problems?"

"Nothing serious Inspector, just the usual manpower issues. It seems we never have enough people to cover all the territory."

"It's the same all over the city, Ian; but I have a problem I don't want to discuss over the phone. How about meeting me tonight or tomorrow morning to talk it over?"

"I'm yours to command inspector; just tell me where and when and I'll be there."

"Since it's a matter of some urgency to me, let's make it tonight at my house. I'll be up whatever time you can get here son." The use of that term made his ears perk up.

"See you between six and seven then, sir."

Ian's father and Art Beseske had been great friends and card-playing drinking buddies before Fred passed away at an early age, if he remembered correctly. Art was a newly appointed police officer while Fred was starting up a construction business that had grown by leaps and bounds just after World War II when the building boom had swept the country. As Fred's business was thriving Art was climbing the rank ladder within the New York City Police Department. However, they still somehow maintained their close friendship and exchanged favors, both money-wise and through political persuasions. When Ian's father died suddenly of a massive heart attack, Art had stepped in as a surrogate father for Ian's brother and himself. That was the motivation for his taking the police examination, thus following the course Art suggested.

"Come in my boy, come in", Art croaked when Ian finally arrived at seven-thirty. One look at the Inspector was enough to tell Ian that here was a very sick man. The once robust person looked like something was eating him from the inside. His once-healthy complexion was now haggard, skin was hanging from his neck in folds, and as he motioned Ian to follow him into the kitchen his steps were short and unsteady. Have you been sick, inspector?"

"You might say that. Sit down boy, what'll you have? Beer, coffee, or some very old ouzo."

"Coffee, but only if it's ready, will be fine, sir."

"You don't have to be so formal in my home, Ian. Coffee is always on." When he returned with a steaming mug he almost dropped it setting it down on the table. "Now, about my health. As you've no doubt noticed already, I've developed a malignant tumor which I've been told is inoperable. I've had so many different opinions I've come to realize the end isn't too far off, which is why I wanted to talk with you so urgently. I've already set the stage for what I have in mind. It only needs your approval now to complete the final steps that can be handled by phone. In the next day or so I intend to put in for sick leave which I know the commissioner will grant." Ian sat looking at Art trying to figure out where this discussion was heading and what part he was to play in it. He was completely at sea.

"Puzzled, son? Don't be. With your moxie there's no telling how far you'll be able to go. It's simple, Ian; you will take my position. Don't believe anything you've heard about this mandatory retirement. It's not going to happen, trust me, I know wherefore I speak. Now, who do you recommend to take your present job in the Bronx?"

"I will have a beer Art. Don't get up, I'll find it." His mind was traveling at high velocity as he moved to the refrigerator. Did Art wield that much influence, the power to bring this about? He returned to the table with a cold brew to listen carefully to Arts plans.

"I can see by your expression you're starting to believe me." Then he unfolded the whole map of plans he'd set in motion. It was a truly amazing story proving to Ian that it had not been a spur of the moment decision because he'd only recently found out about his serious medical condition, this plan had taken some two years of strategy on his part to set up. And then a series of circumstances, some forced and a few by absolute good luck had brought about his desired results.

"So for now just follow your usual routine without making any waves which will allow me to tie up any loose ends. You should also be thinking of someone from your station to be your successor when you leave. I imagine you probably have a likely candidate in mind."

"Yes, sir, I do. His promotion will solve a dilemma he is presently facing", and also put him beholden to me forever, Fuller thought to himself.

"Mind informing me of your choice, Ian?"

"Sorry, sir, it's Stan Modlinski one of my shift lieutenants, the best one I might add. I can count on him for most anything. He's terrific with the paper work and has the respect of all his subordinates so he is most qualified for the station commander's position. I don't believe anyone would dispute his promotion."

"I'll take your word on it Ian, and his slot can be filled by regular Civil Service seniority. Now if everything meets your approval I think I'll call it a night. There is much to do over the next few days and I want to be reasonably fresh and alert to get it done, so if you'll find your way out I'll say goodnight."

Captain Fuller was almost in a trance driving back to the Bronx, his mind racing in several directions at once and only the absence of heavy traffic allowed him accident-free passage.

—

Saturday August 29th was the date Stella had purchased tickets for Yankees-Red Sox double-header. When Felix's party of four arrived at Yankee stadium the temperature was already in the eighties with the humidity equal and rising. The Yankees had lost the previous night 5 to 3 and their hitters were struggling at the plate. Yet some spark had ignited the team in this scorcher. First baseman Joe Pepitone started the fireworks with a bases loaded home run in the first inning giving Jim Bouton all the cushion he was to need. Although he had no strike outs or walks he kept the Red Sox scoreless for six innings losing a shut out by serving up a home run pitch to Carl Yastrzemski with a man on. But Pepitone added another round-tripper with two men on for seven runs batted in. Mickey Mantle added a homer maintaining his 300-plus batting average. Roger Maris had three hits and Elston Howard, the popular Yankee All Star who was being feted as last year's league MVP also had an RBI to give Bouton a 10-2 rout and his fourteenth win of the season.

Felix was getting hoarse by the end of the first game despite averaging a beer an inning which Tom matched. The girls were imbibing soft drinks along with the usual ball park fare of hot dogs, peanuts, and popcorn which had caused them both to use the restroom facilities on a regular basis, thus missing several key plays which then had to be explained to them. "If ya' could hold it ta' the seventh inning stretch ya' wouldn't have ta' have these constant recaps", Felix croaked. "Ya' don't see us runnin' ta' the head all the time." Stella turned to Tom and winked. "I don't know where he stores all that beer. Has he got a hollow leg or something? And you don't do too bad yourself, Tom." "I guess we've built up a tolerance for large sums of beer. We've been doing it for several years now. I don't suppose it's good for either one of us but since neither one of us smoke, well ... a man has to have one or two vices."

"Oh? What's your second one?" Tom just looked at her with a smile to accompany his expression of innocence. That made Stella break out laughing. Felix looked across Tom to Stella. "What's so funny? Ya' can let me in on it." She looked him in the eye, "Private joke, Felix." Tom joined her in the following laughter.

By the time the second game of the double-header was ready to start neither Tom nor Felix were feeling any pain. The temperature and humidity had risen to the point where even the players were starting to grouse. Tempers were at the flash level where just about anything could start a bench-clearing melee. Whitey Ford started for the Yankees and he was sharp and before the game was done he had struck out seven on the way to his fourteenth win of the season. Pepitone had another home run, Maris batted in three and Mantle one, aided by three Boston errors, but Ford had to let Terry relieve him after seven innings because of the heat. The final was 6-1, the Bronx bombers had won the double-header and were now in third place nearing the league lead which was held by Baltimore.

Felix was overjoyed that he had witnessed some of his favorite players in action and although he was almost legless by now and could barely speak he hoped he would be able to see future games as the Yankees pursued the league title.

"C'mon, partner, we have to get you home."

"This is what's known as the blind leading the blind" Gennie quipped.

"Never you mind young lady, we've both been in worse shape than this and still functioned adequately if any threatening situation arose that called for our type of expertise to handle it. Today was simply a combination of heat, humidity, and the excitement of one of his favorite forms of entertainment. He gets three or four hours of rest and nobody will be able to tell how much beer he has consumed in the previous five hours. You can put that in the bank. In the meantime you could be a lot of help if you would accompany us home to put him to bed. Don't worry we'll get you home in good shape. What do you say?"

"Sure, I don't have to be to work until tomorrow noon so there's nothing pressing I have to take care of until then."

When the four arrived at the shop – Stella had agreed to ride with them after which she would cab home – Tom found that all was serene as they had left it. Rocky had entertained Leo sufficiently so that he was sleeping soundly in the third floor kitchen, unlike the disaster Felix had created in that room previously with his form of playtime.

"Nothing out of the ordinary happened while we were gone?"

"Lila Colozzi called twice is all, sir. The messages are on your desk in the office. Beyond those nothing of importance for the team."

With the brevity of that statement Tom wondered if Rocky had received a call from his so-called girlfriend Esther, the tall girl from the shoe store he had been so anxious to get away from a few nights ago. Rather than pursuing that incursion of Rocky's life Tom took a different course. "I'd better contact Lila to see what her problem is before I bed down. Thanks for holding the fort while we enjoyed the ballgames, Rocky, we owe you a favor."

"Not to worry about that, sir; it's the least I could do", he said as he headed toward the stairs. Stella told Tom she would be cleaning up in the bathroom while Gennie was occupied with getting Felix to sleep. "I could hear them thrashing around in the other bedroom when I passed by despite her trying to quiet him, so the sounds of the shower running should alert her that I'll be staying the night, if that's all right with you?"

"You don't even have to ask you know, you're always invited." Tom was thinking ahead. While she was in the shower he could get in touch with Lila, without being overheard, and find out what was bothering her; as if he didn't know. At least he could quiet her down enough to give him time to figure a way to extricate himself from their relationship gracefully, ill advised as it had been. She answered on the second ring as though she had been sitting a few feet from the phone, waiting for his call.

"Where have you been, Tom? I'll take no more excuses from you. You seem to have a way of avoiding me by letting your cronies take my messages which you never answer." Tom could see that Lila was working herself into a rage that was rapidly escalating to a boiling point, never giving him a chance to reply, so he broke in to her ranting. "For Godsake Lila will you simmer down before you have a stroke. I've never heard you rave like this, what's the matter with you?"

"What's the matter with me? Haven't you been listening?"

"Certainly I have, but you're not exactly coherent."

She paused a couple of beats as though catching her breath before resuming her tirade.

"You listen to me, Tom Mueller, and listen good. I'll be over there bright and early tomorrow morning and you better be there." She said that in a calm manner before slamming the phone down on its receiver hard enough to break it.

Tom sensed someone behind him and on turning discovered he was confronted by a naked goddess, his goddess. Stella stood there with all her young beauty bared for his appraisal. Tom stood, all thoughts of Lila and his dilemma vanishing as though only a dream. "You are absolutely gorgeous, Stella."

"Do you have enough energy left to comfort me for the rest of the night or should I go home now?"

"Perish the thought, looking at you standing there like that is like putting a full charge on a dead battery for me." Tom was shedding clothing while moving with her toward the master bedroom, trying to maintain his balance while staring but not touching that beautiful countenance. It wasn't easy.

13

When the calisthenics were discontinued they both fell into a deep sleep, Stella because of fulfillment, Tom from a combination of over-imbibing and being with the woman he loved. And for the first time as long as he could remember Tom slept a full eight hours waking totally refreshed without having memory of his recurring dreams from the Korean War experiences. His eyes opened to find Leo lying some ten foot from the bed, his massive head on his front paws, his eyes open, staring at them.

"Come big boy, I know what you want. After you get your ears scratched you can go out on the roof. How does that sound?" Leo rose effortlessly and rested his head on the bed. "Don't you wake Stella now, Leo; she'll be up later on her own."

After they both had taken care of their respective business and had returned to the kitchen, they found Stella cooking bacon and eggs dressed in one of Tom's white shirts tied at the waist, nothing under but panties which gave him ideas that weren't exactly related to eating breakfast. Tom realized he couldn't pursue his desires because Lila said she would be here "bright and early today," whatever that meant on her time schedule, so he had to get Stella out of there to avoid having a confrontation between them. Tom knew what a loose cannon Lila could be and that she was capable of almost anything when she was riled. He continued to berate himself for getting involved with her to begin with, but how was he to know that a twin of Sheila existed? Leo was watching Stella transfer sizzling bacon from the frying pan to paper towels to cool. The mouth-watering aroma filled the room and the mastiff could sense as treat coming to him. "You just lie there and wait, Leo, I won't forget you." As if he could understand what she said, his tail started swishing back and forth in anticipation.

"That was wonderful last night, Tom; you had enough energy for two people despite your full day at the ballpark."

Stella turned toward Tom and Leo. She bent forward and offered the dog a strip of bacon which he scarfed from her hand with the genteelness of a human. She continued forward and embraced Tom with full-bodied closeness and kissed him passionately.

"I didn't know ya' were busy but the smell of food pulled me out of bed. I'm starved."

Tom broke away from Stella with breathless difficulty. "You can eat while I get cleaned up and finish dressing, partner. Just tell Stella what you want."

Leo's eyes followed Tom as he left the kitchen but he stayed put knowing the nice girl would give him more bacon treats to munch on. Felix sat at the small table and ordered like he was sitting in Fritz's restaurant." Ya' can get me four eggs hard over, fried potatoes, and fill the rest of the plate up with that great smellin' bacon." Stella simply ignored his complicated order and continued to cook as she had been, thinking he'd get what she had at hand and like it or wear it, fried potatoes indeed!

Felix, the galloping gourmet which he wasn't, ate everything that Stella put in front of him without complaint. The absence of fried potatoes was never mentioned because he was too busy with the rest of the fare to be bothered with minor details. Leo's patience paid off with several more cooled strips of bacon hand fed to him.

"Yer' a great cook, Stella. Ya' leave the cleanin' up to me so ya' can finish dressin'. I'll take care of the overgrown cocker spaniel too so ya' won't have ta' stumble over him. He can be a nuisance if ya' cater to him. I should know."

Felix had one of his premonitions of disaster that came to him right out of the blue with no rhyme or reason. He was right in the middle of scouring the frying pan and washing the utensils when it hit him. Quickly drying his hands he made a beeline for his bedroom where he had left his trusty weapon, Leo following. Gennie was sleeping soundly so he returned to his chores, pistol stuck in his belt and Leo in trail; his previous feelings of doom quelled for the time being. His hands again immersed in soapy water his thoughts returned to Toledo and the Marie Fowler fiasco that had wounded him so severely, then the Greco affair where the odds seemed stacked against him only to be reversed, and so many other hair-raising situations that he'd been involved in where those old foreboding warnings had somehow saved him from meeting his maker.

Leo's massive head came up abruptly and cocked to one side distracting Felix from his thoughts. The dog either heard a threatening sound or his powerful sense of protection for his family was aroused. Whatever the reason, he was on his feet, front legs spread slightly, tail straight down and motionless, and a menacing growl from deep within issued forth.

One of the times when Tom was at their newly rented flat and he'd exhausted himself from an extended period of sex, Lila had taken impressions of his keys in a bar of soap that was soft enough for that purpose. She knew they had put in new locks in the showroom front door after the break-in by her Uncle Ferdie's enforcers. When she began to doubt his fidelity to only her she had gone to a locksmith and had them made. She truly hoped they would work when the time came. She also bought a .32 caliber hand gun to use on him. She had sworn to herself if she couldn't have him no one else would either, and by God now seemed to be the time for all her planning to become a reality. The pawnshop owner had guaranteed that the small weapon would stop any intruder who broke into her house, if she was close enough. The only problem she could think of was that she never carried a purse, so she would have to conceal it somewhere in her clothing.

The key worked like a charm and because daylight was close enough for Lila to make her way to the rear of the showroom without bumping into anything she made it to the rear stairs unimpeded. There she paused, listening before starting up the steps, All seemed quiet but she had two floors to negotiate before she would reach his apartment and where was that damn dog? He was never very far from Tom when they were in this building. Lila hadn't taken more than three steps upward when she heard the first sign of life since she entered the stillness here. She hesitated a few seconds fumbling to withdraw her weapon while listening hard for a repeat of the sound. Not hearing anything she continued. She had reached the second floor landing and was about to make the turn when she sensed rather than heard that she wasn't alone any longer. "Is that you, Tom?"

A door opened behind her and she was about to turn when something grabbed the arm that was holding the .32 with such force she was catapulted across the landing bouncing off the wall. Lila screamed, not just from the pain in her arm but in absolute shock and suddenness and brute strength of her attacker. Her scream raised everyone in the building for when she opened her tear-streaked eyes there were three or four persons crowded around her on the landing. Tom was kneeling beside her examining her arm. He called to the big man to phone for an ambulance.

"Whatever possessed you to sneak in here with a weapon, and how did you get in? I don't know, Lila, I realized you were headstrong but I didn't think you would resort to breaking and entering for some foolish notion. You knew Leo here was a guard dog. I'm afraid he broke your wrist along with tearing a nasty gash in your forearm. We'll get the bleeding stopped while we wait for the ambulance." Felix had gone on an errand and returned with an assortment of first-aid supplies which he not too gently applied, muttering to himself while he did so.

"Ya' don't have the brains of a bug. It must be yer' Italian blood that caused ya' ta' pull a stunt like this."

"Ambulance is on the way, Mr. Mueller."

"Take Leo into your apartment, Rocky, while we finish up here. Then we'll take her downstairs to wait for them. Good boy, Leo; I'll take care of you later."

"What do you mean good boy? Are you going to reward that beast for what he did to me? I've never heard anything so cold-hearted in all my life. You're as mean-spirited as that animal, and I don't know what I ever saw in you, Tom Mueller." She was working herself into another rage, crying in between her spiteful harangue, a ruse a good many spoiled women used to both vent their anger and get what they wanted. Tom thanked his lucky stars Stella didn't fit into that category, so he held his tongue and let Lila get it all out. The ambulance arrived just as Tom and Felix half-carried half-walked her to the front of the shop. The attendants took one look at her patched up arm, strapped her into a stretcher and drove off, siren wailing. When Tom re-locked the front door they walked back up to the third floor, stopping long enough to take Leo with them. "It was lucky Stella and Gennie didn't witness any of that."

"It wasn't luck amigo. When I went for the first-aid supplies they were both dressed an' ready ta' join ya' an' I told 'em to keep outta' it."

"Good thinking, partner. Now when we join them let me answer any of their questions. That way hopefully I can avoid the real reason why Lila came here."

"Lotsa' luck, amigo, heh, heh, heh."

Stella had another pot of coffee brewing when the men joined them. She and Gennie were conversing like life-long friends who met on a daily basis for a trade of local gossip.

"We thought you might like some more coffee", Stella said aiming her statement with a wink at Felix. "Beer'd be more like it."

48

"Oh Felix don't you ever get enough?" "What's enough? Heh, heh, heh."

Felix came to the door. "Phone call, amigo, an' you'll never guess who."

"Enlighten me."

"Mr. McHenry, does that light ya' up?"

"All right Felix, I'll get it. When Leo decides to come in would you grab some towels and wipe him down so he doesn't shake water all over the apartment ?" Tom was wondering how much he should reveal to Mr. McHenry on what had happened to Lila and the teams part in the event as he sat down in the office.

"Any progress with those families, Tom ?" Not hello, how are you getting along, or any other cordial opening remarks. But that was McHenry's usual succinct manner as was his way of signing off.

"Not as much as we would like, sir. It would seem they are consolidating their methods and resources at this time for a different tack. It's mostly a wait and see situation lately."

"You still have your place in Franklin Park?" Tom wondered why the sudden change of direction but was relieved he had switched topics.

"Give particular attention to the families for the next week to ten days and push Miss Colozzi for information during that period. Keep someone near your phone after that as I'll be in touch. There are some important issues before Congress which should be coming to a vote about then and all available agents will be called in to D.C." Click, and he was gone in his usual abrupt manner.

"Felix, did you wipe the rain off Leo?"

"Yeah an it wasn't easy. Every time I get near that animal he thinks it's playtime, he's gettin' worse the older he gets. When he was just a pup we all thought it was kinda' cute, now amigo he's gettin' outta' hand."

"Have you been reading the newspapers lately?"

"Ya' know the only section worth my attention is sports, why?"

"It's something Mr. McHenry said. I'm going to the public library to look over some back issues of the Times. Hopefully they will shed some light on the subject. Now, where is Stella?"

"Dunno. Check your bedroom; she might be in there unless she decided ta' go home. I have ta' get Gennie up an' movin'."

"Well,Tom, are you going to explain what happened here this morning or are you using that business ploy again?"

"You get right to the heart of the matter don't you, no beating around the bush, right? You deserve an explanation and I should have done it sooner. As you may have surmised Lila was our inside informant for the mob which is controlling the drug trade in the city this side of the East River. My superiors had told me personally to be nice to her to coax all the information possible about her Uncle and guardian. It all stemmed from her close relationship with Fred, my deceased twin. She misconstrued some of my attention to suit herself so when you entered my life her misplaced jealousy overrode her common sense. This morning's actions were the result. She was deathly afraid of Leo whenever they were near each other and she underestimated his guard duty capabilities which was her mistake. Will that suffice?"

For an answer Stella walked over to the bed where Tom was sitting, pushed him to a prone position and laid full length on him; he didn't resist.

"We could continue this all day but there is work to be done and errands to run and you probably want to get home. So let me clean up a bit and then we'll call a cab. I'll drop you off and then continue with the things I have to do."

UNLIKELY TWINS

On the way to the Bronx they discussed several things, one being his desire to have her quit her job at Yankee Stadium. She was iffy on that subject, not wanting to be completely dependent on someone else for her "daily bread" was the way she put it. He enforced his case by telling her the team might be leaving the city soon and returning to Washington, D.C., where it just so happened he had a house in a nearby suburb. That information made her pause for a few minutes and Tom remained silent while she stared out the window thinking this new turn of events over. Stella turned back to him but before she could say anything he added: "I'm going to hire a moving truck and crew to come over to your place. I'd like you to send all your finished paintings and your most prized possessions, which includes furniture, that you can live without for a couple of weeks. I'll be there tomorrow before the truck is to help you in any way you need." Stella just looked at him open-mouthed. She had always been so independent, making her own decisions, living her own life style within her means, and along comes this man who in a very short time wants to change all that. She knew she loved him despite his occupation and his hard-drive toward total drug eradication. Yet he never seemed to worry about money as though he had some hidden source although he was a man of simple tastes. Quite contradictory she thought. They pulled up in front of her building and Tom walked her to her front door like the gentleman he was. He chastely kissed her cheek, waited for her to unlock the door, and said he'd see her early tomorrow.

Tom had the cab driver drop him off at a jewelry store in Manhattan where he asked to see the manager who was produced at once without any foolishness, unlike the store in Louisiana where he and Felix had taken the emerald he'd discovered in Colombia. When he took the 3 carat diamond out of its pouch accompanied by the two half carat rubies from another and explained how he wanted them set the manager never blinked an eye. Stella's birthday was in July she'd told him, thus why he picked the rubies rather than some other gems from the hidden wall safe. The manager, Mr. Price, did blink when he said it had to be ready by 2 P.M. tomorrow.

The setting should be gold, which was the color of her watch, a rather old Gruen. "Sorry for the short notice but my job necessitates odd hours", and Tom showed his picture identification. He then asked for a piece of paper and drew an overhead view of how the stones should be placed. Mr. Price was all business as he pulled a tray of settings out of a showcase. "I would recommend this setting, Mr. Mueller. The rubies will highlight that beautiful diamond and the tight dovetail will belie gaudiness. Do you agree?" Tom nodded. "Now as for the time limit, I will have to charge you extra for any overtime. Our jeweler puts in to complete the work by 2 P.M. tomorrow, you understand. This type of work is painstaking and only our top man will be used."

"I have faith in your judgment and expertise, Mr. Price. Be seeing you at two tomorrow." Price was all smiles when Tom shook his hand and accepted the receipt for his stones.

Fortunately, the main library was a short distance from the jewelers because the temperature was in the high nineties with humidity to match.

Tom was glad to enter the coolness of the old stone building. An assistant librarian behind the main desk was more than helpful as she pointed out where past copies of the New York Times and Washington Post were draped over dowels in long racks dating back to January 1st of this year. "If you need anything dated before then just let me know, sir, and I'll direct you to our Archives Section." She had to be in her middle to late forties and was rather plain but was over-endowed in the breast department. Wearing a short sleeve blouse, Tom could imagine her duress and embarrassment in her younger years. Even now, they threatened to burst out of her blouse without the slightest provocation.

Tom spent over five hours between the racks and one trip to the Archives Section which was

50

housed in a separate room. Even with the heavy traffic of the building he wasn't bothered in either section and took copious notes before his eyes started to smart from reading all the small print. He read everything available on the J.F.K. assassination, the Warren Commission, the history of L.B.J, the Gulf of Tonkin Incident, and most of the available supporting documents so he now understood somewhat of what McHenry was alluding to. He had his own doubts on the validity of some of the so-called facts. He remembered an old adage: Believe ten percent of what you hear and twenty-five percent of what you read. He thought that was apropos here.

When Tom got back to the shop, he put the beer he'd purchased into the fridge then started making calls to moving companies. He struck paydirt on the third call. A medium size truck with two men would be at Stella's address by 10:30 A.M. the next day. It behooved Tom to be there an hour earlier to help smooth the transition and to allay any misgivings Stella might have. When the movers were through he intended to coax Stella into accompanying him to Manhattan under some pretext, run in and get the ring, and then find some romantic spot to make his proposal of marriage. Maybe the top of the Empire State Building or some ritzy restaurant like the Four Seasons that had private banquet rooms. He'd have to call them for reservations.

Tom wore his only suit, the one he bought at the airport specialty shop. He hated to wear ties and only owned one but it was a mess so he asked Rocky if he had a tie suitable for a formal occasion, not mentioning what the event would be. Rocky had several and told him to take his pick. So decked out in his finery he called a taxi early the next morning for the ride to the Bronx. He arrived at 9:45 and rang her doorbell. Stella left him in dressed in a sweatshirt and blue jeans with a Yankee ball cap on backwards. She looked lovely.

"Aren't you a bit overdressed, Tom?"

"Don't worry I'll shed the jacket and tie so I don't get them dirty. The movers will do any heavy work anyway.

"Sounds to me like you're hiding something from me."

"Not at all, Stell. I have an appointment later today that calls for this get up. So what is going?"

She started pointing at different pieces, a couple of lamps, some books already in a box and labeled. "All the paintings are together in the back room except for what I'm currently working on. Of course none of my materials are to leave. That would be kind of foolish in the event I got an inspiration don't you think?"

"What are you working on now, another portrait?"

Stella passed over the question by pointing to a credenza. "I suppose that should go too. It has no real function but I'm so used to seeing it there. What do you think?"

"You're evading my question. Why?"

Stella turned away, but Tom could tell by the cant of her head she was crying. He went over to her and put his arms around her, pulling her to his chest. "What's the matter, Stell?" She held on to him like he was a life preserver thrown to a drowning person, but the crying stopped.

"It's just the idea of letting go of the life I'm used to for the unknown. I do love you Tom with all my heart. If anything ere to happen to you I'm afraid I'd go off the deep end."

"Nothing is going to happen to me, not with Leo around watching my back. Now straighten up I hear a truck pulling up outside."

There must have been over a hundred paintings and several charcoal sketches, plus some stretched canvases ready for her attention. Tom didn't get a chance to look at many of them because the movers were wasting no time loading them into the truck. The marked furniture came next and by 11:45 they were done and on their way, credenza and all. Tom didn't even have to shed his suit jacket.

"Tell you what, Stell, why don't you freshen up and change into something fancy so I can treat you to a nice brunch or early dinner. We'll make an evening of it and you'll soon forget about what has happened this morning."

"What about work?"

"You can call in sick if it looks like you won't be able to make it."

"Oh all right, I might as well take a shower. Do you want to wash my back among other things?"

"I think I'll take a rain-check on that if you don't mind. If I took you up on your invitation it would only lead to other things and I'd be late for my afternoon appointment. You go it alone for now and I'll make some phone calls. Take your time."

Tom called Rocky at the shop to see what if anything was happening. "Is Felix still there or did he take Gennie home?"

"They finally left about a half hour ago, Mr. Mueller. Leo is in my apartment too so he isn't up to any mischief. Are you going to be late?"

"It kind of looks that way, Rocky. I'm taking Stella out for the evening to make my proposal of marriage." "That's wonderful Mr. Mueller. Congratulations. I'm sure she will accept."

"Thanks Rocky. If it gets past midnight I'll check in again, but we'll probably end up there anyway."

After some thought, Tom next called The Four Seasons Restaurant on East 52nd St. to see if reservations were necessary for a party of two and if a small banquet room was available for same. Tom was assured accommodations could be made to satisfy any of his wishes so he reserved a table for 6 P.M. He also called the Empire State Building Information Center and was informed the observation deck was open until midnight and guided tours were conducted every hour on the hour, so they could take that in before going to the Four Seasons. He'd keep Stella so busy from the time they left her place so she wouldn't be able to dwell on her soon to come displacement.

Stella finally emerged from he bath and bedroom dressed fit to kill for, in a black cocktail dress. Tom guessed that's what you'd call it, not being a woman's fashion expert. The dress was hemmed just below the knees to show off her svelte legs ending in three or four inch black high heels. The front of the dress was cut demurely high not too noticeably accenting her fine breasts but when she pirouetted on her toes to present the full picture Tom almost choked. There was no back, at least until it resumed well below the waist. What held the material up he wondered? Was it somehow glued to her skin?

Tom looked at his watch. It was a quarter to two. He hadn't realized it was so late. They'd be hard pressed to reach the jewelers on time. "You'd better. I don't want to be too late for my appointment."

They reached the jewelers at two twenty-five and Tom had Stella wait in the cab while he went in. Mr. Price spotted him at once. "Ah, Mr. Mueller you have arrived. Your ring is ready", and he presented a fancy box with a flourish. "I trust this will meet with your approval."

The ring inserted so it stood up against the satiny black interior was everything he had hoped for. Tom realized Mr. Price had fulfilled his promise of excellent workmanship by an artist. He presented the receipt but Price told him that wasn't necessary.

Tom looked the bill over and it seemed quite reasonable to him considering the rush order and the delicate nature of the work. He took out the last stone he had in his pocket, a sapphire of about a half carat. "Can we call this even?" Price was astonished. "Where do you keep coming up with these gems?"

"My brother, now deceased, was a collector of precious gems most of his life and on his passing willed them to me. Now, do we have a deal?"

"Of course, but beyond being a good businessman I do have a conscience I have to live with and I feel that I'm taking unfair advantage of your generosity, so to pacify my conscience." Price withdrew a sheaf of bills from his wallet and handed them to Tom.

"You have been more than fair, Mr. Price, and to show my gratitude I will refer anyone who is in the market for jewelry of any kind to you.." Tom put the ring box into the inside pocket of his suit coat next to his heart, pocketed the cash without counting it, and shook the store manager's hand. "Good day, sir." He joined Stella in the waiting cab and told the driver to take them to the Empire State Building.

"Was your appointment successful?"

"Very", and he took out the bills Price had handed him. Counting, he found $100.00 in a mixed denomination of bills which he shoved back into his pants pocket to join the cash he had brought for the evening. There would be no skimping now.

Why are we going to the Empire State Building?"

"I've never been there and now seems a good time to see it. Have you ever been to the observation deck?"

"As long as I've lived in the Bronx I've never had the time for sightseeing. I was either at work or painting." "It might give you a new perspective for your painting; have you ever thought of that?"

Stella just looked at Tom, thinking how involved he was becoming in her hobby. The depth of the man was astounding with all his other pursuits. The more time she spent around him the deeper in love she fell. Her life before Tom now seemed like an empty void where nothing had any meaning or point of purpose. He was an exciting person with multiple facets of character. She hoped that somehow she could realign her own personality to conform with his harmonies. Stella knew she would try her darnedest.

They spent longer than Tom would have thought on the observation deck. Hand in hand they stood taking in the panoramic vistas of New York City, the crossroads of America. Stella was unusually silent but she indeed was admiring the view, her artistic bent comparing one angle to another, and trying to think of how she would recreate the colors and the dimensions.

Tom turned her towards him and kissed her soundly.

"What brought that about?"

"To break you out of your reverie so you would pay more attention to the guy who loves you. Daydreams should be on your own time."

Stella returned his gesture with passion.

When they finally exited the building Tom hailed the first cab in sight which promptly pulled to the curb for the well dressed couple. "Four Seasons Restaurant, please."

"Wow, we're going first class today aren't we? Tell me this isn't a dream, Tom. I'd hate to wake up at work, which reminds me I better call the office to make my excuses for my absenteeism."

"You can do that from the restaurant, and quit looking at me like I'm Mandrake the Magician or something. This is a celebration."

"Of what?" "You'll see soon enough.

The maitre d' checked his list and found the Mueller name. He snapped his fingers and a white-jacketed waiter appeared to show them to a private dining room.

When the champagne was placed in front of them Tom dismissed the sommelier and stood to make a toast. "This is to our future together, Stell, may it be long and fruitful." They linked arms and drank.

Tom removed the ring box from his jacket, got on one knee, and said, "You know how much I love you, Stell. Would you accept this ring as a token of my devotion to you? I'm asking you to marry me." Stella burst into tears. "That's beautiful, Tom, and yes I will." He placed the ring on her finger and they embraced. "God, I've been so nervous all day that you'd reject me."

"That's an absolutely beautiful ring Tom, and I'd never reject you. I want to be your wife forever. We'll have some beautiful children. How many do you want?"

"What, you can order them like out of a Sears catalog? I'm very surprised that you haven't been impregnated as yet with all our love making."

"That's all you know, my love; you've obviously never heard of a diaphragm." Tom just stared at his blond Goddess completely in the dark. "It's a little device women use to avoid unwanted pregnancy, and it usually works."

"What do you mean usually?"

"If it's put in hastily and isn't seated properly or becomes turned someway, but it's more reliable than the pill."

"Can we talk about something else, like what you would like to do next."

"I'd like you to take me home."

"Yours or mine?"

"It better be yours or Leo will have his nose out of joint."

14

When Tom and Stella were on their way home the previous night from the Four Seasons, he had the feeling all was not well, that extra sense that some sort of doom lurked within striking distance despite the euphoria of Stella accepting his proposal. The feeling persisted in his mind the next morning when he regained consciousness. The odor of coffee and eggs was wafting in from the kitchen. Since Stella wasn't next to him in bed she must be at the stove, rather than Felix. Leo who usually was near the bedroom entrance was also absent. Tom slid out of bed, donned some underwear and bathrobe, heading in that direction. Felix had beat him to it. The bottom-less pit was already sitting at the table with coffee in front of him waiting for food of any kind. Tom walked up behind Stella and nuzzled her behind the ear. "No second thoughts about your betrothal last night?"

For an answer Stella turned around and planted an arduous buss on his lips, spatula in one hand, while Felix and Leo looked on.

"Congratulations, amigo, I jus' wondered what took ya' so long ta' get up yer' nerve ta' ask for her hand, heh, heh, heh."

"You are an agitator aren't you, partner? You better be careful how you speak or you might wear that breakfast before you get the chance to eat it."

"Aw, Stella wouldn't do that ta' me, we kinda' unnerstand each other."

"Stella isn't the only person living in this apartment. Stell, when you get done feeding this galloping gourmet come back to our bedroom, I want you to see something that might interest

54

you. I'll either be there or in the shower." Tom sat Stella on the bed, walked over to the hidden wall safe, and pressed the recessed button. Part of the wall slid noiselessly away revealing the face of the safe with its gleaming combination dial which he spun to the memorized numbers. "Pretty neat, huh? Now come over here and see part of my treasure. I say part because the real deal is in New Orleans."

Stella's eyes resembled those of Eddie Cantor as she looked through the pouches of jewels Tom pulled open one at a time. There were also banded packs of large denomination bills Tom had added since taking over the building, from several sources, mostly from expense and salary checks.

"What do you mean by real deal?"

Tom explained his find of the large emerald while in Colombia on a mission then taking it to the largest jewelry store in New Orleans for appraisal and subsequent housing for show and the draw he had arranged for against it. "Now there are some other things you should know about concerning property. I've done a little corresponding with attorney friends of mine from Ohio State about the home Fred owned on Key Largo off the coast of eastern Florida. They are checking with colleagues of theirs who are licensed to practice in Florida so I should be hearing from them most any time. If the outcome of their research is favorable to me we'll take some time to see it. There's a Gresham motor yacht in a repair yard near there that by paying the bill we'll also own."

"Oh that sounds wonderful, Tom, I've never been to Florida."

"Let's not put the cart in front of the horse, Stell; everything has to mesh first. What are your plans for the day?"

"I've got to get back to work tonight; I can't afford to take two nights off in the same week, not if I want to pay my rent and utilities on time."

"Didn't anything I just told and showed you sink in?"

"Sure, but we haven't moved yet and the rest is contingent on when you are notified by the attorneys, right?"

"If your intention is to go to work today then let me call you a cab."

"That's what I'm talking about honey. You spend money like a drunken sailor, never giving a thought about saving any. I'm perfectly capable of taking the subway."

"Dressed in your finery? At least let me buy you some suitable clothing. Then we'll take the subway together. I'm about due to try that out before we leave New York City. It'll be a new experience for me."

"I give up. All right if you won't heed my advice go ahead and spend."

"Any chance for a matinee before we leave?"

"No. Maybe when we get to my place. I'll see."

Tom looked in the Yellow Pages and found the closest women's apparel store and then called a cab anyway. It was too far to walk in this heat. He notified Felix, then Rocky he would be gone for a few hours, leaving Stella's phone number with both.

Wouldn't you know, Tom thought, Stella picked out the cheapest sun dress in the store. Whether she was trying to show him how frugal she could be or not made no difference, she looked terrific in it because it was impossible to hide her physical attributes. But the kicker was the shoes she chose to compliment the outfit, a pair of canvas moccasins. Tom just shook his head but didn't say a word. She'd get over her snit by the time they got to her apartment.

Stella held Tom's hand as they headed for her brownstone. As they neared Tom could feel her tense up. He hand tightened its grip on his and she increased their pace to almost a lope. "Something wrong, Stell?"

She didn't answer until they rounded the corner where her anxiety was now obvious. There parked in front were fire trucks with hoses running to a hydrant and a rescue squad vehicle and another car which they would soon find out belonged to an arson investigator. As they approached a fireman wearing a white helmet said, "I'm sorry folks you can't come any closer as we are still checking for hot spots."

"This is my apartment, sir. Was anyone in the building hurt?"

"The old folks in the lower right were taken to the hospital for smoke inhalation but no burns. They should be all right. No one else was home in the building. And you are?" Stella gave him her name and occupation. "There were a lot of combustibles in your apartment, why?"

"My hobby is painting, mostly in oils."

"I see, now this next question will be rather difficult for you, so take your time."

Tom had stood silent throughout the entire exchange waiting for the obvious. The district chief motioned to another fireman. "Is Pete about done in there?"

"I'll check, chief."

"Do you have any enemies, Miss Bond? This was definitely the work of an arsonist, which is about to be corroborated by the man I just called for. He's a specialist in the field." Tom could wait no longer, having flashbacks of the arson of his Mom's house in Toledo.

Tom flashed his picture ID. The district chief took a classic double-take. "And what does the CIA have to do with a house fire?"

"Miss Bond is my fiancee. The case we are working on was most likely caused by the mob we are investigating in retaliation for some damage we've already done them. This isn't the first time their type of organization has resorted to this tactic. So you see that is my interest in this. Any information you can relay to me will be greatly appreciated."

"We'll do our best But the Bronx Police will have to be involved."

"So be it."

"How large a team do you have working on this?"

"Four."

"That doesn't sound like very many, why so few?"

"From past experience we have found the larger the team the more chances there are for leaks both internal and from other agencies involved."

Pete, the arson specialist, joined them and was introduced to Tom and Stella. "An old-fashioned Molotov cocktail was thrown through the rear window. A very amateurish yet effective fire starter by anyone who is a first timer or in a hell of a hurry. In this case I would say the former because of the estimated time of start based on when it was called in. I'm afraid there is much salvageable in the back half of your apartment, Miss Bond. I hope you have somewhere else to live while repair is under way. The damage back there is extensive."

"Will you be filing your report with the Bronx precinct?", Tom asked.

"Yes, sir. First thing in the morning I will deliver my full findings to Commander Fuller in person. I would imagine someone from his office will want to speak with you shortly thereafter so could you give me a phone number where you can be reached?" Tom did and then asked if they could somehow reach a cab so he and Miss Bond could return home.

When they reached the shop, Tom called Felix and Rocky for a confab while Stella took Leo into the bedroom with her. Her mind was spinning with all the problems that faced her. It was like she hade been backed into a no-win situation which nothing she could do would solve. The full impact of her loss now realized she finally broke down, the tears flowing freely. Leo who had been lying by the door sensed the nice lady's distress, rose effortlessly and trod over to the bed. He laid his massive head in her lap, his expressive eyes watching her intently. "Now I understand what Tom means when he says you're almost human." She took his head between her hands, lowered her head and kissed him on both jowls; Leo almost purred his appreciation. Stella, her tears now stopped, scratched behind his ears with the inevitable results. Stella laughed out loud, her troubles momentarily forgotten.

"So you see, you guys, we now have a semi-permanent house guest at least until we're called back to Washington. I don't expect her to wait on you; she's not a maid. We all have to share the load. I know I can count on your cooperation on this. She has just suffered a terrible loss that for a woman is hard to swallow. I'll make it up to her but in the meantime we have to make her stay as pleasant as possible. One more thing, she should never be left alone here even with Leo left to watch over her. He can do just about anything but he can't talk."

Tom walked over to the hidden wall safe, opening it. He removed two hundred dollars in twenties from the banded cash inside then re-closed it. This money he intended to give Stella to replace some of her lost clothing. He doubted she would give him any argument this time about his wastrel ways. She had to have something to wear around the apartment beside his shirts, even the basics of bras, panties, hose, and toiletries. Every woman needed those. He tucked the cash into a pants pocket and returned to the bed, giving Leo a hand signal to assume his customary position by the door. Leo swiveled his huge head, first looking at Stella then Tom , before deciding to obey. Tom stroked her beautiful hair gently not exactly trying to wake her but just to show his affection.

15

Stella was trying to find places to put her new clothes in Tom's bedroom. It was hopeless. There was only the one closet and it wasn't very large. It contained mostly his shirts and suit. There wasn't even a separate bureau and she wondered where Tom kept his underwear, handkerchiefs, and things like that. She was sitting on the bed looking around in puzzlement, her clothing taking up a good portion of the bed's surface when it dawned on her to look under it. She got down on her hands and knees to pull back the bed covers and found the answer. There were four zippered clothing bags which were used to hang clothes in when traveling, each containing holes at the top for hangers to protrude. Tom's other items were in each, evenly divided with a neatness uncommon for a man. Her only recourse was to consolidate enough of his things into three bags to allow her one. This took her the better part of an hour before she was satisfied his items were as neatly arranged as he had them. Now she was sitting on a neatly uncluttered bed daydreaming about her future with this complex man that she so dearly loved, wondering when she would become pregnant. The last few days she quit inserting her diaphragm and as virile she hoped Tom was it was possible she already was. If so, then they would have to have a quick, no-frills, wedding. Not especially religious, Stella still wouldn't think of having a child out of wedlock.

While Stella was thinking about her future Tom entered the bedroom. "I see you found my hidden stash for smaller items of clothing. I should have alerted you to the shortage of closet space. When Fred had those inner passageways installed some of the second and third floor living spaces were short-changed and inner wall closets were the first to go.

—

Later, on the way to Alfredo's Tom broke up an altercation that attracted several policemen, who were about to put him in handcuffs until he produced his picture ID. One patrolman motioned to the other and they had a quick whispered conference. "Look, mac, I've seen enough fake IDs to last me a lifetime so my partner's gonna' call the district sergeant to check you out. You can put your hands down until he arrives but keep that animal under control." Tom deftly returned the Cobra to its belt holster and in a low tone talked to Leo. "Good boy, Leo, behave now until someone with a little more sense gets here. Sit." The dog acted like he understood every word but regardless obeyed the command.

Within five minutes another patrol car pulled into the alley and stopped. A uniformed officer not much smaller than Rocky had a short discussion with the patrolmen before approaching Tom alone. Tom could tell the officer was a street-savvy veteran by the hash marks on his sleeve. It was obvious he wasn't interested in climbing the rank ladder. "All right, what is your side of the story?"

The sergeant was eyeing Leo while Tom was retrieving his credentials. "That is one beautiful dog you have there. Don't think I have ever seen one that big before. He must eat you out of house and home." The big man had a New York accent you could cut with a knife. Tom presented his ID while the sergeant was still looking at Leo..

"CIA, huh? What brings you to our fair city?"

Rather than going into it, Tom changed the subject. "I can give you several phone numbers in Washington, D.C., to verify my status or you can check with the Bronx Police who will also do so."

"Oh, I don't doubt you at all, sir. Let me get my crew back on patrol then when I return I'll take you and your dog back to your residence." He turned and lumbered away.

"You might as well sit up front with me, Mr. Mueller. Your dog can have the back all to himself."

"His name is Leo, Sarge."

"My name is Patrick O'Toole but most everyone calls me Paddy, everybody but the criminal type."

"How long have you been on the department, Paddy?"

"Twenty-six years. I went on when I returned from the service."

"Have you always worked this area of the city?"

"I walked a beat in Brooklyn until my promotion but yes I've always worked here since. Any particular reason why you're asking?"

Tom figured, why not. "Then you should be familiar with the higher ups in this area. I mean the key figures who run all or most of the rackets here, which includes the drug trade of course."

Paddy looked over at Tom. "Would you care to stop at an all-night restaurant I know of and discuss this further? We both my learn some things."

"What about Leo?"

"He can stretch out on the back seat and take a nap. I'll open a rear window a couple of inches so he'll have some air in here. I'm sure nobody will bother him, no one in their right mind that is. Besides, a police car can be parked anywhere and we'll be able to see anyone foolish enough to approach it."

Tom turned toward the rear seat. "Leo, you guard the car and no chewing, got it?" The dog raised its head at the sound of his name. His tongue hung out of his maw with the expression Tom always associated with a grin. "If you're a good boy maybe I'll give you a treat."

"You talk to that dog like he's a human and can understand you."

"He almost is. I could tell you any number of stories that would prove it."

Paddy was greeted like an old friend rather than a policeman or just a regular customer. He headed straight for a booth along the wall near the front where he could keep an eye on his car through the front window. A coffee was placed in front of him and the older waitress asked Tom what he would like. "The same will be fine."

After Tom was served he waited for Paddy to begin. There were no niceties exchanged. The sergeant asked Tom who he was tracking by being in that particular alley where he was stopped. "Might it have been Ferdie Colozzi?"

"You know who and what he is?"

"I wouldn't be much of a policeman if I didn't. He's pretty high up the ladder of the mob in Manhattan."

"He also has tentacles that reach into Brooklyn you must know. The two families might be competitors yet they are from the same breed, drugs, which is at the top of their nefarious crimes."

"You seem to have more information on them than I do, Mr. Mueller. Finish your coffee and I'll get you home."

16

"Where ya' been, amigo? We were startin' ta' worry ."

"It's kind of a long story, partner. Get me a beer while I get Leo an overdue reward for being so helpful tonight. You'd have been proud of him, Felix; he was instrumental in my making a contact with a new source of valuable information about Colozzi and the family in Brooklyn."

Seated over their beers with Leo by the door making short work of his beef stick, Tom brought Felix up to date on the events of the night which began in the alley behind Alfredo's.

"Here's a little aside. While Sergeant O'toole and I were having coffee and exchanging information he went into some personal history of his. It seems he owns a Irish Wolfhound. Kind of figures doesn't it? O'toole, Irish Wolfhound." Tom let it rest there, sipping his beer while staring at Felix. It didn't take long for the little man to make the connection.

"Ya' mean, naw' that's too much, his dog is gonna' have a litter, heh, heh."

Tom just nodded and let Felix enjoy the coincidence.

"Did ya' confess that yer' dog might be the poppa'?"

"No, I didn't go that far. I forgot to mention Paddy is the same size as Rocky, just older."

"Sounds ta' me like he's a real character."

"You said it. Before he was promoted he walked a beat in Brooklyn and knew about that family too. His superiors told him the warehouse was under surveillance so not to rock the boat by appearing in the area too often so that he was noticeable. It sounded to me as if he was promoted to get him out of Brooklyn."

"A bit of corruption in his bosses huh?"

"Sounds that way to me. To change the subject, I'm itching to get back to the house in Franklin Park. What are your plans?"

"Dunno, amigo."

"Well I'm going to need a lot of help to clean this place out because we won't be coming back and I don't intend to pay anymore rent here. Let Mr. Levine worry about disposing of what's left. In the meantime I'm going to get together all of the usable furniture and appliances which can be used in Franklin Park, all the weapons too."

"Are ya' gonna' do all this before ya' hear from McHenry?"

"Just the gathering. I won't hire a van until he calls. The contents of the wall safe won't be entrusted to anyone. They'll stay with me from here to our house. That reminds me partner, when we get to Franklin Park the house will be a bit crowded with Leo, Stella, you and Gennie, and I. We'll have to find you a place nearby. I imagine you would want to rent a house rather than an apartment right?"

Felix had that blank look while he tried to think of a suitable reply. Tom understood his reticence. He most likely hadn't given it any thought beforehand and now felt like he was being pushed into something or somewhere he had no desire to go. As long as he'd known the little man Tom had always thought he was a happy-go-lucky individual unless riled. He never really cared much for permanence, relying on friends to offer their hospitality for as long as he wished. Now faced with the added responsibility of Gennie he would have to plant some roots however temporary.

"I'll have ta' think 'bout that and ask Gennie what she wants ta' do. It isn't a' easy thing for me ya' unnerstan amigo. Let it boil in my think-tank for awhile." Tom knew better than to push Felix. Now that he had planted the seed he'd give it time to germinate.

Tom was on edge. It wasn't anything he could put his finger on yet the uneasiness persisted. He continued sitting at the table long after Felix left, probably to talk to Gennie, not exactly focused on anything but letting his thoughts wander. It was becoming a habit lately simply because there were so many different things that needed his personal attention, such as the Florida Keys house and boat and his large emerald in New Orleans, plus setting up a studio where Stella could paint once they got to Franklin Park. There seemed to be no end to things that demanded his oversight. He could only be in one place at a time.

Felix shouted Tom's name. "Telephone, amigo, an' it's not McHenry."

Tom reluctantly rolled out of bed grabbed his shorts off the floor, threw on his bathrobe, and walked into the office avoiding Leo who was napping just outside the bedroom door.

"Phone calls come at tha' most inconvenient times, don't they heh, heh, heh? I asked who was callin' an' all he' say was 'an' old friend. I'll leave ya' alone while ya' talk ta' yer' old amigo.'

When Tom picked up the receiver and said hello, the answering voice was recognizable at once without identifying himself. "How you doing, old buddy? I knew you'd be sitting on pins and needles waiting to hear from me concerning the Key Largo, Florida property. Lance Nolte had a distinctive voice that once heard was hard to forget. He yammered on in attorney legal speak about how he had arranged for Tom to take ownership of the Key Largo property and all the difficulties he had to overcome to get the deed transferred to Tom. "You'll have to sign some papers when you get down there, old buddy Do you have any idea when that will be?"

"Probably within the next month. We will be returning to D.C. shortly so there will be a flurry of personal business to take care of. Since I haven't taken any vacation time for more than a year I'll have accrued quite a bit. I'll call you when the time is to begin Lance. Is that all right?"

"Sure, just give me two or three days notice so I can make arrangements with the people down there. Good talking to you, old buddy. Bye."

Tom didn't understand quite how it happened but when Lance said he was going to do something it always got done. He guessed friendships in the legal business were as tightly knit and loyal to their friends and associates as were those in the agency. Whatever the inner-workings, he was more than pleased with the outcome. He had just returned to the kitchen for another beer when here came Felix again.

"Ya' weren't off the phone two minutes when it rang agin'. Ya' sure are a popular guy today, amigo. This time it's ya' know who." Felix reached for Tom's beer. "Ya' won't want this ta' get warm, so I'll take it, heh, heh, heh."

Tom gave him a look that would have frozen the equator but the little man ignored it guzzling at the Bud like a newborn babe.

Mr. McHenry was his usual terse self. "Any new developments there?"

"No, sir, the perps must be re-grouping, but I made a new contact who is very versed on their activities and membership. He's a grizzled sergeant of the New York Police Department named Patrick O'Toole who knows all about the Manhattan and Brooklyn families. You may want to contact him." Tom gave him Paddy's home number.

"Ah, sounds like a good Irishman. I will give him a call. The reason for this call is to tell you to report back to Langley in two days."

Before he had the chance to hang up, Tom interjected, "I'm going to need some vacation time."

"We'll talk when you return." Click. He does that to me every time we talk, Tom thought to himself.

Now Tom really had to get himself in gear. Two days, wow! Where to start? "Felix" Tom called out. His partner came into the office beer still in hand. "Ya' called?"

"Moving orders from headquarters. Run down and tell Rocky then bring him back up here with you. We only have one day to get everything together and down to the showroom for moving van pick-up. Tell him to start stockpiling all weapons down in his apartment, we'll bring what we have here and what's in the inner passageway down to him. I'll alert the girls."

When Stella was told about the time limit for moving she just stared at Tom for a few moments.

"What's the matter, Stell?"

"It's just that this is the final shift from all I've known for a home since college. We're moving to Virginia and a whole new life for me; I guess I'm a little scared."

Tom took her into his arms and whispered in her ear, "You are my life, sweetheart, without you I'd probably wander from pillar to post until retirement or the grave, which ever came first."

"Don't even think that way, Tom; we'll have more than fifty years of marital bliss."

The next ten hours were a frenzy of activity for all. Leo sensed something important was afoot and graciously stayed out of his friend's way only once about five hours into their work stood by the door to the roof until Tom noticed in passing that the dog needed out to use the facilities. "You'll be glad to get home boy where you have your own doggie door." The mastiff looked at his main friend in appreciation. "Home" was a word he understood.

After about nine and a half hours Tom took a break and first called for the van then called the nearest Chinese restaurant that delivered and ordered for the five of them. He picked a variety of dishes with enough egg rolls to afford everyone at least two with some for Leo too. Forty dollars worth of Chinese food in the 1960s was a lot of food, especially Chinese, which was filling anyhow. Tom caught Felix in passing and said, "Notify the troops that chow is being served in Rock's apartment ala carte without the price tag."

All assembled, Tom started passing out the white cardboard cartons. "Rocky, ya' got any silverware; I can't handle chop sticks. I'd starve ta' death before I could get any food in me." Rocky handed him a tablespoon. "What's this? ain't ya' got no forks?" Rocky looked down on the little man. "Have you ever tried eating Chinese before Felix? Forks won't hold the gravy or the rice without dropping it all over the place." "Whadda' ya' think we got that overgrown cocker spaniel for? He's better than a vacuum cleaner, heh, heh, heh. Ain't ya' got no beer here?"

"I have coffee, tea, or ice water. If you want beer you'll have to tap your own supply."

Tom had listened to their good natured banter without interfering but spoke up, "I suggest you try tea, partner; it's better for the digestive system with heavy Chinese fare, but if it's beer you crave go up and get some. Bring me a couple while you're at it. I'd have thought you'd had enough stair climbing for the day." Felix was off like a shot to get his favorite beverage.

Tom cabbed over to the long-term parking garage to pick up the station wagon, expecting it to be filthy and hoping none of the tires had gone flat. When he went to the office to pay the bill he was pleasantly surprised when the attendant told him it was company policy to start long-term vehicles periodically to keep the battery up, wash them monthly, and check the tires to eliminate flats. He looked at a clip board full of papers denoting all such customers. "Your wagon was checked just three days ago, Mr. Mueller, and no problems were discovered." When Tom paid the bill he was handed his keys with a voucher for five dollars worth of gas at any Esso station in New York State, compliments of the management. Nice way to get repeat business, Tom thought.

Never having been active in the business world before but knowing once he had Stella set up in some sort of studio he would end up marketing her paintings and it would be necessary to possess as much moxie as possible to compete, so he filed that little item away for future use. Parking garage, art business - same, same in his mind.

While driving back to the shop it dawned on Tom that the wagon was going to be crowded while returning to D.C. What with the three men, two girls, and Leo it wouldn't leave the dog much room to stretch out. He needed water for the five hour drive plus a pit stop or two to discharge what he drank. And where was he going to house them all once they reached Franklin Park? Mr. McHenry just didn't realize the logistics involved in moving so many bodies, but then he didn't know about Stella or Gennie, yet. He would explain Stella when he asked for vacation time; Felix would be on his own when it came to Gennie. Tom also knew he had better pre-plan his trip to New Orleans and Key Largo with much better forethought than he had used so far. That trip could shape his future in many ways. He was also curious about what type of home Fred had purchased in Key Largo. With the size of the remaining mortgage Tom wondered if Fred was intending to live there full time or just use it to get away from the cold winters of the New York area?

Tom entered the shop and had to be careful of all the furniture which was piled helter-skelter throughout the showroom. In reaching the rear stairs he snapped on the second floor landing light. As he started to make the turn toward his floor he saw the envelope taped to the door of Rocky's apartment. Closer inspection revealed his name written in neat script on it so removing it he continued upward. Leo heard him coming and was right there when he pushed through his door which entered the kitchen. Tom didn't scratch behind his ears because he was distracted by Felix who was head down at the table.

"You all right partner?"

Felix slowly raised his head. "Must a' dozed off amigo. All the Chinese food on top a' the exercise must a' tired me out."

Tom sat down next to him and opened the envelope. Leo, feeling ignored put his head in his friends lap. "All right, Leo" and he scratched behind the dogs ears. "Does that get me back in your good graces?"

While Tom read the note Felix retrieved two beers. "Did you know about this, partner?"

"'Bout what?" Tom handed him the paper. "That does solve a problem but as long as we work together or I even know him, I'll never understand the man. I just can't get a handle on him. He's paying his own way back to Langley so our car won't be over-crowded. Isn't that something?"

"He's a strange one, that's for sure. He took a lot a' ribbin' from me an' just shrugged it off. How long 'til the movers get here?"

"They'll be here at seven in the morning, why?"

"After I finish this beer I'm gonna' join Gennie an' see what she wants ta' do 'bout living near ya' in Franklin Park, then grab some more shut-eye. I hate ta' admit it but I mus' be gettin' old."

"Nonsense, you'll be your old self after a decent nights sleep."

Tom found Stella laying in their bed fully clothed. He lay down next to her not touching and forced himself to close his eyes. He heard Leo thump down on the floor just outside the bedroom door. As he was drifting off he reminded himself to call Paddy O'toole for the disposal of the drugs in the basement safe. That should get him some points with his superiors.

————

The next thing Tom knew when his eyes opened was the presence of Leo with his large bulk bouncing against the bed. Then he heard the ringing of the office phone. He got to it before it stopped.

"Thought you would be up and about, you being such a night person, Mr. Mueller. I wanted to let you know that Mr. McHenry from your agency called me before I came to work. He thinks very highly of you by the way. He said you were a 'valuable asset' to the agency and to cooperate with you whenever possible, if those were his exact words."

"I'm glad you called, Sergeant." Tom looked at his watch. It was 4:30 A.M. "Can you stop by the shop between now and six-thirty? I have something you might be interested in taking with you."

"Sure. I'm calling from the restaurant you were at with me. I can be there in fifteen minutes."

"Stop by the front door, I'll be watching for you." Tom took the inner passageway to the basement and turned the lights on before swinging the doors of the safe open. There it was, a small fortune in cocaine and marijuana that would never be distributed on the streets. He returned to the first floor to wait for Paddy. At 4:45 exactly the patrol car parked at the front door and the big sergeant lumbered his way. Leo had come down the rear stairs in search of his main friend, silently approaching the door when Tom opened it to admit Paddy.

"Top of the mornin' to you, Mr. Mueller. I see your canine companion is on watch as usual, which is good 'cause I brought a little something for him from the restaurant." He produced a wax paper package from behind his back. When unwrapped it revealed a medium-rare T-bone steak. Leo didn't move an inch but his multi-colored eyes were centered on the morsel.

"You're going to spoil him, Sergeant, but you have made a friend that will remember your kindness. All right Leo take it to the back of the showroom and try not to make a mess that I'll have to clean up." Much to the dog's credit he daintily took the steak from Paddy's hand rather than snapping at it hand and all.

"Now what was it you thought I might be interested in taking with me?"

"Follow me. Watch you step, as you can see we're about to vacate the premises. We've been ordered back to D.C." When they reached the basement safe Tom pointed to the various packaged drugs. "Holy Mary, Mother of Christ, is that what I think it is?" Tom nodded. Paddy stared at the cache.

"I won't ask which family you got this from, but whoever it was had to be hurt in the pocketbook. My God! I'm going to have to summon a crew to help carry all this out and witness the withdrawal. Will you and Leo retire to your apartment during the process? I don't want to disclose your presence and endanger your cover."

"Just so they are out of here by seven o'clock. That's when the moving van comes to collect all our belongings to take back to D.C."

"I better get started then." Paddy stuck out his huge hand to shake Tom's. "Now I understand what Mr. McHenry meant by 'valuable asset'. I hope you can understand I'm not being selfish in this recovery but a certain amount of notoriety is bound to enhance my position on the Department which I'll owe all to you. I never forget a debt, so keep in touch. Who knows I might be valuable to you someday."

Tom unlocked the showroom front door on his way to collect Leo and head upstairs. He still had to empty the hidden wall safe of the jewels and cash that would be going with him in his wagon. Tom didn't intend to let them out of his sight at anytime until they were safely back in Franklin Park.

True to his word, Paddy had the drugs removed from the basement safe before the moving van showed up, without any untoward hassles. After informing the company men where and when to deliver Tom took one last look around to see if anything of importance had been overlooked. Satisfied, he put more cash in his pockets before closing the case and locking the door for the last time. Everyone including Leo were already seated in the station wagon. Tom placed the last of his brother's spoils just behind the drivers seat next to Felix and Gennie and told everyone to lock their doors. They hadn't gone three blocks before Stella slid over closer to her man. Tom remembered how Sheila always liked to crowd close when they drove, another trait the twins shared.

By the time they crossed the George Washington Bridge into New Jersey Tom glanced back through the rear view mirror checking how close the truck following him was, and returning his eyes forward couldn't see Felix. The next chance he got he half turned and saw his partner had his head down in Gennie's lap and seemed to be sleeping. Maybe Felix was slowing down with the amount of sleep he was getting lately, although he did have a habit of sleeping in cars. He'd have to keep an eye on him to see if he had some physical defect beyond his former injuries which was causing the excess sleep. Tom thought their annual physical checkups were about due so that might reveal some new malady or other disorder that was bothering him. The next few weeks should prove hectic what with getting him settled into a new residence and Tom's planned trip to New Orleans and Florida on the horizon. He hoped the little man would be capable enough to accompany them. For now, he best concentrate on the road as traffic was building up for some reason and Tom didn't need to be involved in an accident to complicate matters any more than they already were.

17

Tom wasn't certain what instinct alerted him, yet when he pulled into the drive of the Franklin Park house the hair was rising on the back of his neck. The warning was not to be ignored. Something wasn't right so he sat quietly his head swiveling to take in the complete panorama of the property. The other occupants of the wagon were getting antsy to get out and explore their lodging, all except Felix and Leo.

"Whassa' matter, amigo? Ya' seem upset."

"Something isn't right, partner. I'm just trying to figure out what before we enter the house. Leo senses it too. Look at him." Leo was sitting looking out the side window, mouth closed unlike his usual tongue hanging demeanor. Tom didn't want to let the dog out alone. "You girls stay in the wagon while Felix, Leo, and I check a few things. If we get out of your sight and anything out of the ordinary occurs hit the horn and one of us will return. I'm not trying to alarm you, it's just a feeling I have that can't be ignored. We have been gone for a while and the property has stood unguarded."

"What are ya' lookin' for, amigo?"

"Booby traps of any kind around doors or windows so if you spot anything that looks suspicious give a holler. I'm going to keep Leo with me so he won't try to enter the house through his doggie door and set something off."

"I'd bet ya' are thinkin' of that Pepe Basquez character."

"You are becoming more perceptive the older you get, partner, so keep your eyes peeled. His father's compound isn't that far from here and Pepe has a warped sense of revenge stored up in that head of his."

Tom was checking windows for wires with Leo less than a yard away, his nose in the air sniffing for the scent of past intruders. There were so many conflicting odors he was having a hard time separating them. But one stink stood out, he remembered it from when he discovered his main friend's female companion injured in her apartment closet. His first reaction was to drop to his stomach with his rear legs getting a grip in the soil in preparation for a lunge. Tom noticed Leos sudden movement. "What is it boy? Do you see something or hear something?" Leo's response was to let that tongue roll out in what Tom always thought was a knowing grin.

Just then two things happened simultaneously. Felix let out a bellow and the wagon's horn blared. "Leo, stay with Uncle Felix and guard." Tom raced to the front only to find the moving van pulled in behind his wagon.

"What's the matter, Stell?"

"I'm sorry, honey, when that truck pulled in I guess we became overexcited and blew the horn with too much zeal. We were somewhat nervous sitting here alone. Have you found something wrong at the house?"

"Felix may have. I'm going back now to see what he and Leo have found. Tell the movers to wait until they see the front door open."

When Tom rejoined his partner, he found his breath almost taken away by the sight. Felix was on his knees with a loose wire in his hands. "I know this wasn't here when I remodeled the door, which means it has been added since. Now whadda' ya' suppose it's connected to?" "Only one way to find out. I'll go in through the front door. You stay where you are in the event one person is needed outside."

"Ya' think that's wise, amigo? Wouldn't it be safer ta' call Langley for a bomb expert?"

"I'm sure it would, but then Mr. McHenry would be notified we're back and that would mess up our whole timetable. He most likely would want us to report there or the downtown office immediately. No thanks, for once we're going to do this our way. We are on scene; he isn't."

"At least let me go in, I'm a bit more mechanically minded than you. Whadda' ya' say?"

Tom thought on it for a few moments. "You're right there, partner. I suppose that makes more sense, but if it looks more complex than you can handle, we'll revert to your first suggestion. I can't even imagine how they got in to begin with. There were no signs of forcible entry that I could see, how about you?" "Naw, but the fact is they did. I jus' hope whatever is in there isn't set up non a timer or some kinda' motion device. I'm wastin' time; you keep Leo back away 'til I let ya' know. Gimme' the front door key, will ya'?"

So far so good, Felix thought. He locked the front door behind him to prevent one of the girls or the movers from following him. His eyes moved in every direction as he moved toward the kitchen. While in the hall before crossing the threshold he stopped, his eyes bored into every aspect of the room before crossing into it. The goods were half hidden by the stove. He continued to search as he edged slowly farther into the room staying on the opposite side from the charge. He counted eight sticks of TNT taped together over a pot of what smelled like gasoline from his position. The wire he had discovered protruding from the doggie door was now explainable. A piece of tape which had been used to secure it tautly had come loose causing it to drop where he could see it. The only thing he couldn't figure was what the detonator would be. Something had to detonate the charge. He again got down on his stomach to scoot closer. Less than a yard away he hesitated, something was hanging down from under the charge almost touching the liquid. It was so small Felix could hardly make it out. It was a vial of some sort of liquid. The overpowering smell of the gas was making his eyes water and causing a little dizziness. He shook his head to clear both of the temporary maladies off. Reaching in to his trouser pocket he removed his pocket knife, a Swiss multi-gadget model, opening it to the scissors. He reached under the TNT and with one hand cutting through the string attached to the vial, his other hand cupped under it as a catcher's mitt. Withdrawing both hands he could feel the heat the vial was discharging. This was the igniter he thought as he backpedaled away from the charge. Probably some type of acid which would create enough heat to eat through the vial and pow, the gas fumes would do the rest. Muy Dios, talk about overkill, the combination of these two elements would blow the house off its foundation and the following fire would reduce what was left to ashes. Something didn't look right as he got unsteadily to his feet. When he put the vial in the sink he looked out the window between the cupboards. Then it dawned on him. What window? The pane had been removed without breaking it. Here was their entrance point. He unlocked the rear door and motioned Tom in. Tom in turn gave a hand signal to Leo which made the dog stay where he was. "You took long enough. I was starting to get nervous. What did you find?"

Felix just pointed to the charge and with his other hand pointed to the missing window pane. Tom swore under his breath. " I looked right at that window and I should have noticed it was just too clean. So much for my power of observation. I wonder where the glass is?"

"Don't worry 'bout that amigo, ya' have other things ta' consider before ya' let the movers or the girls in. Whadda' ya' gonna' do with that stuff?"

"Is it volatile? You know, explosive?"

"Naw, but ya' don't want it layin' 'round do ya'?"

"I see your point partner. Guess it's about time to call in the experts to come and dispose of it. You might as well wait for them while I take Stella and Leo to the grocery to re-stock our larder which will include plenty of beer, so you don't have to look at me like that." "Take Gennie with ya' so she's out from underfoot. Ya' better bring yer' case of goodies in here too."

"You're absolutely right, partner. I'll call Langley now before we leave. Anything else?"

"Nuthin' I can think of, amigo."

After Tom called Langley and reported what they had found he was assured the bomb disposal team would be there within a half hour. "Just don't touch anything until we get there."

"Mr. Santana will be here waiting for your arrival since I have other business to attend to." Tom brought the case in containing everything he intended to put in the safety deposit box he had rented when the bank was open. It would be safe here with Felix until then.

"Stella, we're going to the grocery after I talk to the movers."

When they reached the business area and Tom had given Stella sufficient money to buy food and spirits, he had a subject he had been mulling over for the whole trip down from New York City. "Before you go in, Stell, there is something I want you to think about. It's time you learned how to drive a car. With everything that's going to happen in our future you'll need your own form of transportation. It's not a luxury but a necessity in this case." Tom could see she was thinking up reasons against the idea so he pressed on. "There's no point in arguing, Stell; there aren't any subways out here and you can't rely on cabs all the time. Leo and I are going to check on this while you're shopping so take your time. Gennie, if you see anything Felix prefers add it right in."

Stella put her hand behind Toms neck and pulled him close for one of her five-alarm kisses. "God, I love you Tom; you're always thinking ahead."

There was a light on in the AAA club office, which Tom figured meant someone was still working so he pulled to the curb.

"Leo, you guard the car. I'll only be a few minutes then we'll go back and pick up Stella, Gennie, and the groceries.

When Tom tried the door it was locked, so he knocked a few times then waited for a response. A bearded man about his size came to the glass. "Sorry we're closed. I'm just here catching up on some paper work. Come back Monday." He was just about to turn away so Tom said, "I just need some information sir. Monday I'll be working too" and he held his pictured identification against the glass. The man squinted through his thick glasses before unlocking the door. When it was re-locked he turned to look at Tom.

"I'll make this short so you can get back to your paper work. My fiancee is from New York City and has never learned how to drive, depending on the subway and cabs to get around. I need the name of some driving school in this area to give her lessons. Some accredited firm who can pick her up and return her home while I'm at work."

"Is that all?" He got up from his desk, walked over to a filing cabinet, and returned with a folder with several sheets of paper in it. "Here are several, but I would recommend Ernie Andrews of the A-1 agency. Of course, it helps that he is my brother, hah, hah. But I'll call him to let him know you will be contacting the agency and since you are a neighbor he should give you special consideration. Since I backed him to get him started that's a given."

When Tom got back to the grocery his timing was almost perfect. The girls were pushing two fully laden carts through the check-out counter. Evidently the money he had given Stella was enough because Tom could see her getting some change. Tom got out of the wagon to rearrange the seats to allow room for everything. "Leo, you have been a good boy so far. Move up so the groceries will fit in."

"They have a wonderful selection in there honey, it will be a pleasure to shop there."

"That's good. Now aren't you glad the arrangements have been made for your driving lessons?"

"Already? That was quick. I swear, I don't know how you get things done so fast. Do you use some form of coercion?" "It's a long story. Right now I'm anxious to get home to find out how Felix made out. The movers should be done so we can have some dinner. I for one am getting kind of hungry."

The movers were gone. Just one car remained parked in the street which Tom knew belonged to one of the bomb experts even though it had no markings. Tom backed into the drive so the rear of the wagon was even with the front door.

"I'll take the heavier stuff in on the first trip, you and Gennie can follow at your leisure. C'mon, Leo, I imagine you're pretty thirsty by now."

Tom wanted to make sure the bomb expert didn't mention anything in front of the girls to explain why he was there. No sense in alarming them.

Both men were in the kitchen when Tom when Tom set the beer on the kitchen counter. He was about to warn the expert when Felix broke in, "Ya' don't have ta' say nuthin' ta' him, amigo, I already warned Mr. Brazelton 'bout sayin' anythin' in front of a' the women. But before he leaves he wants ta' tell ya' somethin'. We can talk in the front yard while the women are cookin'. Don't know 'bout Ned here, but I need a beer."

"Make that two, partner." Leo had been sitting patiently while his friends were talking but now he nuzzled Tom's leg.

"Sorry, big fellow, I'll get your water right now, then I'll get something special for you." He winked at Felix.

In the front yard Ned explained what else they had found while removing the first charge. "Those intruders were leaving nothing to chance. They used that window pane for a second bomb. Whoever opened the oven door would have moved that glass which would have triggered another blast. Quite ingenuous for civilians. You have some potent enemies, Mr. Mueller. Watch your back. That's advice from someone who has had the same problem. Anything further that is the least bit suspicious don't hesitate to call me, for he who hesitates is lost."

When Tom walked into the house he was amazed by how the girls had manhandled all that the movers had dropped haphazardly in the front room. There was actually space to move about without banging into something. He had to give the girls credit; they were tireless workers. All the groceries were out of sight and the pleasant aroma of food cooking made his saliva run. Where did they get the energy?

Felix and Gennie said they were going to stay up awhile longer. They had things to discuss. Tom followed Stella into the bedroom just as the phone rang, he was in a quandary whether to answer it or not knowing full well who it was going to be but on the off chance it wasn't Mr. McHenry he picked it up. "Hello." Silence on the other end. "Hello." Again, still no reply. "If that's you, Pepe, you're going to have to think of some other stupid way to get rid of me before I get to you." Tom disconnected.

"What was that about honey?"

"I'm not sure but it might have been an old adversary of mine. How tired are you?"

"Never too tired for that with you."

Sometime later, Tom snapped awake for no reason he could ascertain. He lay still trying to understand what had alerted him. Stella was clamped to his back, so to avoid disturbing her Tom moved his head enough to see Leo, who was napping just outside the bedroom door. Nothing had bothered the Mastiff so what had caused the interruption of his overly-tired state? Since his hearing was acute he blocked out everything to concentrate on that sense but could discern nothing out of the ordinary night sounds. He was probably still a little jumpy from the bombs which were removed earlier. That was enough to make anyone nervous. He could call Ned Brazelton about it.

18

The next morning, after a delicious breakfast that filled him almost to the bursting point, reminiscent of some of the meals his mother coaxed him into eating, Tom told Felix to get the case that containing the valuables. He was going to transfer everything but the cash and deeds to the Florida property to a leather briefcase he had here at the house.

"You come with me partner and while we're in town we'll check on nearby places for you to rent. Stella is going to take driving lessons as soon as I make the appointment. I'll do that later today when we get back. That also means she'll need her own car. How about you?"

"Yeah, I guess I'll have ta' buy one too. Nuthin' fancy, just a cheap go ta' work car. Ya' know two or three hunnert'."

Tom had to laugh despite trying to suppress it. "You better up your figure Felix. Anything in that price range will probably cost more in repair bills than the cost of the car. Didn't mean to laugh, partner, but some of the things you say are hilarious." Tom got that blank stare Felix used when trying to think of a retort.

While Tom was transferring things Felix went into the kitchen to tell the women where they were going. "An' you, ya' overgrown cocker spaniel stay here an' guard the women an' the house. No sleepin' on the job either."

Tom entered the bank and went directly to the safety deposit desk which flanked the huge open vault door accompanied by the man in charge. They stopped at a row that contained the size which Tom had ordered. The man put the two keys in, pulled out the box and left Tom alone to take care of his business. Tom carefully placed the cloth bags containing the jewels together then added the rest so that the neatly packed box was balanced. He then headed back to the opening where the man met him and reversed the process, handing Tom his key. As Tom was putting the key in his pocket, he glanced out the vault door. He saw a person pass who wore a face mask and was holding an automatic. Tom grabbed the man next to him and whispered, "There's a hold-up in progress out there. You better stay in here."

Tom pulled out his Cobra and edged out for a better view. He kept low so he would be out of the normal line of sight if the bandit happened to glance his way. There were three, masked, gloved, and almost identical in height. It was impossible to tell what race or gender the three were until one of them yelled, "Dis is a hold-up you all hit de' flo'." He at least was Negro, Tom surmised.

He crawled behind the desk for cover, edging ever closer to one unsuspecting hood. Shades of the Wild West, the mask a kerchief pulled up over the nose, and ten-gallon hat pulled low. This desperado was in for a big surprise. Tom rose up behind him and threw his arm around the mans neck in a strangle hold, pressing the Cobra against his temple. He felt the man's knees buckle as he realized he was caught and about to die if he wasn't careful. Tom yelled past his ear at his two cohorts. "Drop those weapons or you die."

The men hesitated just too long.

"Do what he says. One false move an' I'll drop ya' where ya' stand", Felix called out in that deep authoritative voice that Tom had heard him use so many times before. The two he had directed his orders to exchanges glances, One turned toward Felix while the other made a move toward Tom, weapons rising. That was all the provocation the two agents needed. Two shots rang out sounding like one. Both would-be bank robbers fell to the marble floor, one hit in the left knee cap, the other in the right. Both would-bes were screaming bloody murder but were now, for all intents and purposes, harmless.

"Hit the silent alarm button. We need some assistance here." Tom was speaking in a normal voice toward a teller who had risen from the floor. Felix was removing weapons, not too gently, from the perps. Tom had simply rabbit punched his perp who fell to the floor like a rock.

Less than five minutes later, multiple sirens sounded in the street where a mix of sheriffs deputies and state troopers were rushing the bank weapons drawn. The first officer in, a trooper the size of Paddy O'Toole, stopped his rush and holstered his weapon removing a pen and note pad from his pocket instead. He looked directly at Tom Mueller. "Looks like you have the situation well in hand, sir." He turned to the other law men. "Start lining up witnesses and getting names and addresses of patrons and workers alike. Paul, radio for a couple of ambulances and delegate someone for outside crowd control."

This is a good man to know, Tom thought to himself. He approached the trooper with ID in hand. "My partner, the small man over there, and I were here to transact some business when this attempt went down. Naturally, we had to intercede. Criminals just won't listen to good advice, which is why they suffered gunshot wounds, non-life threatening as you can see. We both live near here and operate out of D.C., Langley."

"I live in Woodbridge myself so I'm somewhat aware of the CIA but have never been involved with anyone from your agency before. My name is Terry Connoti. Since we are practically neighbors we should get together socially sometime."

"I'd like that, Terry."

The ambulance crews arrived which interrupted their conversation as Terry turned to supervise the transportation of the perps with officers to ride in each ambulance as guards.

Terry and Tom exchanged phone numbers after the crews left and Tom and Felix had given their statements

When they finally left the bank, three hours had passed. Tom drove over to a realty company which was less than two blocks away. He had noticed it on the way to the bank. "Let's see what kind of rental homes they have here partner. Maybe we'll get lucky so we don't have to traipse all over the area."

"What ya ' tryin' ta' do, get rid of me?"

"Don't talk nonsense now Felix. We already agreed you should have your own place. After we try this place we'll go look at some cars."

"Man, I'll have enough money ta' last me the rest a' my life if I die by midnight, heh, heh, heh."

They went directly to the manager who was recognizable by a plaque on her desk, N. Brazelton. Was everyone in this burg related, Tom wondered? If that was the case they would have to guard whatever they said. He could imagine small town jealousies. Tom explained what they were looking for to the woman. Felix piped up, "Nuthin' too fancy ya' unnerstand', Federal employees don' make big money."

She went through her listings pulling three sheets out of the loose-leaf note book. Looking through them she discarded one then began explaining the features of the other two. "Either one of these two should be just what you're looking for. One is a two-bedroom ranch style, and the other is a two-bedroom bungalow with attached garage. They are both priced reasonably, although the ranch has no garage." She turned the sheets around so Felix could see the diagrammed floor plans and frontal house pictures. While Felix was studying the descriptions Tom was looking over his shoulder.

"That bungalow looks like the ticket, partner."

"I could take you out to see it right now. It's vacated. Oh, by the way, the former owners the former owners left some perfectly good furniture and appliances when they moved. That's a plus that the ranch doesn't have."

Tom and Felix followed the realty representative the short distance to the bungalow and pulled into the cement-ribboned drive behind her.

"I understand we had some excitement in our little town today", she said making small talk while she fiddled with keys to open the front door. "I swear, I don't know what this country is coming to."

Tom ignored her idle gossip; the less she knew about their involvement the better. They walked into a living room about the size of his own. It had old but serviceable furniture, drapes on the two windows, and a worn but still intact carpet. "There isn't a basement, this home was built on a cement slab. The water table is rather high around here so digging a basement was impractical. What makes up for it is the extra storage area in the attached garage. If you follow me you will see the furnace and water heater are in a utility room to the rear of the kitchen. There is room in there for a washer too. It's a forced-air furnace and I understand the utilities are reasonable."

Tom noticed very little had been removed from the house. It was like the tenants either died or moved into a retirement home in a warmer climate.

"Are we talking rental with option to buy or straight rental here?"

"It's your choice, sir. Of course a land contract will raise the monthly payment somewhat but her again that's up to you."

"I gotta bring Gennie here ta' see what she thinks."

"Can we make some arrangements to leave a key here so we won't have to stop at your office and bring you back? If you'll contact your husband I'm sure he'll vouch for me." The startled look was well worth his while. "I talked to Ned yesterday and since we are neighbors so to speak when you talk to him be sure you mention Leo's name."

"Oh, Mr. Mueller, I'm so ashamed. I never connected ... Oh, my goodness." The blush on her neck and cheeks showed her embarrassment was real as she fumbled to remove the house key from the ring. "Please accept my apology."

"There's no need to apologize Mrs. Brazelton." Tom pocketed the proferred key. "C'mon Felix we have much to do before dark."

"Right with ya' amigo, there doesn't seem ta' be anythin' else ta' look at here now."

Before heading back to his house Tom stopped at the Chevrolet dealer. "Let's look around the used car section Felix, maybe we can find something decent for you. If you see anything you like holler." They separated, each taking a different route. There must have been seventy or eighty models, mostly General Motors. Cadillacs on down to the cheapest Chevy coupe. It didn't take long for a slick salesman to show up. "Anything in particular you're looking for sir?"

"Just browsing. We're looking for an affordable car for my friend over there." Tom pointed toward Felix. The salesman made an abrupt about face heading for new prey. Tom had to laugh, that man had better be careful how he handled the little guy or instead of selling a car he might wear one. Tom spotted a green Plymouth business coupe. The two-seater with an overly large trunk. Upon closer inspection it had a minimum of rust, a chrome door strip missing, and a broken plastic tail light cover. Not bad for what he figured was a 1951 or '52 model. "Hey, Felix, have you found anything yet? If not come over here and look at this one." He beat the salesman by about ten yards or so, giving him enough time to say, "The guy keeps tryin' ta' sell me high-priced cars. This looks more like it." When the salesman arrived, he looked disappointed upon seeing hat they were looking at. "I'm sure you want something more recent than that, sir. That relic is thirteen years old."

"So what. Get the keys, so I can start her up. Find out the price while yer' at it."

"Now look, partner, let me negotiate price with this guy. I've had a bit more experience with high pressure salesmen. If I pause at anytime during the horse trading don't you jump in. It's a ploy used to force him into a counter-offer."

"Yeah I've seen ya' in action before amigo so I'll follow yer' instructions to the letter."

The salesman came back with the car keys which Felix grabbed like a fish taking bait. The salesman smiled to himself, here was a live one he thought despite how ugly; he'd have to watch out for the big one though. The starter whirred a few times before the motor coughed to life with a cloud of black smoke rising from the rear end. Felix didn't gun it though, just let it settle into an idle. Tom told him where the hood release was and the little man popped the hood. When Tom pulled it up and looked inside he thought, OK, sharpie, let the games begin. "So what was the asking price?"

"The manager said seven hundred and fifty as is."

Tom smiled in his wolfish manner down at him. "You've got to be kidding. With everything that has to be fixed or replaced; turn it off, partner; we'll go somewhere else." The salesman's complexion changed colors as he looked up at Tom. His sure thing was about to take a hike. "Well, well what's your idea of a fair price?"

"Not a dime over five hundred and that's after it's put up on a hoist where we can see what might be wrong underneath. You relay that to your manager." The salesman practically ran back to the office.

"How're ya' doin', amigo? I'm gettin' hungry."

"We'll know in about two minutes."

The salesman returned almost as fast as he left. "You drive a hard bargain sir. The manager wants you to come to the office while I drive the car over to the shop."

"I have a better idea. Felix can go to your office while I accompany you to the shop. I'm the one who wants to know how trustworthy this car will be on the road. I'm not buying any pig in a poke."

"Oh, you're paying for it?"

"That's right, so let's get this show on the road. My partner is getting hungry."

When the car was hoisted Tom got under and found a leaky tail pipe and a rotted out muffler which would need replacement but the shocks looked all right. "Will you call one of your mechanics over here? There's something I need his expertise on."

A burly man joined Tom under the car wiping his greasy hands on a shop cloth. "Whadda' you need mister?"

"Will you check that oil pan and give me your opinion on whether or not it is leaking?" "Short a' removing it which is a job in itself so all I can do is wipe it off then stand here an' wait for a leak, if there is one. Will that do?"

"It'll have to."

"Ya' know this is an old buggy an' it has seen its better days."

"All this does is determine the price. If it will cost me more to fix than it's worth we'll forget the whole deal."

"What are they askin' for it?"

"They started at seven-fifty but my counter offer was five but if something major like the leak you're looking for is detected then I'll go elsewhere."

"Regardless of that, I wouldn't pay over three hundred for it. You're lookin' at over two hundred at least to fix things an' that's not countin' labor charges. How are the brakes?"

"They seemed all right on the short distance from the used car lot here but of course there were no sudden stops where heavy pressure was needed."

"OK. Let me get a clean cloth to put under the pan, bring it to the floor level so I can check under the hood, and then I can give ya' a better idea if you should go any farther."

"Don't see any major problems, now I'll pull the cloth out. No, it's clean. Tell ya' what I'll do. I live across the road, down a couple of blocks and I add to my income here by fixin' an occasional car or truck in my garage. Strictly on the Q.T. of course but I can guarantee I could bring this green monster up to snuff cheaper than it could be done anywhere else. It shouldn't take me more than a couple a' days." Tom didn't have to think on it long before agreeing to his proposal.

"Give me your address and home phone number and we'll drop it off after I settle with the used car manager. I'll leave my pertinent information under the sun visor along with the keys."

When Tom returned to the used car lot he went directly to the office where he found Felix relaxing in a beat-up old stuffed chair. His eyes were closed and his head lolled to one side and for all intent and purposes he was in his sleep mode. Tom knew better. He simply wasn't one for idle chatter with strangers, unless they were female of course. Then he would switch into his charm mode, regardless of their age.

The manager sat behind an old wooden school desk with a fan blowing from one side. Tom could understand why the salesman did all the running. The manager was beyond obesity. He had to weigh over three hundred pounds. All this Tom took in as he crossed the small room to stand towering over the manager.

"I understand you are the party who will pay for the Plymouth, Mr. er?"

"Tom Mueller is the name. After having one of your mechanics look over the car, your counter offer does not meet with my approval. It seems there is more wrong with it than I originally thought, so I will now give you my final bid. This will be a cash transaction." There was a pregnant pause.

"I'll take it off your hands for three hundred and it will cost me twice that much to get it road worthy."

"You've got to be kidding."

"Come on, partner, we've been wasting our time."

As they started out of the shoddy office, the manager yelled, "Wait, you said cash?"

"Yes, and no." Tom started to reach into his pocket.

"Three fifty and I never want to see you again."

"Three twenty-five" and he pulled a roll from his trouser pocket. "Sign over the title" counting the bills with a theatrical flair. The managers eyes followed the bills and as Tom offered them he reached into a drawer and pulled out a sheaf of titles which he leafed through, drawing one out signing and stamping it. They exchanged money and title, the manager re-counting the bills.

"Come on, Felix, we've been gone from home long enough and we still have another stop to make." Tom winked at his friend.

After dropping the Plymouth off at the mechanic's place, they hightailed for Toms house. Felix couldn't get into the house fast enough to give Gennie all the news. Tom had already told him not to mention anything about their part in the attempted bank holdup.

"Hi, Stell, did you miss me?"

"I thought you had abandoned me honey and it's a tough job keeping Leo entertained when you or Felix aren't here. Of course he spent some of the time out in the back yard."

"That's like him. Where is he now?"

"Probably taking a nap."

"I hope you can rustle up something to eat because we're taking Felix and Gennie in to see the house Felix rented with the option to purchase on land contract. The reason we took so long was because we were horse trading on a car which will be ready for him in a couple of days.."

"You have been busy. I have a meat loaf in the oven that should be just about ready. Combined with veggies and tossed salad, it should fill you up."

"Felix is the one complaining how starved he is. I forgot about my hunger listening to him. That sounds good though. The reason I'm in such a hurry is I don't know if the utilities are turned on so we should get there before dark." Tom sat at the kitchen table watching her as she completed preparing the meal. She was so efficient, no wasted motions in a kitchen that she had only occupied for a few hours. It must be an attribute from her artistic inclinations. Leo wandered into the room and laid his large head in Tom's lap. Tom knew what he wanted so he accommodated the dog with the usual results.

"Soup's on", he called through the closed bedroom door of the room Felix and Gennie were using. "You didn't forget how hungry you are, did you?"

"Be right out, amigo."

"Well hurry up partner so we can get to your house before dark. I don't remember if the saleslady mentioned if the utilities were on or not. Gennie won't be able to appreciate the place by flashlight."

The hasty meal consumed, they all piled into the wagon, even Leo. He loved to take rides, always had ever since he was a pup.

Upon arrival Tom was pleased to see the overhead front stoop light on. Mrs. Brazelton must have returned earlier to turn it on. That seemed to solve the utility situation. They all piled out eager to see Felix's new digs. Leo began sniffing around the front yard but always keeping Tom within sight since the surrounding territory was unfamiliar to the dog. Tom had already been through the place so he remained in the yard with Leo to allow time for Felix to play tour guide to the girls. After about fifteen minutes they came trooping out and Felix re-locked the front door like a prudent home owner should. Stella and Gennie had their heads together discussing re-decorating changes and Tom could see more of the little man's wages escaping his grasp; he might even have to cut back on his beer consumption - or even quit entirely. Tom snickered to himself, that would be the day. Gennie had better watch her P's and Q's or Felix would give her up first. He was an independent man, as she would find out if she pushed him to far.

As they all got into Tom's wagon he turned to Felix. "You want to see if the mechanic has statred on your car before we head to my house?"

"Might as well, amigo; it's on the way ain't it?"

They pulled into the mechanic's drive which led up to his double garage. The Plymouth was no longer where they left it earlier and lights showed from underneath the overhead door. Tom and Felix carefully dodged scattered car parts strewn helter-skelter on the path to the entry door next to the overhead. They could hear grinding noises coming from inside so rather than knock Tom just opened the door and they entered to find the mechanic hard at work cutting off the muffler and tailpipe from the Plymouth. Tom got his attention by nudging his protruding legs and the mechanic rolled out from under the vehicle.

"Didn't hear you come in, Mr. Mueller."

"Felix here just wanted to show his fiancee the before and after of their new car."

"Sure, I can do something else until they are finished."

Tom took the mechanic off to one side while Felix went out to get Gennie. "What do you think?"

"As I said before, she's up in years but I think I've got her figured out. Now it's all accordin' to how much you want to spend to make her presentable again. The only major things I haven't checked yet are her brakes and cooling system. If nuthin' is seriously faulty there we'll be in

74

business again. Her cosmetics can be remedied easy enough. I can find used parts for that. Seat covers will do wonders for the interior. That answer your worries?"

"Yes and by the way what is your name? We've only referred to you as the mechanic."

"Don Prince, most people just call me Princer, don't know why though."

"OK, Princer, what do you think about some body work and a touch-up paint job. Would that be out of your field of experience? This is to be my wedding present to my partner and his girl and I'd like it to look as spiffy as when it came out of the showroom."

"I can handle that, Mr. Mueller. It just might add a bit of time for the paint ta' dry."

"Well, go to it, Princer." He handed the mechanic fifty dollars. "That's on account, to show you how serious I am about your project. Here's my phone number in case you have any other questions or needs. Progress reports would be appreciated, too."

Tom passed Felix and Gennie on the way to the wagon. "Don't take all night, partner. I still have some phone calls to make."

19

"Do you hear something?" For an answer Leo moved toward the front room slowly, but with enough urgency to let Tom know he wasn't playing any games with him. After Tom grabbed shorts, bathrobe, flashlight, and his Cobra he followed. Leo was sitting by the front door similar to the position he'd taken yesterday morning when Tom had spotted the car pulling out of the cul-de-sac. As he stood next to the dog listening he could just make out the sound of an idling car engine somewhere close by. This was no longer coincidence. Two mornings in a row was more than mere chance of a lost motorist making a wrong turn. It showed real purpose on someone's part. The only way to relieve his own mind on the seriousness of the situation was to confront the occupant of the vehicle. Here he had mixed feelings on how to do it. Sneak up on the car in his state of undress or wait long enough to put on trousers and shoes and grab a shotgun? Or wake Felix to accompany him? Tom chose the latter. If the car was gone by the time they were ready, so be it. They would be gone tomorrow anyway. Tom knocked softly on the bedroom door where Felix and Gennie were staying. When his partner answered sleepily through the door Tom said simply, "I need you right now, Felix."

Felix opened the door and Tom explained the situation in few words. "Grab your weapon and we'll use the back door and circle around. I'm going to load a shotgun." Within seconds, Felix was by his side. Tom hadn't even finished loading the shotgun when the little man joined him.

"Who da' ya' think it is, amigo?"

Tom shrugged his shoulders. "No idea, but I'm hoping it's Pepe."

"Yeah, that'd be good. I'll trade ya' weapons." Tom handed over the Remington and they quietly left the house by the rear door. Leo stationed himself right at Tom's side without command. Nearing the front, Tom could now plainly hear an idling engine nearby but as yet couldn't see anything. A roadside street light would sure come in handy here he thought. They were at the front corner of the house when Leo emitted the deep sound from his throat that was as close as he ever came to an actual growl. That noise always stopped Tom dead in his tracks for he knew it was his signal of approaching danger. Although his eyesight wasn't as acute as Leos he focused on the direction the dogs head was pointing where he could just discern the silhouette of a high-standing vehicle. He instantly remembered where and when he had seen a similar replica of that image. Two times actually; once in Colombia when Felix's friend delivered the armored Whizzers, and once when he and Pepe had followed one to his father's compound. So he immediately realized it was the property of the elder Basquez.

Tom reached to his left to forewarn Felix but his partner was no longer at his side. He must have seen or heard something which drew him away, something he'd had no time to alert Tom of. Turning his head to the other side Tom could now see Leo crouched in his attack position so he quietly dropped to his side. This standoff was quickly getting out of hand. For some reason Pepe seemed desperate to eliminate Tom. What potential danger did he now pose to Pepe family that he hadn't previously? Was he in possession of information he wasn't aware of?.

Tom had his hand on Leo's back and could feel the dog quivering. Two things happened in quick succession. The meaty smack of a rifle butt striking human flesh and Leo launching himself in the same direction. A gunshot rang out, not a shotgun blast, then a high pitched scream that denoted Leo had made some sort of contact. Tom was up and running toward that sound.

"Don't worry 'bout Leo, amigo, he's got some guy pinned to the ground. Come aroun' here an see if ya' know this one. He won't be awake for awhile."

Tom followed his instructions but couldn't identify the man. When he turned toward the jibbering captive of Leo's, that man wasn't recognizable either. He was yelling in what sounded like Spanish. "What's he yelling, Felix?"

"Aw he's just wantin the dog offa' him. Pay no 'tention, he'll live ta' answer some questions later, but I don't know 'bout this one. I suppose an ambulance will have ta' be called. Maybe I hit him a little too hard, heh, heh, heh."

The front stoop light snapped on. One of the girls must have been awakened by the gun shot." Go in and calm the girls down, Felix. I'll keep an eye on the perps. If you think an ambulance is necessary call one along with the Sheriff's Department, or else wait for them to arrive - your choice. Just make sure the girls stay inside. There is no reason they should be exposed to the results of this seamy side of our work."

Leo looked over at Tom with that questioning expression that almost spoke out loud. "Did I do good?"

Sirens could be heard in the distance closing fast. Tom knew that before everything quieted down again several hours would elapse. It didn't look like he'd get much sleep before he made his morning phone calls.

When Tom talked to the accommodations reserver at Union Station in D.C., he was assured that a double pullman stateroom direct nonstop to New Orleans would be available, leaving at 6 P.M. that evening. Also the baggage car would only be one car forward to house a large dog for the trip, easily accessible for owner visits. With that assurance Tom booked the passage. Long-term parking nearby was also available, serviced by insured drivers. It seemed like the railroad had thought of everything to obtain new business threatened by airline travel. With that out of the way he next called Lance Nolte to inform him they would be on their way to Florida via New Orleans tonight so he should arrange the paper signing meeting with the attorneys there. Tom was eager too see the Key Largo property.

Rather than letting his imagination run away with him, he wanted first-hand concrete proof of its possibilities. He knew Fred did things up right. The proof of that what he had accomplished at the so-called computer shop in Chelsea with all the hidden passageways. Not only the work involved, but the ingenuity of its creation. If only Fred had channeled his creativity along legitimate lines. Look what he had done with his stock portfolio.

It seemed he was putting the cart before the horse, so Tom next talked to Stella before making any further calls. With her usual unflappable manner she accepted the short notice of the trip without reservations about what to pack for a month-long journey. "I'll get together with Gennie to see what we can take that will be suitable. We'll make do."

"Anything you don't have can be picked up once we're down there. I don't imagine either one of you have swimming suits, nor do I for that matter."

Tom made two more calls then told Stella to wake him by three o'clock. He crashed and was asleep in minutes but again his dreams made him restless and the tossing and turning was not conducive to the deep sleep that he sorely needed. Thus when Stella woke him at three he felt disoriented and groggy. He took a quick cold shower which helped somewhat then threw a few things into a suitcase before putting on his freshly cleaned suit and heading to the kitchen for some coffee to cleanse the remaining cow webs from his head.

"Ready to leave, Stell?"

"As ready as I'll ever be. Everything is in the wagon and all that's left to be done is to collect Leo who is out in the back yard."

"I'll do that, you just get Felix and Gennie rounded up."

"I think he is taking a nap too."

"Naw, I'm awake, I smelled the coffee."

"This is the last of it so it may be a little strong."

"Thass' all right with me since I won't get a chance ta' have any beer 'til we're on the train."

The last call Tom had made that morning was to Terry Connoti, the state trooper. He just happened to catch him before he went to bed, which meant he was working nights, so he gave him the address and location of his house and asked him if he could swing by a couple of times a week to check the property since no one would be here for the next four weeks and they'd already had two incidents in the past ten days.

"Be more than glad to, Mr. Mueller. In fact, I'll do you one better. We just had a graduating class of new officers of which three were assigned to this post, one per shift. You know how gung-ho new patrolmen can be. I will guarantee your property will be checked every night." "That would be great, Terry, and you don't have to be so formal; the name is Tom." He then gave him the particulars on what had happened just that early morning. "We'll get together when I get back."

Tom went to a closet and got the dog's body harness which had been extended to its maximum to fit. If Leo put on any more weight he'd have to get the next larger size, and he didn't know if a larger one was made or a custom-made harness would have to be ordered.

Before Tom had left the bank after the aborted robbery he had returned to his safety deposit box and removed several stones of lesser value. These, rubies, garnets, sapphires, and smaller diamonds he put together in one pouch. The reasons were twofold. They were easier to carry than bundles of cash and secondly when he got to New Orleans he wanted to pay back his cash advance on the emerald. That gemstone was his ace in the hole. Tom had thought quite sometime about removing it from the jewelry store and putting it in a deposit box closer to where he called home. His main reason had to do with meeting and falling in love with Stella. The gem would eventually be used to pay the ever-increasing cost for their children's college education wherever they decided to go. But go they would because in this more modern world the lack of that degree would mean a life of struggle to eke out a living at menial jobs that took brawn over brains.

They pulled up to the depot with time to spare. When the wagon was unloaded, a redcap wheeled their sparse amount of luggage to the waiting train. A fuss was made by every railroad employee who saw Leo. The dog mostly ignored the attention plodding along between Tom and

Stella, keeping his eyes on both as well-mannered as Tom could hope for. The redcap picked up their tickets on the way and everything meshed perfectly when the red cap handed them off to the porter, accepted his tip, and the porter showed them to their connecting pullman suites. The porter then showed Tom where Leo would be housed for the trip, one car forward from theirs. The dining and club cars were two cars back. He handed Tom several papers which were for meal times, ordering forms, and price lists. "If there is anything you want special just push the white button near the door of your suite at any hour and I'll take care of it."

So Tom explained what Leo would need in the way of food and water. "It will be taken care of, Mr. Mueller, rest assured, sir."

20

He had to show his winnings to all to prove what an astute poker player he was

Tom figured he was up three hundred, not too shabby for a little over four and a half hours play, but a far cry from what he had expected.

Then Miss Luck had a change of heart. His hole cards were an ace and a king of clubs and his first card up was an ace. His first reaction after scanning the rest of the hands was to jump on it and bet high but after looking at the grin on the shark's face he calmly waited for his move first so he just called the two hundred bet. Everyone stayed except the old executive. Tom's next card was an ace, which made up his mind. The shark had two high cards showing, a jack and queen. He immediately raised the Mexican's bet of three hundred by another three. When it came to Tom, after the railroad dick called, Tom raised five hundred, which the Mexican called with a pair of fours showing. The shark licked his lips which told Tom almost certainly what his down cards were. He figured his foe had either two high pair, jacks and queens or an open-ended royal straight flush. That nervous lip-licking gesture almost surely indicated the latter. It was the first outward sign that the shark did have less than iron nerves. Tom figured there was over two grand in the pot. The shark raised again but only three hundred, probably to keep the railroad dick in who couldn't have more than a full house, low at that. Tom's last card was dealt down and he resisted the urge to take a look, just staring at the shark. Put up or shut up, he thought. Tom could see Bernie, the porter, hovering by the car door not advancing but obviously waiting to rearrange the car for breakfast. While the shark was checking all the cards on the table Tom raised the corner of his down card. It was the fourth ace. He had him, because his king stopped his royal straight flush. The railroad dick called, so he raised three hundred. The Mexican folded and the shark called. Tom flipped his fourth ace over and said, "Read 'em and weep, gentlemen." The stunned look on the two remaining players was priceless. "It seems your luck was golden tonight, Mr. Mueller; lets see how you do tomorrow night."

Fat chance of his playing another night, he thought as he raked in the cash. When Tom happened to look over at the executive he saw a definite wink on the old man's deadpan face. He assumed that was a wink of approval for nailing the shark.

When Tom got to Bernie he handed him a twenty. The porter nodded his thanks as he let him out of the car. Mission accomplished, Tom thought, as he entered his compartment. He sat at the window table counting his winnings. Twenty-four hundred bucks over his original stake, and now he would give his sleeping beauty five hundred for any purpose she wished. Tom looked over to where Stella lay in all her innocence, he hair spread out in a fan on the pillow. He marveled every time he looked at her, when she was not aware of his inspection, that God had allowed him this beautiful yet complex woman to enter his life. He thanked his creator every day for his benevolence.

Stella stirred in her sleep almost as if by some form of ESP she was aware of Tom's presence. Her eyes flickered open and looked directly into his. She held out her arms in a come to me gesture and Tom rose, never breaking eye contact, and moved to her arms. Not a word was spoken as they joined just holding each other in a tight embrace, each it seemed, content for the body contact. There was little doubt they were made for each other. Tom kissed her soundly before pulling away enough to retrieve the cash he was still holding. He offered the bills to her as a supplicant would bestow a gift to a goddess. Her eyes questioned the offering but she still held her tongue patiently waiting for Tom to explain. Instead Tom unclothed, hanging his apparel on a hanger, and stripped to his shorts returned to her embrace. "That's some of the money I earned last night in a card game; the remainder will be added to my nest egg to help pay for this trip. All is not fun and games you see."

"I love you so much honey and I couldn't ask for a better benefactor. You always seem in charge of every situation. I don't know how you do it but I've quit questioning and just accept the results. Now let's stop all this conversation and sate our desires."

It seemed the rest of the trip was going to be uneventful. They were nearing Biloxi, Mississippi, and nothing out of the ordinary had befallen them. To be on the safe side they had taken all meals in their separate compartments. Bernie, the porter, had been quite accommodating to their wishes. He made no reference to the poker game Tom had missed on purpose. Leo was returned to his shipping cage in the baggage car for the remainder of the trip. Both Tom and Stella visited him on a regular basis.

The last night before reaching New Orleans when Tom returned from another visit with the mastiff he found Stella sitting at the window table with her sketch pad busy at work. What caught his immediate attention though was her choice of dress, his old OSU jacket unzipped and panties – nothing else. "Comfortable?"

Stella looked up from her work with a radiant smile, her eyes sparkling as much now as the night she had accepted his proposal and engagement ring. "Yes, and the reasons are twofold. First, this drawing is finished ready for the transfer to an oil. But that can only be done when I have the materials needed and the work space to do it in. I'll show you this in a minute."

She placed the drawing face down on the table and stood, shrugging the jacket off of her shoulders as she moved toward him. " The second reason is of a more intimate nature." She put her arms around his waist and looked Tom directly in his eyes. "I've missed my period, honey. I'm afraid you have a pregnant woman on your hands." She kissed him tenderly. "What are you going to do about it?"

"How would you like to get married in New Orleans, the city of romance and intrigue? We should be pulling in there sometime around three or four in the morning. We'll get a good hotel room for the rest of the night where we can sleep in comfort and I can make the arrangements for our ceremony. Felix and Gennie can stand up for us if that's all right with you, and Leo can be the ring bearer."

21

Tom booked them into the Roosevelt Hotel when they left the train. This was one of the oldest and best hotels in the city. There was no point in second class when he had the money.

Stella was enthralled. "God, Tom, this place is beautiful."

"Nothing is too good for the mother of my child. You see, Stell, money is just about everything; without it you're just an also-ran."

"Do you think Leo will be all right where he's at?"

"The night manager assured me he would be all right down there, and it will only be for a few hours anyway. He's had worse accommodations than that before. I explained to him that we would be on our way shortly so to behave himself. He seemed to understand and didn't make a fuss when I left. I think we'd better get some shut-eye ourselves; tomorrow is going to be a busy day and I have to make several phone calls to set everything in motion. I left instructions for an eight-thirty wake-up call so let's call it a night." Stella wrapped herself around Tom like she was afraid he might vanish. For Tom it was a pleasurable experience.

The ringing of the phone woke Tom from a dreamless sleep, no flash-backs which sometimes caused him to awaken in a cold sweat. He believed it was accredited to the peace of mind that Stella's presence made in his life. He reached over to the night stand and answered he was awake. "Send up a double order of coffee and those beignets New Orleans is so famous for." Stella was still glued to him so he had a difficult time extricating himself from her grasp but nature was calling and he had to answer the call.

When room service delivered, Tom met the bellman at the door so as not to let him enter the room and see Stella in her state of undress. That vision was for his eyes only. Tom woke his sleeping beauty. "Breakfast is served, dear lady, and since you are eating for two it is my pleasure to serve you four beignets. It will be nine-thirty or ten before we're ready to leave, and I still have several calls to make."

While Stella was in the bathroom Tom got on the house phone and with the help of the directory began making his calls. But first he rang Felix's room and spoke to a just awakened Gennie; his partner was still pounding his ear, so he explained to her what he had in mind for the day and asked if she had any suggestions for making things go smoother. That was like turning on a water main. Most of her ideas he mentally discarded as frivolous and it was difficult to end the conversation without hurting her feelings. "Have Felix call me when he wakes up, hopefully in the next fifteen minutes."

Next, he called a car-rental agency that advertised General Motors vehicles. They would be happy to have a new Chevy station wagon available for him within the hour. The rates were acceptable to Tom so he reserved one on the condition they would deliver it to the hotel along with the necessary paper work. Agreed. Now, not being a particularly religious person he had to rely on the directory for wedding chapels. There were five pages full of every imaginable service for the to-be celebrants so he had his pick. Seeing it was now nine o'clock he first called City Hall to arrange for the blood test. It would take three hours for the documents to be issued for the license to be issued to be registered. That would work out perfectly, Tom thought, giving them enough time to get to the jeweler to complete his business there. He wasn't going to warn them he was coming as he wanted to see how his gem was displayed and what safeguards the owner had devised for its protection. Tom knocked on the bathroom door. "You about ready, Stell?" She opened the door and stuck her still wet head out. "In a minute, honey. Just let me finish drying my hair." She left the door ajar so they could converse without yelling while she finished her toiletry. "What would you have me wear for this important occasion?" She re-entered the room in panties sans bra. She really knew how to arouse her man.

"Well a little more than that although I like your taste in clothes."

"You may look but not touch, dear sir." "That's not going to be easy but I'll try." Then Tom explained what he had done so far while she had been taking her shower.

"You've done well, honey; it deserves a kiss." She started toward him. "Oh no you don't, not until you put some more clothes on or you'll need another shower." Just then there was a knock on the hallway door and she shot back into the bathroom. There stood a bleary-eyed, tousled-haired Felix. "Ya' really set Gennie off; she was jabberin' a mile a minute 'til I had ta' leave the room ta' get the straight story from my amigo. What's the scoop?"

"Come on in here, you don't have to stand out in the hallway. Stella's in the bathroom." So Tom went through his findings again - a condensed version. "So when the rental station wagon arrives here, Stella and I will go to City Hall to get our blood tests, then head for the jewelry store to retrieve my stone."

"Where are ya' gonna' take it? An' I suppose yer' gonna' do this alone since ya' got all this thought out."

"I'll take Leo along for protection, he'll be happy to get out of the basement I'm sure."

Felix looked like he was in deep thought for several moments but before he could say anything more Stella stuck her head out of the bathroom. "Honey hand me my black dress please, as you've already mentioned times awastin.' Oh, hi, Felix everything satisfactory in your room?" As Tom was taking the dress to her, the phone rang. "Get that, will you partner? It seems everything is happening at once."

"Yer' car is waitin' for ya' amigo. Yer' rental agent is waitin' at the front deak; what's yer' pleasure?"

"Tell him I'll be right down." In an aside to Stella, Tom said, "You have ten minutes to join me at the front desk so don't rush yourself, I can't have my future bride sweating when she gets her blood test. What would the city officials think?"

"What are you planning to do now, partner? That is until you stand up for us at the regular wedding ceremony?"

"If I remember right when ya' first too the stone ta' that jewelers ya' had i t taped to yer' chest an' ya' wanted me with ya' for protection. Ya' didn't know yer' way around this town anymore then than ya' do now. So even if ya' have Leo with ya' what makes ya' think ya' don't need me. I'm goin' ta' my room now an' make myself presentable so that when we see that Saltzman guy at his store he might not know me right away an' think I'm a hired bodyguard, heh, heh, heh." Tom just looked at the little man and shook his head. His partners sense of humor was as always, a bit weird. But he did have a point. If Mr. Saltzman had any thoughts of pulling a fast one on him it wouldn't hurt to have added protection along. He could always go out to the wagon and take Leo back in with him. Tom had to have that emerald.

Everything was completed in less than the ten minutes he had given Stella. The rental agent assured Tom he could drop the wagon off at one of their offices in Miami if he didn't plan on returning to New Orleans. He also refused a return ride to his office saying it was part of their service. As Tom stood waiting for Stella here came a spiffed up Felix with Gennie in tow. "Well, quite a change, partner, and since Stella hasn't come down yet why don't you two wait here for her while I go down and get Leo."

Parking in front of the jewelry store in a no-parking zone, about where the cab had originally dropped them off all four of them trooped into the store. Leo was left behind with orders to guard the car. He was so happy to get out of the hotel basement he was obeying Tom to the letter. He somehow sensed this was an important day in his friends life just from the way he was talking to him. Anyone foolish enough to approach his ward until his friends returned was risking bedlam.

Tom stood next to Stella slowly surveying the showroom. He couldn't see the emerald displayed anywhere. If Saltzman was showing it, where was it? The same character that Tom remembered as the flunky that took his orders from the manager was about to make an approach to his party when he saw Tom. His face blanched and he took an abrupt about face, disappearing into the rear office area. Now Tom hoped there would be some sort of a favorable development. When Tom glanced over at Felix he could see the little man was getting antsy looking all around the showroom the same way that Tom was. He sidled over to Tom. "Where is it, amigo?"

"That's just what I'm about to find out. Stay here with the girls unless you hear any sort of scuffle coming from the offices. If so, hightail it in there to back me up."

It turned out not to be necessary to use his partners help. Tom almost ran Hector down. "Mr. Saltzman is on his way here, Mr. Mueller. He's coming from a branch office. Can I get you anything until he gets here?"

"I think you know what I'm looking for, Hector. Where is it? I don't have a lot of time today, I'm on a tight schedule as it is."

"Mr. Saltzman will explain everything when he gets here, I'm sure, sir."

"He'd better and quickly because I'm about to have my partner bring in my enforcer from the car and I can't guarantee what steps he'll take. You can get me a bowl of water though."

As soon as Mr. Saltzman saw Tom he became "Mr. Cordiality." By this time Stella, Felix, and Gennie had joined Tom in the office. Spotting Stella he immediately made quite an ado over her engagement ring. "Congratulations, Mr. Mueller, you found a beautiful woman to marry" and on and on becoming more effusive as he continued. Tom had to interrupt to get to the point of his visit. "I suppose you know why I'm here."

"Another advance on you emerald, I imagine."

"On the contrary, I want to repay what I've already borrowed."

Saltzman blinked several times, the indicator of his surprise and/or astonishment. "I hope you're not carrying that much cash on your person."

Felix jumped in. "Where is the stone? Ya' don't seem to have it on display here that we could see? An' where is your manager?"

"He is now the manager of both my branches since I've decided to open a third branch in Baton Rouge this year."

"Business must be good then if you're expanding out of town."

"Yes, and I can thank your emerald for a big part of it. I'd never seen such interest in a gem in private hands before; in museums of course but not in a retail outlet. I've doubled my annual net profit here alone."

"I hate to relieve you of it then, but I have other plans for it. So if you'll get it we'll transact our business an be on our way. We have to get our blood tests and the sooner we get to City Hall the quicker the results will be available."

"You're in luck, then. My sister works in Vital Statistics there. One call to her will give you a rush through. Now let me get your gem, it's always in the safe when I'm not present."

The gem lay in a black velvet-lined tray covered by a domed glass contraption that Saltzman had to unlock with a key that was on a sterling silver chain around his neck. Stella gasped and squeezed Toms arm in astonishment. "Oh, honey, it's just beautiful. I've never seen one that huge. I'll have to paint that."

Tom winked at her. "Now, to business." He extracted the bag of gems from his jackets inner pocket pouring them out in his hand. Saltzman grabbed for a nearby loupe. "Where are you getting all these gems?"

"My deceased brother was a collector, and he willed them to me."

"These are exceptionally fine-grade stones, especially the diamonds and sapphires. The sapphires are a very rich blue." He did some figuring on a calculator. "All told, I'd have to offer thirty thousand for the lot, and if you have any more I hope you'll keep me in mind. I'm always in the market for good quality gems. Let me return to the safe and get your five thousand." That was what Tom liked about the man, no haggling. When Saltzman left the room, Tom again winked at Stella and Felix. "That was painless, was it not? That's a nice way to do business, no muss, no fuss." Mr. Saltzman returned with a packet of bills, mostly of high denomination which Tom promptly broke down to individual piles that he then parceled out to his merry little band before asking Mr. Saltzman if he would lend him a piece of that black velvet and some surgical tape. "That is the way the emerald was originally brought into your store and it's only appropriate that it leaves in the same manner don't you think?" "You never cease to amaze me, Mr. Mueller, with your ingenuity and resourcefulness."

When he returned this time he also brought the contract Tom had dictated at their first meeting. "If you'd please sign off on this our profitable business will be terminated, then I'll call my sister to expect your arrival forthwith." Then he stuck out his hand to shake. "It's been a pleasure dealing with you, Mr. Mueller, and don't forget me in the future if you ever decide to part with more of your gem stones."

Once in the car Felix said, "How come ya' gave us that money, amigo?"

"You didn't expect me to carry it all did you? I'm running out of pocket space."

When the reached City Hall and parked close by, Tom ordered Leo to guard the car and they would be back shortly. He'd found a tree lined boulevard where the wagon was somewhat shaded in the rising temperature, but first he let him out to empty his system along the trees. That accomplished, they returned to find the others in deep conversation that ceased when they noticed Tom

"What's the verdict? The secret session you held while we were gone must have been serious enough to warrant me an explanation." Stella spoke up. "Felix and Gennie have decided to take their blood tests too, so there will be a double wedding ceremony."

Tom looked at his friend and partner who stood nervously alongside his prospective bride. "So that discussion we had on the train was all camouflage huh?"

"Ya' can't believe everything ya' hear, amigo, but let's get it over with. I'm kinda' nervous when it comes time ta' get stuck with needles."

Tom got Leo back in the wagon, poured him some water, and holding his massive head between his hands looked him straight in his multi-colored eyes and said, "This is important to us, big guy. Bear with me a little longer and I'll make sure you have a reward for your patience." Tom stroked, not scratching behind the dogs ears to avoid getting his reward.

They were a handsome, yet somewhat peculiar-looking foursome who strode hand in hand toward City Hall. Tom was thinking this would cause somewhat of a dilemma . Why couldn't Felix have confessed to his intentions while they were still at the jewelers. He was sure Felix didn't have a ring to present to Gennie at the coming ceremony. He could have bought one with the money he gave him at the time. Of course Felix usually did things on the spur of the moment, bass-ackward. While they were heading for the car Tom had excused himself saying he forgot something, returned and plunked down cash for a diamond-covered wedding band.

"What is it, honey? You look deep in thought. You aren't getting cold feet are you?"

"Not on your life, Stell. I've never wanted to do something more than what we are about to perform. You are the love of my life. I was just regretting that my Mom didn't live long enough to see my happiness and look forward to spoiling her future grandchild. She so hoped one of her sons would provide her with that blessing before she was too old to enjoy them. Let's talk of more pleasant things like who you are going to get for a doctor once we get to the Keys?"

"I don't know if I'll need one that soon honey and don't worry Tom, you won't be cut off that soon. Maybe you can double my pleasure" and she gave out her sultry laugh.

"Easy girl, you know how that laugh affects me."

Stella clamped her hand over her mouth in a mock gesture of stopping herself from laughing again.

They entered the building and quickly found the office of Mr. Saltzman's sister who appeared to be younger. She was a small woman with close cropped blonde hair, a style not common as most women let their hair grow longish. She had a pleasant sounding, deep voice when she greeted them.

"Abe described you to a T when he called that you were coming, Mr. Mueller. He is quite a fan of yours since you brought him that huge emerald. It has helped his business immensely to the point he has expanded beyond his wildest dreams. We constantly discuss his promotions because he likes my woman's viewpoint. But enough of my idle chatter. Abe said, 'Barb, you take good care of these folks because they are in somewhat of a hurry.' I've got the necessary paper work ready so you will have little to fill in before signing. Now your friends here are going to stand up for you?"

"My partner and his fiancee have decided to take the plunge along with us so they will need the same service. We only have a month vacation and we still want to go to Florida for some further business of mine."

"I understand. While you are working on yours, I'll prepare theirs. We have a doctor on site which eliminates the three-day waiting period. This is not for the general public, only for special situations like yours," she laughed. "Your only charge will be ten dollars a couple." When all was completed she closed the office with an "out to lunch" sign and escorted them down the hall to the doctor's office and introduced them. Forty-five minutes later everything was finished and as they headed back down the hall Tom asked his now solemn cohorts to wait a minute he wanted to thank Barb in person.

"Hi again. There is one more thing you might help me with. Is there a non-sectarian chapel that could perform the rites somewhere nearby? Cost is not an issue."

"There are several, Mr. Mueller. Would you like me to call one and set it up? All I have to know is what time."

"That would be wonderful, Barb. Make it one-thirty and make sure a dog is allowed at the ceremony. That is a must." She laughed again. "You certainly have some strange requests. But hold on, I'll get right on it." She consulted a notebook from her purse and dialed a number. She relayed all that Tom had asked for and added a few suggestions of her own. Then she wrote the name, address, and phone on a slip of paper and handed it to him. "Everything you might want to know is itemized there and, yes, they will allow a dog to be a part of the wedding party. To solve my own curiosity what kind of dog is it?"

"Leo is a two hundred and eighty pound mastiff that is a part of my team. He has saved my life on more than one occasion and is loved by all of us."

Tom went to hand her a twenty dollar bill for all her help but she refused it. "Let's say that is another wedding gift." When Tom rejoined the others Felix asked "What took ya' so long amigo?"

"Just some last minute arrangements, partner, now let's make haste. We have about an hour before the ceremony." He handed Felix the slip of paper with all the information on it. "You might want to study that on the way back to the wagon to see if you are familiar with the area. We still have to let Leo out to stretch before we start for the chapel."

The temperature was rising rapidly along with the humidity and Tom for one was starting to perspire under his lightweight suit. He could feel his shirt starting to stick to his back, an uncomfortable sensation he would have to endure at least until the ceremony was over.

Leo didn't even attempt to rise when they arrived at the wagon. He was obviously suffering the same discomfort as the rest of the group, with the exception of Felix who the climate didn't affect in the slightest but of course being raised closer to the equator explained his indifference. Tom could understand, remembering a like situation at the Yankee-Red Sox game they had attended. Tom finally coaxed Leo out of the wagon by mentioning the magic word yummie. When he followed his main friend in among the trees, with his long tongue protruding almost to the ground, Leo changed course to one of them to release his bladder then returned to Tom's side, where he sat waiting for his treat. A slight wind, although hot, suddenly blew through the glade bringing a bit of relief from the highly heated stillness. Seeing no special treat in sight Leo swung his head in the direction from which the wind was coming to enjoy any relief it might afford. The mastiff would have stayed in that position had not Tom started back to the wagon. When they were alone together from a group Leo never let him distance himself farther than six feet away so he dutifully followed. Back at the wagon everybody but Stella were standing in the partial shade of the trees. The cars buzzing by were also creating a bit of moving air. "Stella you don't happen to have anything in your purse that resembles a snack for Leo do you? I had to use that word to get him outside." Stella looked but came up empty. "Maybe we'll pass a store on the way to the chapel that carries meat of some kind where I can get him something."

"If we do honey get us all something cool to drink. I know I'm parched. Does this car have an air conditioner?'

"I haven't really checked it out yet, Stell." Tom removed his suit jacket folding it neatly and placing it over the back seat where the precious contents would not fall out of the pockets and slid in behind the steering wheel. "Open the glove box and see if there's an owner's manual inside, push that chrome plated button right in front of you." She handed him a half-inch-thick booklet which Tom studied for a few minutes flipping pages back and forth to pictured diagrams. He compared the pictures to the dashboard in front of him and murmuring to himself set the knobs accordingly. When he started the wagon a rush of hot air spewed out but after about a minute grew steadily cooler so by the time he beeped the horn to alert Felix and Gennie they were about to leave the wagons inside temperature had dropped to where they could close the windows and cool off. When Felix and Gennie got in they were greeted by almost frigid air. Tom moved steadily into the flow of the increasing traffic and following the directions given by Felix had soon separated themselves from the heavy traffic and were tooling along on a two-way street below the speed limit. Stella spotted the delicatessen up ahead on her side and pointed it out to Tom. "I think that's just what you're looking for, honey." Tom left the engine running but lowered the air conditioner blower to a more moderate air flow. He turned in his seat. "Anything special you two would like?" Felix spoke, "Do ya' have ta' ask?"

22

Tom entered the smallish store front, to be surprised by its depth. It must extend all the way to the next street or an alley, but just scanning the immediate area to his front, he saw a series of refrigerated meat cases in a row along the left wall manned by a little woman pushing eighty. She was a true Cajun by the looks of her mixed ancestry, and when she spoke the dialect proved his surmise to be correct. "May ah' help yas' sor?" Another thought passed through his mind. He didn't see anyone else working here. How could this pint-sized old woman protect herself in the event of an armed robbery?

"I'd like two of those T-bone steaks wrapped separately please and a six pack of Budweiser, two bottles of cold Coke, and some any-colored ribbon you might have on hand. She moved about like a whirling dervish, quite agile for a woman her age. "Ten-fifty, sor'." Tom handed over thirteen dollars telling her to keep the change for her kindly service and with his bag of goodies returned to the wagon. Stella reached over and unlocked his door so he handed her the heavy bag and slipped into his seat. Tom started to disburse the contents handing a cold Coke to Stella and Gennie before handing Felix the Bud, then retrieving one of the steaks he unwrapped it and gave it to Leo.

"Now Felix, how far are we from the chapel?"

"Less than a mile, amigo; jus' keep goin' straight and I'll tell ya' when ta' turn."

The chapel itself was nothing much to look at from the outside. The only thing that set it apart from the other buildings nearby was a large brass cross embedded in the green brick. There was an adjacent parking area for about six cars so Tom pulled in right next to the canopied side entrance. They all piled out except for Leo who was still gnawing on the steak bone.

"Why don't we all go inside and check on the interior then I'll come back out for Leo."

They were greeted by a middle-aged man dressed soberly in a dark suit who showed them into an anteroom where several chairs and a sofa were scattered around. The room was cooled by a window air conditioner.

"You folks are the Mueller and Santana party?"

They all nodded. "Good, the chapel proper is ready whenever you wish to commence the ceremony. I was told a dog would also be included. Where is it?"

"He's finishing a snack and I'll bring him in shortly."

"May I give you women corsages? You have a choice of wrist or apparel pin-ons. Lapel flowers are provided for the men. I'll wait in the chapel while you bring in your dog."

Tom went out to the wagon. Leo saw him coming and got to his feet. Tom let him out. "Do you have to release anything?" Leo just sat looking up at his main friend with what Tom always associated as a knowing grin on his face. So Tom tied the ribbon with the wedding band attached around his massive neck. You won't need your harness or leash today, big boy. I know you're going to behave." Man and dog reentered the building like they had so many times before. The wedding party was standing outside the anteroom waiting. Stella placed the flower in his lapel and petted Leo. "I guess were as ready as we'll ever be ", she said. They entered the chapel proper en masse, Tom and Stella with smiles on their faces, Felix and Gennie just looking nervous. Standing at the head of the aisle on a raised platform stood the greeter who Stella just told him was Mr. Bell. As they started toward him a recording of a pipe organ playing the "Wedding March" started. A woman who Tom figured was Mrs. Bell was handling that assignment. When the reached Mr. Bell the organ stopped and dead silence reigned. "Dearly beloved -------------." I now pronounce you husbands and wives." The diamond wedding band had been removed from Leo's ribbon earlier and placed on Stella's ring finger and Felix came up with a wedding band for Gennie. It was a bit large but it satisfied her. The little rascal went ringless, he didn't want any visible proof that he was still not available.

Tom paid Mr. Bell and thanked him for the short noticed use of his chapel. Mr. Bell handed him both signed and witnessed certificates of marriage that bore the official Louisiana State seal and they left the air conditioned coolness of the building to what felt like walking fully clothed into a sauna. After a short time the wagon's air conditioner brought the temperature down to a bearable level and Tom headed for the nearest route out of town. Leo decided this was a good time to take a nap so he stretched out in the rear of the wagon and was soon racing after an Irish Wolfhound in his dreams.

Tom found what he was looking for just short of Biloxi, Mississippi, a decent looking motel with a restaurant and cocktail lounge. A flashing neon sign said vacancy. He pulled in parking next to the office. "Come on, Felix, here's where you can spend some of the cash I gave you. We're going to have a small celebration before we sack out for the night and consummate our vows. Leo, wake up and guard our wives until we return." The mention of guard brought Leo awake from his dreams and his huge head arose to tend to business. Tom and Felix weren't gone for more than ten minutes before coming back to the wagon, "You ladies are going to like this place even though we'll only be here overnight. Tom had chosen a room on the ground floor at the end of the row where he could let the dog out to take care of his business without anyone being wise to the fact there was a dog in his room. For a one night stay, they would be gone tomorrow if any complaints were lodged. When all were settled in their rooms Tom and Stella took turns using the bathroom to freshen up. Neither could leave the other alone physically for very long, therefore a lot of kissing and touching ensued, but finally they were ready to meet Felix and Gennie in the cocktail lounge. It was surprisingly crowded but they were given a good table along the interior wall, at Felix's insistence, his being forever watchful for trouble. As they proceeded to their seats most heads in their path were turned to admire the beautiful woman Tom was escorting. If Stella noticed, she certainly didn't bask in the adulation, her eyes were only for Tom.

Of course Felix wanted his cold Budweiser when the waitress arrived to take their orders but Tom asked for a bottle of champagne; after all, this was a celebration. The waitress asked what the special occasion was. "We're all on our honeymoons."

"What do you mean all?"

"Just that , all four of us pledged our vows earlier today and are on our honeymoons. We chose this establishment to celebrate, then rest up before continuing our trip to Miami."

"That's wonderful. If you'll excuse me a moment, I'll complete your beverage order now."

"Ya' better watch this guy, Mrs. Mueller. He's tryin' ta' compete with me on butterin' up ta' the opposite sex."

"Your so-called buttering-up days are over buster," Gennie said. "I ever even suspect you are trying to make time with another woman you'll never see the next sunrise, I kid you not." Felix took a sideway glance at his new bride. "It was only a joke, Mrs. Santana; ya' don't have ta' get uptight over it."

Tom had never heard Gennie get her back up like that before or suspected she had the attitude of a green monster in her. But his surprise over her diatribe was interrupted by the return of their waitress with their drink order accompanied by a small man just a bit taller than his partner who the waitress introduced as the lounge manager.

"Debbie here tells me the reason for your celebration, and as the house manager I would like to provide a gift of this bottle of Heldsleck Blue Top champagne which is of a excellent vintage." A white jacketed boy arrived carrying an ice bucket on a stand which contained the bottle wrapped in a towel. Debbie produced four champagne glasses. The manager made quite a production of opening the bottle which emitted a resounding POP, and caught the ensuing foam with the towel wrap. He poured each glass half full deftly and stepped back to allow Tom to propose a toast. Tom stood extending his glass over the table and with formalese started, "May God bless us and ours hereon. May we fulfill our destinies to His satisfaction and be models of integrity for our children." He raised his glass in true Teutonic fashion and took a sip before reseating himself. Stella took hold of his hand again. That toast was lovely, honey. I didn't realize you had clergyman leanings."

"I don't really, those words just came to me when I stood. They just seemed right for the occasion. Now drink up, Stell, this is supposed to be a party and tell me if and when you are hungry. Remember you have two to feed."

Felix who had sat uncharacteristically subdued since being dressed down by Gennie could not maintain his silence for any extended period. "That was quite a toast, amigo. Ya' do have a way with yer' words not that I unnerstood' all of them." He turned to his wife. "Mrs. Santana, ya' had every right ta' take offense ta' my words about my dealins' with women an' I stand corrected. I guess I'm not fully used ta' the idea of marriage yet." This half-apology was made sotto voce where only those at the table could hear it, but Gennie's face lit up with a radiant smile. I kind of understand your Lothario leanings, sir; you belonging to that hot-blooded race. It will simply take you a little time to get used to being a one-woman man", and she gave him a hardy buss on the cheek. Tom again thought his partner had met his match. It would just take a little time for him to be house broken and Gennie was just the woman to accomplish that. In retrospect Tom could remember all of the women in Felix's life sincle he had known him, and although his partner would never admit it , he had always been taken advantage of.

"Since all is once again in the state of happy bliss, is anyone hungry?"

When the waitress had passed the four menus around she stood to Tom's left, pencil and ordering pad poised. Tom didn't really need a menu. He knew what he wanted; they were for the benefit of the others. Stella seemed to be having trouble focusing on the entrees so he leaned closer and said he'd help. "Steak or fish, Stell?"

"Oh a small filet mignon I guess, a Waldorf salad, and no potato" she slurred. Tom passed that on to Debbie. When the others had finished ordering, Debbie, the waitress, looked back at Tom, ready to take his choice.

"This might sound strange but there is a method to my madness. One porterhouse steak medium-rare with steak fries, no salad, and one of the same cut very rare, alone."

Debbie's eyebrows rose a little but she continued writing. "Two more Buds also and that will do it."

Tom looked over to see Felix watching him with that silly expression he had whenever he was about to wisecrack.

"Devious ya' are, amigo. Looks like Leo is gonna' enjoy 'nother treat."

"He's more than earned it don't you think? Once we get to the Keys he'll have the chance to run the extra weight he's gaining now off at the same time he's exploring his new territory."

"Yeah, an' hopefully he'll be out from under foot so we can relax , ya' think?"

The food and beverage arrived and once served Debbie stood out of the way. They all dug in earnestly with the exception of Stella who picked daintily at her salad and all but ignored her filet. She had a hand on Tom's leg under the tablecloth and was rubbing him absent-mindedly getting ever closer to forbidden territory in public. This was enough to distract Tom from his dinner though and he grabbed her roving hand covering it with his and keeping it stationary at a discreet distance. "Later, Stell. I hope you can save those amorous feelings until we get back to the room plus you'd better take it a little slower on that champagne so you don't pass out on me."

The meal finished, the beer gone, Tom raised his hand to beckon Debbie. She saw the signal and within moments stood at his side. That steak was delicious Debbie, my compliments to the Chef, but I guess my eyes were bigger than my stomach. Could you furnish a doggie bag so I can take the second steak with me?: I'll be able to have that later on in our trip. Oh, and bring the bill." She returned less than five minutes later with everything he had asked for.

"Let me pack this for you, Mr. Mueller."

"I wouldn't think of it, Debbie; it's my mess so I'll handle it." Tom reached into his pocket taking out a wad of bills. Looking at the bill he quickly figured he gratuity. Rather than paying the customary fifteen percent he upped it an additional five and handed her the total. She almost curtsied her thanks. He looked at Felix who was about to add another quip and held up his hand to stall it until Debbie was out of earshot.

"I knew what you were thinking, partner."

"Aw ya' take all the fun outta' life, amigo, with yer' serious ways. He continued jamming what little food was left on their plates into his cheeks until he resembled a chipmunk. The galloping gourmet was at it again. I'll see you two in the morning, say about six-thirty so we can hit the road. I've got to get a little sleep." Now came a difficult chore for Tom. He had to steer Stella, who had overindulged on champagne, the distance to their room while juggling the doggie bag until they finally reached the room. Stella, realizing Toms dilemma removed her high heels. Tom had to admire her level-headedness; she always accepted whatever situation arose with a cool calculation that got her through it. Life seemed to be a constant challenge that she must meet head-on and solve. They made it to the room without incident.

"I'm going to take a shower, honey, so by the time you take Leo out for his constitutional I'll be fairly sober and squeaky clean."

"Sounds good to me, Mrs. Mueller; just don't drink too much water or you'll be right back where you started, trust me on that."

When Stella was in the bathroom with the door closed, Tom took the other porterhouse out of the bag and told Leo ," You can have this after your walk, big guy, so you have something to look forward to. C'mon we're going outside."

Outside was another word Leo understood and he was right on Tom's heels at the door, which Tom carefully locked behind them. Tom walked Leo far enough away from the room so when he emptied his bowels there would be little chance of anyone stepping in it. As was the usual case the dog never let him far from his sight, not only because Tom was the human that fed him most of the time but because he was raised to guard and protect his main friend with that inner instinct to sacrifice his own welfare for the sake of toms well being.

When he returned, Stella was still as amorous as at dinner. "What do you say we make this a quickie so we can get some sleep."

"Don't quickie me, honey. You don't know the meaning of the term."

She was right of course. Tom went to sleep with her clamped to his back and the last thing he heard was the sound of Leo gnashing the steak.

23

About five-thirty in the morning, Tom was awakened by Leo who laid his massive head on the bed by Tom's face, practically breathing in his face. "What is it, Leo? Do you hear something or do you want to go out?" Even half awake, Tom knew to be careful of how he spoke to the dog, not using any of the key words Leo understood. Tom unglued himself from Stella's embrace, then swung his legs out of the bed to sit up. His hearing was no match for Leo's by any stretch, but he sat with his hand on Leos flank listening anyway. The reason for the placement of his hand was that if Leo was shivering it meant that he was either excited or in his protective mode. He was shivering. Tom walked over to the door, parted the drapes covering the window next to it and looked out toward where his wagon sat. There was a car about five feet away in the adjacent parking slot which hadn't been there when he took Leo out earlier.

"Stay, Leo" he commanded, as he walked to the telephone to first call the office to find out if they had some regular patrol that checked the perimeter at night. The phone rang several times before a sleepy voice answered. "No, Mr. Mueller, we have only the Sheriffs Department checking periodically but on no regular basis. Why?"

"Something woke me up but I'm not sure what, but thank you anyway" and hung up. His second call was to Felix on the second deck. An equally sleepy voice answered, it was Gennie.

"It's Tom. Wake him up, will you?"

"Yeah, amigo, what is it?

"There may be some funny business going on in the vicinity of our wagon. You have a better view from up there so take a look. I'll keep the line open. Leo alerted me, and you know he doesn't fool around."

Two minutes later he was back "It looks like some broken glass near yer' wagon, whadda ' ya' want ta' do?"

"Get some clothes on and grab your weapon, I'm going out there to check and you can back me up if necessary. I'm leaving Leo inside to guard Stella."

By the time Tom got his shorts and pants on, grabbed his Cobra and gave Leo his instructions, he was ready to find out if the glass Felix had spotted was from his wagon. He didn't bother putting on a shirt remembering how humid it was he'd taken Leo out for his walk. Tom approached his wagon with extreme caution not really knowing what he'd find but hoping for the best which would mean no damage to the wagon at all. He stood motionless letting his eyes quarter both vehicles in his usual methodical manner borne from his teachings and experience in the Marine Corps. The longer he stood there concentrating on the scene the more he came to realize it wasn't the simple smash-and-grab caper he had originally thought.

He crouched down, moving obliquely closer on an angle to get a different perspective.

"Felix, come down here", he shouted after seeing the true results of what Leo had heard. Slumped over the steering wheel of the car next to his wagon was a person who wasn't just sleeping off too much to drink. Tom crept closer. Whoever had caused this mayhem didn't care how much noise or bloody mess they made. What looked like an iron reinforcement rod protruded from the victims neck. Felix pulled up next to Tom. "Jesu Christo," he muttered. "Somebody sure didn't care for that guy much. Talk 'bout over-kill."

"Run up to the office and have the clerk call the sheriff's office to report a homicide. I'm going to make sure Stella keeps Leo in the room while all the clamor goes on out here."

"Ya' got it, amigo, be right back."

Stella was awake when Tom reentered the room. Leo was laying close to her bed. "What is happening, honey? I woke up and you were gone."

"Nothing for you to be upset about, Stell, just an unrelated incident in the parking lot, but I'd like you to put a nightgown or one of my shirts and keep Leo in here with you. There's going to be several police and emergency vehicles out there shortly so lock the door behind me." To back up his statement the wails of approaching sirens could be heard. Tom put on a lightweight jacket unzipped, put his Cobra in the belt holster, and got his picture identification to verify his need for the weapon. "You guard Mrs. Mueller, big guy." So far, three deputies with flashing red and blue overhead lights had bracketed the victims car, as if it was going anywhere. More sirens could be heard in the distance. Felix joined him. "If any more lawmen join this crowd, it's gonna' look like a three-ring circus an' ya' could set up a food concession an' make a fortune, heh, heh, heh." To add to the confusion, several unmarked cars and vans were pulling into the now congested parking area and it, and it sounded like more were on the way.

"Do you have your ID with you?"

"Yeah, I stopped by the room on my way back from the office. Gennie might sleep right through this mess. After ya' called she went right back ta' sleep like someone had given her knockout drops."

"Now, don't volunteer any information until we find out who the head honcho is and then only pertinent information. Refer anything you don't understand or aren't sure of to me. I believe we'll soon be visited by a plainclothes detective. The only thing that ticks me off is it looks like we'll lose another day of our vacation, and to tell you the truth, partner, I'm starting to get a little tired and we have three states to traverse yet."

They didn't have to wait long before the office clerk pointed them out to a large red-faced man who flashed a detectives shield and introduced himself as the homicide department head. He got right to the point in a Southern drawl you could cut with a knife. "Ah understand ya'll discovered tha' victim. Did ya'll touch anythin'?"

"No, that wasn't necessary we could see he was quite beyond any medical treatment."

"Now before we go any farther cahn' ah' see some picture identification?" Tom and Felix both produced their agency IDs that the detective eyed suspiciously. "And what, pray tell, are y'all doin' in our fair city?" So Tom went through the same story, for what seemed like the tenth time, of being on vacation, both he and his partner combining their marriages in New Orleans to their honeymoons in Florida where they had further business, and just by chance stopping here for a dinner celebration and a night's sleep before continuing their trip. To his credit, the detective didn't interrupt Tom until he was finished. Then he turned to Felix. "Don't y'all evah' speak?"

Tom broke in to answer the question for Felix. "He seldom says much; we rely on hand signals mostly for communication. He's Colombian you see."

"Well, ah' guess that rules out holdin' y'all as material witnesses, but ah' would like some way ta' get in touch with y'all if we need any further testahmony'." Tom removed his wallet and found a card with Mr. McHenry's name, address in D.C., and telephone numbers where he could be reached, and handed it to the detective. "That's our immediate boss who we check in with periodically even when on vacation."

"Thanky'all, and that 'll be it, and have a pleasant trip," he said with all the cordiality of true Southerner.

Before they parted, on their way back to their respective rooms, and were out of earshot of the lawmen, Felix said, "Ya' sure have a way with words, amigo; ya' had that guy eatin' out a' yer' hand before ya' were done. Now no more 'mergency calls 'til we leave. I gotta' get some shut-eye fore we leave this 'fair city" heh, heh, heh."

Tom knocked on his room door, "It's me ,Stell." She opened the door on its chain, saw Tom and re-closed it to remove the chain. She was wearing one of his shirts which did little to hide her natural beauty.

"You were gone so long and there was so much activity out there I was becoming worried, honey. Here we are in a strange territory and without you to guide me I'd be stranded here alone."

"You have plenty of money, Stell, so you could get just about anywhere you wanted to go by plane or train, and you know how to get in touch with Mr. McHenry and I know he would help you in any way possible."

"Yes, but I'm not in love with anyone else but you so it's not the same, and what would I do with Leo?"

"It's a moot point anyway, sweetheart, I'll always be with you. Now, let's get to bed; my gas tank is running on fumes."

Even though his body was tired he couldn't turn off his thoughts and recollections of past events. Somehow he always got involved in other peoples problems by being in the wrong place at the wrong time. Was it in his genes? Was it something he had inherited from his father? God knows he had picked up other useful traits from him such as his expertise with weaponry before he had enlisted in the Marine Corps where it came to such good use..

"Honey, are you still awake? Are you thinking about something that might concern our future?" Tom rolled over so that he was facing his wife who was attired in her usual bedtime clothing, nothing. Trying not to look below her perfectly shaped lips he stared directly into her eyes. "Most of my thoughts these days are about you sweetheart, you and our child."

"Oh, Tom, I love you so much. Every day I thank my maker that he allowed you to come into my life, to give me a purpose to look forward to what each new day will bring. I know you're tired, honey, but I'd like to show my gratitude in more ways than just words. You just lie there, and let me minister to you." And she did.

24

They slept like two fallen logs, both from exhaustion and exertion side by side covered only by a sheet in the pleasant air-conditioned room. Leo, not completely asleep, lay near the door where any intruder would have to get past him to bother his main friends. All three remained like this until just before five that evening. Stella awoke first and headed directly for the shower. Tom was still dead to the world when the bedside phone began ringing. Stella couldn't hear its persistent ring because of the running water so Leo took it upon himself to notify his main friend of the irksome noise by using his massive bulk as a battering ram along the side of the bed until the constant vibration brought Tom out of his fog enough to see the light of day. When Tom saw what Leo was doing and only then did he hear the phone and understood why the dog had resorted to his action. "I'm going to teach you to talk yet, big guy." Tom picked up the receiver but didn't speak.

"Thought maybe ya' were in the shower foolin' 'round."

"You're just lucky I picked up instead of the Mrs."

"Aw, I knew it was you, amigo 'cause she wouldda' been civil, 'nuff ta' say hello."

"Now that you have my attention, what is it?"

"Doncha' think we outta get started for the Keys amigo or do ya' intend ta' spend the rest a' our vacation here? I'd a' thought we've had 'nuff 'citement in this berg." Only then did Tom look at his watch which had been pushed behind the lamp. 5:15 P.M. Where had the time gone? He swung his legs out of bed and sat up. Leo moved aside during that maneuver.

"You're absolutely right partner, it's later than I thought. Are you dressed and ready to go?"

"We have been over an hour."

"Well give me about a half hour then come down and knock."

Tom went to the bathroom and opened the door letting out a cloud of steam in the process. "Felix called while you were in here I guess. Leo answered the phone, I'm being facetious Stell. He woke me up. I didn't realize it was so late but he and Gennie will be down here in a half hour. Will you be ready?"

"I will be honey if you'll keep your hands to yourself."

"I'll try but it won't be easy. Just looking at you causes stirrings of my libido."

"You're insatiable, honey. Think about something, anything, else before you make me lose control again. That would mean losing another day."

"A short, cold shower should do the trick if I can stand it. If not, I'll call Felix back and delay our departure for a couple more hours."

"Make that a long, cold shower to slay the beast in you." She closed the door on him.

Tom was still chuckling as he shaved and almost cut himself in his haste. He got into the shower, soaped himself thoroughly, and washed all the sex off of him before turning all hot water off to kill the beast in him as his wife would say. He took it as long as he could, then got out shivering. A brisk rubdown returned some heat to his body and he was glowing pink as a new born babe. The word "babe" triggered the thought of his wife bringing a blessed creation of his into this world. Boy or girl he wondered, not that it made any difference, he would love and cherish whichever.

Tom was dressed and out the door to turn the wagon around so the rear end was facing the room, so Leo could get in un-noticed. There was no sense in advertising the fact of his presence. Felix and Gennie were heading toward the wagon with their meager belongings, a small duffel bag and carryall thrown over his shoulder. Gennie again was very subdued unlike the wildcat side she had shown last night at dinner. "You two ready to go?"

"Yeah an' the sooner the better 'fore somethin' else happens. This place has been bad news, amigo."

"Pile in then, I've had the same feelings. Stella should be done packing by now so I'll get her and Leo and we're out of here."

They were nearing Tallahassee, Florida, with only one pit stop for Leo to unload as the sun was rising in the east. Traffic was getting heavier by the minute, causing Tom to reduce his speed somewhat.

Tom tried to skirt the capital but it was no use, he was caught in a gridlock with nothing to do but grin and bear it.

"I sure wish you knew how to drive, Stell, but this is not the place to learn."

"I'll learn soon enough, I've been watching you since we left New Orleans. It's just a matter of judgment isn't it? Oh and of course knowing the basic rules of the road."

"I wish more people would think in those terms, there would be fewer traffic fatalities if they would follow the basics. Speeding, assured clear distance, falling asleep at the wheel, and of course driving under the influence of alcohol or drugs are other factors which contribute among many others I could name, but I'm beginning to sound like a lecturer."

"No you aren't, honey; that's another reason in a long list of rationales I'm adding up for the reasons why I love you so much, and I must say that list i getting longer everyday."

They were nearing Ocala when Tom pulled to the roadside to let Leo out and to switch places with Felix. They had found a small Ma and Pa diner and loaded up with cold cokes and a variety of sandwiches that were split up between them. Five rare hamburgers were purchased for the dog. At least a half dozen were wolfed down by his partner while the girls had one each. Again Tom wondered how such a small man like Felix could put away so much food in one sitting.

"Wake me up when you're nearing Fort Lauderdale partner and I'll take over again to get us to the Keys. If the banks are still open I'll rent a safety deposit box for the stone. If not it'll have to wait until the next day. I have to call the attorney either way. Take it easy with the wagon, Felix."

"I'll treat it like my own, amigo, doncha' worry 'bout that." Now Gennie got in the front seat with her man while Stella chose her former place so Tom was in the middle where most of the luggage was. As soon as he was settled Leo moved to his left side,. luggage or not. So Tom had his right hand on Stell's leg and his left hand on Leos flank. It didn't take him long to nod off.

Gennie wasn't exactly a nagger but she kept up a constant chatter, not expecting any answers, to keep Felix awake. She had discovered whenever he had a full stomach he had a tendency to get sleepy. Felix let his woman drone on not paying much attention to its content. He kept his eyes always looking ahead for any hazards that might loom up unexpectedly. The miles passed by along with little towns he'd never heard of. Winter Garden, Kissimmee, for God's sake why would anyone name a town that he wondered? Not Not understanding the local lore of the region. A five-foot-long alligator waddling along the berm broke him out of his reverie. "Did ya see that babe?"

"Yes. Ugly looking brutes, aren't they. I wonder what brought it so near a highway? A passing semi could run over it and make a lot of purses, wallets, and belts to sell." She laughed at her own humor. Felix laughed with her. Now this is the way she liked her man. Never taking anything too seriously unless she was in danger or a part of his job warranted it. She slid over and gave him a kiss on his cheek. "What was that for?"

"For being you, babe." Then she aped his laugh, "Heh, heh, heh." Felix took one hand off the wheel long enoughto caress her cheek. I'm gonna' really enjoy being married to ya' babe. It was long overdue ya' know? I was kinda' tired playin' the field plus it got me in all kindsa' trouble. I wasn't always this ugly ya' know. Course I was no Cary Grant but heh, heh, heh." Gennie stayed where she was and husband and wife discussed their life together as married couples should. The miles continued to pass. They passed a couple of beautiful inland lakes with surrounding orange groves laden with the succulent fruit. Because of the climate Florida furnished a good part of the nation with much of its citrus . "Look at the size of this lake coming up Felix, you can't see across it."

They were approaching Fort Lauderdale where his amigo wanted to be awakened to take over the driving again, so Felix began looking for a suitable spot for the change over. The dog would probably have to make a deposit too. What looked promising on his side ahead had a few palm trees that looked stunted for a little shade so he began slowing to make his left turn. The traffic wasn't too heavy here so over he went.

There didn't seem to be any point in rearranging the wagon because they wouldn't be stopping again until they got to Miami. Ten minutes later they were on the road.

25

Tom realized it was too late to rent a safety deposit box, so he had the added worry of keeping the stone with him for another night. Just another problem to be solved. That kind of burden was really a pleasure. The emerald was his ace in the hole, and someday it would pay for his child's college education, or children's if Stella decided to have another. That would have to be her decision depending on how hard this pregnancy was. Some women dropped babies with comparative ease. All their men did was plant the seed. "You're very quiet, honey; what are you thinking about?"

"I'm always thinking about you, sweetheart, you should know that."

"Yes, but about what?"

"Just that I hope your pregnancy and delivery of our child isn't too hard on you, so you might consider having more."

"Oh, don't worry about that honey; my mother told me after my brother was born she had no problems with Sheila and me. In fact, she was thinking about more. "Let's hope that is the case with you. Wouldn't that be something if you had twins, too?"

Stella laughed. "Now, you're wishing for the moon. Be careful of what you wish for was another one of my mothers sayings. Your wishes could backfire. It seemed she had a drawer full of those kind of axioms."

"She sounds like an astute lady. I'd have liked to have met her. We'd have got along famously." That exchange caused Stella to cease conversation and drop into deep thought. Tom took a sideways glance at his wife. "I didn't mean to say anything wrong, sweetheart."

"That's all right honey; it just took me back a few years to when I still had a happy family. You couldn't say anything wrong, loving my sister the way you did. But fate intervened, luckily for me."

"I've got to find a public phone to call Lance Nolte in Columbus before it gets any later and his office is closed. Or else, we'll have to rent hotel or motel rooms for another night, something I'm sure none of us want to do after the experiences we've had in them lately. Keep your eyes peeled for a booth or and outside phone on a stand where we can park close so everyone can hear my end of the conversation."

It started raining, not a slow start either, a deluge with the sun still shining brightly to the west. Where did that come from, Tom wondered? as he slowed to be able to see. The windshield wipers were hard pressed to clear the glass and as they progressed, Tom saw several cars pulling to a stop along the berm to out wait the worst of it. They had the right idea and he was about to follow suit when it stopped as if God had turned off the tap. He glanced at Stella. "Wasn't that strange?"

"It sure was, honey. I wonder if a rainbow will appear now? I haven't seen one of those in quite awhile."

"Here's a phone booth coming up on the right. That's our pot of gold, rainbow or not." Tom went through his wallet to find Lance Nolte's office phone number. He ought to have known it by heart now but with all the other numbers lodged in his memory that one always got lost in the shuffle. When he found the card, he took it and a handful of change with him to the booth walking carefully to avoid water standing in puddles that might be deeper than they appeared. He got the local long-distance operator on the first try, a good omen to start.

"Your card-playing luck is holding, Tom, you got me just as I was about to shut up shop for the evening. Where are you?"

"Just on the outskirts of Miami. Lance we're all bone-tired and hoped to avoid checking into motel or hotel rooms again. Is there anyway you can reach the holders of the Key Largo house keys yet tonight. I'd appreciate it more than you'd know."

Lance erupted with one of his high-pitched laughs. "Miracles I can perform, ole buddy; the mundane takes a little longer. By the way you don't have to pay for these calls, I'll just add them on to your bill. Give me the number where you are calling from and wait there a few minutes for me to set it up and I'll get back to you."

"Sounds great" and he relayed the number. "I'll be waiting." Tom hung up and the phone sounded like a slot machine paying off with the return of his coins. "Did you hear most of that, Stell?"

"Yes, and your former classmate sounds like he's as efficient as you are honey. Ohio State University must have a patent on that."

"I'm going to let Leo out. You listen for the phone in case I don't hear it. Just yell." Leo stepped down from the open tail gate and within four feet let out a stream that would match the earlier down pour in velocity without a tree to aim at. He turned, looked at his main friend a moment then jumped back into the wagon pretty as you please. Tom shut the tail gate shaking his head. "When you have to go you don't mess around do you?" The phone rang just as Tom was heading toward it. He answered on the second ring.

"One miracle executed; don't ask for another one yet tonight. My powers are spent for the evening." Again the high-pitched laugh-giggle. You have pencil and paper available so I can tell you where to go?"

Tom said, "Give it to me slowly so I can relay it to my wife. Wait a second. Stella, write this down somewhere as I give it to you."

"Wait, honey, until I can find some paper." Tom could see her rummaging in her purse. "OK. Shoot."

"Go ahead, Lance." He started by saying, "First let me congratulate you, ole buddy, for tying the matrimonial knot. May you have many years of bliss and let me be godfather to your first born son, if you will." "Thanks, Lance, I'll keep that offer very much in mind. Now go ahead with the info. Tom relayed the instructions very slowly to Stell and when finished had her read the full text back to him. It was complete.

After thanking Lance profusely, he hung up and returned to the wagon. "What do you think, can you find the place following those directions?"

"I'd better or else we're in trouble."

It was a two story building tucked away behind a row of retail stores that the average person would never see unless he had personal business there. Tom could see there was a light on behind the shade of the door glass so he went to the portal and tried it. It was locked. Since he didn't see a bell he knocked on the door glass. An few moments later, the shade was pulled and a man stood there. "Are you Tom Mueller?" Pressing his picture ID against the glass seemed to satisfy the man and he unlocked the door. "Can't be too careful these days, Mr. Mueller; senseless crimes are running rampant. It's not like a few years ago when people could leave the doors unlocked in their homes and offices and no one would think of trespassing. It must have to do with the sudden influx of all the Cubans. However you are not interested in our problematic situations; you are here for the keys to your Key Largo mansion. There are several papers you need to sign to take over the property. You will have copies of everything, don't worry. The utilities have been turned on,, so all that is necessary for your habitation is to purchase foodstuff. I would suggest you shop at a super market on the mainland for economical reasons you understand. There are several fine restaurants on the other Keys but I am certain you wouldn't want to make a steady diet of them."

Tom had listened to all the advice the attorney had shared but really didn't need anymore. The papers were all signed and copies were in a folder in front of him when Mr. Goldberg retrieved a ring of keys from a desk drawer.

"You will note all of the keys have a tag attached so you will have an easier time recognizing which one is which. It has been a pleasure doing business with you, Mr. Mueller. If you need any further information here is my card so don't hesitate to call. Goodnight sir and I'll unlock the door for you. Oh, one more thing. Do you know how to get there in the dark?"

"I've never been there, but I'm sure I will find it."

Mr. Goldberg returned to his desk and shuffled through some papers and handed Tom a map complete with mileage, yardage, and arrows pointing to the estate. "That should simplify it for you."

Tom knew the first thing he had to do from Goldberg's list of advice was to stop at a supermarket before they got to the Keys. There was a list of things growing by leaps and bounds in his mind.

"Stella , do you have anymore paper handy that I can dictate a growing list of necessary to you that we'll need from the grocery?"

"I'll find some, honey, hold on." She was going through her purse again. How can women pack so much miscellaneous junk in such small containers Tom wondered?

"I've got some, it's a little bit wrinkled but with pen it should be readable. Go ahead."

Tom started at the top. Dog food for the big guy, coffee, fresh fruit, vegetables, sugar, beer, soft drinks, butter, bacon, eggs, flashlight, batteries, and on he went until Stella stopped him for a moment. "Where are we going to put all that stuff honey? The wagon is practically full as it is. Do we have to get all this yet tonight?"

"I can put some of the foodstuffs off but most of the non-food items are vital and they won't take up that much space. We just don't know what Fred had on hand until we get there. The attorney told me the utilities were turned on so at least we won't have to grope around in the dark. All that paperwork in the portfolio he gave me has to be read by both of us in the next few days too. We have some hard decisions to make about the property and the Gresham while we're there, plus I have to call Mr. McHenry to give him our phone number there, so you see this is a working vacation for us, and I just can't lay back and relax while we're there. Mr. Goldberg, that's the attorney's name by the way, was very helpful to me but I'm not sure what his assistance is going to cost us yet or if it will be consolidated with Lance Nolte. Oh, here's something else Lance said that I forgot to mention to you. If our first born child is a boy, he wants to be the godfather. That would be very useful for our son in his future."

Tom saw a Piggly Wiggly supermarket ahead that was huge. He pulled into the parking lot that was about a third full attesting to the market's popularity for around-the-clock shopping.

"The choice is yours, Stell. You can come in with me or stay in the wagon. She decided to accompany her husband to make sure he didn't buy any items frivolously. The air conditioning inside the store was like a blast of artic air and Stella commented at once. "It's downright cold in here, honey. Let me hold on to you for body heat. Tom took a cart that was proffered by a fancifully attired store employee and stood a moment checking the overhead signs of the different departments. He spotted one that gave him an instant flash of an idea. It was set aside from the household items and was marked automotive. Tom saw at once what he was looking for. There were plastic tarpaulins of all sizes and thicknesses arrayed on a shelf and right next to them were elastic stretch cords with metal hooks on each end. He stopped a passing department employee and explained his problem. "What make and model is your vehicle sir?" Tom answered and the employee looked that up in a manual and found the specific material needed. Stella had been diverted by something she was interested in and missed the whole transaction, so when she joined up with Tom again she was unaware of what had transpired. "I saw this light jacket that will be perfect for any rainy weather. It has a hood too."

"Good, sweetheart, now get that itemized list of yours ready we're going shopping for real now."

"Honey, we just don't have the room in the wagon. I already told you that."

"I've got that problem remedied my dear. Now we can take the luggage out of the inside too." Stella looked at him totally at sea.

Tom went food and beverage shopping in earnest then. He had the cart filled to overflowing and was thinking of getting a second when Stella grabbed his arm. "Honey, look over there. I don't know if I'm imagining things or not but I swear I just saw Rocky Newbole pass by that aisle over to your left. He is rather hard to miss being as large as he is."

Tom looked to where she had indicated but didn't see anyone who resembled Rocky anywhere. He thought for a few moments. "I'm not leaving you alone with this cart to investigate further for him. I believe you, Stell, so there are two ways to confirm your suspicion. We'll check out now and have the counter employee contact the night manager. He or she can then page him to report to the office. If he is here incognito we can watch the exit doors after we're checked out and catch him outside."

Tom passed on his original plan to the check-out girl. She picked up her inter-store phone and asked whomever she was talking to if they would come to counter ten. Meanwhile she began checking out his purchases. An older man showed up within minutes so Tom showed him his picture agency ID to authenticate his request. The manager nodded his assent and left on his mission. The store's public address system called out his request so they waited for the results. The check-out girl had finished Tom's purchases and everything was in plastic bags re-packed in his cart. The total was $73 and change. Tom and Stella were ready to leave the store thinking their original plan had failed and they would have to watch the exits because Rocky was indeed undercover, when the check-out girl called his name. "Mr. Mueller?" Tom nodded. "Whoever you wanted to contact will meet you in the parking lot."

Tom nodded again and they wheeled the cart out.

There he stood bigger than life, leaning against a black closed van watching their approach with that nonchalance he always maintained. As they neared Tom could see his eyes, ever sweeping the immediate area for any signs of threat or recognition belying his outer coolness.

"If I may be so inquisitive, why are you in Miami, Rocky? There is no reason why you have to tell me, of course, but this is the last place I expected to see you."

"It's a long story, Mr. Mueller, and rather than getting into it here where I stand out like a black swan in a gaggle of geese maybe it would be better if we could meet somewhere a little more secluded. By the way may I congratulate you and Miss Stella for entering into marital bliss. That is a beautiful ring Mrs. Mueller. Your husband has great taste in many ways."

"You might be surprised to hear that Gennie and Felix are also married. In fact it was a double ceremony in New Orleans."

"That is surprising. I never expected him to tie the knot."

"Look, Rocky, let me re-arrange the load in my wagon, which won't take long, then you can follow us down to Key Largo in the Keys. That way you won't stand out so much and you can relax and we can talk. Leo would enjoy seeing you, too."

"It's a deal, Mr. Mueller just as long as I get back sometime tomorrow."

"Of course. You can get into your van now and after I'm finished with my loading I'll drive by and blink my headlights twice." Tom pushed the cart over to his wagon and with the help of Felix began re-arranging the contents of the car and cart. In fifteen minutes the job was completed. "Someone you know is going to follow us partner so don't be surprised when you find out who it is."

"Ya' jus' gonna' leave me hangin' like that, amigo?"

"Turn about iis fair play, Felix, if you know what I'm talking about."

"You see all the room we have in here now, Stell? Just using a bit of ingenuity can work wonders."

"Last stop before our destination, Leo. Do you want to go outside?" The dog was up and waiting for his main friend to open the rear hatch and again didn't need any nearby tree to unload. Leo hopped back into the rear hatch without command and settled down to see what would come next. He was asleep before they had left the parking lot. Tom flashed his lights twice as he passed the van and saw Rocky fall in behind him as they gained access to the main road South, Route 1. According to his map furnished by Mr. Goldberg it was exactly 43 miles from his office to Key Largo and Fred's estate. Tom figured the longest that would be in time was forty-five minutes even not knowing where they were going and in the dark. Fortunately, Mr. Goldberg's map was quite explicit.

"Stell, watch for mile marker 38 on the causeway. Mention it if you see it before I do."

It was pitch black to either side of the causeway, no lights of any kind showing. It must be overcast above because not even the stars or moon were visible. Their headlights stabbed into a nothingness so dense they could have been on another planet. It was eerie and gave Tom an empty feeling in the pit of his stomach. "Isn't this weird, sweetheart? Without your closeness to comfort me I might as well be in a casket."

"Don't be so morbid, honey. I think it's very peaceful after the hubbub of the last few days."

The wagon rose suddenly like it was going to take flight, then as it started downhill again there spread out before them was Key Largo.

"There's the mile marker you were looking for honey and a sign naming the Key. Do you feel better now?" Tom just grinned to himself. "Sure do, Stell. We are within minutes of opening a new chapter in our lives."

26

It turned out that 234 Shady Palms Rd. was a lark to find even in the dark. It was on the Atlantic Ocean side of the Key, and the closest neighboring dwelling was over three hundred yards distant through a virtual forest of palms. Tom could understand why Fred had chosen this particular property over others. It was isolated enough to be perfect for an enterprise such as he was undertaking: innocent appearing to distant neighbors but suitable for meetings with others of his ilk who could arrive under the cover of darkness, discuss business during the day, and leave the next night. Mr. Goldberg had explained about the deep channel that came into the property for ingress and egress. What Tom couldn't understand was how Fred had amassed such wealth from his college days at Harvard, to the rental of the computer shop in New York City, to buying this property at Key Largo. Not forgetting his stock market portfolio, which was so lucrative, there was a time gap there.

When they pulled in and parked, Rocky right behind him, Tom left his headlights on so they could see their way to the entrance without falling into the pool. Everybody including Stella was given something to carry, mostly the perishables that wouldn't take long to go bad in this heat and humidity. Tom unlocked the door and they filed in.

Soon Stella had coffee brewing. Gennie was going through cupboards and drawers making a list of what appliances and canned goods were on hand. "Your brother had just about anything you could imagine in appliances here. Look at the size of that double-door refrigerator, the most up to date commercial stainless steel model available. As far as we could see he spared no expense in furnishing in here."

"I'm going to fill Leo's water and food bowls, then I'll have a cup of that coffee while you and I go over some of the paper work from Mr. Goldberg's portfolio, that is if you're not too tired."

"I'm practically wide awake, honey. I can hardly wait to see the grounds and the outside of the house in daylight. So far I just love this wonderful place. It's like a dream come true."

"You artists are romanticists at heart, Stell. If you still feel that way tomorrow when I take the stone into a safety deposit box and after I call Mr. McHenry we'll see if we can't make this your permanent residence. Would you like that?" For an answer Stella turned to him and gave him one of her five-alarm kisses with the body work that went along with it. When they both breathlessly came up for air Tom said, "No more of that, sweetheart, or we'll never get any paper work done tonight - not that I don't love it."

When Leo was finished investigating every room in the place he finally sauntered into the kitchen heading directly for his water and food bowls that Tom had placed on a piece of the tarpaulin that had been used for covering their goods from the grocery. Tom thought there was no point of having to clean the spotless kitchen floor after every time he ate or drank. He could be very sloppy at times. The way the dog was lapping up the water you would think he hadn't had a drink all day. After he had filled up his tank he made straight for his main friend and plopped down with his head on Tom's feet. Tom looked down and shook his head. "It doesn't look like I'll be going anywhere for awhile. He's got my feet pinned to the floor. It'll be up to you for coffee refills, Stell."

"I'm here to serve, O master."

"Let's see here, since you have your heart set on living here year around that eliminates one problem but creates another. Where and for whom will I work? This is part of Mr. Rowens' territory, a man I've an experience working for before. He's from another agency and we have always had a personality clash. Felix belonged to his agency before being transferred to ours, so I don't relish the idea of working for him again. But if that is to be the case, I guess I will have to swallow my dislike and work for him. Maybe Felix will have some ideas on that. You do what you have to do. Boy, Mr. McHenry will have a fit when he hears this. I don't know how I'm going to break it to him."

"You'll think of something honey, you always do."

"Maybe, but I've got bad feelings about this." They were staring at each other both with their own thoughts when the silence was interrupted by the ringing of the telephone. "Oh, oh, will you get that Stell? I don't even know where the instrument is. And be careful of how you answer and what you say. If by chance it's Mr. McHenry stall him by saying I'm out walking the dog."

"Don't fret over this, honey; I'll handle it." She gave him a kiss on the cheek in passing. Tom reached down and scratched Leo on the neck. "You're going to have to move, Leo; I have to get up." The dog gave out a noise sounding like a groan but slid his huge head off Tom's feet. The rest of his bulk didn't move a fraction. Tom got up but had to hold on to the table a few moments waiting for the numbness in his feet to pass so he could walk without falling on his face. He could hear Stella talking from the vicinity of the main living area toward the front of the house but couldn't as yet make out her end of the conversation. Stella saw Tom enter the room and put her forefinger up to her lips, an indication to remain quiet.

"Yes, I understand and will relay the information when he returns." She removed the receiver from her ear, staring at it a few seconds before returning it to the cradle.

"Let me guess. Mr. McHenry right? He is always succinct and hangs up without saying goodbye."

"You've got it, honey; you know your boss better than I do."

"What is the message and how did he get our phone number?"

"He was very polite even calling me Mrs. Mueller from the start. He had me write down a phone number where you should call Rocky Newbole, a former team member of yours in New York City, who is now on the job in Miami undercover. When I asked how he got our number he said they had ways, and left it at that. I knew better than to pursue it."

"Am I supposed to call him back?"

"No just call Rocky, who will explain everything."

"Right, where the devil is he? Felix I can understand. He's most likely sacked out somewhere with Gennie but that big galoot never seems to get tired. Have you seen him?"

"Not since he helped carry things in from the wagon."

"He's too big to hide anywhere. Let me get the flashlight and look to see if his van is where he parked. Leo, wake up and guard Stella."

When the mastiff heard the word "guard" he was instantly on his feet moving in to the main room.

Rocky's van was still parked in the same position where he'd left it, so Tom moved toward it in a roundabout manner approaching from an angle, his head turning from one side to another, to get the best overview of the vehicle. When he was at the rear, he took a more direct path to the driver's side window where he could look directly inside. There he was, kind of folded up, sprawled across the front seat. From what Tom could see he was breathing normally, at least his chest was rising and falling in a regular pattern indicating normal sleep. Rather than shaking him awake, Tom chose to take the flashlight and blink it on and off in his face. It had the desired effect except that Tom found himself staring into the muzzle of a wicked looking hand gun. "What are you doing out here, Rocky? You would me much more comfortable in the house and cooler too." "Sorry about the weapon, Mr. Mueller; I didn't know it was you. The reason I'm out here is I didn't want to intrude in your family affairs and I'm rather used to fending for myself." All that was said in his usual unruffled manner that Tom was getting used to from the man.

"Come on inside so we can discuss some issues about why you are down here in the relative comfort of air-conditioning. My wife talked to Mr. McHenry, who told her you would explain what you are working on in detail. Lock your van and follow my light. I'm still not too familiar with the layout here never having seen it in daylight." Rocky followed as obediently as Leo had until they got to the front door. Inside Tom called to Leo. "You can relax now, big guy, and go back to sleep unless you want to see Rocky. The dog stuck his head around a corner and saw the big man who he recognized instantly. He made a beeline for him then stopped short of hitting his legs. "My God, he's bigger now than the last time I saw him if that's possible. How much does he weigh now Mr. Mueller?"

"Close to three hundred now. He's really been spoiled on the trip down here, food wise, but he'll run it off quickly enough in checking out his new territory and returning to his regular dog food without all the special snacks."

Rocky leaned down and scratched behind Leo's ears with the usual reward which made even the stoical Rocky laugh out loud. "At least his personality hasn't changed."

"Let's go to the kitchen and have some refreshments while we talk. Stella is out there and she can give you a firsthand account of what Mr. McHenry said. He can be very devious, as you should know by now."

Stella gave him a recapitulation of her conversation with Mr. McHenry, which Rocky absorbed without interruption. He nodded a couple times as though agreeing with the facts as he knew them..

After a few moments of silence, he began. "There is no reason to withhold anything from you, Mr. Mueller, because I'll never forget your kindness and influence in getting me the position I now hold. When I returned to Langley I was at loose ends until Mr. McHenry called me into his office and asked, not told, if this undercover job in Miami would be of interest to me. He sketched out some of the details without any of the names or any exact locations of ingress or specific delivery schedules. When I agreed tentatively he gave me a thick portfolio to take with me to study and memorize over the next few days. He explained there would be a van fully equipped furnished that would be at my disposal for the trip down and subsequent transportation while here. As you know, sir, I'm quick study but it took me six days to digest all of that material which included faces of the kingpins of the organization. My mind was full of facts and figures."

Now Tom knew he was leveling with him and would include all in his methodical manner, so he waited for the rest of the story to unfold.

Stella excused herself so as not to deter Rocky from revealing agency information that shouldn't be heard by anyone not in it. Tom loved her for that wisdom because he knew why she left the table. "You have to be hungry or thirsty, Rocky. Can I get you something before you continue?"

"No thanks, Mr. Mueller."

"How about some tea, hot or iced?"

Rocky sighed audibly. "You have all that here when you just arrived so short a time ago?"

"You saw how much was in that shopping cart. There wasn't much we didn't buy in the way of staples. Now what will it be ?"

"I could handle some iced tea if it isn't too much trouble, sir."

"Comin' right up. You can continue your story. I can hear from here while I work."

"Right. As I was saying these aliens have tried every method that the agency knows of to bring in the marijuana and cocaine and deliver same to their contacts in the South Miami and Keys area. Their latest ploy is to use cigarette boats which can outrun the patrolling Coast Guard. They were using small single and twin-engine planes, but the Naval Air Station in Key West quickly put that idea out of business by either forcing them back to where they came from or shooting them down. Those fighter jets are nothing to fool with. Now one of the main contacts in the South Miami area is a frequent shopper at the Piggly Wiggly you saw me at. It seems like he has a large family which demands constant shopping trips to nourish. I've only been there two days but still haven't spotted him or his Mercedes convertible. All this information on him and his car has come from multi-agency cooperation through their surveillance and contacts, then compiled by ours where Mr. McHenry has passed it on to me. What do you think?" Tom sat the ice tea with an extra bowl of ice in front of the big man, and turned to the fridge and took out a cold Bud for himself, he'd had enough coffee. "What did you mean by what do I think? It's your operation, Rocky, I'm on vacation."

"Mr. McHenry may have other ideas about that, sir. He said that since you were coming down here, I should enlist you to take over the operation after you had time to study the data I already have."

Tom stared at him, temporarily speechless. Then, after he got over the initial shock of the idea, his mind calmed and his usual cold, calculated, reasoning kicked in. Here was the perfect solution to what he had been discussing with Stella earlier. Now he would know who he was working for, it would mean some rearrangements made in the properties in Franklin Park and Felix would have to decide where he wanted to live and work. He would prefer having the little man here with him because they were a team. Tom could always count on him for needed backup when Leo was unavailable. All this was running through his mind while he continued to stare at Rocky.

"Let me have the info you have with you to read over while I work out some sort of plan of action. We're going to need some two-way radios with a range of fifteen to twenty-five miles to begin with – smaller than the service walkie-talkies. Do you think you can arrange that?"

"I'm sure we can and welcome aboard, Mr. Mueller."

"Oh sure, there's nothing I appreciate more than a well organized setup.

Tom left Rocky sitting at the table and went to find Stella. She was in the main living area with Leo at her feet. "Everything has changed, Stell. Now instead of worrying who I'll be working for I got suckered into taking over Rocky's operation. I have yet to talk to Felix but I want him here with me. That shoots down his returning to his house. You wouldn't believe how I got sandbagged into this however now we don't have to worry about moving."

"I knew it would work out, honey; everything does in the end."

"Now we have to make some changes. First, we need to change your driving lessons to here instead of Virginia. Second, I have to buy you a car and no jalopy either. Third, if there was ever a time for additional help it's now. I wonder if Paddy O'Toole is available? Now is the time for his help. It's a certainty there won't be anyone else we can call on. Now I'm pooped sweetheart, let's hit the hay.

Tom had a restless sleep with images of all he had to do in the coming week flashing in his mind so it was no surprise that when dawn came and normal household activities resumed he was awakened by a combination of sunshine and Stella hovering over him in her usual bedtime attire he felt like he hadn't slept at all. "Wake up, sleepyhead, so we can go out and see what our property looks like in daylight. I'll put some coffee on in a minute but first ..." Forty-five minutes later both soaked in sweat from their exertions they finally parted. Stella bounded out of bed heading for the shower while Tom was a bit slower, looking for a pen and paper to make a list of today's phone calls and a chronological roster of immediate things to be done. The more he thought about it he decided to call Mr. McHenry about the chance of getting Paddy O'Toole detached from NYPD and put on loan to the agency. If anyone could set that up it would be McHenry.

27

"All right, Leo, lets go out and check your new territory now that its daylight. "'Out" was the key word, and the dog was standing at the front door waiting for his main friend to open it. Leo took everything in order. First he watered down several bushes, then laid the foundation for a mortared wall, all the time keeping his eye on where Tom was. They started out near the stand of palms at the rear of the house and worked their way counter clockwise to the channel. All this time Tom was talking to the dog as if he were human.

"You see, Leo, there is a lot for you to guard, not only the house but all the rest of the property surrounding it. Soon Stella came out in a house dress. She wanted to see what the house looked like in daylight, too.

"This is beautiful, Tom. Could we ask for anything more? I want to stay here forever."

"You can, sweetheart; it'll all be worked out. I have some things to solve first, but when they are you'll be secure here. Man, there are a lot of things that have to be done later today so we better head in so I can have some coffee."

"C'mon, Leo, we have to go in."

For once, the dog obeyed without an argument. He was getting acclimated to his new territory and didn't feel he should give his main friend any static. Felix smelled the coffee and was in the kitchen when they entered. "Where ya' been, amigo? Ya' never let me know nuthin'."

"Well, if you would stay awake once in awhile I'd explain things to you. As it is, you have some serious decisions to make. You can consult Gennie or not, that's up to you, but since Mr. McHenry has dumped this load on me, no thanks to Rocky, they include you."

"OK. Lay it out for me."

"There's a drug ring running out of South Miami that has connections to both Colombia and Key West. Do you want to stay here, which I would prefer, or return to Virginia? We can get your Plymouth down here but it would mean giving up your house. There's plenty of room here, Felix, and with your own transportation you would have enough freedom to go your own way when not working. With your love of baseball you could go into Miami and see the Penguins play, I think that's the name of the team. "What do you think?"

"Sounds ta' me like ya' already have it figured out for me like always. I'm for it but Gennie had her heart set on that house."

"I told you they were tough decisions, partner. I don't have to know right this minute; tomorrow will do."The phone rang in the main living area and Tom went in to answer it, letting Felix alone to mull over how he was going to con Gennie into agreeing with him. The little man did have a way with women. Without any greeting, Mr. McHenry started his dialog. "Your Sergeant Paddy O'Toole is now Lieutenant O'Toole and is the new station commander in the Bronx. When I talked to him and explained your situation down there he jumped at the chance to assist you in anyway possible at his own expense. He is quite taken with you, Tom. He said he owes his promotion to you. He has some built up vacation and sick time coming to him and will be down there in three days at your disposal for at least fifty days.

Talking to your wife, she sounded like a very intelligent woman, she'll be an asset to your career in the agency." "Besides being intelligent, she is also beautiful and I trust will bear us beautiful children."

"Your team should now be complete so make the most of the full term you have them all assembled. Keep me informed." Click, he was gone. Tom went back to the kitchen to find the whole team present including the women. Leo was lying by the table. Tom looked first at Felix who just nodded which must have meant he was in. "What's the occasion for the gathering?"

"Just compiling a list of needs honey."

—

Five days passed, in which Tom accomplished just about everything he could Locally or at least within twenty-five miles north or south of Key Largo. The women had given him several lists of small items that would fit easily into the wagon. Tom was most often gone from nine, after breakfast, until dusk. The emerald was now secure in a safety deposit box in a branch of First National , one of the largest banks in the Eastern half of the country, along with all the gems he had brought South with him. Rocky had returned to the Piggly Wiggly to resume his watch for the South Miami contact with instructions to call Stella twice a day whether any progress was made or not. After the third day, he returned to Key Largo with a nifty pair of hand-held radios no bigger than man's hand with telescoping antenna and a range of fifty miles. They had their own frequency with a life of two days before being re-charged. Tom had turned the station wagon in, and leased a pickup truck, after the girls cleaned it out and washed it. The pickup didn't have air conditioning but the days were in the middle eighties with sporadic rain showers that would pass quickly, the humidity remained high however. He had also spotted a private-owned Pontiac with a "For Sale" sign in the window parked in the driveway of a nearby residence. He wrote down the phone number and intended to call the owner when he got back to his house that evening but was sidetracked by the arrival of another closed truck in his parking area. There was no mistaking the driver. It was Patrick O'Toole. In one of his purchases from their lists he had run across some battery-operated floodlights that he picked up cheap. They came on at dusk and went out with the rising of the sun. Those lamps showed Paddy lumbering toward the front door. Tom had it open before he could knock to greet the older man who was visibly sweating from the high humidity. "Come on in to the air conditioning Paddy and meet my wife."

"Is it always this humid down here? I sure have the wrong clothes with me for this kind of weather."

"We can also remedy that. There is another member of my team just your size and can outfit you with anything you need. I don't know about shoes though, I think his feet are longer and definitely wider than yours,16 EEEE, if I remember correctly."

"Not to worry, I suffer from what all beat men have, flat feet." All this was said before they entered the kitchen. There sat Stella.

"This is my wife, Paddy."

"You sure know how to pick 'em, Tom; she is a raving beauty."

"Thank you, kind sir; all compliments like that will put me forever in your favor. Now if you'll sit down here, Tom has some pictures he wants to show you, and I'm sure you'll be interested in what new methods the bad guys have dreamed up to bring in their product. It's absolutely amazing. After you're done, you should get a good night's sleep. Tom will show you to your own cool bedroom. So until tomorrow, I'll bid you good night."

Stella had got along with the big New Yorker as if they had lived on close streets in the city, understanding his heavy brogue like it was her second language, and it was spoken everyday at the dinner table. Tom thought he had married an amazing woman with so many different facets that he was discovering almost daily that he couldn't have done better in picking a lifetime mate, had the practice of polygamy had been still in effect. Tom was about to enter his bedroom when his hand-held radio went off with its buzzing sound. When he pulled out the aerial he could hear Rocky, but faintly. So Tom went out the front door where the reception was much better. "Go ahead, Rocky."

It was still faint but Tom covered his other ear and could just hear the big man. He was whispering. "I'm on him, Mr. Mueller, but this van is steaming up and I'm afraid to go much farther lest the engine seize up. He's heading home. I can tell by the affluent neighborhood. He's almost a block in front of me."

The hissing sound wasn't Rocky whispering as Tom first thought. It was the van's radiator. He must be leaning out the window to see ahead.

"He's turned into a drive and entered the garage so I'm continuing on past. I've memorized the location, so I'm going to try to coax this heap to the nearest repair shop wherever that may be. I'll let you know, so keep your radio handy."

Tom was back to their bedroom door ready to finally get some sleep when he stopped to listen for any sounds that were out of the ordinary. He was like Leo, his territory was becoming familiar to the point where any unfamiliar sound stood out. Everything seemed normal so he opened the door and slowly walked in. Ever thoughtful, Stella had left the bathroom door cracked to shed enough light to get undressed by. She was in bed covered by a sheet only. Tom quickly disrobed and slid in next to her after placing the radio on the bedside table along with his wristwatch. Even in her sleep Stella sensed Tom's prescience and automatically reached over to place her hand on him for her own reassurance. Tom enjoyed her caress of possession and left her hand stay right where it was as he drifted off to slumberland. What a woman he had. Tom never heard the radio buzz but Stella did. She shook Toms arm until he came to and opened his eyes. It took him a few moments to understand the why of it then he swung his legs out of bed and reached for the instrument. "Go ahead, Rocky." This time he didn't have to extend the antenna or go outside. Rocky came through loud and clear.

"I'm sorry to call you so early in the morning, Mr. Mueller, but I'll be without wheels for the better part of two weeks and that's only an estimate; it could be longer. There was more internal damage than I thought; also I either have to rent a vehicle or have someone from your place pick me up."

"If you will give me your location, I'll have Felix pick you up in my truck." After getting the particulars with the shortest route to get there, Tom signed off, threw some clothes on and went to find Felix. When putting Paddy into a room alone Tom knew where he was but that left two other bedrooms to choose from for Felix's location. This place was as bad as a hotel. Tom chose one of the two and knocked several times, then opened the door. Empty. He repeated the action on the other. A sleepy-eyed Gennie opened the door. "Can you wake your husband and have him meet me in the kitchen?" She nodded and shut the door. When Tom got to the kitchen, Stella was already there brewing some coffee, Leo by her side looking as alert as ever. A half awake Felix stumbled into the room and parked at the table next to Tom. Stella served them both steaming mugs then left the room Leo in trail.

"We have a little problem, partner", and he went on to explain Rocky's situation and how Felix could remedy it along with explicit directions of route and address of Rocky's exact location. "I'd suggest you go armed too because you just never know. Tomorrow I'm going to have your Plymouth shipped down here. We suddenly have a shortage of vehicles, which I intend to take care of. It seems it's one thing or another lately and I hope it will let up soon so we can get back to our main objective which as you know is stopping the influx of foreign drugs."

"I hope ya' have those directions written out for me, 'cause I don't have total recall the way ya' do. Give me 'bout five minutes ta' go back ta' the room for my stuff then I'll be ready ta' go."

Tom quickly wrote out the directions so Felix wouldn't get lost, refilled both their coffee mugs, and waited impatiently for his partner's return. Felix came back looking much better than when he left. It was like he'd taken a magic pill that caused the transformation..

"I guess you won't need any more coffee; it looks like you're ready to go." Tom handed him the directions and the keys to the truck. "Don't let Rocky talk you in to making other stops. Come back here as soon as you can."

"Don't worry, amigo; he might be bigger than me but what I'm carryin' makes us the same size. Keep the home fires burnin' sport, ta' quote a friend a' mine heh, heh, heh."And out he went. Tom heard the truck start and leave and then he heard something else, something he'd never heard before. It wasn't exactly a scream yet the noise seemed to rise and fall in harmony with a bellow of injured rage of a grizzly bear. Tom just didn't know what to make of it. If he never heard it again it would be too soon. He wondered what was causing it. Stella must have heard it also because she emerged from the bedroom with only a light wrap on. She looked at her husband with a questioning expression on her beautiful face. Tom just shook his head not knowing what to say that would explain it. She moved into his arms. "I'm frightened, honey; what can it possibly be?" Tom held her close in an attempt to quell her fears. If he had an explanation he would give it to her but there was no point in lying to her with some made up fabrication that she would see through anyway. "I think you better get more clothes on, sweetheart. Some kind of trousers and a blouse with maybe those canvas shoes of yours, then come into the kitchen. I'm going to wake Paddy then we'll meet you there. Don't waste any time either. Whatever is causing this, it will be better to be all together."

When Tom rapped on Paddy's door the man opened it fully dressed. "I've had the radio on all night, Tom, which is another trait of my patrol car days. It seems like second nature to have that as a background. That roaring noise you hear that sets your teeth on edge is from Hurricane Betsy. To paraphrase the news report, its eye is right over Key Largo as we speak. Winds of 155 miles are expected tomorrow. So this is just the beginning, my friend. I don' t know about you but this would be a good place not to be."

They found Stella in the kitchen with Leo at her side. "Paddy, why don't you explain to my wife what you heard on the radio while I fill a couple of thermos bottles with coffee and tea."

"Do you have a plan in mind, honey, you usually do."

While she was listening to Paddy she was absentmindedly petting the dog who seemed quite content for her attention. The two had become very close since their arrival at Key Largo what with Tom being gone during the day and only giving his attention solely to Leo for two or three hours before he went to bed. Then the mastiff roamed the house at will before returning to his nightly customary position either inside or just outside the open bedroom door. After all, he was a guard dog, which his breed was raised to do. "Paddy, do you want to risk a run up the causeway to the mainland yet tonight to outrun this thing before those 155 m.p.h, winds hit us tomorrow? I know it will be perilous but since there is no place to find shelter on this island I really don't see an alternative. I'm going to try to radio Rocky and Felix to stay put rather than returning here as was originally planned. we can meet up somewhere in Miami or maybe inland like at Homestead or Florida City."

"I know my truck will make it, it's just getting to it without getting soaked to the skin."

"I saw a couple of raincoats for the women and there's a large slicker for you, Paddy. Rain isn't going to bother Leo or me one bit. Sweetheart, go collect Gennie and get her down here. Explain what we are going to do and why on the way. We'll wait here for you.

To say the trip to the mainland was harrowing would be an understatement. Between the rain and wind there was little to do but hang on for dear life. Tom held on to Stella's hand and hoped she was depending on him for support. He'd told her he would always be there for her and he intended to be but Mother Nature had her own ideas how and when earthlings could fulfill their promises. The rain was falling so hard the trucks windshield wipers were useless, and Paddy couldn't tell where the causeway was intact or not. He was only going just over stalling speed just in case. He was saying every prayer he knew to himself often repeating them. The truck was getting warmer by the minute inside but he didn't dare open a window even a crack lest the wind driven water soak the interior. He shed his raincoat right at the beginning and was down to a T-shirt and was still sweating profusely. He wondered how the women could stand it but neither of them complained at all. One good thing about this storm though no drug runners would dare try to ply their trade in it and survive. A Navy aircraft carrier would be hard pressed to maneuver in a full blown hurricane. All these thoughts ran through his mind as he continued his silent chanting of the rosary.

Tom had dried from the initial run for the truck but was soaked again in his own sweat. Stella had her head on his shoulder and was either asleep or doing a good job of feigning the fact. He looked at his watch to see how long they had been on the causeway and was somewhat surprised, over two hours. When they had first traveled the causeway after shopping in South Miami it had taken less than fifteen minutes from store to property at night and never having been there before. There was the difference a severe storm could make.

When Tom talked to Rocky on the radio, he described Paddy's truck and they decided to meet at any restaurant that was open on the main street of Homestead since he said most of Miami and all of Fort Lauderdale were flooded with water standing a foot deep and more in some places. Now that they had finally reached the mainland, Tom tried Rocky again to see if Felix had picked him up and they were on the way to Homestead. They were , yet some bad luck had befallen them too. The rear of the pickup had collected a copious amount of water due to the heavy rainfall and with nowhere to go it was sloshing around in the bed of the truck causing it to slue in different directions according to whether Felix was turning or stopping. Even at their slow speed it was causing their heavily weighted rear end to alter his steering ability. Felix mentioned this to Rocky who told him to find a partially covered spot where he could let the tailgate down to release the buildup. The only thing in sight was a combination gas station, carryout with gas pumps covered by an overhead metal roof - pumps only. The place was closed.

"Pull in there, Felix, and I'll open the tailgate." Rocky went behind and unpinned the gate and pulled. It wouldn't give. So he figured because he was on an angle at one side he was working against himself torque-wise so he went to the center and pulled again. The gate dropped and water and assorted flotsam shot out of the opening looking like Niagara Falls. Unfortunately he was standing directly in its path and couldn't backpedal fast enough to avoid a soaking from the knees down. He let out a howl that could have been heard in Jacksonville which brought Felix rushing back thinking the big man had somehow injured himself. Instead what he saw made him laugh. "Looks like ya' got kinda' wet there, partner heh, heh, heh."

"My shoes, look what it did to my shoes. Well for anyone else it wouldn't be such a calamity, just dry them out and wear another pair but when you have 16EEEEs it's not that simple. Rocky had the strength of three men, the patience of a saint, and the coolness of one who never gets riled but his Achilles heels were his feet. He got back into the truck muttering to himself. Felix took one glance at the big man then busied himself with driving. They still had a way to go before getting to Homestead.

"You did a fine piece of driving there, Paddy, now let's hightail it for Homestead before anything else happens. I don't know about the women but 'm getting thirsty and Leo looks like he's getting restless and I know what that means."

"So do I. My wolfhound is the same way. She can hold her water for just so long then look out."

"Honey, I don't feel well." "What's the matter, sweetheart? Is it the heat in here? Paddy can open a window now that we're off the causeway." "That's partially it but there's something more", and she cupped his ear to whisper in it so the others couldn't hear. "I feel like I'm going to throw up. God forbid but I might be getting morning sickness. I feel bloated."

Paddy had been watching Stella in the rear view mirror. It was the first time she had complained since getting in to his truck but of course he didn't know she was pregnant. Tom was trying to soothe her and they were exchanging whispered messages which could only mean there was something seriously wrong with her beyond the heat. He rolled his window down half way and was going to do the same on the other side when Tom asked him if he would pull over at the nearest opportunity. Tom got Stella out just in time. He held her by the waist as she retched. He pulled a sodden handkerchief out of his rear pocket and gave it to her to wipe her lips, never letting her go from his grasp. It was a good thing too because she let go again. By this time Gennie had joined them. She took over like a mother hen. "This is woman's work Tom. You just stand by to make sure she doesn't fall." Gennie was sweet talking Stella and wiping her mouth from the now dry heaves. Here was a midwife who had never given birth herself. She was a blessing in disguise. Yes, Felix had himself a winner here. They had both lucked out.

Paddy had let Leo out on the other side of the truck where he accomplished his duty out of the way from Stella. The rain had slackened to a steady drizzle as they loaded back in. Everyone seemed to be feeling better now that they had some relief and they continued their journey to Homestead.

28

They all met up at a diner on Elm Street with a large sign above that advertised "EATS." It was surrounded with pickups, old and new, of citrus pickers who were trying to salvage some of the crops being ravaged by the winds and rains.

Rocky was still carping about his shoes but he squished across the street into the diner. Stella thought some ice cream would settle her stomach, so Tom helped her into the place. Leo had the truck to himself with Tom's order to guard and he would be given a treat later. So this motley-looking group entered the diner and found themselves a table that would seat them all. Even as disheveled as Stella was, she brought stares and whistles of admiration for her beauty, which she totally ignored, not even gracing them with a smile of acknowledgment, which proved how poorly she felt. A waitress pushing sixty with a coffee pot in one hand and five ceramic mugs in the other stopped at their table. "Who'll have coffee?" After she put those on the table, she pulled out an ordering pad and waited for their wants. Tom had his mug down in front of him and ordered a dish of vanilla ice cream for Stella then bacon and eggs for himself. He looked toward Paddy who had the same but asked for tea , hot or iced , either one. And so the rotation continued until every one had made their orders. Felix was last and of course wanted two cold beers with his meal. He also wanted a full breakfast for Gennie, and he intended to finish whatever she didn't eat. Much to his credit, the little man didn't turn on to the waitress which showed that he was starting to take his marriage vows seriously. As the waitress was leaving Tom asked her to make a special trip to bring Stella her ice cream. She nodded in agreement.

"I'm sorry to be such a baby about this, honey, but my mother didn't forewarn me that this could happen in her family. She never experienced morning sickness, so why should I."

"I'd have to say the conditions are quite different for you, sweetheart. Your mother wasn't living through a hurricane, being bounced around in an airless truck, or getting wet without a chance to dry off or clean up properly. It will be a miracle if you don't catch a cold or worse out of this."

The ice cream, four scoops in a banana split dish, was delivered and Tom told her to dig in. All this time Paddy had been watching and listening to Tom and Stella without out being overtly conspicuous. Never having been married, he had little personal experiences with pregnancies. Now everything that had happened in his truck began to make sense. The more time he spent around Tom Mueller the more he learned, not that it would profit him monetarily. It just seemed the man was a fountain of information. He kind of wished he had him working for or with him on the NYPD. With his drive and moxie, Tom would make him a captain in no time. The food was delivered and devoured and Stella had a second dish of ice cream. When the bill was brought Tom asked for any kind of large steak, raw to be added on. The waitress' eyebrows rose but she quickly filled his request. A sirloin that must have weighed two pounds was put in wax paper and bag and brought to the table. Tom went to pay the bill but Paddy spoke up first. "I'll split it with you Tom", and they did. The waitress just wanted to be rid of this crazy bunch. She wouldn't put anything else past them. Stella asked where the powder room was and was directed. Gennie went with her. When they returned, Stella had some color in her face , her hair was rearranged, and she flashed her usual beautiful smile to all the onlookers. The rain had stopped momentarily, but the wind was still strong. She guessed that while she and Gennie were preoccupied the men had decided where they were going to spend the rest of today and tonight. They all got back in the two trucks as before with the exception of Gennie who joined her husband and Rocky in the cab of the pickup. They started off with the pickup leading and didn't go more than two miles when they pulled into a motel parking lot.

It was one floor in a vee shape with the office at the point of the vee. Tom, Paddy, and Felix went in. The owner was at the desk playing solitaire. "Do you have four rooms for a few days?"

"I can fix you up, but they won't be in a row." He quoted the price and also said that since he and his wife were alone now that his maids had fled north he could furnish clean towels and linens, but they'd have to change the beds themselves. Everyone agreed and he handed out the keys after they signed the register.

"I see one of you is from Key Largo. I know some folks down there and at our last communication they said that they were really taking a beating. It seems this damn hurricane sat right on them for several hours before moving north. We have been lucky so far sheltered as we are here. You better get some sleep while you can." Tom, Stella, and Leo took the room at the far end of the vee where Tom could let the dog out unnoticed when nature called to him. As motel rooms went it was average, nothing fancy, but sturdy furniture featuring a queen-size bed and two night stands flanking it, a table with two chairs, and a small settee against the wall next to the table. Sand-colored walls without pictures completed the decor. One thing in its favor, it was exceptionally clean. The bathroom was spotless, cleaner then the previous rooms they had stayed in. While they were getting undressed for bed, Tom unwrapped the sirloin steak for Leo and took it to the bathroom . "Try not to make too much of a mess with your treat, big boy. I know where you'll get your water but this will only be temporary until I can buy you a proper dish. Enjoy, you earned it."

When he joined Stella in bed he asked her how she felt. "I think I'll be all right now, honey; that ice cream settled my stomach. I'll be able to tell you more when we wake up." Tom kissed his wife then rolled over so she could clamp her body to his. His last thoughts before drifting off to sleep were of Fred's estate, wondering when he could return to assess the damages and instigate repairs so the could return . The howling wind outside was a cacophony which accompanied those thoughts.

Tom was still groggy when something woke him out of his deep sleep. His eyes were open yet it took several moments for him to understand where he was, nothing seemed familiar in his field of vision. Then it dawned on him, there was the lack of a howling wind. It was deathly quiet which should be the case on a fall night. He lay there trying to remember the date. He knew it was the first week of September but what date? His usual meticulous mind was at a loss. What he needed was some coffee to jump start his brain. He carefully detached himself from Stella's embrace and got up to don his still soggy clothes to go in search of the stuff. He looked toward the open bathroom door and saw Leo watching him. "C'mon, Leo; let's go outside" he whispered . The dog followed him obediently. He didn't go ten steps before the dog let go. "You have to back in and guard Stella while I look for some coffee." Leo understood and returned to the room door on his own and waited for Tom to open it. The sky was overcast yet there was no rain or wind. He looked into the bed of the truck and saw some standing water but it was only about a half inch deep so he got into the cab. It started right off so he pulled out of the motel parking lot back toward Homestead proper. If nothing else was open he could at least return to the diner of the previous night. It was on Route One, which was also Elk Street in the business section. Traffic was still light so he made good time. Tom glanced at his watch only to find it had stopped. It suddenly dawned on him that there was a plug in the bed to let any accumulation of water out. It would have eliminated Rocky's shoe problem had he known.

The diner was open with fewer trucks at it than his previous visit. He entered and sat at a stool at the main counter. When his coffee arrived he started looking around while sipping the hot brew. The closest person near him was a swarthy hued man about the size of Felix who kept his eyes roving between the cash register and the counter waitress. Tom had that feeling he always developed that something was about to happen. He had just received a refill of his second cup of coffee when the little man made his move. He jumped up on the counter and with a small nickel-plated revolver waving it around and shouted, "Everybody take their wallets out and put them in front of you and keep your hands where I can see them. As he edged toward Tom, the CIA agent made his own move. It was so fast the would be robber never knew it was coming until his head bounced off a stool and he lay unconscious on the floor. Tom held up his CIA credentials and told everyone to stay put until the police arrived. Then he turned to the badly shaken waitress and in a lower, soothing tone, told her to call the police. "You're all right now , don't think about anything but getting the law here. I need a wet bar towel to subdue this guy until they get here." She obeyed like a robot, handing Tom two wet towels. Tom tied his wrists together with one around the base of the stool and used the other to wipe his own face. When the waitress returned to tell the police were on the way he asked for a fresh mug of coffee? "It seems mine got spilled during the fracas." Three Florida State Police entered the diner weapons drawn. "Everyone stay exactly where you are," shouted one. "Who's in charge here?" asked another in a quieter tone. The third trooper walked over to Tom. "Is this the perp on the floor here sir?"

"Yes it is. Can I show you my credentials?"

"Sure, go ahead." He read everything twice. He was quite thorough. "And what were you doing

111

here, Mr. Mueller?" "Just a patron like the rest, having some morning coffee. My team is working another case down here but Hurricane Betsy interrupted all that. I live on Key Largo and I'm just waiting to return and assess the damages. I understand they are extensive.."

"I think you can leave anytime you want, Mr. Mueller. I'm just going to check your actions with that young waitress for my report. She seems to be in shock but she should become lucid enough to corroborate your story soon. In any case we know how to contact you if need be."

"Fine, officer. I'd like some carryout coffee for my wife before I leave. She's pregnant and has had a rough time of it for the last couple of days." The young waitress sidled over just then and Tom asked her for the to-go coffee. She seemed to have snapped out of her stupor enough to get back to business and accommodated him. Tom asked her for one of her for one of her order checks and wrote Mr. McHenry's name and telephone number in D.C. to give to the State Policeman. "That is my immediate supervisor who will vouch for my authenticity. He will want a copy of you final report. By the way, this clown will probably need some medical attention. He doesn't seem to be coming around. I must have hit him harder than I thought." Tom paid his bill and left the diner. It would be a cold day in hell before he returned, he thought.

Hurricane Betsy wasn't finished yet. She was heading north off the coast opposite Jacksonville heading for the Carolinas when she took an abrupt about face and started back south by west. She was a category four storm with winds just short of 155 m.p.h. When she hit New Orleans at the mouth of the Mississippi River Delta she flooded a great portion of the city. The worst was over for Miami and the Keys. Tom would have to contact Mr. Goldberg again to find out how much his insurance covered. Money was soon going to be a problem, which meant returning to the bank for cash. How long could he keep draining it he wondered?

As Tom was heading back to the motel, he spotted a smallish delicatessen he had somehow missed before . It sat back off the road a bit but had a lit neon sign on the doorway, so he pulled in on the off chance it was open. Maybe his luck was changing for the better, because it was open. It had just about anything in the way of prepared foods you could think of. It reminded him of the deli in New Orleans only on a smaller scale. So he went about shopping with a vengeance. He even found a substitute water bowl for Leo. By the time he was finished he had over twenty dollars worth of goods that fit into three large paper bags. "I'll have to pay for these now but I'll have to make two trips to get them out." Once back at the motel he made another two trips before opening the door, knowing that as soon as Leo recognized him he'd be all over him. Such was the case and Tom had to order him down . Stella was up and dressed sitting at the small table so that's where Tom took the bags. "Honey, I'm home", he said cheerfully, remembering an old radio program he used to listen to as a child back in Toledo. "Wait 'til you see what I have for you both. He started unloading the bags. There was a pint of vanilla ice cream still hard, plastic spoons, a six pack of cold Coca-Cola, some sketching paper and crayons, six large cans of Alpo dog food, a can opener, and lastly a water bowl for Leo. "Oh, honey, that's wonderful. You do think of everything . Where did you find all these items?" So he explained about the deli he had missed before. "It reminded me of that deli in New Orleans we stopped at when you were still single. "Oh ,those were the days, footloose and fancy free as they say. I trust they will never come back. I like it just the way it is." Tom wasn't about to tell her about his fracas at the diner earlier. As long as she was feeling better and in a loving mood why spoil it.

"I don't know about you, honey, but I'm getting horny." "My God, woman, you're insatiable. But before we commence our fun and games I have to feed and water Leo. There's one more item still in the truck that I'd better get while I still have clothes on. So, first things first. Tom went into the bathroom and filled the water dish setting it out of the way then opened one of the cans of dog food. Leo came in and sniffed the dog food but went to the water dish first. When Tom returned from the truck with the small radio and reentered the room the first thing Stella said was, Leo decided to eat the Alpo since he wasn't going to get any more special treats from us. I guess he figured it was a case of eating what was served or starve. Is that the other thing you had in the truck honey?"

"Yes, and it has two very important functions. One is to get the weather and news, the other is more romantic in nature. It should be fun for background music to make love by and it will provide a provocative beat for something else, if you get my meaning." Stella actually blushed at that as it did dawn on her. Then she giggled. "Get those clothes off right now, honey; I can't wait to try it." Tom placed the radio on the night stand and tuned it in. He kept the volume down until he found a station playing big-band selections, at which point he turned it louder. After the last tune which was a golden oldie the disc jockey was announcing the next several numbers he would spin following the commercial. The first would be Artie Shaw's "Begin the Beguine," which Tom knew had a Latin beat with a vigorous tempo. "Now we're in business, sweetheart. The number should get your motor running at high speed."

"Turn the light off, honey; that way you won't know from what angle I attack you. He did as she commanded, and it was well worth it. Tom had no idea those innovative ideas, surely not from Gennie, but she was the only female that Stella had contact with. What followed for the next fifteen or twenty minutes was totally beyond his sphere of experience with women. Tom was certain he would remember every detail for as long as he drew breath. They both fell into exhausted sleep and were oblivious of their surroundings or for anything but themselves.

The radio continued playing but had switched to a news and weather format. Had Tom been conscious, he would have heard that Hurricane Betsy was ravaging New Orleans before blowing itself out in the Gulf. When Tom woke this time it was to the persistent knocking on the room door. He unglued himself from Stella's embrace, threw on some shorts, and grabbed a shirt to answer. There stood a sheepish-looking Felix. Tom turned to see if Stella was amply covered; she wasn't so he called Leo out and closed the door behind him. The dog took about ten steps and discharged. Once that was accomplished he returned to his main friend and sat by his side with that pleased look on his face that Tom always associated with smugness. Leo didn't have to talk; Tom could read him like a book." All right, Felix, what's so important you had to wake me?"

"It's like this, amigo, I'm jus' 'bout starvin' ta' death. When are we gonna' get sumthin' ta' eat?" So Tom told him to take the truck and gave him directions on how to find the little deli down the road. You can buy just about anything in prepared foods. You can tell if it's open if the neon light on the door is lit. Just turn left out of the parking lot and it's on your right. Get me a bag of ice while you're there. C'mon, Leo, let's go see how Stella is feeling."

Taking his clothes off he slipped back in into bed with Stell, Tom had the sudden urge to play the keyboard, he was running riffs over in his mind as he dropped off, a pleasant way to enter slumberland.

This time when Tom awoke and opened his eyes he was looking directly at Stella sitting at the table stroking Leo who sat by her side. She was clad in bra and panties which only made her look more alluring to him. He swung his legs out of bed dressed only in shorts. "How are you feeling, sweetheart?" "Much better, thank you, and if you'll look outside you'll be happy to see the sun is shining and there isn't a cloud in the sky."

"If that's the case, I've got a lot to do so I better get dressed and round up the troops and get to a public phone. It wouldn't be a bad idea if you followed suit, getting dressed I mean."

"I will. You must have had a pleasurable dream last time we were in bed. I hope it was about me."

That caught Tom by surprise. "Why, was I talking in my sleep?"

"No but you were kind of humming and your fingers were flying on my leg." Now Tom remembered, the riffs he put himself to sleep with but it was embarrassing to think it woke Stell.

Tom went to all the rooms and notified his team members to gather in his room in a half an hour. It was indeed a beautiful day. The temperature and humidity were low enough to be comfortable in shirt sleeves so none of them would have to worry about their clothing. Tom had given Rocky his hand held radio the day they arr4ived at the El Dorado motel so he could charge them both up. When Tom notified Rocky about the meeting he gave him the fully charged radio before he left. Felix was the last stop to make before returning to his room. He answered Tom's knock himself, a complete reversal from the usual front of Gennie. "Gen's in the shower so we'll be ready by meetin' time, amigo." When Tom passed the truck, he knocked out the plug in the bed to let the little bit of remaining water drain out. When he was let in he found that Stella had changed the bed linens and tidied the place up. Ever the busy housewife she always wanted her surrounding rooms in neat order. "You know, Stell, it's nice to have a tidy place but you have to slow down some. Think of our child."

They started drifting in. First Paddy, then Rocky who joined him on the settee. Last, the Santanas. Felix was carrying a cold Bud; he must have bought some ice from the deli too.

"Now that we're all here I thought we should discuss our future plans for dealing with the drug runners and their stateside contacts. If you have any suggestions or questions feel free to interrupt at any time. Nothing that we discuss here will be withheld from the women for obvious reasons they are usually going to be nearby when the radio communications are exchanged. I'm also going to admit my using my wife as a sounding board for ideas I have concerning tactics to be used to curtail shipments, and I'm sure the Santanas discuss our business when they are alone." Tom looked over at Felix who just nodded in agreement. "So here's my first thought on the subject" and he went to cover all the points he'd been thinking of since before Hurricane Betsy struck. "Now when the meeting is over there will be different seating arrangements in the two trucks. This will only be temporary until more vehicles are obtained. Stella and Leo will ride with me in the pickup. Paddy, you'll have everyone else because I think we'll be going in opposite directions. I have to return to the bank for additional funds first, contact Mr. Goldberg, then Mr. McHenry. Therefore, gaining access to a public telephone is paramount, and not a phone booth either. Since Rocky has the handheld radios fully charged we'll have to keep in touch that way if any further truck problems develop. Does anyone have anything to add? No? Then let's get moving."

Paddy took Tom aside before leaving the room with the others. "Are you coming back here tonight?" "That depends on the results I get from those phone calls. Why?"

"I'm not a rich man by any means but I do have access to certain funds and if you need cash now or tomorrow let me know so I can get to those funds."

"I appreciate the offer, Paddy, I really do but let me see what those calls dictate, then I'll have a better handle on what we're faced with."

Tom got to the bank by way of various side streets. Miami was flooded in many of its low lying areas right up to the edge of its main business district. They saw many smaller businesses on the way leading there that had broken plate glass windows caused by high winds and flying debris. These shop owners were scurrying in and out trying to salvage goods and sweep up out front.

Insurance adjusters were going to be inundated with claims for many days ahead. When they arrived at the bank Stella and Leo stayed with the pickup while Tom transact his business. He could see they were operating with a skeleton staff, many of their regular employees including executives were absent. Finished with his safety deposit box he asked if they had a telephone where he could set while taking copious notes? The woman he asked told him to wait a moment while she checked. "Go to the desk of Mr. Berra and he will accommodate you, Mr. Mueller." Berra set him up in a closed area where he would be alone. "Any long distance calls, Mr. Mueller?" "Several, one to our head office in Washington, D.C., but they will all be reverse charged."

"Fine, take your time. There is a scratch pad and pens for any note taking. Forty-five minutes later he was finished with several sheets of note paper filled. Mr. McHenry congratulated him for foiling the restaurant robbery in Homestead and remarked how Tom seemed to attract trouble wherever he went but came out of it smelling like a rose. "The report I received From the Florida State Police praised your actions in saving lives. A newspaper reporter present at the time was especially impressed and wrote a story for the Miami Herald saying so. Now concerning vehicles. You can lease whatever you need and have them send copies of the agreements to us." Click, he was gone. Tom called the mechanic where they had bought the old Plymouth for Felix. He told him it didn't look like they'd be back to Virginia for quite a long time if ever. So he gave him instructions how to ship it down to Miami along with his wagon and where to send the total bill. You won't recognize the car when you see it, Mr. Mueller. I've made it kind of a hobby. I've already given this gyp artist a two-week notice because I have enough outside work that I don't have to worry about whether I'm going to get paid or not every week here. I think you're going to be very pleased with the Plymouth. She has some of my most artistic work in her and if you are as pleased with her as I think you'll be if some time in the future you can send me a testimonial to that effect I'd appreciate it."

Rather than call to cancel his lease of the rental property in Franklin Park, Virginia, where he couldn't reverse the charges, Tom decided to write his landlord to that effect. His only regret there was he wouldn't be able to get together socially with the big State Trooper Terry Connoti. The trooper had been very helpful in checking the house and yard of his rental property in Franklin Park.

When Tom had finished his phone calls he gathered up his notes, thanked Mr. Berra for his consideration, and returned to the pickup. There he found an impatient Leo being soothed somewhat by Stella. "Did you find everything you needed, honey?"

"Yes, they were quite cooperative for being so short-handed. They were operating with a skeleton crew. Mr. McHenry gave me carte blanche as far as leasing vehicles so there won't be any problem on that score. There are a couple of letters I have to write yet because I couldn't reverse charges to those people but other than that I'd say this part of the trip was successful. Now let's see if I can raise the others on the hand-held unless they're out of range. Tom was shuffling through his notes as he spoke. "Do you remember where they were headed, Stell? It's completely slipped my mind with everything else that's been going on."

"Can't you get them on the radio?"

"Not at the moment; they must be out of range, yet these are supposed to be good for fifty miles. Where the devil could they be?"

"I don't know, honey, but I know where I want to be and pretty darn quick. I must make for the girls room. The dog can go anywhere but I can't and still maintain my decorum."

"Sorry, sweetheart. I'll find a place a.s.a.p. Hold on." As Tom worked his way south trying to avoid still flooded streets, they began entering the seedier parts of the city, mostly industrial in nature, warehouses, lumber yards and the like where restaurants were nonexistent. To tell the truth, he was getting lost. Street signs and state route numbers were either blown off or twisted so you couldn't trust their veracity. Tom was about to give up when like a mirage appeared a little greasy spoon that had to have a bathroom. He parked on the street among tipped garbage cans and scattered contents letting Leo out first then telling him to guard the pickup until he and Stella returned. He escorted his wife inside where he found they were only the second customers there An older man was sitting at the counter sipping a mug of coffee. The waitress behind the counter was the old duffer's age or older. She looked up when they were seated but was in no hurry to serve them. Tom looked around trying to spot the restrooms. There didn't seem to be any at least that he could see and the place wasn't that big so where were they? The old crone finally waddled over to them. "What'll it be?"

"First, you can point out the restrooms. My wife is badly in need of one."

"They're around that corner. I guess they're not to plainly marked if you are a stranger here. Our regulars know the place inside out." Tom pointed this out to Stell who was clearly fidgeting in her need. Tom said, "I'll have a mug of coffee until she gets back." Tom's mind was racing, wondering why he couldn't reach Paddy's truck on the radio and thinking ahead and thinking ahead to his next moves on Fred's estate. Stella returned relief showing clearly on her beautiful face. "Do you want anything, sweetheart?"

"No, I think I'll pass; go ahead and finish your coffee, though."

"Ma'am could I have the bill and some directions."

"That'll be fifty cents and where are ya' headed?"

"The Keys", he said as he laid a dollar on the counter. She grabbed the bill and stuffed it into an apron pocket where it would probably never see the cash register. She gave him instructions that were easy enough to understand and they left. When they got outside Stella said "That was the filthiest restroom I've ever been in. I had to practically hold my breath in it. No paper towels, rusty water in the tap, and I had to use toilet paper to wipe my hands. Let's get away from that horrible place. I take it you're heading for Key Largo."

"Yes, and I'm going to try to raise the others unless you want to while I concentrate on driving."

"Sure, honey, I can do that." Tom opened the tailgate and told Leo to get in. He did obediently and stretched out for a nap and wait for their next stop.

The devastation in Key Largo was incredible. Every home they passed had broken windows or torn off roofs, or cars turned over in driveways. As they neared Fred's estate, he turned to Stella. "You don't suppose those guys came back here do you?"

"I certainly couldn't contact them on the radio, honey." Tom's question was answered as they pulled in to their grounds. There stood Paddy's truck amid ripped out palm trees and flotsam of every description.

29

Tom couldn't see where any of his team were, which meant they must be inside. "Be careful where you step, Stell; there's broken glass and twisted metal all over the yard. That downed palm tree doesn't look like it was uprooted anywhere in the front yard; at least I don't see any gaping holes."

"I'll stick close to you, honey. What a mess. I can only imagine what the inside must look like.

Oh, that beautiful kitchen." They carefully opened the front door, which was ajar. There all the rest of his team were busy sweeping, putting everything and anything they found scattered about in orderly piles on the furniture. They had found brooms and dustpans somewhere and were making good use of them. Very little idle chatter was heard as they stood watching the work in progress. Leo had hopped out of the pickup bed and followed his main friends but stayed just outside the door out of the way. He was getting hungry again but knew to wait. His main friend would feed him soon. In the meantime he would investigate his territory outside.

"Rocky, why didn't you answer Stella's calls on the radio?"

"I'm sorry, Mr. Mueller; we have been so busy here I left it out in the truck. You might want to check those piles of documents on the furniture for anything important only you would recognize."

"Good idea. Where are Felix and Gennie?" Rocky just pointed toward the kitchen. He was still a man of few words.

"Stell, do you want to see what they're doing?" "Sure, honey. I'm anxious to see what damage has been done there anyway." Her friends were hard at work. Water had seeped in from overhead somewhere and was still dripping in to the mop bucket that Felix was using to squeeze out what water was still on the floor. He had his eve-present can of Bud sitting on the counter top close at hand.

"Who says men can't do women's work? What does this look like?"

"Do we have lights?" Gennie shook her head. "The lines must be down somewhere."

"How about gas?"

"I don't know I haven't tried it." Stella walked over to the stove and found that they did so she went about making coffee after she found the coffee canister. Soon the aroma of fresh coffee wafted throughout the kitchen. Knowing that Paddy only drank tea, she put a pan of water on another burner then started rummaging through cupboards looking for any canned goods she could use to slap together a hapharzard meal that would be at least a snack for everyone. She knew not to open the refrigerator that had survived Betsy intact because without electricity any coldness that remained would escape. Tuna, peas, and an unopened box of Ritz crackers before she found a two pound box of Velveeta cheese, were all she could find so she forgot about the peas and made a large platter of hors d'oeuvres with the rest. It would have to for now she thought. Stella found a serving platter in one of the cupboards and loaded it with everything including condiments. In the same cupboard a box of eight-inch candles that placed on saucers could be used tonight if the electrical power had still not been restored. Upon completion of loading the platter with the finger food and coffee, tea, and styrofoam cups she found the loaded platter rather unwieldy so she went to the main living area to get some help. Tom saw her coming and stopped looking through the stacks of papers to go to her side. "What kind of shape is the kitchen in, Stell?"

"It could be worse. There is an overhead leak that is keeping Felix and Gennie busy mopping up. I came in for some assistance in carrying a tray of foods I prepared in here."

A while later, Tom found Stella sitting on the bed with wet papers spread out all around her. She wasn't exactly crying but close to it. "Look, Stell, there's little you can do here until we get the roof tiles replaced but in the meantime we have things to do. Come with me while I find some food to feed this horde. Leo is fed and he'll watch the house while we're gone."

"I can't go out looking like this honey, I'm a mess."

"You'll never be a mess, sweetheart, not with your looks, now let's go." Tom told Leo to guard the house and to stay awake.

When they got into the pickup Tom didn't bother looking into the other truck, he knew independent Rocky would be in it. "First stop, food. That's your department, Stell; you know what to and not to buy. We'll pick up a charcoal grill to cook outside on and I'm going to look for a generator to provide lights in case this ever happens again."

"Where are we going for all this."

"Back to the Piggly Wiggly. It has almost everything and you can be sure it'll be open." It was more than just open, it was thriving. The huge parking lot was almost full. When they entered the store which had sustained minimal damage they were surprised by the amount of not only shoppers but employees present. Every cashier line was open and doing brisk business. "Stay close, Stell; this place is a madhouse. If we do get separated go to the raised managers office and have him make an announcement over the intercom." They started in the grocery department where Stella was picking out the necessary items that were needed, then to meats. There Tom was loading steaks and chops with abandon. He found a cheap grill for outside with barbecuing utensils and he bought ten pounds of charcoal with lighter fluid. The cart was almost full at that point but they headed for the appliance department anyway. He found what he was looking for in generators but it was a monster. His truck could handle the bulk and weight of it but it was getting it out and in to it. That was solved by the department head. "You say you have a pickup truck?"

"Yes, but it's pretty far back in the lot." The department head eyed his loaded cart. "When you get to the check-out lines Have the cashier call this department and I'll have someone meet you at the main exit door to help put it aboard your truck." He handed the slip showing the cost to Tom, who was surprised how reasonable it was. On the way up front, Stella asked Tom to stop a minute, as something she needed caught her eye. He waited while she shopped. She returned with her arms full of women's apparel. "Yes, they do have almost everything here, honey."

On the way back to Key Largo, Tom told Stella after they unloaded everything with whoever was available she should cook up a good meal for them all. "I have to go where Fred's Gresham is housed and settle up with Mr. Gomer then see about making a trade for the fastest boat he has."

"I'll be all right now, honey, what with my new clothes and everything, and don't worry, they'll eat well today."

When Mr. Gomer was pointed out to him Tom found an older, white-bearded man who couldn't be more than five foot three or four inches tall. The shipyard owner looked up from his task just as Tom approached. "Well, youngster, I never expected to see you again. You just get out of jail or what?"

Tom produced his picture agency ID and handed it to the man. "That was my twin brother you're talking about, Mr. Gomer, and I don't take kindly to that kind of reference, even though I now know what his occupation entailed." Gomer backed off abruptly. "I thought you were him, er', you know what I mean." Tom let that pass, retrieved his identification, and continued "It's about his Gresham yacht. Where is it?"

"That's it over there. I didn't continue its hull repair because I knew I wouldn't get paid for the job. It's sat on blocks taking up valuable yard space ever since."

"Let's have a look." Tom let the sly old bastard lead the way to the yacht gabbing in a nervous manner as they walked. As they stood looking up at the huge boat Gomer kept praising its value, obviously thinking Tom would pay the repairs, but Tom had other ideas. "What do you put its value at?" Gomer gave him an inflated price, higher than Tom would have thought. "If that's the figure, then, I'll hold you to it. Now, what's the fastest boat you have in stock?" The switch of topics caught Gomer by surprise. He had both a crestfallen expression and one of expectation to over price a new sale. "I've a new cigarette boat just delivered this morning. Let me show you this beauty. She's over here." Tom followed the old duffer, thinking he was playing right into his hands. This might be better than poker.

"I'm surprised you didn't have more damage from the hurricane then this. I live on Key Largo and we had quite a bit." "Oh I had some to the showroom and it destroyed some of my floating docks on the inner jetty but I'll survive. What do you think of this? Thirty-five feet long, ten foot wide, twin three hundred and fifty horsepower Rolls-Royce engines with a draft of three feet, capable of speeds over fifty-five miles per hour. She holds twin fifty gallon fuel tanks etc., etc." He went on with mundane facts and figures that didn't interest Tom at all but leading up to an inflated price tag. The final figure was five hundred dollars over what he had valued the Gresham. The only things Tom didn't like about the boat was its flashy red paint job with yellow jagged lightening streaks down each side of its fiberglass body.

"All right, Mr. Gomer, here's what I'll do. I'll give you title to the Gresham in exchange for this boat, with two conditions. You repaint this boat matte black, eliminating those lightning streaks, and you reinforce the cowling just forward of the cockpit to handle a twenty-millimeter cannon on a swivel plate. All that has to be finished in one week and delivered to my Key Largo estate."

"And where and how am I going to buy the cannon that ya' want," he sputtered.

"I'll furnish the armament, you just install it."

"Looks like you have me over a barrel, mister, I hope you remember to give me some protection if these smugglers find out I helped you and decide to retaliate in some way."

"I don't think you'll be targeted in any way but I'll give you my home phone in case you need us. You just hold up your end of this deal or you'll have us to contend with and believe me the choice of which force is more formidable is no contest. See you in one week. I'll have a man with the armament here in two days."

As Tom was driving home he thought getting the artillery piece would test Rocky's resourcefulness, especially with the two-day time limit. He doubted if the silent one would call on Mr. McHenry for assistance on this job. He also had to lease a vehicle. Yes, Rocky was going to be a busy boy for the next two days.

When Tom entered the house he could actually feel the change of atmosphere. Paddy's truck was gone, which should have been an indicator that something was up. He found Stella in the kitchen washing pans and cutlery, the remnants from a recent meal. "Where are the troops' Stell? I see Paddy's truck is missing."

"He and Rocky went to lease a van. They didn't say where, honey. In fact, they were almost secretive in their preparations. I honestly don't understand Rocky's mood swings at all anymore. His personality seems to have changed from that of when in New York and I don't know why. Personally, I don't know him anymore. How was your errand?" Tom explained it all to her. "It sounds like you consider it a successful outcome. I don't know about that cannon business though. Why do you need something like that?"

"These smugglers mean business, and I want to be ready to meet force with superior force. It's not a question of overkill."

"Well, you know best. Did you notice the electricity has been turned on? Felix lit the pilot light on the water heater so I have hot water. When I'm done here I'm going to take a leisurely shower if I can get anyone to wash my back."

"That anyone had better be me, sweetheart, and your back isn't all I'll wash." Leo had had been on the floor farther back from his main friends just waiting for something else to happen when his tail started swishing back and forth in anticipation, he had heard something outside that the others hadn't picked up yet. First his massive head rose then he was on his feet, head cocked to hear better before alarming his friends. Tom noticed the dog's sudden movements and raised his index finger to Stella to stay quiet, pointing to Leo. The mastiff took off for the front door, Tom right behind him. "Stay where you are, Stell, until I see what's bothering him." Tom had his Cobra in hand when he reached the door. Mr. McHenry had it right when he insisted Tom be armed at all times.

"What do you hear, boy? Should I let you out alone? Tom decided against that. Leo was too valuable to him to let foray alone. "We'll do this together like we always do. You stay close and watch for my hand signals." Now the dog sat waiting for the door to be opened. He understood his main friend by the tone of his voice. The late afternoon was still pleasant as the sun began its descent to the western horizon. Tom couldn't figure out what had alerted Leo, the dog had powers of sight, smell, and hearing way above the capacity of man. Then he heard it, a sound resembling that of a tractor or bulldozer, faint but discernible. Somewhere on the Key, a crew was removing debris, whether it was a private party or the homeowners association remained to be seen. If it was the latter his taxes would include his property for clean up too. "We'll just stay inside boy. You can continue your nap for now. I'll take you out later before we retire for the night." Since the power was now restored it meant the phone was working so Tom decided to make a few calls before it got any later on the off chance he could connect on a few things that were bothering him. The phone book was soaked so he had to rely on the long distance operator to find numbers for him. This was a slow and tedious process and after forty-five minutes of no answers and wrong numbers he gave it up as a waste of time. He was about to join Stella for a frolicsome shower when the unmistakable sounds of vehicles outside interrupted his intentions. This time he beat Leo to the front door. Paddy and Rocky had returned. "All right, Leo, you can go outside with me but don't stray too far from the house, You understand?" The dog went one way while Tom joined the returnees. Paddy handed Tom all the paper work for the new vehicle which was a GMC enclosed van, ebony in color. "That seemed to satisfy Rocky's need in vehicles Tom. I don't understand why he wants that type of transport but he must have a reason that he didn't wish to divulge, at least to me."

"That's the way he is, Paddy, at least as long as I've known him but I have a real problem for him to solve tonight. You are very welcome to sit in while I break it to him. If this doesn't open him up nothing will." Tom called Leo in . He must have been close for he was at Tom's side in a matter of seconds.

"Time to stay in for the night, boy. You can go out again in the morning." Tom scratched behind his ears with the usual results.

When he told Rocky he wanted to talk to him in the kitchen on a matter of great importance the man simply nodded and followed him into the house. Paddy was already seated at the table when they entered the kitchen. Felix appeared from nowhere as was his custom, opened the refrigerator and grabbed two cold Buds, handed one to Tom and sat uninvited at the table. "Thanks, partner, I was ready for this", and took a healthy slug. "Now Rocky I have an important assignment for you. You have your own wheels again so you'll not have that as an excuse for not completing this job. There is a two-day time limit for completion. I'll get into the reason for that shortly. You seem to be a resourceful person so this should be a piece of cake for you. We need a twenty-millimeter cannon with at least fifty rounds of ammunition, half armor piercing. The barrel of the weapon should not exceed fifty inches, breechblock loading. The weapon should rest on a tripod or some other contrivance that will connect to a swivel plate attached forward of the cockpit of a cigarette boat we now own. The reason for the two-day limit is the shipyard doing the work needs that time to repaint the boat and construct the swivel plate. Think of the weapon as a recoilless rifle mounted on a boat instead of a Jeep or tank. It bothers me not how or where you find it, legal or not, just have it at the shipyard within the time allotted." Rocky sat silently staring at Tom. The silence lengthened until it was broken by Felix. "Amigo, I wonder if Master Sergeant Maddox is still with the Guard in New Orleans? He could get a weapon like ya' want or know where ta' tell ya' ta' go."

"There's an idea, Rocky; you can call the old veteran and mention you were referred by either Felix or me and I'm positive he would help you. You can use our phone and charge the long distance calls to us." Rocky still had not said a word, but Tom could practically hear the wheels turning in his head. "Well, gentlemen, it's been a long day and may be even longer tomorrow so I'll say goodnight."

Stella was asleep when Tom undressed so he quietly entered the bathroom for a much needed hot shower. He had just lathered up with soap even on his face when those hard breasts dug into his back. Why, you faker, I thought you were sound asleep; that's why I didn't go directly to bed and disturb you." "You promised you would wash my back among other things so I'm holding you to it." A whole lot of grabbing and giggling followed before they finally climbed into bed where Stella assumed her usual position clamped to his back. They were both asleep in less than two minutes.

Tom and Stella were awake almost simultaneously but this morning there was no sex even thought of by either of them. Tom was anxious to see if Rocky had left yet and to talk to Felix while Stella was ready to cook a big breakfast for all and to plan other meals. She was into her tasks when Leo came into the kitchen hoping for some sort of a treat from the food she was cooking. Stella noticed him almost crowding her at the stove so she put aside several strips of bacon to cool.

Tom found Felix coming out of his bedroom with what looked like clean and pressed clothing on. Gennie must have been hard at work. "Have you seen Rocky yet this morning?"

"Naw', I just got up; I smelled bacon fryin' an' it is pullin' me straight ta' the kitchen. Is his van outside?"

"I haven't looked yet."

"Well after ya' do, there is away ta' find out if he called Sergeant Maddox ya' know. Jus' ask the long distance operator if any calls were charged ta' this number in the last six hours or so."

"I didn't have very good luck with them last night when I tried to make some calls. All I got were no answers and busy signals for my efforts. I gave up after forty-five minutes."

"Yeah but ya' know what they say, amigo, if at first ya' don't succeed, try again so what have ya' got ta' lose."

"Oh you're just full of wisdom this morning, go eat your breakfast." Tom called to Leo, "You want to go outside?" The dog had finished his bacon and met Tom at the front door. "You stay close, boy; don't go wandering off out of my sight." Rocky's enclosed van was gone. Only Paddy's truck and his own pickup remained in the parking area, so it seemed Rocky was on his quest. Tom looked around his property trying to determine what damages from ground level were the most pressing to be repaired. The pool was a disaster. It had everything imaginable in it, and the roof of the pool house containing the filtering system and chemicals was blown off completely. Betsy had done a job on his property and he was certainly glad that he had hurricane insurance. "You ready to go back inside, Leo, or do you want to stay out here for awhile?" The mastiff didn't move and Tom took that as an answer and returned inside to make his phone calls. He was determined to get some answers today. His first call was to the homeowners association and they assured him they would be working toward his property today and questioned him on the amount of debris he wanted removed. Tom didn't pull any punches, and if anything, he exaggerated somewhat. He also

121

got a list of reputable contractors to call for repairs to the house. On his third call, he came up with a jack-of-all-trades who said he would be there in the afternoon to give him an estimate and if he was satisfied with the price could start work the next day. Emboldened by his successes so far, he next called the New Orleans National Guard Armory and asked the clerk who answered if Master Sergeant Maddox had retired yet. "No, he is still at his post; who is calling?" "An old friend; would you connect me, please."

"I don't have too many old friends left, who is this?" Tom identified himself and heard, "The shooter; of course, I remember you. One of the best shots I ever saw, second only to Hathcock. How is Felix Santana these days?"

"Just fine, he is my partner in the agency and he recently got married."

"Well I'll be darned, I never thought that womanizer would ever settle down. What can I do for you, Tom? I'm sure you didn't call me to pass the time of day." So Tom explained what he needed and wondered where the cannon could be purchased.

"You must be hunting pretty big game nowadays to want one of those." But he gave Tom a list of suppliers who handled large-caliber weapons. "Thanks much, Sarge. I really appreciate it and it was good talking to you again." So Rocky didn't call him as Felix suggested. That meant he had other plans to obtain the weaponry needed. All the more power to him, just so he did it in the time frame, of course nothing ever worked out as planned. When Tom called the railroad to find out about Felix's Plymouth, he was informed he could expect delivery in Miami the next day. That done, he went in search of his partner. He found him in the kitchen alone, the ever present Bud before him on the table. "What are you doing sitting here all alone Felix?"

"Had ta' get away from the wife for awhile. She was gettin' on my nerves grousin' 'bout learnin' ta' drive."

"That's what I came looking for you about. Your Plymouth will be in the Miami freight yard tomorrow. After you get used to driving it again, you can teach Gennie yourself. Also I talked to Sergeant Maddox and he gave you his regards and congratulations on your marriage. Rocky hadn't called him as you suggested but he gave me a list of suppliers of heavy-caliber weapons, the closest one being in Savannah, Georgia, quite a drive from here. I only got the list in case Rocky flubbed up."

"I can hardly wait ta' see that boat ya' bought. From yer' description it must be somethin'."

"It is that. Now what we need is the highest candlepowered portable searchlight available. Something that will blind the smugglers if they look into it. Can you imagine their annoyance when a very bright light coming from nowhere pinpoints their location?"

"Yeah that oughta' be somethin' amigo. I jus' hope I'm aboard when it happens."

"Oh you will be, partner. You'll be my co-pilot because you speak their language if they pretend not to understand or speak English. You will also be my backup with a shotgun at close quarters, so you see you'll always be present. I'll bet an Army-Navy store in Miami will have what I'm looking and if not there's always the Key West Naval Air Station. You and I are going to be busy tomorrow because I'm also going to show you the boat. So get a good nights sleep tonight."

30

Bright and early the next day, after a hearty breakfast Stella furnished, Tom and Felix kissed their wives goodbye, saying they had a long day ahead of them. Tom told Stella he would call her every couple of hours just in case Rocky returned and needed anything. "You can also keep me informed if the workman needs any further money. You have your nest egg but I'd prefer you use mine, that way if I'm laid up in any way you'll have cash of your own. I think you understand. You ready to go, partner?"

Stella had paled somewhat, thinking his discourse over. The hidden meaning is what caused her complexion change.

"Leo, you guard Stella until I get back."

The Miami freight yard was easy enough to find. The yard foreman pointed out the Plymouth which was covered by a full-bodied protective wrap. After exchanging the proper papers, Tom helped Felix remove the wrapping. There sat a fifteen-year-old car which appeared to have just been driven out of a showroom floor. To say it was beautiful would be an understatement. They both stood there and gaped. "Looks like you have a new car, partner."

"Yeah, that Pricer is somethin' isn't he. Hope she runs as good as she looks."

"Let's find out. You follow me down to the shipyard, and I'll keep an eye on you through my rearview. If it acts up in any way, blink your headlights." They entered Gomer's shipyard in tandem, parking near his showroom. "Man, she runs even better than she looks. Wow!, I'm impressed." Gomer spotted Tom's truck and hurried over. He took one look at the Plymouth before greeting his newest customer. "That's some car; where's it been all these years? A '51, ain't it?"

"Right; it was my wedding present to my partner here, Mr. Santana." The two eyed each other but didn't attempt to shake hands. "Partners, huh? You sure have a strange lookin' team, Mr. Mueller, another one of which was here earlier. He must have been darn near seven foot tall. You have some pretty good pull too."

"How's that, Mr. Gomer?"

"He brought the cannon and ammunition for it. Didn't say much after he showed his credentials but I got the drift when he pointed out the armament." Tom and Felix exchanged glances and smiled at each other.

"That's Rocky, all right. The paint job finished?"

"Sure is, and to your specifications."

"Where is it?"

"On a skid in the back of the showroom where nobody can see it. My men are putting on the swivel plate right now."

"Come on, Felix, you have to see this. I traded that big Gresham over there", he pointed, "for it."

"Was that Fred's boat?"

"Yes, and I came out of the deal smelling like a rose." Felix followed Tom into the rear of the showroom and there it sat, a menacing looking vessel even out of the water. Gomer called Tom to one side. "He also dropped these off." he opened a locked cabinet to reveal an assortment of weapons. Tom couldn't believe his eyes. Where did Rocky come up with all these in two days? Surely not legally. "I'm not finished yet, there's more. I didn't have enough space in that cabinet."

Ever inquisitive, Felix walked up behind Tom. These weapons were not hand guns. There was every weapon here Tom had ever handled and some he hadn't.

"This gets more interestin' by the minute, amigo. I wonder what armory he broke into? Just jokin' heh, heh, heh."

Tom turned and looked at his partner and could tell by the expression on his face he wasn't joking at all. There were .45-caliber risers, a submachine usually fired from the hip because of its tendency to rise as fired, two ten-gauge shotguns with double-ought shells by the box, a bazooka with ten rounds of rockets, an English Bren gun, and of course the cannon with five napalm shells in canisters alongside, a particularly malevolent form of shell. All in all, weapons and ammunition not to be used by amateurs. "I've seen enough. Keep everything under lock and key until you're finished with the installations then call my home phone then instead of you delivering, three members of my team will come here to assume control, take responsibility for loading the weapons, and that should be the last you see of us unless you call for assistance at a later date. Gomer nodded his agreement and relocked the weaponry. "I need to use your phone before we leave, local."

Stella answered the phone on the second ring as though she had been expecting the call. "Oh, honey, I'm so glad it's you. The contractor is here for house repairs and needs your go-ahead before he'll continue. Can you hold on while I get him?" Tom waited. When he was connected he listened while the man told him the problems and what they would cost. "I'll be home in less than two hours, go ahead and I'll pay you when I get there. Put my wife back on, please."

"Yes Tom what is it?"

"He seems satisfied for the moment. Who is there with you besides Gennie?"

"Just Leo and Paddy. I haven't seen Rocky or his van at all if that's what you're getting at."

"No, he's done what was asked of him, if and when he shows up there and I'm not there yet tell Paddy to stall him until I do return. I'll be there in less than two hours. Love you, bye."

"C'mon' partner, one more stop and then home. The post office. Since your hot rod could probably out run my pickup you better continue to follow me. Wait until Gennie gets a look at it. She'll probably be after me to have a garage built on the property to house it out of the weather."

"She more than likely will be after me ta' teach her how ta' drive soon as she sees it ya' know. It's not like before we were married when she did like I told her, now she tells me. I tell ya' amigo bein' hitched has its drawbacks."

"Maybe so, but you have a woman that loves you and from what I have witnessed will be a loyal, courageous soul mate for life. Maybe you should think about starting a family, unless you're shooting blanks." Felix stopped dead in his tracks. Tom turned to look at him and saw that expression he always had when he was trying to come up with a suitable answer. "What's the matter, partner, did I hit too close to the truth?"

"Sometimes I jus' don't know 'bout ya' amigo; ya' seem ta' want ta' plan my life for me. Has the ownership of the emerald made ya' into a mother hen? Let's change the subject before I say somethin' I'll regret."

Tom went into the Post Office which doubled as a Western Union depot and sent a wire to Pricer congratulating him on a job more than well done. That document when delivered would be suitable for framing. "I'm done here partner so let's go home unless you have something else to do."

"Naw, home sounds good ta' me , I'm gettin' hungry." When they pulled into the parking area of the estate only Paddy's truck was there, but no Rocky.

Stella was in the kitchen talking to the big man as if she had known him from childhood. That attested to her usual bubbling personality. When she sensed Tom behind her she was up and in his arms without hesitation mindless of who was witness to her passion. "Where's Gennie? Felix has something to show her." His wife shook her head. "We haven't seen much of her since this morning and it's not like her to keep to herself when Felix is gone. Felix, you'd better go and see if she's all right."

Felix was gone an exceptionally long time and when he returned alone, Stella asked where Gennie was. "She isn't feelin' so good but she's not sure what the matter is."

"The food is on the stove; help yourself. I'm going to check on her. When Stella returned she was all smiles. "For your information, Felix, your wife is going to have a baby." Felix dropped his fork midway to his mouth. "Gesu Christo, it's catchin'" and he actually blanched. "All of a sudden I've lost my hunger. He looked at Tom. "Did ya' know 'bout this or are ya' a seer?" He got up from the table to rush for the front door. Stella calmly took his half full plate and put it near Leo's eating area. "You might as well finish this' Leo. Your Uncle Felix has suddenly lost his appetite." Leo didn't understand what it was all about, but food was food. He gobbled it up then sprawled out near his main friends waiting for further handouts.

Tom had noticed scaffolding erected alongside the building when he and Felix pulled into the parking area but with all the other commotion had let it slip his mind. "How's the workman coming along, Stell?"

"He was working on the roof tiles earlier honey, I imagine he still is."

"I'm going to take the dog out for a walk so I'll check.,All right ,Leo, let's go outside." The mastiff beat Tom to the door. Tom found the handyman at the side of the house chipping the edges off tiles to specific sizes to fit pre-measured roof tiles. He was a burly man wearing coveralls and a T-shirt which showed well muscled arms. Tom interrupted his work by saying he saw no reason to piecemeal his wages on a daily basis. "I'll give you two hundred tonight then the balance for the week each Friday night. I expect detailed lists of materials at that time. Is that acceptable?"

"Fair enough, Mr. Mueller. I hope you don't mind my driving my truck close to the house. Your lawn is already well torn up, and that way I don't waste time carrying materials back and forth from your parking area."

"That's perfectly all right, anything to speed up the job. Things will be getting hectic around here within the next five days or so and I'm going to have you sign a paper swearing you will not divulge anything you see or hear which might endanger our operation in any way. Nationals security, you understand." The workman had that dumbstruck look on his face that Felix often had when lost for an immediate reply. About then, Leo came wandering around the side of the house looking for his main friend. The handyman saw him first and grabbed for something to defend himself from the wild beast. The dog didn't let the strangers action faze him the slightest, just sitting by Tom's side. "What is that thing?"

"Don't insult him; he understands key words by the tone of your voice. Leo is a very valuable part of my team plus being my friend. He is a guard dog supreme. No one in their right mind would dare encroach on my property or team members. They would end up missing some body parts if they survived at all. He is devoted to my wife and watches over her whenever I'm not here." Tom hoped he hadn't scared the workman off before completing the repairs but it had been necessary for him to understand what Leo was capable of. He finished his explanation by toning it down somewhat. "Now that he knows you'll be working around the property you will automatically fall under his umbrella of protection. Come on, Leo, let's go back inside and let the nice man get on with his work." Leo first looked up at his main friend but instead of following Tom inside approached the workman and sat a foot in front of him. "Put a hand in front of his nose and let him pick up your scent. He'll file that away in his mind so you'll be covered by the same protection while you're on the property." As Tom turned to go inside, Leo in trail, Rocky's van pulled into the parking area. Tom waited by the front door for him to come into the house. The vans door swung open, yet Rocky didn't get out. Tom was puzzled but it was explained soon enough. The big man almost fell out. Tom ran toward the van yelling for help. The workman heard Tom shout and putting two and two together followed behind him. Rocky was definitely injured,. He had one foot on the ground but was still holding on to the steering wheel, blood running down the other arm. "What happened, Rocky?" "Help me into the house, Mr. Mueller, so I can lie down. I'll try to explain everything then." Mr. Ajax, whose first name Tom never knew, but turned out to be Cliff, took one side of Rocky's body effortlessly while Tom carefully supported the injured side and they almost carried him to the front door. Inside they placed him on one of the longer sofas that could contain his tall frame. Felix heard the commotion and wandered in, took one look at Rocky and said, "Ya' don't look so good, Rock."

"Felix go knock on Stella's door. She's good at first aid, and maybe she can figure out if we have to call an ambulance or not. I would like to hear how he got the weapons and if he was hurt doing it." When Stella looked at Rocky she just shook her head. "Felix will you get that first aid kit out of the kitchen and put a pot of water to boil on the stove while you're there? I hate to use you as a go-fer but you know your way around that room as well as anyone. If you've regained your appetite there is still meatloaf left to warm up."

About then Cliff excused himself. "You don't need me here any longer Mr. Mueller I'm just in the way, so there are a few things I can still do outside before it's too dark to see, but I'll be here bright and early in the morning to continue. I hope your friend is better by then."

Felix brought the kit before returning for the hot water. Stella took out sterile wipes and began applying them to some of the wounds. She cut away some of his clothing to get a closer look at some of the bleeders. "This in his thigh is definitely a gunshot wound. I can't tell whether the projectile is still in there or not. From the angle of the entry only an X-ray will show whether or not it struck the bone. This shoulder wound is the same."

"Can you bring him to long enough for me to find out what happened?"

"Sure, honey, but you better call an ambulance in the meantime. He needs better care than I can provide."

She snapped a vial of smelling salts under his nose and Rocky's eyes opened as his head turned to escape the fumes.

"Stell, just dial the operator and ask for the closest ambulance service to come to this address. Don't tell her gunshot wounds are involved or we'll have an assortment of police here most of the night. I'll question him while you're doing that."

When the ambulance arrived and they were assured he was a government employee and the ensuing bills and best of care would be paid by the Federal Government, Rocky was taken away. Tom was satisfied with Rocky's explanations of the events of his being wounded. He had gone to Fort Stewart just outside of Savannah, Georgia. There is where he found the cannon, ammo, and assortment of small arms using a government voucher for them. After delivering the arms to Gomer's shipyard, the trouble began. The illicit arms dealers had a network, which from Fort Stewart extended southward to the Key West Naval Air Station. They knew the man who purchased the assorted inventory drove a dark van with Florida plates so they assumed he was heading back to that state but lost him somewhere near Boca Raton or Deerfield Beach, where Rocky made an inland detour to avoid heavy flooding from Hurricane Betsy he had seen on the way North. So Rocky had delivered the weapons to Gomer's shipyard and was returning to Key Largo when they intercepted him again. Not knowing the weapons had been delivered, the hijackers tried to force him off the road. When Rocky eluded that maneuver they fired at the van. Rocky was hit twice but had enough savvy of the area to outwit the highwaymen and make it back to the Mueller estate.

Tom had to call Mr. McHenry to bring him up to date on Rocky's injuries and to let him know they would be a man short and what his plan was to thwart the smugglers with his own high-powered cigarette boat. "It didn't cost the agency anything, I traded for Fred's yacht so it came out even. Felix, Paddy, and I should be able to handle this job."

"Just make certain Paddy doesn't get hurt or I'll never be able to ask the NYPD for another favor."

"Oh, Felix and I are expendable huh?"

"That doesn't sound like you at all, Tom. Has marriage softened your zeal for the position? Are you ready for a desk job at headquarters? Just get it done and keep me informed." Click, and he was gone.

Tom was up and out of bed earlier than he needed to be. He supposed it was the dreams that reoccurred whenever he was overly stressed with a subconscious goal. He wondered if Fred had felt anything similar. Tom was thinking about his brother more and more lately; it had a lot to do with living here in Fred's house, he realized. Everything he touched Fred had handled at one time so that might add to the feeling of closeness. He went to the kitchen for coffee and to ponder further on his thoughts of Fred.

Tom was successful on his trip to the Army-Navy surplus store. He bought a 10,000-candle-power spotlight with a loud-hailer that ran off the same battery pack. That moved the schedule ahead, they could pick up the boat later in the day so their test runs could begin in earnest that night.

31

They were out in front of the estate waiting for any smuggler to come near in their powerboats. So far all was quiet but they knew that wouldn't last long. It didn't. Two powerboats running abreast like they were racing each other were cutting an an angle across the bow. "Looks like we're in business, amigo. I'll turn the spotlight on 'em while you use the loudhailer. This oughta' be fun. Too bad Paddy isn't here; he'd getta' kick outta' this."

"I got strict orders from Mr. McHenry not to put him in harms way, so he won't be joining us out here. Load a round in the cannon, partner; I have a feeling these cowboys aren't going to be bluffed by a voice out of the dark. That won't even slow them down like a shot across their bow, and if my aim is off and hits one of them so be it."

"Yer' gettin' kind a' ruthless aren't ya' amigo?"

"Well, they aren't out here this time of night on a pleasure jaunt, partner, so whatever they get they deserve." Tom's aim wasn't off. The round struck the nearest powerboat in the bow slicing it off so that the craft was out of commission. "Get your shotgun ready, partner. I'm pulling along side. If anyone makes the slightest hostile move, don't hesitate to use it." The snick of a round entering the breech showed that Felix meant business too.

There were two men in the powerboat, speechless in shock. One came to his senses in time to swing a nasty looking submachine gun toward them, but his head blew apart from Felix's double-ought slug. "Whatta' we gonna' do with his partner, amigo?"

"We don't take prisoners, Felix. I'll notify the Coast Guard there is a drug smuggler in a disabled powerboat floundering in this area then it will be up to them what happens to the man. Now I'm more interested in finding and disabling the other boat before they reach their destination."

"How ya' gonna' do that?"

"They most likely will come back nosing around here to help their comrades, so we'll just back off a bit and wait. If they don't return, we'll take a tack heading in the direction they were. Keep your ears attuned for their engines sounds Load a round of napalm in the cannon."

"Ya' sure this ia the way ta' go, amigo; sounds like overkill ta' me."

"Let me explain something to you, Felix. Do you remember how you felt when you had the run-in with the hammerhead shark trying to make the landing in Colombia? At that time there was just you and the shark, winner take all, right? Well, this situation is the same thing, us versus them, winner take all. This is just one example and believe me there will be others before we stop the smugglers, or they find a different method. Speaking of systems, do you hear what I hear?"

"Sounds ta' me like they're back. Ya' want me ta' use the loud-hailer or spotlight?"

"Go ahead if it makes you feel better, but remember what I just told you." When the spotlight was turned on and before Felix could say one word they were greeted by a hail of gunfire. Tom could hear several rounds striking his powerboat and he fired the napalm shell in retaliation without thought. Felix yelped, so Tom knew he had been hit. The shell he let loose must have struck a gas tank because when he looked up from administering to Felix there was a secondary detonation that left little doubt as to the fate of those aboard either of the smuggler's crafts. Tom didn't hesitate; he headed his boat directly for home. Cliff Ajax could help him check the boat for damages in daylight which would dictate whether it would have to be returned to Gomer's or not. "How bad is your wound, partner?"

"It's a good thing I'm right handed 'cuz I won't be usin' the left for awhile. Why do these things always happen ta' me? It's like a black cloud is hangin' over my head ya' know?"

"If this keeps up the attrition is going to put us out of business. Whether Mr. McHenry likes it or not, it looks like Paddy is going to be pressed into service while you recuperate. That should make him happy, I know he feels left out of the action. I just hope the loss of two powerboats doesn't alter their mode of operation. Hopefully, they'll just add some armament or run in more than two boats similar to the method used by the Nazis with their U-boats during WWII."

"Ya' know yer' history too. Seems like yer' college gave ya' a rounded education. Now if ya' would quit usin' all those big words so I could unnerstan' what all yer' talkin' 'bout..."

"Hang that arm over the side, you're bleeding all over the seat."

"Sure, an' have a shark take it off an' me with it. That's the thanks I get for bringin' Stella inta' yer' life."

"I'd better stoke up the burners and get you back to the estate pronto. Your loss of blood is causing delirium."

"See what I mean about the big words?" And then Felix passed out cold.

When Tom pulled into the slip and tied up to a stake, he lifted Felix and headed to the front door. He doubted if his partner weighed much more than a hundred pounds, despite all the food he consumed and beer he drank, so getting him into the house was no problem. "Stell, where are you? I need some help here." Stella came in to the living area from the opposite direction than their bedroom. "What has happened, honey? I've been nursing Gennie, she's not handling her pregnancy too well. She took one look at Felix and turned back to the kitchen for the first aid kit. "He took a bullet in the hand from one of the smugglers while trying to give them a chance to surrender. You know how bullheaded he can be; you'd think he was German."

Tom made his calls, then went looking for Leo. "Where are you big guy? We have to check things outside, are you with me or not?" The mastiff appeared from the kitchen where he had been napping and stood by the door waiting. Tom knew the dog needed watering so he opened the door and Leo was out like a flash. Tom followed and waited for him to take care of his business before looking at the boat. There were several bullet holes along the side but none he could detect below the water line. It would probably have to be hoisted out of the water for a closer inspection, a job for Gomer's shipyard. Just then Paddy came wandering out of the house. "You're just who I was about to come looking for."

"I happened to see your wife bandaging Felix in the living area where she told me he had been shot but didn't have any details of how or who so I thought I'd better see you."

"I'm glad you did, Paddy, because you are about to find out first-hand what Felix and I have been doing. Since Felix will be sidelined until his hand heals there is just you and I to continue to go after the smugglers in their powerboats. There is only Cliff Ajax left, and I can't very well enlist his aid out at sea. He can be a great help here on the property since he got over his fear of Leo but that has to be the extent of it.."

"I'm willing, Tom; just show me what I have to do." Tom explained a few things ending with, "The main thing to remember is not to give them a chance to take a crack at us; we're not the wrongdoers. That's how Felix got hurt, by giving them the fair chance they didn't deserve."

Cliff pulled into the yard while Tom and Paddy were looking at the boat and joined them. "Problems?"

Tom explained the bullet holes. Cliff stood looking at the boat for a few moments. "If you want to check below the waterline let me pull my truck down here. I'll fix a sling on my hoist, wrap it around the center, and I can elevate it enough for you to look there."

"Sounds reasonable to me, so while you're moving your truck I'll get some waders on. I want to be certain no holes are underneath so when Paddy and I are out at sea we don't have to be worrying that water will be entering the hull while we are stationary. Patience plays a big part in our work. We're not running from pillar to post searching for narcotics runners lest we burn up fuel too fast. Our strategy is to lie in wait letting them motor near us using our guile to outwit them. My call to the Coast Guard earlier proved worthwhile. The sea will be calm tonight, weather that is favorable for their powerboats."

Tom and Paddy were sitting quietly, each with their own thoughts, when they both heard the approaching vessels. From the sounds of them there had to be three or even more. Since a shell was already in the breech all Tom needed was a target. Those boats were making a God-awful racket as they neared. "Hit the spotlight just long enough for me to aim and fire then switch it off and load another shell. We'll try to get as many as possible until it looks like we're overpowered then we'll skedaddle for home while we're still in on piece and can strike again another night." They bagged two, reminding Tom of pheasant hunting with his father in his youth. Racing back to the estate Tom's thoughts returned to his early years just before he joined the Corps. He owed his proficiency with weaponry to his father for giving him the proper instructions for the handling of small arms, from shotgun to rifle, which put Tom in such good stead as he grew older. He hoped his father was looking down and was proud of his son's marksmanship and the way he was using it. Not being particularly religious, although raised as a churchgoing Episcopalian, Tom felt fulfilled at the moment. He wasn't proud of some of the stunts he had pulled, especially with women, but first Sheila and now Stella had straightened him out and showed him where the path of true love led.

The first thing Tom did when he reentered the house was to call the Coast Guard and give them the bearings of the two boats they had crippled, answered the questions they asked, and accepted their praise for another job well done. After a cup of coffee he went into the bedroom, quietly undressed and slipped into bed, being careful not to disturb his wife. She seemed to be sleeping soundly. He was just about to sleep when Stella rolled over assuming her normal spoonlike sleeping position which brought him fully awake. "I'm sorry for being so bitchy yesterday, honey; it was simply that I felt overburdened with everyone else's problems, and I took an unfair swipe at you. I'll try not to let that happen again. It's just that I worry so much about you being hurt or worse; now, roll over here and make love to me." Tom couldn't refuse that offer and didn't.

Tom hadn't forgotten his promise to buy Stella a car and provide her with driving lessons, if not by him then a sanctioned, reputable agency, so he called around finally finding one that picked their pupils up and returned them after the lessons. The next step was to shop around for a decent car for her. Maybe he could contact Mr. Goldberg again; he might have some connections in that area too, and Tom had never received a bill from him or Lance Nolte. He shuffled through his notes looking for the attorney's unlisted phone number. He really ought to rearrange this mess of notes putting them in some kind of order where he wouldn't waste time every time he needed information. He could only keep so many numbers in his memory but it was not another thing he could put on Stella's shoulders. Time was of the essence; there never seemed to be enough of it. Tom found the number and when Mr. Goldberg answered he seemed delighted to hear from Tom again, and, yes, he did have a good friend who sold fine used cars. A trustworthy man who stood by his word, backed by a guarantee to repair or replace any vehicle he sold if the customer was dissatisfied. Tom thanked the attorney adding, "You're a great help, Mr. Goldberg; you have never given me bad advice yet and I'm more than grateful for your assistance. If there's anything ever anything I can do for you don't hesitate to call on me." With that information in hand, Tom thought he could combine his search for a car with shopping for additional provisions to restock their pantry even though there were fewer people to feed at the moment, with Rocky still in the hospital and Gennie not being able to hold solid foods down because of her nausea. But Leo needed more of his regular dog food so he asked Stella to compile a list of her needs and left the estate to see how much he could accomplish before the next nights foray with Paddy. Tom headed directly for the car dealer rather than the supermarket to avoid having any perishables lying in the bed of the pickup in this heat. The dealer, Mr. Scott, was in his building alone tinkering with an old Studebaker when Tom arrived. He was a low-key salesman unlike some others he had dealt with. Mr. Goldberg had already called to inform him Tom would be coming so introductions were unnecessary. "See anything you like, Mr. Mueller? I have more in the back room if nothing catches your fancy in here. Feel free to look around until you spot something."

"A later model Chevy sedan, automatic shift would be the ticket; it's for my wife who will be taking driving lessons shortly. She is also pregnant with our first child so that kind of car would be more sedate for her. But she is quick-study and will master driving readily."

"Please follow me, sir; I think I have something in the other room." There sat a '62 Chevy station wagon on blocks, its tires off the floor. It seemed to Tom he had been saddled with station wagons for the most part of his driving life. Since he had Leo it was a blessing giving the dog room , as he grew ever larger, an area to lie down full length and play with his toys which kept him occupied while Tom was out of the vehicle.

"I bought this from a recently widowed woman whose husband was killed in the hurricane. She didn't drive, so the wagon was useless to her. If you'll check the odometer you will note there are less than two thousand miles logged. The owner's manual and guarantee are in the glove compartment intact, so this would really be a steal for the buyer."

"That may be so, but I'm not sure I could afford it."

Mr. Scott said, "You haven't heard my asking price to you yet, Mr. Mueller, a price that is only good for you since you are with the agency that is getting rid of these drug smugglers that are trying to bring cocaine and marijuana into our country to hook our young people and ruin their lives. Could you afford five hundred dollars?" Tom couldn't believe he heard right. "Did you say five hundred?"

"That's correct, and I'll have it delivered to your home on Key Largo with a big red ribbon on it. How does that sound?"

"I don't know how to thank you Mr. Scott; that's the most generous offer I've ever had. How can I ever repay you?"

"Just keep up the good work, that's all the thanks I could ever hope for."

Tom shook hands with the man and walked out to his pickup with a light headedness unbecoming to him and drove on to the Piggly Wiggly to buy the foodstuffs Stella wanted.

When Mr. Scott departed, Tom told Cliff he had more work for him. "We need about a five-bay garage built over there", he pointed," with an apartment upstairs. Hire as many men as you need to complete it in one month. There will be a bonus for you if it's done in that time frame. Agreed?"

"You keep these improvements up, Mr. Mueller, and I'll form my own construction company instead of just being a lone-wolf handyman."

"I might invest some money into a venture like that, I so believe in your aptitude. Now if you'll excuse me I have to present my wife with her newest gift. Think hard on my proposal, I have all the confidence in the world in you."

Tom went back into the house with another load of edibles from the bed of the pickup to find Stella about ready to come looking for him. She had put everything away he had brought in so far and despite his warning not to lift anything heavy she figured there would still be some lighter packages she could transport.

"Here, this is it except for the fifty pound bag of dog food. So put this on the counter and come outside with me. I want to show you something. Close your eyes, no fair peeking." Tom led her toward the station wagon his arm around her shoulders until they were about ten feet away. "Now you can open your eyes."

"Oh, honey, it's beautiful" she gasped "But how can we afford it with all the expenses you have in paying for the work Mr. Ajax is doing?"

"Sweetheart, you don't ask how a gift can be afforded; it's just not proper. It's like asking how much a gift costs, besides you wouldn't believe me if I told you. I've already arranged for a reputable agency to give you lessons. They will pick you up here and bring you back. Now you can use their car or yours, your choice. Your wagon is only two years old and has less than two thousand miles on the odometer and it's fully insured."

"Oh, honey don't get me wrong, I love it and the thought behind it – how much I'll show you tonight if you and Paddy don't go out but in the interim how about letting me show you what I've learned just watching you. Just fifteen or thirty minutes. Then maybe you won't have to waste more money on driving lessons." Tom pulled the ribbon off the roof of the wagon stuffing it in the bed of the pickup, handed Stella the keys, and got in the passenger side of the front seat. "You're on your own now, sweetheart. Where do you want to go?"

"How about if we just traverse the Key? You tell me when to turn right or left, stop or slow down, and pick the route."

Stella drove with the deftness of a much more experienced driver. She never hesitated when following Tom's commands and directions, using her turn signals where appropriate. When they were close to the Atlantic side of the Key Tom looked out at a turbulent sea with high waves that would cancel tonight's foray.

32

Six months passed where the powerboat had mixed results, mostly depending on the fickle weather conditions of the Atlantic. Maybe two of five nights were suitable for interception and destruction of the smugglers runs, but the agency was pleased just the same and was even considering adding a fleet to operate in the Gulf putting Tom Mueller in charge of training the new units based out of Fort Myers and Pensacola, Florida, and Galveston, Texas, with a suitable raise in pay and higher expense checks to cover his additional costs for lodging and meals

Paddy O'Toole had been returned to his precinct in New York City and a fully recovered Felix took over his position with Tom, much wiser than before he was hurt. Rocky was released from the hospital and was convalescing in the apartment over the newly constructed garage that Cliff Ajax had completed on time to collect his bonus. Stella received her driver's license without formal training and she had consulted a female pediatrician with an office adjacent to her home. She had advised Stella to curtail any sexual activity for the duration of her pregnancy, as it appeared she was to have multiple births. Tom discussed his new position with Stella when he was notified by Washington. It meant being away from the estate at least one week every month and possibly more depending on the amount of boats and personnel available at each location. He told her he would keep in constant phone contact with her, not only so she would know he was all right but so he could keep track of her physical condition. Felix and Rocky would be there if any critical change developed. If so Tom would drop everything and hotfoot it for home.

Suddenly money spent by the agency flowed like wine. There didn't seem to be anything they couldn't afford. Tom had thousands of dollars at his disposal, no Government vouchers or checks, but greenbacks. He had never known the agency to be so loose; yet again, he thought they might have learned their lesson of being such tight-wads. Whenever he called in to notify them where he staying for a night or two there came a courier with cash in bundles. It got so he bought a money belt to wear under his clothes, which made it rather awkward what with his sidearm and extra rounds. It looked like he had put on weight.

Tom called Stella to check up on the Mueller household. "Honey. I'm so glad you called. Wait until you see what was shipped to Felix late yesterday afternoon from New York. When will you be home?"

"That's a good question, Stell. I wish I could give you an answer but it depends on a multitude of circumstances. Right now I'm calling from Galveston, Texas. Don't keep me in suspense, Stell. What did Felix get?" The operator interrupted, asking for more money. After satisfying Ma Bell, he continued, "You there, Stell?"

"I hear you, honey."

"So what did Felix get?"

"The shipping crate contained a dog from Paddy O'Toole along with pedigree papers and feeding instructions. The dog, puppy actually, is so ugly he's adorable. A mix of Irish Wolfhound and mastiff. Felix seemed delighted. He's out right now buying food and toys for Brutus."

"How is Leo taking the addition of another dog in the household?"

"He just sniffed the rascal then laid down while Brutus climbed all over him in a playful puppy manner. Leo acted like he was bored with the whole scene letting the pup have his own way. It's funny to watch the two together and believe me honey it takes a load off of me. I don't have to entertain Leo now."

It's like Paddy knew Leo impregnated his female Wolfhound but I don't remember it ever being mentioned around him. Even when we were exchanging drug information in that restaurant it was never brought up so how did he get wind of it?"

"I don't have a clue, honey, but you be careful out there and get home a.s.a.p."

When Tom got through to Mr. McHenry and vented his spleen about having all this cash on hand he was told there was a good reason for it but he wasn't let in on what the reason was. "You're being paid well enough to handle it, Tom. It's not like you to question the home office, so don't." Click, and he was gone. Just another wasted call, Tom thought; why did he even bother?

He walked down to the wharf where his two newest cigarette boats were housed. The new trainees were to arrive at nine o'clock for briefing . There were to be four. One, with qualifications similar to Tom's own bore watching. Jim Gross was a recent Southern Methodist University graduate, a German who had been an ROTC lieutenant who was a crack shot on the rifle range. He just finished grad school in physics. A side note: He was an accomplished tenor saxophone artist who put himself through the university by playing gigs. All these attributes and he still wanted a position in the agency. Tom was intrigued as to why although he understood the Government was beginning to draft people for the escalating war in Vietnam. Could that be what his motive was, to avoid the conscription? If so he would be jumping out of the frying pan into the fire. It would just remain to be seen.

Both of the powerboats were matte black as he had specified, at least the agency was getting something right. Tom sort of wished he had Felix here with him. It was going to be rather difficult to train these new men alone. He could only use one boat at a time. There was no point in trying to teach them anything now except how to handle the craft. Besides there was no armament yet so even if he wanted to pursue smugglers tonight they'd be toothless. It was almost dusk when he ceased instructing the four men in relays of two staying mostly in Galveston Bay. There seemed to be two who caught on in minutes while behind the wheel controlling the boat. Jim Gross and Fletch Beaumont were no problem at all thus far. The other two seemed skittish when in control and would need either more extensive training or replacement. Some people were simply not suited to handle boats of any kind. It was not that they were stupid; it was beyond their touch. The two in question, Whalen and George, would most likely flourish in some other capacity within the agency. That was the main problem in being the sole instructor in such a widespread area. He couldn't spend enough time with the slow-learners to satisfy himself that he wasn't sacrificing men and equipment needlessly. Tom thought about this over his dinner at a different restaurant from the one he had breakfasted in. This establishment was on the mainland where he could enjoy a few Buds with his meal. A person's temperament also played a major role in his performance. Finished with his steak, he sat back trying to relax and allow his normal thoughts to replay his actions and decisions of the day. He came to the conclusion, new puppy or not, he needed Felix here. There wasn't any other way he could accomplish his goals. His little partner could share the load and contribute with his practical experience and know how of the boats, and contribute to their commitments of personnel and equipment.

Again that night, as soon as he had showered, Tom went to bed and was out cold within two minutes. Now since he had made his decisions, his mind was at ease. First thing in the morning he'd call the estate to check on Stella then notify Felix to join him. His partner would simply have to forget about his puppy and handle business first which is where his paychecks came from.

It was eight before Tom awoke, totally refreshed. After dressing hurriedly he headed for a phone to call the estate to inform Felix of his decision. The phone rang and rang with no answer, making Tom think he had mistakenly dialed the wrong number so he hung up and tried again. Same results. Now he was worried. Fire, another hurricane, an explosion, what? Who could he call to check the house? He decided on the State Police, asking the operator to connect him to the nearest post to Key Largo, Florida. After a few moments a dispatcher picked up asking if this was an emergency. Tom identified himself and explained the situation and where he was calling from. "Have there been any reports on a disaster on Key West last night?" The trooper checked his log and replied in the negative. "I will send a car to check your property if you'll give me your exact address, Mr. Mueller. That's the only suggestion I have." Tom gave him the house number and directions of how to get there then gave the number from where he was calling. "I'll stay near this phone until you call me back. You can reverse the charges if your budget doesn't allocate funds to cover such long distance calls." After hanging up Tom was in a quandary of how to pass the time while waiting for a return call. He didn't have much change with him if it would be necessary to pay for a return call. He hoped the operator would charge the call to his home phone. His mind was jumping from one scenario to another as he stood next to the booth. Looking at his watch only made him more nervous. Instead of the time passing quickly as it had yesterday now it seemed to be dragging. He was leaning against his pickup trying not to check the time when the phone rang. He almost jumped out of his skin at the noise but picked up on the third ring.

"Hello" Now he looked at the time. Forty-five minutes had elapsed.

"This is the Florida State Police, Mr. Mueller. A car checked your property which had no signs of damage. No one responded to our knocking but there was a note taped to the front door. It seems the occupants had taken your pregnant wife to the nearest hospital with stomach pains. It seems like you are about to become a father, Mr. Mueller. Mr. Mueller, are you there?" But Tom wasn't. He was already driving to the closest airfield to charter a plane if no regular flight to Florida was available. Tom drove to the Coast Guard Station instead (it was closer) and explained his predicament to the station commander. The lieutenant commander, an older married man himself, with five children commiserated with the CIA supervisor and unfolded a plan to get him to Florida. He had already been informed of the presence of the powerboats that the man commanded and was all for any assistance he could get in that regard. He got on the phone, made several calls, and within minutes a helicopter was warming up on the launching pad. It would take Tom to Baton Rouge, Louisiana, where a connecting flight to Miami, Florida, could be had. The way, he explained to Tom, he would be in Miami in the late afternoon. Tom hadn't been on a helicopter since Korea when he was wounded, and then it had been on a stretcher on the outside of the plane. The urgency of his problem would just overshadow his fear of flying. Tom thanked the Coastguardsman and ran out to the launching pad, his only thoughts those of being at Stella's side when she delivered their children. Tom was mulling over children's names as the whirlybird lifted into the sky. The names would depend on the sex of the twins. Please God, he said a silent prayer to himself, not to protect him during the flight but to have one of the children born to be a boy so as to carry on the Mueller name – and of course to be christened Fred for his deceased twin.

By the time Tom got to the hospital it was late afternoon and the first thing he saw was a nervous Felix pacing the floor of the maternity ward like his wife was expecting instead of Tom's.

"How did ya' get here so fast, amigo?"

"It's a long story, partner, which I'll explain after I see how Stella is doing."

"That lady doctor of hers came out once a couple hours ago wonderin' where ya' were but I haven't seen her since."

"I'm going to the desk for information. Somebody there must know something."

134

"I just came on duty, sir, and I'm not familiar with all of the patients yet. Let me call the floor supervisor." An older woman appeared at the desk. Tom told her he was looking for his wife Mrs. Mueller who had come in to have a baby.

"Oh yes, Mr. Mueller, let me get you a cap and gown then I'll take you to your lovely wife.

Stella was lying on her back with her knees up in the air covered waist down by a sheet. She looked like she had just jumped into bed without toweling off after a shower. Her beautiful hair was plastered about her head wetly in a haphazardly manner and she was breathing hard like she had just finished running a four-minute mile. But when she saw Tom her beautiful smile lit up her face while she extended an arm toward him to hold his hand. Her grip was as strong as ever demanding that he continued to hold on to give her needed support. Though she hadn't said a word Tom could tell she was in pain so he bent down and kissed he forehead.

"I'll stay here as long as you need me, sweetheart, you can count on that."

"All right Stella now push. Your first baby is about to emerge", said her obstetrician, who up to then had been unnoticed being completely covered by the sheet at the foot of the bed between Stella's upthrust knees. Stella's grip on his hand tightened as she followed her orders. More sweat trickled down her face from the exertion. If Tom had known there was this much pain involved in the delivery he'd have used prophylactics during their sexual activities. As he stood there helplessly he could only hope that Stella's ordeal would soon be over.

First to be born was a boy followed by the messy placenta. "Keep pushing, Stella; you're doing fine. Here comes the next, it's a girl so you can relax now, it's all over." But Stella didn't relax; it was if she knew something the doctor didn't. Not a minute later, a third head appeared as if by magic struggling to get free of its containment. Now the doctor needed help, and the older nurse stepped in to assist. First, the swat on the bottom to clear the breathing passages, then the cleaning and foot printing of the triplet, another boy. Tom couldn't believe it. Sure, Stella's stomach had enlarged somewhat in the last month, but to birth three seemingly healthy, heavy kids was to him beyond remarkable. Now he thanked his maker for the emerald. He hoped its value increased over the years, it would be needed to put three through college. The last son to be born had a head start on a thatch of blonde hair, a compliment to his mother. "How do you feel now, sweetheart?"

"Just a little tired, honey, but after a nap I'll be fine, and ready to nurse my brood.

The doctor and older nurse were busy cleaning up so Tom sat by the bed still holding Stella's hand. He watched her eyes close as she drifted off to sleep matter-of- factly as if this were an everyday occurrence. So many thoughts were running through Tom's head about the preparations needed at the house for the children's welfare that he was getting drowsy. It had been a long and nerve-wrecking day. And how would Leo accept them with the love he felt for his two main friends and having to share it with three babies? It would remain to be seen if he would continue to have the run of the house that he was so used to. Felix's puppy would also have to learn to either stay outside or be confined to their own living quarters. The next thing Tom became aware of was Felix shaking his shoulder to rouse him. The room was crowded with two nurses, Felix and Gennie, and he and Stella. Stella had her arms full of blanketed babies. Her hair had been combed and she was wearing a housecoat Tom had never seen before. Someone had brought flowers and they were in a vase next to the bed which now had clean bedding.

Tom knew he would have to start buying baby furnishings in threes for the house and there would be the possibility Cliff Ajax would be called on for an addition off the side of their bedroom to house the cribs, bassinettes, and other furnishings that would take up so much room that at present there was no room for. After the three grew out of such needs the room could be converted into a day nursery or music room depending on whatever the desires or aptitudes of the children dictated. Stella would also need a studio for the continuation of her drawing and painting, something she had relinquished during her initial duties of running the household and the feeding of everyone in the aftermath of the hurricane. Tom also understood she would need additional help when the kids grew into the "terrible twos," that stage in their growth when they were walking and getting into all kinds of mischief. By then a nanny would be needed, at least days and possibly on a twenty-four hour basis to take up or at least share Stella's burden. Another reason for the addition which might have to be two-story to provide her with living quarters readily accessible to the main floor. Yes, Cliff would have his hands full of improvements at the estate. Tom had made another wise investment when he backed Cliff to form his own company. He had already received dividends from that.

He had to bring his new family home in two days so he had better get cracking.

Tom had just purchased three bassinettes and arranged for diaper rental from a company that picked up and delivered weekly and was heading for the next stop on his list when a beer truck ran a stop sign and blind-sided his pickup. That was the last thing he remembered.

33

Tom Mueller at last came to from the coma he had been in for five weeks remembering nothing of the traffic accident he had been involved in. He finally opened his eyes to a world of hurt. He had sustained numerous injuries in the truck collision including a skull fracture, broken left tibia, badly lacerated left upper arm, and broken left ankle all because of the carelessness of a five-ton beer truck driver who had run through a stop sign while trying to read a route assignment instead of paying attention to the road. He escaped serious injury with only a cut lip and broken nose. The state trooper who investigated the scene cited the beer truck driver who just happened to work for a Budweiser distributor, a beer that Tom normally drank. When the beer truck slammed into the side of Tom's pickup, the force flipped his smaller vehicle twice and all the contents in the bed were strewn across the road, causing a car following the pickup to hit the bassinettes, damaging them slightly. It was that family who went further down the road to call in the accident and report the injuries. It was a coincidence that Tom was admitted to the same hospital he had left earlier in the day. Stella was not informed of his arrival, through some glitch in the record department, and didn't realize it until the next day, when Felix was notified at the estate. He tried to break the bad news to the happy mother of triplets, but somehow it was botched in his explanation. Felix had a tendency to garble his metaphors when either excited or trying to play down a serious situation.

Now it was up to Felix to call Mr. McHenry and notify him he would be taking over the training of crews for the cigarette powerboats for Tom while he was recuperating. "We'll need some new blood down here, ya' know; I can't be everywhere at once, an' Rocky ain't up ta' snuff yet. So I don't care what ya' do, but do sumpin'." Click, and he hung up, not giving McHenry the chance that he was notorious for. That'll teach him, he thought.

In the meantime, it was up to Felix to spend what little money he had put away to buy necessary furniture for Stella's babies, buy needed groceries so Stella could cook for them all, and generally oversee the running of the estate. The two dogs were behaving better than he could ask for. Leo had taken Brutus under his wing, so to speak, both staying outside most of the time. That was a godsend because they weren't underfoot to complicate household operations. What little time Felix was there he tried to share with Gennie and the puppy so they wouldn't feel ignored. It wasn't easy for him to become so domesticated with all these added responsibilities in such a short time, but he was kept so busy he didn't have time or energy to think too much about it. At least his pregnant wife seemed to understand because she spent most of her time helping Stella with her triplets and was only actually with her husband when they shared a meal or slept together. When they were in bed, Felix usually dropped off within two or three minutes so if she did have complaints he didn't hear them. The following mornings he was most often up, dressed, and gone before Gennie awoke. Out of desperation Felix, finally called on Rocky for some assistance; he just couldn't handle it alone any longer.

"What do you expect from me, Felix? It's all I can do to take care of myself in this apartment. I never realized it before but I'm a slow healer. Maybe it's because I'm getting older." Felix couldn't remember ever hearing Rocky talk with such a defeated attitude before; in fact, he couldn't think of a time when the big man strung that many words together at all. He was always referred to as a "Silent Sam." Was it possible that run-in with the hijackers changed his personality that much?

"Ya' wouldn't have ta' exert yer' body ta' any extent Rock; jus' be ready ta' take and make a few phone calls. That would be a big help ta' me.

"The only problem with that, Felix is there isn't a phone from here to the main house."

"That ain't no problem; ya' can either move back over there or we can get Cliff Ajax ta' lay a line from there ta' here. Which would ya' prefer?"

"Who is Cliff Ajax?"

"I guess ya' don't remember, but when ya' pulled in ta' the parking area after those would be hijackers lost ya', Tom and Cliff Ajax carried ya' on inta' the house where Stella tried ta' patch ya' up. When she realized ya' needed regular doctors help, Tom called an ambulance that took ya' to the hospital. I guess ya' were kind of delirious, accordin' ta' the way the story was told ta' me, but I'm getting away from why I'm here. Ya' see this Ajax guy is who built this place yer' livin' in. He started out jus' repairin' hurricane damage, but Tom talked him in ta' formin' his own company which he backed so there ya' are up ta' date. Are ya' gonna' help me or not?"

"I guess I'd better if you're in as much of a bind as you say you are. Maybe I do understand, more than you think."

"Fine, but what option have ya' decided on, ta' stay here or go ta' the main house? I gotta' know that."

"I hate to be any more of a burden than I already am but if a line can be laid from there to here then I'd rather stay up here."

"All right I'll set it up. It'll take a couple days ta' arrange, but expect Cliff ta' be knockin' on yer' door shortly?"

After Felix left, Rocky sat wondering what he had let himself in for. He wanted his privacy but he also knew he couldn't continue to freeload on Mr. Mueller's largess without contributing in some way. He still felt guilty for dumping the burden on Mr. Mueller's shoulders in collusion with Mr. McHenry to take over the operation here. Could it be he was more naive than he had imagined? Had Mr. McHenry gulled his ego to that extent? Whatever his motive could have been, Rocky still owed more to Mr. Mueller than Mr. McHenry.

Two days later, Cliff was knocking on his apartment door over the garage. "Mr. Newbole, you probably don't remember me but I'm Cliff Ajax, the fellow who built this apartment you are living in. How do you like it so far?"

"You did fine work, Cliff. I haven't left it since I returned from the hospital. Come on in, I imagine you're here about laying a phone line from the main house that Felix wants."

Two days later, everything was completed so Rocky and Felix figured out a code they could use for incoming calls. It consisted of simple tappings on the mouthpiece which seemed to satisfy both men. No one else in the household was to answer incoming calls, but they could call out as much as they pleased. That seemed to satisfy the wives, but Stella was becoming more and more unsettled that she was housebound taking care of the babies and couldn't get away to visit Tom in the hospital now that he was awake. They had to talk soon about christening, so she decided to take matters into her own hands. First she called a hospital equipment company that rented what she figured a person with Tom's kind of injuries needed for home care. Then she called her pediatrician, who after all was a doctor, even though for children, and told her what she had in mind for Tom's home care. The doctor agreed to be on a call basis but warned her about taking on a too big a load in her husband's care. "Nonsense, doctor; physically I feel strong as ever, it's my mental state without Tom here to guide me that's bothering me. The longer we're apart, the more depressed I become, so which is worse?"

Tom had been ensconced at the estate for a period of six weeks under Stella's tender loving care healing slowly, but healing. She split her attention effectively between her husband and their offspring all the while discussing items of household activities she knew Tom would be interested in. In the beginning days, while Tom was still slowly recovering it was mostly about the quirks of each of the triplets. They had decided on names. The girl was easy: She would be Sheila Gennie after her deceased aunt. The first born would be Thomas Lance and the youngest son Frederich Felix.

"Soup's on, Felix, " Stella said as she entered the room. "The way Gennie is wolfing down the chow you'd better hurry if you want any. What can I do for you, honey? Back rub, change bandages, or any other way I can please you? Don't get that look in your eye; you're not ready for any of that yet. I should think you'd be somewhat gun shy of that for awhile unless you think you could support a few more children."

"I can dream about it though, can't I? Just watching you make your normal movements as you go about the room is enough to start my juices flowing. Childbirth has made you more desirable than ever sweetheart, if that's possible."

"Thank you, honey; you must be feeling better if you're getting those pre-accident urges. That's progress. I knew home care would be better for you than that cold, impersonal hospital care. Now that we have agreed on names we have to discuss baptismal arrangements. The sacrament can be performed right here since you are immobile. Felix and Gennie can be the witnesses unless you have someone else in mind."

"No, you're doing just fine, Stell."

"The only question then is when. It'll take a couple of days to get a pastor who will agree to come here and bring his own equipment to our house, then with any last minute unexpected problems that arise. How about a week from next Sunday? That'll give us ten days."

As Tom lay in his sick-bed, one compartment of his mind was trying to think of some way to escalate the efforts and to attain better results with less risk to his team. One night the womp, womp of a passing helicopter gave him an idea he couldn't wait to try out on Felix. The thought wasn't as crazy as it sounded at first. It would extend their reach tenfold and reduce team injury at the same time. He needed some manuals from the library to study and when he could get up and around he knew people he could call on for further assistance and instruction. Anything could be accomplished if you put your mind to it, even his fear of flight could be overcome. One or two bad experiences did not mean he would always be blighted in that respect.

The christening went off without a hitch, with the exception of the youngest son Fred, who didn't like water dripping on his forehead and let all the inhabitants of Key Largo hear about it, completely the opposite of his namesake. When the ceremony was concluded and the babies taken away to be fed, Tom asked Felix to remain so he could discuss something with him, an idea he had been mulling over for some time.

"All right, muy amigo, let's have it," never expecting to hear such an idea, knowing Tom's aversion to airplanes. "Now let me unnerstan' ya' here, ya' want ta' learn how ta' fly one of those things. Are ya' losin' it? I can't believe I'm hearin' ya' right, with yer' fright of airplanes?"

"Look, Felix just get me those manuals for the time being then let me worry about what happens afterward. A lot of time will pass before I'm even out of this bed and I'm tired of watching that stupid boob tube with its re-runs and soap operas. Before you leave, where is that list of your expenditures that you made for baby furniture and the like, I'm sure you can use the money so you can cash the check on the same trip you make to the library. How does that sound?"

"I'll get back ta' ya' with a list, maybe not today but soon." His partner left the room grumbling to himself. Tom wondered how many times he would have to remind the little man before his instructions were followed, knowing how Felix could evade things that were against his ideals or too meticulous to delve into. He had many faults, yet Tom couldn't have a better partner when it came down to any rough stuff, which he had proven many times over to numerous to count.

Tom read the list Rocky left for the Canadian exercises wondering how soon he could begin the regimen without causing further damage to his injuries. He hoped it wasn't his imagination but he could feel his body trying to knit itself back to pre-accident form, a sign he might be ready to try the easier movements. Some pain would be necessary for a gain in mobility. He also knew he couldn't let Stella catch him trying any over-exertion. She would have a conniption fit. This he didn't want to cause, what with all her other worries and responsibilities because when she found out what he had in mind concerning the helicopter training, which Tom was sure she would, there would be hell to pay. Tom knew he could only go so far in riling her before she got her back up. She was a strong-willed woman which she had proven by removing him from the hospital for home care.

Three uneventful weeks passed before the proverbial shoe dropped with a resounding thud, the reverberations heard and felt throughout not only Key Largo but the agency as a whole. Seldom had so many detrimental occurrences of earth-shaking magnitude happen in such rapid order. First, Mr. Welsh, the Director of the CIA, died from a sudden heart attack altering the hierarchy of the agency completely. Mr. McHenry became interim Director and Mr. Rowens of the Southern District moved up to McHenry's slot, leaving his position open. Secondly, on a Sunday when Felix was home at the estate, two things happened in rapid succession. A threatening phone call from Pepe Basquez that was taped by Rocky and less than an hour later Gennie went into labor. Felix broke all speed limits getting her to the hospital where a baby girl was stillborn. That broke Gennie's spirit, while Felix didn't know how to comfort or console her. He was more upset when the doctor told him his wife would never conceive a child again without killing herself so they best look into adoption if they felt children were needed to keep their marriage intact. "Does she know 'bout that yet, doc?"

"No, that's something you should break to her, Mr. Santana. Of course I will corroborate your explanation if she needs proof."

"How soon can I take her home?"

"Give it two days so we can run some tests, I want to monitor her heart during that period, and good luck to you, young man. I think you're going to need some in the days ahead."

Felix returned to the estate, his mind dragging along behind the Plymouth, his usual happy-go-lucky demeanor broken like Gennie's spirit. When he broke the news to Stella, Toms wife broke into tears before she controlled herself enough to say, "You must be starved Felix; what can I fix you while we talk?"

"Anythin'; I don' care."

As Felix unfolded what the doctor had told him, the reference he'd made to looking into adoption of a child was disclosed. "He said if Gennie didn't show signs of mental improvement that might be the only way ta' save our marriage." Stella had her back to him while she prepared a large portion of food for him.

"Look at it this way, Felix. Women are very complex creatures, something like a finely tuned engine in your car. We operate on an entirely different cycle from you men and if our balance is upset a quick trip to the repair shop doesn't always fix our maladies whereas your car can be returned to you almost showroom new."

"What are ya' tryin' ta' get at? I'm not sure I'm followin' yer' drift."

"Let me put it this way if I'm being too obtuse."

"Now yer' soundin' like Tom, heh, heh, heh. If you'll jus' say what yer' thinkin' in words I can unnerstan' maybe I can get on the same track with ya'."

"I'll have ta' think some on that Stella. It's just not my decision ta' make. When I bring her home and she calms down some we'll have ta' discuss it."

Tom had read through the five manuals Felix had picked up from the library several times until they had been due for return. Flying a helicopter was more of an exercise in dexterity and balance than a fixed-wing aircraft demanded. The dashboard dials and knobs were similar but the hands and feet were used more to control the up, downs, and other movements it could make that were impossible to duplicate in an airplane. The chopper could hover like a humming bird, something an airplane could not accomplish.

Tom was now able to leave the confines of his sick bed to use the bathroom and sit in chairs. Leo was allowed into the bedroom to spend time with his main friend, time he had been denied while Tom was incapacitated. His casts had been removed and he began to regain the weight he had lost and re-build muscle tone with the aid of the Canadian exercise program. He had worked diligently to return to his former physical fitness, but it was going it was going to take more time to bring him fully back. "I'm starting to feel better, big boy, how about you?"

34

"Look, " Benito said," this is no big deal; yuh take Jose wit' ya'an' jus' plant about four sticks of dynamite close to the front corner of the house. Yuh either light the fuse an' throw it or plant it an' set it off wit' yer' pistol. It's not like when ya' threw the fire bomb at his mother's house in Toledo, no chance a' gettin' hurt this way."

"Where ya' gonna' be?"

"Back where I drop yuh off with the engine runnin' so I can get ya outta' there fast soons I hear the blast

Leo was lying in the yard of the estate working on a large beef bone Stella had given him as a treat when he was alerted to the stealthy approach of two men moving toward the house. Brutus was closer to their route but apparently asleep. The bone forgotten, the mastiff instantly switched into his guard mode, stretched out full length his front feet splayed out to assist him for a quick take-off when he decided which one to attack first. He was picking up a scent that he remembered from when he was younger, a smell he associated with death. The man closest to the house was carrying a package and had stopped for a moment when Leo pounced knocking him off his feet where he could clamp down on his arm while swatting his head with a large paw. The man let out a blood-curdling howl of both pain and fright. That scream alerted Brutus who charged after the man who was running away from the scene, bowling him over before he could reach the parking area then standing on his chest looking down on the terrified man with all his teeth showing as if daring him to move. The continued screaming of Leo's prey brought Rocky out of his apartment over the garage armed with a handgun and flashlight to find out what was happening. One look at Leo was enough to convince him of the seriousness of the matter. "Hold him, Leo, while I round up some reinforcements." A spotlight on the main house snapped on brightening the whole front yard. Felix came charging out of the front door as if shot out of a cannon, skidding to a stop when he saw who Leo had pinioned to the ground. "All right, Leo, let 'im go, I got 'im." He saw Jose wasn't going to use that mangled arm again for quite some time. When Leo released him, Felix used one hand to pull him up and the other on a pressure point on his neck which shut his howling off like he'd used a sap on him.

"Do ya' know what he was doin' here, Rocky?"

"No, I was alerted by his screaming." Leo took off again to where Brutus had another victim grounded. Felix followed the dogs path with his eyes and saw his Brutus standing on another man. "I'll give ya' odds that's Jose, an' if I'm right that means Pepe's 'round someplace. Ya' better go have Stella call the state police while I check on — whoa, what's this?" He moved over, reached down, and picked up the package of dynamite.

"Now we know why they were here. Double quick, now, Rocky, this bozo won't be comin' to for sometime. Even when he does ya' can imagine where he'll head, straight for their getaway car that has ta' be parked near here." Felix went to where the dogs had the other person pinned to the turf, called them both off and looked down at him. "Well, well, Jose, ain't it?" He petted his dog then told Leo to guard before performing the same maneuver on him that put his lights out. When are these guys gonna' learn they're not foolin' with amateurs? he thought. I sure would like to have another crack at that Basquez because the next time I do it'll be for keeps.

Pepe was getting nervous sitting in the car waiting for the explosion that as yet had not happened. What could have gone wrong? he wondered. His two compadres weren't the brightest guys in the world but they had always faithfully followed his directions before. When a state police car passed him with flashing lights but no siren sounding, he knew the plan was somehow aborted and it was time for him to move out. He would re-think a plan for gaining his revenge on Mueller yet.

35

As Tom had predicted, the war in Vietnam had escalated to the point where so many troops were being sent over there, that men from National Guard units who had joined those outfits for a free ride – being paid a princely wage for one weekend a month and two weeks once a year of fun and games called training in the field with their wage counting toward time accrued for not only college credits but also for retirement if they could make rank and re-up for twenty years -- suddenly found themselves shipped overseas to fight a war where the odds were stacked against them. The prospect of being returned to the States in a body bag was causing a mass exodus to Canada to avoid the slaughter. Drugs, from marijuana to hashish and even heroin, were easily available for even the lowliest grunt, which also helped fill those body bags. To top it off, a major portion of the nightly news was dedicated to showing the American public the results of being involved in a war against North Vietnamese, Chinese, and even Russians who were outnumbering them, panicking South Vietnamese and even American Guard units to drop their weapons and flee. The American youth, mostly college students who had deferments, were also into drugs, mostly pot and were protesting the war. Even the fortunate few returning Reserve Officers Training Corps officers were targets of their disdain. Wearing a uniform with ribbons and medals was found to be a no-no, quickly discarded for the anonymity of civilian dress. All this had the forty-and-over people shaking their heads in wonderment. What was this world coming to? LBJ was not going to run for a second term because of the uproar paving the way for 'Tricky Dicky', who ended up disgracing himself.

While all this was going on nationally, Tom Mueller's body had healed to the point where he was again in 100 percent shape from before the accident. His children were growing and had gone through the 'terrible twos' where they were able to walk and climb without falling or otherwise injuring themselves and getting into everything they weren't supposed to, keeping Stella constantly on her toes. Both boys delighted in playing with and riding Leo who watched over them like a mother hen, always mindful that they wouldn't get into serious trouble. There was no sibling rivalry between the two boys, and Sheila somehow knew how to get most things she wanted from her daddy. She was a beautiful child, the mirror image of her mother and namesake aunt. She liked both dogs but preferred to be picked up and held by her father whenever he was available, which wasn't too often anymore. Tom had been promoted to replace Rowens as the Southern District Supervisor a position he really didn't want, but since Mr. McHenry was now the permanent Director he was ordered to accept with the condition he could take Felix along as a personal assistant. His little partner had also mellowed since he and Gennie had adopted a Colombian orphan son. The boy was just short of a year younger than the triplets. They named him Tomas, a derivative of Thomas, his amigo. As the boy aged, he and Sheila were inseparable and played together constantly.

Since the attempt to place dynamite on the estate property to blow up the main house by the cohorts of Pepe Basquez which was foiled by the dogs, both Leo and Brutus were elevated to new highs of esteem by the women who were so often left alone at the main house with the four children while their husbands followed their career paths with the agency. Brutus was now full grown and topped out at over 125 pounds, half the weight of Leo, but since he was three years younger he was more agile than the mastiff, and with a completely different personality. For instance: he wouldn't allow the children to ride him like Leo did, and no one could feed him except Gennie or Tomas which, although a nuisance, was really a blessing in disguise. He would never be poisoned by accepting food from a stranger. Of course, Felix was included as a feeder because Brutus knew him as his main friend. He had another trait similar to that of Leo's: He was a staunch protector of all the children, keeping constant watch on them while they were outside the main house, and Stella and Gennie knew they would come to no harm while the dogs were present. This greatly relieved their states of mind so they could both go about household duties without having to constantly check on their offspring.

Rocky was becoming a regular visitor to the main house, where he usually showed up near mealtimes. It became obvious to Stella that the big man was tiring of his own cooking. Although he was friendly to the women, he ignored the children when they were inside. They sensed his antagonism and left him alone also. Whenever he was talking to one of their mothers, they knew better than to interrupt regardless of their needs of the moment. Being preschoolers, they had been taught proper manners when around grownups. Stella was contemplating whether she should take on the added duties of teacher to the four for home schooling rather than allowing them to be enrolled in an elementary school, where they would be susceptible to all the childhood diseases and have to be bussed to the site. The next time Tom was home they would have to discuss such an important issue. In the meantime, she had been able to concentrate on her sketching, usually far into the night when everyone in the house was asleep.

It was inevitable now that Rocky was again physically sound he would be called back to duty in the agency. Now there would be no men full-time at the estate, no one to count on if a calamity should strike except the state police, but could they get here in time? It was up to her and Gennie to, as Tom would say, hold the fort. So Stella again took the matter into her own hands. She talked to Gennie and explained what she intended to do. "But I've barely held a handgun, Stella; I wouldn't have a clue how to load and fire one without shooting myself in the process."

"If you think you might be frightened with a pistol, how about using a shotgun instead? They have more power but at a shorter distance. Tom told me they have something called a choke that closes up the pattern of shot. You just keep the stock close to your shoulder and pull the trigger, we can ask Rocky to show us before he leaves. I'm going to use a handgun, though, so it can be carried around with me whenever I leave the house." Stella called the apartment over the garage hoping Rocky wasn't sleeping or otherwise busy with something so she could explain her idea to him and ask for his assistance. He answered in a gruff voice as if he had been awakened, but when he recognized her voice modulated it somewhat asking if anything was amiss.

"No, Rocky," she said sweetly, "I was just checking to see when you were leaving to return to duty, since you haven't joined us for a meal lately."

"I have four more days before I have to catch a plane for headquarters. I was going to come over to the main house to see if I could bum a ride to the Fort Lauderdale airport for my direct non-stop flight to Andrews Air Force Base . It' a government flight rather than commercial."

"That can be arranged. Why don't you come over this afternoon to give me some instruction. We can talk about it, but bring a handgun with you." She hung up before he could question her further, a trick she had learned from Mr. McHenry.

The kids were badgering her to go swimming, but she put them off by saying she had a meeting with Rocky scheduled so to play in the yard until she was finished. The mention of Rocky's name quieted them instantly; they were all somewhat held in awe of the big man who never played with them like their dads, so they obeyed Stella, playing a game under the watchful eyes of the two dogs. When Rocky knocked on the front door, Stella let him in and headed directly for the kitchen.

"I suppose you are wondering why I asked you to bring a handgun." Then she spelled out what she had in mind and why. "Gennie is deathly afraid of handguns but could handle a shotgun if absolutely pressed to. I would like some instructions from you before you leave in one's use. What do you think?"

Rocky knew Stella was a very headstrong woman, so he removed his weapon from under his shirt. It was a Model 1911 A1 .45 Caliber Colt pistol. "This baby may not be exactly your cup of tea, Mrs. Mueller; it takes a strong hand and arm to handle it because it bucks like a rodeo bronco when fired, but if you hit a human anywhere in the torso he's dead, an arm or leg hit will just tear the limb off and he'd probably just bleed to death without proper immediate medical attention."

"As gruesome as that sounds, I wouldn't pull the trigger unless the children or myself were in a no-win situation. When can I try it out?"

"If you'll meet me out by the slip tomorrow morning at dawn we can shoot. Wear old clothes you don't care about and a bandana to cover your hair then you'll be in the proper dress. We'll start shooting at cans that I'll throw out, from both the prone and sitting positions so you can get the feel of the weapon before you actually try hitting the targets. I'm also going to bring my private pistol which is a .38 caliber Smith and Wesson six inch barrel for you to try. One other thing : bring along ear protectors. If you can't find any rubber ones cotton balls from a first aid kit will do. Do you have one of those?' Stella nodded that there was one. "I'll see you in the morning, Rocky, and thank you."

"Don't thank me yet; it's entirely possible that you won't be suited to handle weaponry."

"Don't bet on that," she said to his retreating back.

When Stella met her teacher at the powerboat slip, she wasn't in the least surprised to see him doing pushups. He was obviously still exercising to be fit when he returned to active duty status. Other than the white scars that showed on his body he looked pretty trim to her. For a man that large he would be a formidable opponent for any three men in a hand to hand struggle without weapons.

First Rocky showed her the nomenclature of the .45, how to load and release the clip, where the safety was on the trigger guard, and which position it had to be in before the weapon would fire. He had her run through it several times so she was comfortable with it. Stella put the cotton in her ears when she saw Rocky insert a loaded magazine into the handle and hand it to her. He threw two lidded coffee cans out into the water before sitting down on a spread blanket motioning her to do the same next to him, watching her every movement closely. He pointed to the cans . "Go ahead." Stella didn't really aim, she just pointed the gun in the general direction of the cans that were bobbing slightly in the wave action and fired. The first shot was low and to the left of the right hand can. Her next shot was more careful, and the bullet hit the same can, hurling it four feet in the air. She turned her head a little to glance at Rocky, who had a shocked expression of amazement on his face, like he couldn't believe this woman had actually hit a can with her second shot. Then he pointed to the other can which was drifting off to the left and nodded. Stella aimed, fired with her two-handed grip with the same result. Then she released the clip, ejected the round in the chamber, and put the safe weapon down.

"You don't need any more practice, sharpshooter." He stood giving her a hand up and while she removed the cotton said, "Keep that, Mrs. Mueller; I'll bring a couple more loaded clips and a holster down to the house later. You are an amazing woman." Stella accepted the compliment graciously. "You are a good teacher, Rocky."

When Stella reentered the house she went directly to the kitchen, put a pot of coffee on, and hid the .45 on a high shelf. Then she sat at the table waiting for the pot to brew, tears running down her cheeks.

36

Pepe Basquez's father Juan told him, "This is the largest shipment of cocaine I've ever attempted to bring into this country. It will flood the market here an' make us a fortune an' eliminate our biggest competitor to make us numero uno. I want you to forget about getting revenge on Tom Mueller. It is just stupido, as you should know by now, since you lost your two compadres on your last try. They may not have been the smartest guys, but they were faithful to you an' went back many years. I have tried to impress on you since I brought you into this business the value of our people from the lowest pushers to mid-level guards and enforcers to higher reliable district managers. The only thing more important than our people is the product. You don't seem to get that straight in your mind an' if you continue on the track you are running, you are going to be on the outside lookin' in, because nothing is going to impede my movement to the top rung of the ladder."

"Are you threatenin' me? I don't like to be threatened."

"If that's what it sounds like, so be it. I know what I want an' nothing or nobody is going to get in my way, you should know how ruthless I can be. I have spent a ton of dinero an' called in a lot of favors to allow you a free reign after you recovered from your injuries suffered in Colombia for again being stupido an' that's not counting your protection costs since."

"Protection from what? I don' need that; I can take care of myself."

"There you go again. You seem to forget important things like what you went on that raid to Colombia for. Of course from what I was told about it, you didn't know what Tom Mueller accomplished there. You should have known since you were in training with him. His proficiency as a long-distance marksman is almost unequaled in this country, in fact there are but a handful in the world who can match him. He could take you out whenever he chose to an' you'd never know what hit you, that's protection from what."

All the more reason why I should get rid of him now before he has the chance to set me up for a long-distance hit, Pepe thought, not voicing his ideas aloud to his father. He'd have to think the method over carefully before making any rash moves and enlist some outside the family help, some people who would work for reasons of hatred of the man not just money. There had to be men inside the business who fit that category; it just meant finding them.

"You've become awfully quiet, Pepe; are you taking my advice into consideration?"

"Yeah, I see yer' point. I was just wonderin', you remember the family in Brooklyn that had the operation goin' combined with their olive-oil business? You sent me there to bargain for some product and a way to ship it. There was some kind of a sting goin' on an' I was lucky to get outta' there without gettin' caught."

"Vaguely, why?"

"Are they still operatin'?"

"I have no idea, I could check but where is this going? What do you have in mind?"

Pepe wasn't too sure himself what so he couldn't answer that question readily. It was something he remembered about that fiasco, something concerning one of the partners of that business. He had sustained some kind of a leg injury which had immobilized him for a lengthy period, and Pepe thought it had been caused by that Santana character who had pulled some kind of a jujitsu move on him when he had been nosing around the equipment on that airplane that took them down to the submarine on their way to Colombia. What was that big man's name? He would certainly have a motive to want revenge, wouldn't he? All the same he kept his parting with his father cordial enough so that Juan would have no suspicions that Pepe might rock the boat by going against his orders to leave Tom Mueller strictly alone. He would also be more careful in his movements so that he could spot and shake his so-called protectors before they could report back to Juan what he was doing. One thing was for sure, he'd have to get rid of this car that was a dead giveaway connection to his whereabouts. He hated to trade it in because despite its shabby appearance it always got him where he needed to go. He had put quite a bit of money into the souped-up engine and reinforced suspension to deal with the lousy washboard roads surrounding the Basquez compound. Rather than trade it in, Pepe decided to rent a garage where it could rest hidden for future use. He'd lease something newer that would blend into urban driving where he wouldn't have to care much about damage because he would dump it somewhere after it had served its purpose. He had no intention in paying off the lease; that was suckers' worries. He found a new black, enclosed Ford van that would be just the ticket. It hurt his feelings to put out 1,800 bucks plus tax and insurance for a vehicle he would have for such a short time, but it was necessary. If he had protectors following him they were pretty good, he couldn't spot anyone in particular but if they were there he'd run them a merry chase where they'd earn their money.

He was tooling down the Pennsylvania Turnpike, obeying the traffic laws and speed limit when the name just popped up out of nowhere – Dominic Greco, the enforcer and bodyguard for Livio Stefino of the Brooklyn mob. There would be his man. He only hoped Dominic was still alive: bodyguards and enforcers had a short life span protecting their bosses' backs. This turnpike fused into the New Jersey Turnpike, which led to the Holland tunnel, and shortly he was approaching his goal. The only problem was that he could hardly keep his eyes open. It had been a long drive, and besides it was four o'clock in the morning, not exactly a time to go calling. So he parked the van on a side street, lay down in back, and was soon asleep. At 9 A.M. he woke up with a start, looked at his watch and wondered where he was. Then it dawned on him where he was and why. Pepe looked out the windshield and it was pouring down rain. That's what woke him up. Now what was he going to do, short of driving the van right up to the front door of the olive-oil business, leaning on the horn until somebody came out with an umbrella? Ridiciulous, but he had to do something; his great idea and the long drive weren't going to go for naught. As if to answer his thoughts, God turned off the tap, the rain ceased. You'd think you were in Florida where you could stand dry on one side of the street and watch it pour twenty foot away. Pepe drove right to the company and parked near the front door. There were puddles of standing water everywhere but he didn't try to evade them. He wouldn't melt. He rang the buzzer next to the door several times before it was opened and there stood Dominic filling the door space from jamb to jamb. "Yeah, whadda yez want? We're not open for bizness yet."

"I'm here to do another kind of business, Dom."

"So yez know my name, so what? Come back later" and he started to slam the door but Pepe stuck his foot in the way hoping the man wouldn't break it off.

"Look, bub, I may have to rattle your brain, don't yez unnerstand plain English? Come back later."

"How would ya' like ta' get even with the guy that did that to yer' leg?"

"Oh? Keep talkin' if yez know about that. Now I'm interested. What's yer name?"

"Pepe Basquez. Is that last name familiar?"

37

Tom Mueller was having a devil of a time getting used to his new position as the Southern District Supervisor. First, he had more people he didn't know because the were on assignment and away from the area, plus the paperwork was overwhelming. If he ever got back to Stella for weekends it would be a miracle, and man he needed her, not for sex but for her level-headedness.

She always could figure out the answer to his problems. Sometimes when he was puzzled, he wondered what he ever did without her. He missed his kids and didn't want them to get older and have an absentee father. Felix tried to take some of the load, but because of the difference in their personalities he wasn't always successful. Still, Tom didn't know what he'd do without the little guy. For instance, an old-timer who got along famously with Rowens was upset with this new boss. He didn't understand why Mueller did things the way he did and was vociferous about it. Felix told him if he didn't like it to either quit or ask for a transfer, and if that choice wasn't to his liking to step outside and he'd make him understand within thirty seconds. The agent immediately backed off, he was aware of Felix's reputation and wanted to keep his body intact. From then on, he followed orders to a Tee and was as docile as a kitten.

One day when Tom had been in his new position for over a month, he was at his desk doing the inevitable paperwork and threw up his hands in disgust, exasperated with the whole mess. Felix was at another desk across the room talking to someone on the phone, and when he saw Tom's emotional outbreak, quickly hung up the receiver.

"Whassa matter, amigo?"

"It's this lousy paperwork; I'm just not cut out to be a secretary, my place is in the field where some action is, even if it's only a surveillance task."

"Well, then, why doncha' hire one?"

"Hire what, a secretary?"

"Sure, yer' the main man aren't ya'? Ya' can do what ya want 'round here. I know I would if I was in your shoes. I'm surprised its taken ya' this long ta' figure that out."

"I don't know if I have the authority to do that; after all some of these documents are classified and I think you have to get someone out of a Civil Service pool where they have different ratings for classified information, all the way up to Top Secret."

"Well the only way ta' find out is to call headquarters an' see. I hope ya' can get a woman who knows how ta' make a good cup a' coffee and not this instant junk we been drinkin'. Maybe ya' can talk 'em inta' a refrigerator too ta' keep cold beer in 'round here. Might as well go for broke, heh, heh, heh."

It was Tom's bad luck to be connected to Mr. Rowens. Mr. McHenry was otherwise occupied at the moment, and when Tom stated his needs, the man turned into a surly bureaucrat acting like to grant his desires would be tantamount to paying for them out of his own pocket. Tom wasn't going to give up that easily. "If I remember correctly, you had a dozen or so office employees here when Mr. McHenry first brought me down here, what happened to all of them?"

"Look, Mueller," no mister either, which showed Tom how low Rowens held him on the agency totem pole, "yours is not to reason why. Simply make do with what you have down there." And he broke the connection ala Mr. McHenry.

"What was the verdict, amigo?"

"I'm sorry I called. Your old boss gives me a pain where I sit so I'm going to circumvent his so-called advice and do what you first suggested. We'll go out on our own and hire a secretary. Concerning any secret or confidential papers, we'll just have to lock them in the safe or shred them. Now all we have to figure out is how much salary we should pay and how to go about finding one. If nothing else comes up I'd like to go home for the weekend, I miss my family."

Finding a competent secretary was easier than either Tom or Felix would have thought. Felix looked up employment agencies in the telephone directory and struck paydirt on his first call. Yes, they had a glut of secretaries and could begin sending them by the next morning at 10 A.M.

At 9:30, both men were there dressed in slacks, white shirts, and ties, with CIA windbreakers on that should set the tone of formality which hiring a new employee deserved. After the interviews were completed, they would shed the jackets and ties to be more comfortable as the temperatures and humidity rose. A bevy of women began arriving at fifteen minute intervals promptly at ten, whom Felix met at the front door and began shuttling to Tom via an electric golf cart. His interviews never lasted more than fifteen minutes, enough time to read their resumes and ask a few rudimentary questions, thus getting an instant impression of the woman's abilities and experience in that type of work. At 1:30, after a dozen women had passed through his office and been returned to the front as Felix brought another, Tom had made his choice and a hastily printed sign POSITION FILLED was taped to the front door to turn away anymore aspiring applicants for the job. Christine Cabroulet was a stunning woman of Creole heritage, a widow of a Korean War combatant killed at Chosin Reservoir. She had been the Girl Friday of a two-man law office. One partner recently died, dissolving the firm. She had put herself through secretarial school existing on her husband's G.I. insurance until she graduated and found employment. Thankfully, they'd had no children for her to support. She wore sensible clothing, nothing garish, and her posture for such a small person was erect, sitting or standing. Her coal black hair worn long shone like a new car's paint job. She was both outgoing and quick-witted, something that both men admired. After discussing what her position would entail ,Tom told her what he and Felix discussed earlier and said, "Your hours may be rather erratic in the beginning until we develop a workable system that you are comfortable with but shouldn't require you to put in more than a half day on any Saturday unless an unforeseen flap occurs. Those may arise from time to time depending on situations our field agents get involved with. You are expected to keep your own time sheets since there will be no time clock to punch. Paydays for you will be every two weeks nearest the first and fifteenth as possible. If at any time you have an emergency of a personal nature, feel free to let me know so I can advance you cash to see you through. We have your phone number, and Felix will give you ours, and since you live so close I'll have spare keys made so you can enter at will. Do you have any questions?" She had been taking notes while Tom was running through her job description and shook her head indicating there were none. "Well then, Chris, since we both have families and live in the Florida Keys we planned on returning home for the upcoming weekend. I'll pick up a good drip coffee maker while we're there so we can have better brew and while we're gone. If you know of anywhere we can get a small refrigerator, write it down so we can pick it up on our return. Here's my Key Largo phone number if you think of anything that can't wait until we get back. We will have a sixteen hour drive ahead of us so if you'll stay and talk to my partner here I'll go get those keys made for you. Back in a bit."

Tom returned with all the duplicate keys for Chris, each marked with a tag designating which lock they were for. "If you can handle that overhead door in front, you can drive almost to the office eliminating a long walk, especially if you're carrying anything bulky or heavy. There's a light switch on the first straight ahead beam which will show the painted arrows on the floor to direct you, or you can use the electric golf cart so long as you plug it into the charger at this end. Here's our Key Largo phone number if you need to call. Tomorrow will be a short day for you because we will be heading home by 2:00 or 2:30. Get a good nights rest so you can absorb the rest of my instructions that you can mull over while we're gone."

Chris arrived at 9:45 AM the next day, almost beating Tom and Felix, and she did indeed know how to handle the overhead door. She brought in a coffee pot and coffee and started some brewing. "If you would help me, we can bring in the other item I brought." They followed her to her car, a

148

five-year-old Ford station wagon that was shined to a high gloss, and weighing down the back end was a three-quarter size refrigerator.

Tom and Felix took turns driving the flashy Plymouth stopping only once to buy some carry-out food and use the head thus they arrived at the estate in thirteen hours, it was 5 A.M. on what promised to be a gorgeous morning and day. So much for Felix's wish for rain. They were greeted by Leo and Brutus, the two dogs napping outside on permanent guard duty for the household. When Tom looked at Leo, not seeing him for quite sometime, the mastiff appeared bigger than ever which made him wonder what Stella was feeding him, surely more than his regular dog food. "Aren't you getting any exercise, boy? You must be just lying around soaking up the sun." Leo sat looking up at his main friend with an expression of puzzlement on his massive face like, where have you been? "We'll take care of that this weekend if I have to run you ragged myself. We can't have you going to fat now can we, big fellow?" Tom reached down and scratched behind Leo's ears with the usual reward from a now satisfied dog. So far as Leo was concerned all was again well on the home front.

Felix played with Brutus for a few minutes before disappearing into the house so Tom knew where he was going and following his lead headed for his own bedroom and Stella. They had a lot to talk about but that would come later. Tom just wanted to hold her close to his chest to get the feel and smell of her that he had so missed. She must have sensed his presence or else she'd heard him playing and talking to Leo in the front yard. She raised her arms in a come-to-me fashion and Tom quickly disrobed, heeding her call. Their embrace was long and breathless and when they finally parted for air he said, "I have missed you so sweetheart; no job is worth being apart this long. In any case if there is a solution, it escapes me as to what it would be. How are the kids?"

"They're fine, honey, and they miss their daddy almost as much as I do. Sheila asks me every morning at breakfast when are you coming home to her. No amount of excuses seem to pacify her. She's not like the boys who just wonder what you'll bring them when you return. Your little girl includes you in her prayers every night first even before her `Now I lay me down to sleep' prayer. It's not bless mommy and daddy, just daddy. That's devotion, honey. When your little girl grows into a big girl, you're going to have your hands full. The boys I can handle, but Sheila I don't know, even now at her tender age it's scary how much we think alike. Are you tired after your long trip?"

"Not really. We took turns driving and napping with only one stop between New Orleans and here. Why?" Stella had that look in her eyes that Tom knew only too well. An hour later as they lay back, spent but still holding each other Tom began explaining about Chris, the new secretary they had hired and what a find she was in relieving him of all the paperwork and how they had gone about hiring her despite the advice to the contrary from Mr. Rowens at headquarters. "You know how much I dislike him and I thought his living in D.C. would be a godsend that I wouldn't be saddled with him any longer. Well, I was wrong; the distance between us is measured by more than just miles. That was when I began to wonder how you would handle it with your usual no-nonsense, straight from the shoulder reasoning. The more I thought about it the more I missed you and here I am.."

"Forget about all that while you're here, honey, there's time enough for those things when you go back. I have a letter I received from that beer distributor whose driver ran into you. It looks rather official. I'll give it to you over breakfast. Now I'm going to take a shower, alone, please."

Tom couldn't resist, alone my eye, we'll see about that.

At the breakfast table, Stella handed Tom the registered letter and he was about to open it when the triplets descended on him like a swarm of locusts. Sheila crawled up into his lap, threw her little arms around his neck, and clung to him as if she feared he would leave again if she didn't anchor him down. "I missed you daddy, don't go away again puleeeze."

"Dad has to work, honey, so you can have nice clothes and food for your tummy. I don't like to leave you, but it's my job. I hope it won't always be like this, but for the present it is. Have you boys been behaving and helping your mother around the house?"

"Sure, dad," they chorused. "We're the men around the house now that Mr. Newbole is gone."

Tom took a quick look at Stella but she was avoiding his glance. "Let your father open his letter now and eat your breakfasts." Tom tore the edge off the envelope and pulled out the contents. There was a cashiers check for $25,000.00 in the middle of some typewritten pages that explained the check.

"Dear Mr. Mueller, we hope the enclosed check will somehow cover your loss of work due to the negligence of the distributor's negligence, causing you serious injuries that we hope you have recovered from. If you accept this settlement by depositing same, you will release the company from further claims." It was signed by a law firm and dated two weeks earlier.

"Take a look at this, Stella, and tell me what you think." She leaned against the counter and read the letter slowly twice. It sounds reasonable to me, honey, but when you add together all the expenses not covered by your agency insurance, of which there is a long list, I think you'll find those costs almost equal to this check so you're not being compensated for the suffering you tolerated while the slow process of healing occurred. Your pickup truck alone was a large fraction of this amount and I'm not even counting the hardship that was placed on me which would entitle me to punitive damage awards as wll. If in doubt, I would suggest you call your lawyer friend in Columbus for further advice. I can compile an actual list of costs if you want."

Tom walked over to her, put his arms around her and whispered in her ear so the kids couldn't hear, "I always knew you were more than just a pretty face attached to a terrific body, your opinions are always beneficial."

"You don't have to follow all my suggestions you know but thanks for the flattery anyway, it's always nice to hear especially when I'm feeling rather blue."

"After the kids are done eating we'll send them outside to play while we discuss a few things." Tom returned to the table to be with the children as they finished their meal correcting the way the boys were eating. "You don't have to wear your food; a little restraint is needed here. That means slow down, there is nothing so pressing that you have to be in such a rush. If I had ever showed poor table manners like that when I was your age, my parents would have cracked a spoon across my knuckles. My brother had it happen to him several times before he got the message. That was the old German way."

The kids went outside after eating to be under the watchful eyes of the dogs. Nothing yet had been heard from the Santana family, they must all have slept in. So while there was relative quiet and before he called Lance in Columbus he had several questions for Stella. "The boys mentioned Rocky was gone, when did he leave?"

Stella knew exactly when, yet she didn't want to open up that can of worms and ruin Tom's weekend so she offhandedly said, "Oh, maybe ten days or two weeks ago, something like that ..."

"Well, where did he go, and how did he get there?"

"He mentioned something about going to Washington for reassignment but you know how closed-mouthed he is, and I didn't pry. I drove him to the Fort Lauderdale airport. Now what else is on your mind?"

"You mean to tell me you drove him all that way and didn't find out anything?"

"Oh for God's sake, Tom, leave it alone." Tom just stared at her knowing something disagreeable had happened that his wife just didn't want to discuss. He'd leave it alone now but before he returned to New Orleans he would bring it up again. "OK, this is something I've been thinking about and it's another subject you won't want to talk about. The last time I broached it, you just about bit my head off." The Santana threesome picked that moment to troop into the kitchen, so Tom had to let the topic die on the vine until later.

"Sorry we overslept but we were up late talkin'; is there anything left for breakfast?"

Stella jumped up, "I'll make a good meal for you all after I get these dirty dishes off the table. Sit down, the coffee is always ready, and I'll pour a glass of milk for Tomas. Tomas took right after his father, everything put on his plate disappeared. At that rate, he might turn into a Goliath instead of a runt like Felix. Gennie watched her son eat with total adoration in her eyes. It was obvious to Tom their adoption proceedings had been the salvation of their marriage. Tomas was finished eating, drank the last of his milk, and said, "May I be excused?" showing that Gennie had been coaching him on his table manners which she had undoubtedly given up on with her husband.

"I'm going to call Lance now, Stell, to see what he recommends I do with that settlement check. I'll tell him what you said about expenses so you won't have to compile a list now, only if he thinks you should at a later date. Then I want you to go with me to look over the garage apartment before I contact Cliff Ajax." Now what? Stella wondered to herself but continued doing dishes and cleaning up the kitchen. Felix and Gennie returned to their rooms which left Stella alone. She glanced up to where the .45 was stashed on the top shelf over the kitchen sink wondering if she should leave it there or move it to a more secure hiding place until Tom left for New Orleans. She never knew when he might go rummaging around in search of something else and accidentally discover it by mistake, then she would have to explain why she had it and where she got it. Her thoughts were interrupted when Tom called her from the main living area. "Do you know where the registration papers are for the wrecked pickup?"

"I imagine the whole packet is in our bedroom where we keep all the other important papers. Do you want me to go look?"

"No, Lance says there is no rush just so you know where they are when we go to litigation, plus he reiterated what you already said about the hardship it had placed you under. I just have to make copies of the contents of their letter and mail it to him."

"All right, Lance, yes I'll pass that along to her."

"He said to give you his love and for you to take good care of his Godson. After this is over he's going to try to arrange his schedule so he can visit us, most likely this coming winter after the football season is over."

"That would be nice. I'll finally be able to meet him in person."

Stella was reluctant to enter the apartment where Rocky had lived for so many months lest she would be reminded of the last incident on the way to the airport and his inference that she might use the weapon he had provided her for something other than protection, but Tom insisted she accompany him. His agenda lately was often at cross-purposes with her own that she supposed was the result of their living apart for such long periods where their thoughts were out of sync with each others.

"Here's my idea, sweetheart. You need somewhere to resume your painting. To avoid building a new structure from the ground up on property, we don't really have as yet what about modifying this space to suit your needs? Cliff could remove part of the roof and replace it with glass panels to allow for the most advantageous sunlight at most times of the day which only you could judge, the direction I mean. Shades inside could be installed with better lighting in the event of rain or if you were struck with an idea at night. What do you think?" Stella looked around the area with a new perspective. Her husband was always planning ahead, and his thoughtfulness for her well-being was one of his traits that so endeared him to her. This really could be done and her aversion to the former tenant would be cut out and replaced by an enhanced amount of creativity.

"What did you mean about property we don't have as yet, honey?"

"That was something Felix joked about when he heard what I was planning which got me to thinking about talking to the Home Owners Association to see if the vacant land to our north was available for sale. At the time I wasn't aware that Rocky had vacated this place. It's still not a bad idea because property values have to go up as more people from the north are fed up with the weather up there and the higher heating costs. Now it would just be a good investment whether we ever used it or not, and it's not like it could be used as a trailer park because the association rules stipulate the type of dwellings meet their code of standards. It's just not so pressing now that you have agreed on the renovation up here. I see that Rocky didn't remove much of his possessions other than clothing, I wonder why? How much luggage did he have when you drove him to the airport?"

"Just a duffel bag, Tom, why?"

"Well then I'll have to ship everything else back to Langley. I wonder if I can send it C.O.D.?" Tom laughed out loud.

It had been quite some time since Stella had heard Tom out and out laugh that way, even if it was at his own wit. He was always so serious about everything. Maybe it was being away from the job, and the responsibilities it entailed despite it only being a few days from it. Whatever, the change of scenery was something she was going to take advantage of. She looked out to see what the children were up to and found them playing some sort of game out by the parking area. At least they would stay occupied for a while and couldn't get into too much trouble because Gennie was close at hand plus both dogs were near.

"Honey, are you about done with your calls?"

"I was just talking to Cliff. He is going to meet us here in the morning to discuss the changes so it looks like we're going to be here an extra day. I'm calling Chris to tell her of the delay so she doesn't start calling state patrol posts checking for injury accidents then we'll rejoin the kids out…"

One look at the way Stella was dressed or undressed as the case was enough to make him forget further phone calls.

38

True to his promise, Tom took Leo for a run/walk after he was fed. Naturally, Brutus wanted to tag along, but Tom told Felix to order him to stay on the property to guard the children while they were gone. The Irish wolfhound was now fully grown at 140 pounds would obey his master completely whenever he was at the estate, but when he was absent followed Stella's instructions because the dog knew by instinct she was the boss, and no dog would bite the hand that fed it. Tom hadn't needed anymore exercise that day after the bout with his wife but a promise was a promise so after he gave Stella strict orders about only feeding the mastiff his regular dog food, man and dog struck northward into the adjacent property that Tom was interested in for investment purposes. The land was a mess. Betsy had seen to that, felling most of the palms, which the Home Owners Association had as yet not removed. That made for slow-going, so instead of running most of their journey was spent climbing over tree trunks and dodging crater-like holes filled with dirty water. The association would be hard-pressed to restore any resemblance of normalcy here. They pursued their zigzag course until they came to an access road that led to the next house, if you could call it that, a mansion that made Tom's estate look inconsequential. The palace rose three stories, pillared on two sides, the surrounding lawn smooth as a putting green. Stately trees rose to a canopy higher than the roof. The whole scene was almost as majestic as pictures he had seen of the Taj Mahal. They stood staring ,and Tom wondered who had that kind of money to own anything so huge. There didn't appear to be any damage from Betsy at all. How could that be when his own place, a quarter mile south, had sustained so much? "That's really something, isn't it, big guy, or have you seen it before in your wanderings? Sure makes our place look insignificant, though." Leo sat by Tom's leg. He wished he could tell his main friend about the nifty, female bull mastiff who lived here. They had a great time when he first met her and he told her he would be back whenever he got off sentry duty. He wondered where she was? He couldn't detect a sniff of her particular scent anywhere near. Oh, well, he'd give her one more chance to prove she wasn't just another fickle female then he would explore greener pastures elsewhere.

"I think what we'll do Leo is follow this access road to see where it goes instead of traversing that obstacle course area the way we came, so we can do some flat out running. You won't lose any weight otherwise. So stay close until we see where it head beyond that bend." They hadn't covered more than fifty feet when they first heard, then saw an approaching vehicle. It was hard to describe coming head on. It wasn't a car but it wasn't exactly a truck either. They moved to the extreme edge of the dirt road to give whatever it was room to pass, but it slowed to a stop before it reached them and a brusque voice from the interior called out, "What are you doing back here? Those no trespassing signs posted along this road mean just that."

"We didn't come up this road, we came cross-country, so we didn't see any signs. My estate is the next property south of here."

"Well then, stay there, you have no *@%*~* business back in here." Tom wasn't used to being talked to in that manner or in that tone of voice, especially sworn at by a total, faceless stranger and he was quickly becoming more than just irritated. "Look whoever you are, watch your manners, I don't appreciate having anyone giving me orders or cursing me, so we'll be on our way unless you want to step out of that contraption and try to stop us." At this point, Tom was so annoyed he hoped his challenge would be met. Leo noticed his main friends' vexation by the tone of his voice, his huge head lowered to meet any oncoming threat. Tom saw this and softly ordered the dog to sit. If the situation so dictated he was armed with his .38 Cobra but he hesitated to draw it unless he or Leo were threatened with bodily harm. The stalemate was de-fused as the vehicle was put into gear and with a belch of black exhaust smoke moved away. "Let's go home, boy. I want to call the Association to find out who owns that place. Something just doesn't feel on the up-and-up here. That clown acted like he had something to hide."

After identifying himself to the woman who answered the Homeowners Association phone Tom asked for the director or the person in charge, because this was important Government business. It seemed Government was the operative word, because within seconds the head honcho himself was on the line. "What can I do for you, Mr. Mueller?"

Tom had to be careful in his inquiry not to reveal his true reasons for the information he was seeking yet to make it sound official enough to force the director into giving out the facts he wanted. "As you should know by now, the principal aims of my agency is to forestall drugs of any type from reaching our shores. To facilitate our goals we need inside data concerning certain individuals who may be involved." The director remained silent waiting for and wondering how much this CIA operative would want him to reveal. "I was exploring the property just north of mine with my dog with the intention of contacting you to see if it was for sale. It's really a mess in there, which leads me to believe it must be because no attempt has been made to clean it up since Betsy struck. Is that the case?"

"I would have to check my charts to find out."

"Please do that at your earliest convenience. But to get back to the other information I'm seeking, rather than return through that quagmire we stumbled on to an access road to return and in so doing came across this palace just beyond the unkempt lot. My question is, who owns it? As I'm sure you know we can subpoena you to release that information, but since my family intends to live here on a permanent basis I'm bending over backwards to allow you to release it of your own accord without taking any drastic steps."

"Since this is connected to your agency's quest, I see no reason why I shouldn't give you what you need Mr. Mueller. That property is owned by a New York City based company, well actually Brooklyn, an import olive-oil company owned by Mr. Livio Stefino. He isn't always in residence, though. I have been led to understand almost eight months a year he sublets it. Since there has never been any complaint brought up before we don't closely check who is there at any given time. Are you lodging a formal complaint?"

Bingo, Tom thought, the very company that Paddy O'Toole mentioned when Tom had first met him, the company his superiors on NYPD had told him to steer clear of and Paddy had found out why, thus being promoted to sergeant and transferred to Manhattan to keep him away from there. Now it all rang a bell. Small world, he thought. "No, director, you have been most helpful, but when you check your chart to ascertain the ownership of the other lot just north of mine I wish you would call here and leave a message with my wife if I'm not here."

"I will do that."

Tom told Stella about the association director's call she could expect anytime concerning the cost for the adjacent property to the north of them but was careful not to allude what he'd learned about that lot. He thought she would probably nix the whole deal if she knew what kind of people would be their new neighbors.

It was time to put in some family exposure. The boys were always wanting to go in the pool but Stella would have none of it unless they were properly supervised. Now was a good time to get in with them, tiring them out just before bedtime so they would sleep the night through. Cliff would be here early in the morning, and he didn't need any interference from the children. They splashed and frolicked until even he was worn out.

Cliff came bright and early and Tom and Stella accompanied him to the apartment to explain the changes they wanted. After looking the problem over, drawing a few sketches, and making some measurements, Cliff told them he could manage it with the help of some glaziers; it would be too tricky trying to do it alone. "Is there a rush on this?" Stella, ever frugal, answered, no, she had done without a studio for several years now and could wait awhile longer. "I could complete this project within three weeks but it would greatly depend on the weather. "A rainy spell would complicate matters because part of the roof will be opened so it might ruin the interior and cause mildew. Mr. Mueller, you will get your discount per usual because thanks to you I never would have had so much business. As it is I have a five-man crew on permanent hire. Soon I'll need an accountant because I just don't have time to keep a running ledger."

"I'm glad to hear that, Cliff; it couldn't happen to a better workman. One other thing, though.

I don't think you have seen the Irish wolfhound since it's grown up. It weighs 140 pounds now, so you better honk your horn like you used to do for Leo until it gets used to your scent. The only difference between the two dogs is: you won't hear Leo coming at you like a runaway freight train whereas Brutus is a barker. I don't mean you, per se, but any intruder." After Cliff left, Tom asked Stella if she was satisfied with what the contractor was going to do?"

"It sounded like it will turn out just fine, honey, but you know you didn't have to shock him again about the dogs. You have a tendency to scare people unnecessarily by the use of your language; you even scare me sometimes with your innuendos, and I'm your wife." The phone rang. It was Chris. Tom listened for several moments before saying anything, "What were their names, and are they on our roster? All right I'll take care of it when I get back. I was going to call you later today anyway. Something came up here so we'll be a day late returning. Where did you say that letter was postmarked from? Well put it in a safe place and I'll deal with it when I see you." When Tom hung up Stella asked, "Trouble?"

"It seems like that's all there is with this job, both internal and outside the agency's field of operation. At least I don't have to think about any of that until the day after tomorrow."

They took their time returning to New Orleans making several stops for breaks to get something to eat or just coffee to break the monotony of the drive. Although the non-stop on the route home was faster, it seemed that neither man was in a great rush to get back. Even though Tom realized there were pressing matters to take care of – most of all finding out what those agents who had come to the office that Chris mentioned were involved in, plus his curiosity about the letter marked personal that their secretary hadn't opened. That was bothering him, simply because anytime you received a missive of that sort it was like getting a phone call in the middle of the night, it boded bad news. Tom told his partner what he had found out from the Home Owners Director concerning the property to the north of his that was owned by that Stefino character of the Bronx and after thinking about it for several miles, Felix said it sounded to him more than just coincidence. "I certainly didn't tell Stella about it, she would have had a fit knowing low-life of that ilk were living so close."

"That was probably best, amigo; it even makes me kinda' nervous with my family so close. If I thought for one minute they were in any immediate danger ya' would have ta' run New Orleans alone."

"Let's not dwell on that, Felix. Stella would be on the horn to us if any life threatening problems arose, and with Cliff Ajax being around for the garage improvements our families won't be exactly alone." The last stop they made before New Orleans they agreed to split the cost of several cases of Budweiser to stock the refrigerator Chris had brought so they could enjoy a few at the end of the day while discussing events.

"Ya' know, amigo, I been thinkin' 'bout that Stefino guy. Isn't he the boss of that Greco I had the run-in with at that Times Square restaurant? That was before Gennie was my wife, but she was with me. Ya' don't suppose that letter Chris is holdin' for ya' is from them do ya'? Wasn't it postmarked NYC?"

"Yes, that hasn't left my thoughts since she told me. I guess I should have had her open it right then but because she said it was marked personal she didn't want to intrude."

"Yer' gonna' get upset at this since I'm bouncin' around a bit but did ya' know 'bout the .45 pistol Rocky gave Stella for her protection while we're gone? Gennie told me 'bout it, even though she was sworn ta' secrecy. She doesn't keep any secrets from me. She's scared of guns herself but Stella showed her how ta' load an' point the double barrel ya' have from the powerboat in case a' trouble like the dogs handled before," Tom just looked at Felix who was driving when he divulged that information, but the little man never took his eyes from the road. He was a good cautious driver. Tom was flabbergasted by the revelations but turned his head forward not wanting to break the driver's concentration on the road. What else did his partner know that he hadn't as yet revealed? As long as he had known and worked closely with him there were times he thought he didn't know the man at all.

Something else had been in the back of his mind all these years. It was the circumstances surrounding Fred's death. All he had ever said was nearby on another matter and talked to the Coast Guard. There was another person who obviously knew something too, Gomer, the marina owner who had taken Fred's Bertram in exchange for the powerboat. It all seemed to be connected, yet he was the only person who didn't have the actual facts. Would he ever? Even if by dumb chance he stumbled over the facts would he see the truth? Tom knew he wasn't qualified, outside of his chosen field, to be a detective; he was more of an action person who had a gift of marksmanship and inside organization and even there he had made some poor decisions in the past. Now with the added responsibilities of a large family he had been thrust into a position he didn't want without the proper training or adequate supervision and was supposed to ad lib his role to everyone's satisfaction. Without the support that was necessary he wondered how he could accomplish much under those circumstances.

"Ya' got that thousand-yard stare again, amigo, what are ya' thinkin'?" A variety of topics, Felix, and none of them are much to my liking."

They had timed their arrival to the warehouse where their office was located to coincide with when Chris was due to come to work. They had the coffee brewing and were enjoying their first cup when she drove in, again, proving she could handle the overhead door easily for such a small woman. A bag she was carrying contained two more three-pound cans of Maxwell House coffee. "Good morning. I had coupons for these that had to be used before they expired, and since I don't drink that much coffee myself I knew it wouldn't go to waste here. How was your long weekend at home? I'm sorry I had to call but when those agents came in I was somewhat startled. They were the first I had seen."

"I'm glad you brought that up, Chris. Did they mention where they were working and on what?"

"Just something about the Bijou Club and they were looking for expense checks. I couldn't find any that matched their names although there are some for other agents."

"What were their names again?"

"Just a minute; that information is in my desk. Oh, here's that letter for you." She found what she was looking for. "Mr. Stone and Mr. Price, both rather short men." Tom had slit open the letter as she spoke, and Felix noted he had lost some of his facial color before he looked up and nodded to him. That meant the letter was from who they thought. Now Felix's curiosity was aroused, and he wondered how long his amigo would sit on it before he shared the contents, surely not until the end of the day.

Come with me, partner, I want to show you where ...." When they were away from the office and out of hearing range of Chris, Tom stopped and gave the letter to Felix. After he had read it he handed it back. "I told ya' what my position was on this. Ya' wanna' flip a coin ta' see who stays here and who goes home?"

"Sounds fair to me. Who performs the toss? This is not a football game; it's a much more serious event, so I would suggest we use Chris. She doesn't have to know what it's for so she will be impartial. Agreed?" Felix nodded and they headed back to the office both in a somber state of mind. If Chris noticed their sudden change of attitude she didn't let it show when Mueller asked her to flip a coin for them. She dug into her purse retrieving a half dollar, put it on her thumb and up in the air it went. Felix called tails while it was airborne. It came down on their secretary's desk – heads. Felix looked so crestfallen Tom had a notion to relinquish his victory but then had a flash of his kids innocently playing in the yard without any idea of what danger lurked nearby. He couldn't and wouldn't take the chance of not being there to protect them. After all, he had three to his partners one and he would watch over Tomas as if he were one of his own, and he assured Felix of that before he got on the phone to rent a car.

Chris had no idea what the content of that personal letter had wrought-up but she could sense the seriousness of it by their demeanor. When she heard Mr. Mueller calling for a rental car she was certain it must be of a life or death decision. Tom stopped mid-dial and turned to Felix. "We'll both go, partner; it makes no sense to split our team at a time like this." He then called the estate to warn Stella and Gennie to keep all of the children indoors until they got there. "Keep those weapons handy too without alarming the kids."

"Can you tell me what this is all about, honey? You're starting to scare me again." Stella knew the cat was out of the bag when Tom said "weapons." There was no point in quarreling with Gennie now for breaking their pact of secrecy about the .45 Rocky had given her if their children were in some kind of danger.

This trip to the Keys was nothing like the one four days ago, whoever was at the wheel pushed the Plymouth for all it was worth. When Felix drove, he treated the car as if he were driving for a NASCAR racing team or at Indianapolis Speedway, all the time keeping a close eye on the dashboard gauges to make sure all was as it should be. There was little if any conversation between the two men and neither took a nap while the other was driving as previously. They made one stop for gas just outside of Tallahassee, picked up some carryout coffee. No engine oil was needed as the car continued to perform perfectly, and they resumed their high-speed journey Tom at the wheel. Tom knew kidnapping was a death penalty offense in most states, Florida included, after the infamous Charles Lindbergh case but it still hadn't deterred the crime. Ransom money was the usual expectation of the perpetrators but in this case a misbegotten sense of revenge seemed to be the motive but Tom wondered to whom it was aimed, Felix or himself. Pepe Basquez had some strange ideas even before his head injury suffered in Colombia and how to gain revenge and he was a consummate liar. All in all a dangerous, untrustworthy individual . Tom also knew the FBI should be notified since it was their area of expertise, but he was loathe to call in an outside agency before the fact. But why wait until an attempt was made? And another thing , it would put more armed men on the premises. Tom kept thinking of more reasons why they should be called in: With the dogs out in the yard he was not going to take the chance of Leo being killed accidentally or on purpose. The mastiff meant too much to him, almost as much as one of the kids. They certainly had been through enough together to qualify that thought. "I've decided to call the FBI in on this, partner; there are more reasons for that idea then against. Sound reasonable to you?"

"I got nuthin' 'gainst it if ya' think it's needed. They prolly could be some help."

They were just short of West Palm Beach when Tom noticed the oil-gauge light on the dashboard start to blink red so he started looking for an all night gas station. He was surprised it had taken so long the way they had been pushing the car. He had the gas tank topped off so they wouldn't need to later. While Felix used the restroom he asked the attendant for two coffees to go but was informed this particular Citgo station didn't have a coffee machine so he had to settle for two Cokes to give them the needed caffeine to keep them awake and alert until they reached the estate. Felix took over the wheel for the last leg. When the arrived on Key Largo Tom told his partner to be especially wary for any vehicles that looked strange or out of place. "Watch for out of state license plates and pull right in to the garage. Back in after I open the doors and take care of the dogs if they're outside."

Felix remembered the beer they had bought and never unloaded at the New Orleans office so he grabbed a case of Bud before heading for the darkened main house. Tom had followed after closing the overhead door. "Strange that Stella doesn't have the outside spotlight on," he whispered to Felix when they met at the front door. "I don't like this. Skirt around to the rear door. Leave the beer sit here. You have your house keys?"

"Yeah."

"As quiet as possible go in to survey the situation, if everything is copacetic come straight through and open this door. If you're not here in three minutes I'm coming in gun drawn. The dogs aren't outside which indicates to me they must be in there somewhere and I haven't heard a sound out of Brutus." Felix took off running for the rear door. He must be able to see in the dark Tom thought. If he tried that he'd most likely run into something. He looked at his watch with the luminous dial, this would be the longest three minutes he'd have experienced in a long time. He always conjured up the worst case scenarios first he thought. While continuing to stare at the watch he took out the Cobra with his other hand readying himself for the worst when Felix opened the door. "Yer' not gonna' believe this, amigo" handing him a note. Everyone, which included women, children , and dogs were in Rocky's old apartment over the garage. Tom just shook his head in disbelief. Why in such a cramped area he wondered? Here they had all the room the main house afforded yet they chose there. It seemed there was little point in contacting the FBI until morning after they found out from their wives what made them opt for that location so Felix took the beer in putting it in the refrigerator and they both headed for the garage leaving the outside spotlight off for now.

You would have thought they had been gone for four months instead of four days with the reception they received from the women. Neither of them wanted to let go of their men long enough to explain why they were up here. Soon they separated and Stella the strong-willed one of the two explained. "We had a strange phone call this morning just after you called telling us the children couldn't be watched all the time so we put our heads together and decided on this move. The kids think it's great fun, like camping out in their sleeping bags without any mosquitoes. They're all in the bedroom sawing logs and no one wanted to use the bed so guess who is on it?" Tom didn't have to think twice. "Leo, I suppose."

"Bingo, right on the button. Sheila is using him for a pillow. It's cute, their both content. We heard you pull in downstairs but you were gone before I could get down there to catch you. There's coffee if you'd like some, all the comforts of home." While Felix filled two cups Tom told the women about the threat contained in the letter marked personal that their secretary had held for him and their subsequent decision to return quickly as possible. "I'm calling in the FBI in a few minutes so this place is going to be over-run with good guys before long. They take threats of this nature seriously so we're going to have to keep the dogs indoors for a short while. We won't feed either one of them today so they won't have to go outside until tomorrow, and keep the toilet lid down unless you want that smell around. If they have to go yet today we'll let them use the garage, we can air that out later. Tom called the number in the book for the FBI. It didn't signify where the office was located but when he asked for the agent in charge a recording played giving him several options to select for service. Since this was a rotary phone he hoped the last choice, dial zero to speak to an agent, would work. It did. "This is agent O'Brien, how may I help you?" After Tom had laid out the complete story he gave his address and directions how to find it. At the end he gave his agency, job title, and location for his office for additional authenticity and was gratified with the agent's responses. When he hung up two things happened almost simultaneously, three things actually: The phone rang, Leo came out of the bedroom, followed by a half asleep Sheila who immediately crawled into his lap, putting her little arms around his neck in a strangle hold, and Leo sitting in front of him with that supercilious expression on his face. The phone call was agent O'Brien calling to verify that Tom's call wasn't a hoax. Tom motioned Felix to take Leo down to the garage so he could hose it down then motioned to a giggling Stella to retrieve her daughter so he could finish his coffee before it got spilled in his lap. Again hanging the phone up he breathed a sigh of relief. He looked at his returning wife, "What was so funny?"

"You you big clown." She promptly sat in his lap, giving him one of her four alarm kisses which had its desired effect on him. Tom looked over to where Gennie was sitting on the floor, her head leaning back against the wall sound asleep before returning Stella's affections. There was wasn't much time to play as Felix would soon be returning with Leo but he' give it the old college try. Tom heard Felix clomping up the inner stairs so he lifted Stella up off of his lap telling her to go into the bathroom and make herself presentable. Felix stomped into the room with a disgusted look on his face. "Between your dog and mine I'm gonna' have ta' open all the garage doors in the mornin' and hose the place out; then I'll have ta' find some kinda' deodorant ta' get the smell out. Havin' dogs is great but they sure are messy."

39

Tom Mueller was having reoccurring thoughts and flashbacks of experiences he had witnessed and taken part in during his escapades in Korea. It had been brought about by reading an obituary in the Miami Herald. One of his team had just killed himself. He'd left a note why he was leaving his wife of five years, no children thank God, because he could no longer bear the thoughts of what he had done by ending the lives of so many men who would never have the opportunity to enjoy what he had because of his ruthless use of marksmanship. Why would he feel that way, Tom wondered? They would have killed him, never giving it a second thought. He and Frank had been in the same three-man team for two months before it was broken up by Toms being wounded by one of those gooks Frank was so worried about. When Tom returned from the Naval Hospital in Japan, Frank was no longer there. He didn't ship over, and returned to the States, while Tom did another tour.

In the field of battle there is nothing more terrifying than the cough of a heavy mortar, whether friendly or not. Cough refers to the hollow sound the projectile makes when leaving the tube. Secondly in hair-raising sounds is the pop of the fuse heard in close quarters as a hand grenade comes your way. All other sounds are insignificant to the ground-pounder except the meaty smack of a rifle round striking a friend or team member, which is the cause of many nightmares after the fact. A Marine Corps tradition is to never-ever leave a KIA behind to the murderous, butchery of the gooks, a philosophy not taken lightly. Tom would not for a moment have a nightmare or any misgivings about pumping a round or two into Basquez. This world would be better off for it. That went for his father Juan, too.

Maybe Tom was biased but he didn't care what other people thought.

The new job, with offices in New Orleans, separated Tom from his growing family in Key Largo. Tom fervently wished to be returned to his former field job where he could practice his chosen vocation unhindered by unwanted bureaucratic obstructions. So far this wish had not been granted. Instead, he was becoming embroiled in unrealistic problems on two fronts. Never the bashful type, Tom was determined to buck the system by any method necessary to return to his choice. It seemed the only way he could contact his mentor would be by personal letter, the same type Tom had received threatening to kidnap one of his children although this would not be a threat to Mr. McHenry. It was the only way he could contact him without being rebuffed by Mr. Rowens again. Tom would enclose it in another envelope and mail it to Lance Nolte so it wouldn't be postmarked from Florida. It wasn't that he wanted time off or vacation time; he just needed advice on how to handle this predicament. Coming from old German stock, he had a stubborn streak inbred which made it almost impossible not to attain wanted goals. Felix on the other hand, could be a bit more devious. His ancestry dating from Colombian heritage had a cross breed of the Incan Royal family on his father's side, thus his short stature. He had shown both sides with traits of his own stubbornness, strength, and loyalty. Another reason why he and Tom made such a good team. That Felix had proven by leaving one agency to join Tom in his. Add Leo and the threesome was formidable, each part complementing the whole. Now adding the FBI to the cauldron would create such a maelstrom of affairs that any incursion of the estate could touch off a BANG that might be heard as far away as Washington, D.C. The Basquez congregation didn't fully understand what they were about to tackle – the full power of the two largest quasi-military agencies in the country with unlimited resources. If ever there were such a foolhardy exercise that would be it.

The phones were monitored around the clock with recording and tracing devices, some of which Tom didn't know even existed. Trained personnel worked four on, four off which caused a glut of incoming and outgoing people who had to be housed and fed. Tom had to call Cliff Ajax to postpone the garage apartment alterations because the space was being used by the off-duty agents, each of whom had been warned by their supervisors not to wander around the grounds while off duty unless accompanied by Tom, Felix, or Stella, who the dogs knew, thus avoiding any accidents from mistaken identities. Tom made certain the rule was followed by printing large signs which he fastened to both doors of the apartment. They read: Due to the seriousness of this warning please OBEY!! If that didn't get their attention they deserved to get mauled, he thought. Then let his risk insurance that he paid so much for take over. At that point their attorneys could take over litigations. As he had heard, most FBI agents had law degrees anyway so that would be interesting. But he was not going to keep Leo in the house.

Three days passed without a threat, and the tension was building. Every time the phone rang, four people would jump, three agents and whoever was close at hand. Tom began to wonder if somehow if Pepe got wind of the FBI presence and was waiting until they pulled out for lack of action. Did he have some eyes watching the compound, Tom wondered? The supervisor had made several outgoing calls that either Tom or Stella knew about, so it was possible he was thinking the same thing. Now a week had passed – nothing. Tom was actually avoiding the supervisor lest the man brought up his misgivings and set a deadline for pulling his people out.

Tom finally got his call from Mr. McHenry, and it was all he could have hoped for. The CIA director commiserated with his present situation, saying nothing was more important than one's children. "As far as your concern about the FBI ceasing coverage there, because of inactivity I'll talk to the powers here in D.C. to prevent that happening. Now, according to your letter you aren't too happy with your position in New Orleans. Mr. Rowens has some comeuppance due him. I realize in some of his dealings he can be rather abrasive and there are some who refuse to work under his direct supervision but I hope you're not one of them. I have all the confidence in the world with your abilities so hang in there for awhile longer, Tom. You never know, something more to your liking may come along. Don't worry about returning to New Orleans until your present problem is resolved, and happy hunting. Is there anything else? If not, keep me informed. My personal secretary will put you through direct whenever you call. Her name is Denise. Oh by the way, you just send us a pay voucher for your new girl Friday Chris; you don't pay her salary out of your own pocket. We'll reimburse you for what you have already paid her. We'll be talking again soon, I'm sure, so keep up the good work. Goodbye." Tom was absolutely amazed, dumbstruck to be more precise. Not only had the director gained polite telephone manners, no sudden hang-ups; but how did he find out about Chris?

The second non-threatening phone call for Tom came on the next Friday but it was a local call made from Miami. It took Tom a few moments to remember the caller, Terry Connoti, the State Trooper from the attempted bank robbery in Fairfax, Virginia, who had assisted in guarding his residence while he was occupied elsewhere. "Good to hear from you again, Terry; what brings you down this way?"

"A combination of an extended vacation and hunting for a future permanent home. The Virginia winters are getting too much for the wife and me. I had a tough time finding your phone number because I couldn't remember where in Florida you were living. I hope and pray that isn't the beginning of dementia."

"I don't think you're old enough to start worrying about that yet, Terry. Where are you staying?"

"We're at a motel just south of Florida City. If it's not too far from where you live, I thought we might get together tonight for dinner and a few drinks, my treat. You and your partner, Felix, wasn't it?"

Tom told him to hold on a minute while he talked to his wife. "I would have you down here; we have some terrific restaurants in the Keys or we could even have a cookout here at the estate, but unfortunately the place is overrun with FBI agents at the present, but let me talk to my partner and our wives. Give me your number and I'll call you back in fifteen minutes."

Tom found Stella with the children all together playing some sort of arithmetic game making it both fun and educational at the same time. These were her ideas of prepping them for preschool learning and he had to admire her patience with them. He took her aside to explain about the Connotis.

"A night away from here would do you a world of good sweetheart, with all the pressure cooking atmosphere of the last days around here, what do you think?"

"That sounds wonderful, honey, I'll order pizza for the kids right now and get them to bed early. Are Felix and Gennie included too?"

"Terry specifically mentioned Felix but he wasn't aware that we were now married. I have to call him back shortly to arrange a meeting place. They're staying in Florida City."

Gennie begged off saying she would stay with the kids and help them eat their pizza. Felix was disappointed that she wouldn't join them but saw the practicality of her staying at home. "I'll bring ya' a doggie bag of goodies from wherever we decide ta' eat, so don't eat too much pizza."

They decided to halve the distance to meet. Tom told him to watch for a Chevy station wagon so they could join up. Then they could decide where to eat.

Stella looked ravishing in a light green cocktail dress that complimented her complexion and physique, and as usual Tom marveled that he had been so fortunate to claim her as his wife. Not many men had a woman who was the envy of all when she entered a room, envy of the men, jealousy of the women. But Terry's wife Lisbeth proved equal to the challenge. The woman, not three inches shorter than her husband, had a body to match Stella's, but there the resemblance stopped. Her hair and complexion were dark, probably from her Italian heritage, and she was of Amazonian proportion. The two women hit it off immediately like they had been close friends for years. They decided on a seafood house. Tom was delighted; he loved any kind of fish, broiled, sauteed, or deep fried. The next thing was to catch up on past histories. Tom explained his, Felix added his two cents worth, then Terry told them what had happened to him since they last saw each other. Those reviews lasted through their meal and included some outrageous events from both sides of the law enforcement divisions. Terry's state police covered much larger ranges of criminal occurrences than Tom would have imagined. Tom always thought their main concerns were the patrolling of business and residential areas to show the taxpayers they were getting their money's worth of protection with an occasional attempted robbery or burglary thrown in to break the monotony. But he was surprised to hear they were so involved in tracking, and with the aid of drug-sniffing dogs, intercepting drug traffickers on state highways and toll roads. During one of those stops Terry received a gunshot wound from an especially adroit suspect who his rookie partner of the evening had failed to search thoroughly. After recuperation from the chest wound, he was relegated to a desk job when he returned to duty. That was his reasoning for coming to Florida to search for a vacation/permanent retirement dwelling. Now, the meal over, they began on alcoholic beverages, both women abstaining under the excuse of being designated drivers. While the women talked about womanly concerns, Tom asked Terry what price range of home he was thinking of, not really expecting the answer he got. "Somewhere between two hundred and three hundred fifty thousand depending on the type of mortgage rates we can get. I know that won't buy anything large but we don't have children so our needs don't demand that much. The climate is our main concern. Neither of us can handle any more harsh winters with snow and icy conditions to contend with." Tom thought a few moments then said, "I don't suppose you want seaside property."

Here Terry hesitated. "Not much could be had in our price range for that I would imagine, if I thought it possible I might jump into deeper water. I'd have to discuss it with Lisbeth first but she loves the water. She belongs to a health club at home and constantly swims in their pool to stay in good shape. Do you have something like that in mind?" Tom was thinking of the investment property just north of his and that Cliff Ajax could build something suitable there. Then they could use our pool anytime they wanted. The big lawman would be a good neighbor to have to worry about his or Felix's family being protected while they were in New Orleans. It had great possibilities if Terry would agree. His own cost would be negligible compared to the peace of mind provided. Felix had quietly taking this all in downing Buds as fast as they were served. The little mans capacity seemed bottomless but he winked at Tom, "Where's the can, amigo; I have ta' make room for more a' this stuff." Tom noticed he hadn't eaten all that much of his dinner most likely going to take it home for Gennie. "We'll find it partner, I need the same services." As they were washing their hands, Felix said, "I'm startin' ta' figure yer' methods, amigo; no wonder you're livin' so high off the hog. Ya' get what ya' need almost fer' nuthin' an' in some cases ya' make money off the deals. Got ta' hand it to ya' though yer' pretty slick an' it's all legal, heh, heh, heh."

"I have an idea, Terry, that you and Lisbeth might like to think about. It has many benefits for you and one or two for my family also. I can either call you tomorrow when we're both dead sober or we can meet half way again, your choice." Terry looked at his wife and she gave him some signal only happily married couples would understand, so without a word spoken between them an agreement was reached. "Tell us where and what time and we'll be there. That's a promise we don't intend to renege on."

"Fine, you won't regret it, because I do believe you're going to be pleasantly surprised."

Tom didn't have the chance to explain Mr. McHenry's call completely to Stella completely before they became involved with the Connotis so he did so while she was driving them home. Felix was napping in the seat behind them so wasn't privy to his conversation. Stella remained silent during his discourse, taking it all in then abruptly changed the subject. "I heard a good deal of your proposition to Terry but where is that heading honey? You must have an ultimate object in mind."

"What would you think about having them as permanent neighbors to our immediate north, I mean on a year around basis? If I buy that property which I fully intended to do anyway that could easily become a reality."

"I like Lisbeth well enough for just meeting her tonight, yet I'd have to think about that proposal of yours before giving you a final answer."

"Would you prefer total strangers to occupy it?"

"I would hope you would be more selective than that."

"Look, Stell, once your studio is completed and things calm down around our area it would be a boon to have them there and also give me much needed peace of mind while in New Orleans. How else could you have ready-made, instant police protection practically on your doorstep? You've often said you wondered how long it would take for police of any kind to arrive if something you and Gennie couldn't handle alone took place so think about that for awhile. I know how you covet your independence but think of your kids as they grow older."

Stella pulled into the parking area then slowly headed across the lawn toward the garage watching for the dogs. Of course Leo saw his main friends coming and waited to see if they brought him anything as they often did when away for any length of time. Felix woke up when the wagon stopped. "Home already? That was fast." He got out with his doggy bag and Leo was on him almost before he slammed the car door. "Don't got nuthin' fer' ya', ya' overgrown cocker spaniel, ya don't like fish anyway, so get lost." But Stella the ever resourceful one produced a bone as if by magic which Leo daintily accepted from her hand. "I wouldn't forget my protector would I?" She handed another smaller bone to Felix. "That's for your Brutus."

"I won't ask where ya' got beef bones in a seafood restaurant but thank ya' kindly."

When Stella pulled into the garage after Tom had opened the doors she waited for him to close them before walking to the main house alone. After his dissertation on how she enjoyed her independence, therefore the need of the Connotis as immediate northern neighbors, it wouldn't do to flout it so quickly. But as she was checking on the children before heading to bed herself she had to admit there was a certain amount of wisdom behind his words. Was she simply being catty because she was misinterpreting his need for that particular family to protect them because of a latent attraction to Terry's wife? Stella could have bitten her tongue off in penance for thinking such a thing. Tom loved her as much as she loved him without any doubt. He was more than just her husband; he was her best friend and confidant. Proof of that thought was the adoring look he gave her as she unclothed in front of him for bed.

40

The first item on Tom's agenda the next morning after coffee was to call Terry and give him explicit instructions on how to find his estate. "When you pull into the parking area, honk your horn twice then I'll come out to meet you, but stay in your car until I get there. I have a guard dog on the premises who won't know you until introduced."

Next on his list was Cliff Ajax who had to be paged but would return his call shortly. Stella was feeding the kids and would call him in when Cliff called back, so Tom chose the moment to spend some quality time with Leo. The mastiff could easily get his nose out of joint if his main friend was home and ignored him. Tom hadn't taken three steps out the door before Leo spotted him, rushing toward him like nothing else mattered than reaching him before he disappeared again. Tom gave him a hand signal and the result was instantaneous. His rump hit the grass and he skidded to a stop one foot in front of his main friend before he would have bowled him over or else pinned him painfully to the house. "Good boy, Leo; you have that move down to a science."

The call from Cliff came. "Thanks for getting back to me so promptly, Cliff. Can you be here in about an hour? I think it will be well worth your while. Someone will be here about then who'll want you to build him a house on the property I bought just north of mine. He's talking between two and three hundred thousand. Interested?"

"Interested? That is a dream come true. I'll be there before you change your mind. I don't want to miss out on this." Just as Tom hung up, he heard a car horn honk twice. The Connotis had arrived earlier than he had anticipated. "Stella, do we still have those coveralls here from when we were cleaning up from the hurricane?"

"All washed and folded, honey. Why?"

"If I'm taking Terry and Lisbeth out in the north lot they'll need them to cover whatever they are wearing. It's kind of nasty out there. I wish the association had made time to clean it up some before I showed it, or decided to use it myself, but, of course, how were they to know this opportunity would come up so quickly? Hold on to these while I go out to bring them in." Tom saw Leo crouched in his attack position as he headed for the Connoti car. "Relax, Leo, they are friends of ours."

The dog looked up as Tom approached, wondering how he was supposed to know the difference between friend and enemy.

When Tom reached the car, the quite shaken Terry rolled down the window.

"I, I see why you wanted us to stay in the car, Tom; that animal is huge."

"You can come out now, Terry, so Leo can meet you. Once he gets your scent he'll never forget and you'll be able to come and go freely without escort unless I tell him differently." Terry got out hesitantly and joined Tom. "I don't remember him being this big; what do you feed him, hormones?"

"He was much younger the last time you saw him. Reach down and let him smell your hand. Where's Lisbeth? She should do this too." Terry motioned to his wife to come out and join them. Leo had to strain his neck to look up at these big people so he sat up. They both extended their hands downward. "One word of caution, don't scratch behind his ears unless you are prepared to get his idea of a reward, a sloppy kiss." They followed his instructions then three people and dog started for the main house before Leo veered off to resume his guard duties. Terry was looking around like a sight-seer, or the policeman that he was, taking in everything. When they reached the main house and entered Tom asked if they would like some coffee while they waited for his contractor to show up then they would survey the north property. "He built that garage with the apartment above it you noticed on the way in. He's a very capable builder. All you have to do is give him your idea of style, floor plan, and special amenities you desire, and he'll take it from there. He'll make a rough sketch then hand it over to his draftsman for exactness, then show it to you to see if you have any last-minute changes to make before he brings in his crew. You also have to give him a time frame. I was amazed at how fast he put the garage up because one of my team needed a place to live in and recuperate after his stay in the hospital and we didn't have enough room in the main house."

Sheila wandered into the kitchen while the grownups were talking looking for her daddy. She looked especially cute this morning wearing a new little dress Stella had made for her, her longish blond hair done up in intricate pigtails. "Oh what an adorable little girl," Lisbeth said. "Is she yours?"

"Yes, she is one of the triplets, the only girl", Tom answered. It was obvious she was the apple of his eye as he scooped her up placing her in his lap. She sat there quietly as though sitting on a throne. The resumed their conversation waiting for Cliff, Lisbeth continuing to watch Sheila as though she wanted to take her home for her own, a natural feeling for a woman who could not bear children of her own, similar to Gennie.

Cliff arrived with another man Tom had never seen before, and Tom assumed he was just a new draftsman. After all the introductions had been made and small talk completed, Tom handed the coveralls to the Connotis and the group headed for the northern property. The new man had been introduced as Tim Mathers, and he was more than a draftsman. He had been hired for his ability to crunch finances in materials and workmen but also for his knowledge of tax preparations in an ongoing field that was becoming more complicated every year – one smart fellow to have aboard.

Of course, Leo had to tag along, whether to be with his main friend or for some personal reason only he knew and since he couldn't tell Tom it would have to remain a mystery. But Tom didn't tell him to go back because he enjoyed his company at any time, that was how closely bonded the two were. Tom only wished Leo had a twin brother so he could take one of them to New Orleans with him while the other guarded the estate – wishful thinking.

There was a slight breeze coming in from the Atlantic that proved to be a godsend because it was enough to break up the insect population that formed around the pools of stagnant water where the hurricane had uprooted stately palms. The shape that the land was in now without extensive cleanup would present a virtual minefield for anyone walking through, especially after dark. Tom wasn't going to point out any of this and he tried to steer the party clear of the worst of the downed debris. Tom picked a fairly clear area fifteen yards from the water where one or two stunted cypress trees grew that had withstood the high winds of Betsy because of deep gnarled roots. When he stopped Leo sat next to his leg waiting for further developments. "We're about one third of the way in from my property line. As you can see, this might be a choice spot to build. You would be close enough to the water for some spectacular vistas day or night and whichever direction you decided your house should face. If you planted some palms large enough they would provide you with some shade in the short run and as they grew more, in the long run. By belonging to the Home Owners Association you are entitled to various services including garbage pickup, the building of an access road, electricity to your home site, and cut-rates on a number of other things maintenance of appliances and a variety of other problems that might arise. So you see there are a host of services available to you free of charge. I'm going to leave you for awhile to talk with Cliff and Tim. There's something I want to check on but I'll return within a half hour to get you back to my estate safely."

"C'mon, Leo" and they headed north and were out of sight within moments. Tom wanted to get close to the huge, hidden building just north of his property without being seen. "Stay close, Leo. I don't want you running off where you might get shot at, you understand?"

Tom was crouched behind some bushes looking across the perfectly mown lawn at the huge place. All was quiet without a soul in sight. The windows reflected the sun so he couldn't tell whether anyone was behind the panes looking out or not. He looked down to say something to the dog, but he was gone. One minute there, the next moment, poof, vanished. Where could he have gone so quickly? Tom thought maybe he had to relieve himself but in scanning all around the area that wasn't the case. Then out of the corner of his eye he saw movement. Leo was belly-crawling on the ocean side of the mansion toward something out of the line of his vision. Curiosity got the better of him so he carefully moved to his right in an attempt to discover what Leo was creeping up on. He pulled his Cobra out of its holster under his shirt and he would use it on any person who threatened Leo without hesitation. When he had full view of that side he didn't have much cover but he didn't need it. He almost laughed out loud at Leo's antics but checked himself as he put his weapon away. The mastiff was rutting a bull mastiff only slightly smaller than he was. So he had snuck over here before when he wasn't guarding the estate, else they wouldn't have been acquainted. Leo must have smelled that she was in heat. Now he could believe Felix when he told how he could have easily been hurt had he not dropped the leash when the dog turned into the alley after the Irish wolfhound, hence Brutus the gift from Paddy O'Toole. After the dogs were finished, they actually nuzzled, a sign of post- lovemaking often used by humans when they were finished. To see dogs doing this was mind numbing. It was like a kiss goodbye until next time. Leo finally turned away, reluctantly it seemed, and headed back toward his main friend, with never a backward glance. Parting is such sweet sorrow.

"If you're as potent as I think you are, you might become a daddy pretty soon big guy. And I think I told you before about any additional progeny at the estate would cut into your own supply of food. We can't have the place overrun with watch dogs. However, your offspring just might be what the doctor ordered." Having a carbon copy of Leo in New Orleans, after complete training, of course, would be a great addition to his team there. It would have the run of the warehouse-office at night and taken with him when his work called for a menacing presence. Most bad guys were deathly afraid of vicious animals whether they really were or not. Just the intimidation was enough.

"Let's get back to the others, it's been longer than a half hour and we don't want them to think we deserted them. Cliff and Tim should have a fairly good idea of their wants by now." Leo was again matching strides with his main friend but his long tongue was hanging down with saliva dripping. The coupling had obviously taken its toll. He most likely would lap up a half gallon of water when they returned to the estate, then watch out trees. If further evidence was needed when they rejoined the group, Leo dropped down seemingly asleep and stayed that way until they were ready to return.

"Is everything settled, or do you need further consultations?"

Cliff spoke first. "Our main objective is to get the access road in place so we can get equipment and materials in. That will be the only thing holding us up. Mr. and Mrs. Connoti have agreed in principle and will wait for our finished blueprint to decide if any changes should be made. We'll have that ready for them tomorrow." He looked at the buyers. "Agreed?"

"Yes and we're going to get a motel room closer than Florida City, I'll call you tonight when we're situated."

"Well let's get back then."

"What's the matter with Leo?" Cliff asked.

"Nothing a good drink of fresh water won't cure."

When they got inside the boundaries of the estate and Cliff, Tim, and the Connotis had all thanked Tom for his assistance and left, the first thing Tom did was fill an extra large bowl from the kitchen with cold water , adding a tray of ice cubes and took it out to where Leo was lying by the garage panting heavily. The dog couldn't even stand up to drink so Tom scooped water out and rubbed it on Leo's muzzle until he could get up, about eight hands full. The longer that process went on the stronger Leo became until he finally lifted his massive bulk and finished off the bowl ice and all. While he moved toward the nearest tree, Tom went back into the house to refill the bowl sans ice. Returning to where now Leo was looking more like his usual self, he put the bowl down in front of him then sat and watched him guzzle half of that before taking a breather. "How does a dip in the pool sound to you, big guy? You wait right here until I change then we'll both take a swim. "Guard, Leo." Tom knew by saying that the dog wouldn't wander. He changed into swimming trunks and told Stella what he intended doing.

"The children are occupied for awhile, so I just might join you. I need some exercise before I gain any more weight. It seems the only exercise I get now days is in bed with you." She laughed that deep-throated guffaw of hers.

The heat outside was rising into the upper eighties when Tom dove into the water. He came up in the shallow end and coaxed Leo in. You talk belly smackers, the pools water lapped at the sides as if ready to overflow. He dog paddled to the other end where the steps were and lazed there almost floating. True to her word out came Stella carrying two cold cans of Budweiser for her man, ever thoughtful Stella. God, he loved this woman, but she had to start thinking of her own welfare instead of everyone else's. Hopefully when her studio was completed and she could resume her artistic bent she wouldn't have the time to wait on everyone else. She was clad in a blue swimming suit that was cut dangerously low in the front and if any of the FBI agents came outside and saw her they would most likely trip over their own feet in an attempt to ogle her body. It certainly had that effect on him so he was glad he was in the water to hide just how much. Stella was an excellent swimmer but at least she had the decorum not to use the backstroke in daylight with so many strangers around.

For some unknown reason, Tom was getting a headache. It was powerful, throbbing just over his left ear and he felt dizzy like he was about to lose his balance. Of course being in the pool where could he fall to? As the throbbing increased he hand over handed his way along the pool's edge until he reached the built-in steps. He crawled up them and sat there, feet dangling in the water holding the bass drum in shaking hands.

"What's the matter, honey, too much sun?"

"I have a headache, Stell ,and it's a beaut. Would you help me into the house so I can lie down for awhile?"

Stella was out of the pool in a flash. Tom didn't normally ask for help under any circumstances so this could be serious. The sun had dried his body off so all she had to do was drop his trunks then seat him on the edge of the bed while she retrieved a towel from the adjoining bathroom to dry his hair and lower body. His torso felt cold to her touch, so she manhandled him to where she could lay him down and cover him with a sheet. "I'll be right back, honey." She returned to the bathroom, stripped, and took a shower as hot as she could stand, careful not to get he hair wetter than it already was, toweled completely dry, and naked crawled into to bed to give Tom her body heat the best way she knew how. His whole body was shockingly frigid to her touch and he was shaking like he had a case of malaria. He didn't complain, he never did regardless of the severity of his ailment. Stella cuddled him as he alternated between hot and cold all the time pressing the sides of his head with his eyes closed tightly. Finally he started to relax and was soon asleep. She waited about five minutes before slowly extricating herself from the bed so as not to disturb him, quickly dressed, and went out to the living area to call her pediatrician. Maybe she could give her some answers. "Oh the kids are fine, that's not what I'm calling you about. It's my husband" and she explained what his symptoms were and how they came about. "I don't like the sound of that, Stella. Can you transport him to the hospital or would you have to call an ambulance?"

"I can get him there, although it'll take some doing, you know how bullheaded he can be about hospitals."

"Just get him to the emergency room within the hour. I'll meet you there with a specialist to run some tests. Don't panic, Stella; it's just a precaution and it could be related to his truck accident; we'll see."

Stella told Felix what her doctor had said and what she needed his and Gennie's help in doing in as short of a synopsis as she could manage in the allotted time and Felix gave instructions to his wife of where and why he was helping Stella with his amigo. "Ya' get 'im ready ta' move an' I'll grab one a' these big FBI agents ta' help. Tom was as obstinate about leaving the estate as she knew he'd be but the three of them got him in her wagon despite his protestations and delivered him to the same hospital he had been in as the result of his truck collision. Stella wondered if this was an evil omen, now that they had thought their future was so promising. If she lost Tom, who her world so completely depended on, what would become of her and the children? She couldn't imagine a life without him to guide them. Her nerves were starting to jangle while she waited for the specialist, a Dr. Brice, to show up. Why did she always imagine the worst case scenarios? Was this some fault in her genes? Her twin sister Sheila, despite all her problems, had made her course and stuck with it come hell or high water even though it ended up killing her. What went through her mind when she realized she'd never hold Tom again? Dr. Brice showed up and talked medicalese for several minutes with her pediatrician before motioning Stella to join them. "I'm taking your husband into the X-ray department for a brain X-ray. It's something like an X-ray yet using a procedure more intricate so as not to put full X-rays on the brain pan. That will give me a better picture of possible injury there. After I've studied those shots I'll be able to tell you more. It won't take more than a half hour." He scurried away to make the arrangements leaving Stella and Felix to twiddle their thumbs while waiting for the results. "I don't know 'bout this but let's go to the cafeteria for coffee. They'll find us when they know more." As Stella led the way she said, "I have a bad feeling about this, something just isn't right here."

"Whadda' ya' mean ain't right; don't go gettin' spooky on me."

"You should have seen his pallor when I took him from the pool into the house. That was before I called my pediatrician for advice. He was white as a sheet."

"Yeah he still is, so what?"

"You know full well he had a tan as dark as yours; how could his complexion have faded so quickly? I mean what has that to do with his brain? Why a brain X-ray? It simply doesn't sound right to me."

"I don' think ya' need any coffee, Stella; yer' jittery 'nough as it is. Why don' we just have some ice cream? That should put less acid in yer' stomach. It worked like that before if ya' 'member. Whadda' ya' say?" Stella nodded her agreement with a faraway look in her eyes not really comprehending what Felix was talking about. Her own train of thought was on a different plane altogether. When Felix returned to the table he sat a dish of three scoops of vanilla ice cream in front of her then sat across from her with a huge banana split with all the trimmings. The little man dove into it like he was famished. Felix was always hungry.

"Ya' better start eatin' that, Stella, 'fore ya' end up with a milkshake" he said between bites. Stella was staring at the wall clock oblivious of his words. A half hour, then an hour, an hour and a half passed while a state of catatonia prevailed over her. She hadn't noticed when Felix, finished with his split, had reached across the table and taken her dish of ice cream because her state of suspended animation, only the wall clock mattered to her. When two and a quarter hours had gone by the P.A. system announced her name to come to room 25 and ask the head nurse for Dr. Brice. The message was repeated bringing her out of her stupor. She rose from the table quick stepping toward the designated room unaware of Felix trailing her. The head nurse pointed her to room 25, where the doctor was still busy looking at negatives attached to the wall over a lighting strip. Another man dressed in the white coat doctors wore was using a pointer, comparing one photo to another. "This needs to be reviewed by a real specialist," Dr. Brice said.

The thing for Stella to do now was to get Tom home in the friendly confines of the estate and to bed, and to arrange for him to see a specialist. She was sure the children were hungry by now so she would feed them before seeing if Tom would eat something. He still hadn't uttered a word which made her nervous but she would hide that nervousness around the children. Felix, sensing Tom's discomfort, kept his mouth shut until they got home where he could unload on Gennie when they were alone. Until then he would feed and play with Brutus for awhile.

Little Sheila was the first to ask, "Where's daddy, how come he's not eating with us?"

"Your father isn't feeling well, sweetie. He had too much sun in the pool today. Remember what I've always told you? Never go into the pool unless you have lotion on your skin or for two hours after eating because you could get sunstroke. Your father got a dose of it today and he's in bed now recovering. He should be all right in a couple of days but until then we mustn't bother him. Daddy gets sick just like you youngsters. After you're finished eating we have some lessons to review before bedtime because there is a test next week and the highest grade gets to have their favorite dessert for a whole week afterwards and everybody wants that, right?" They all nodded their heads already thinking of their favorite. Children were so easy to please.

Felix had just come back into the house after playing with Brutus and was relaxing with Gennie, drinking some ice tea for a change, and watching the news on the television hoping to get some late baseball scores when a news flash interrupted the program. He swore to himself under his breath and was about to switch channels when the mention of an explosion in South Miami made him hesitate. Two men were assembling a time bomb earlier that had exploded, killing sixteen people in the motel, four more in a convenience store across the street, and three pedestrians besides themselves. The State Fire Marshall called to the scene said it was the most blatant act of disregarding human life he had ever witnessed and a full investigation to determine where and how these men obtained that amount of explosives to begin with. One of the two perpetrators had identification salvageable enough to name him: Dominic Greco of New York State. The other would have to be identified through FBI fingerprints. Well I won't have ta' break any more a' his bones, Felix thought. "Did ya hear that Gennie? Heh, heh, heh. Wait 'til I tell Tom and Stella. Things are gonna' get back ta' normal 'round here damn quick. Boy oh boy, I gotta' have a beer ta' celebrate this one." There was no doubt now that Dominic Greco was no longer among the living but Felix wondered how he had been recruited to begin with. The only thing he could think of was an act of revenge for Felix crippling that big dummy. That had to be it. When he went to the kitchen after his beer the children were just finishing their meal and on the way for more home schooling. "Stella, if ya' have a minute there's sumpthin' I'd like ta' tell ya." After he explained what he had just heard on televison it was her turn to blanch. There is a Supreme Being up above granting our wishes after all. You couldn't have given me better news, Felix; thank you." She hurried out of the room probably to tell Tom, he thought. That news should bring him around if anything could.

41

Tom wasn't out of the woods yet. He wasn't exactly comatose but still sluggish enough that when Stella suggested soup he looked at her as if she had committed a faux pas, rolled over and returned to wherever his mind had wandered, eyes open. Stella just sat on the opposite side of the bed wondering if he would comprehend the news Felix had told her or not. She had to get with the children soon as promised but she was loathe to leave Tom without trying to get through to him in some way.

She answered the knock on the bedroom door to find the on-duty FBI supervisor standing there looking very ill at ease. "Sorry to bother you, Mrs. Mueller, but I just received a call from headquarters informing us to pack up our equipment and return to base now that the immediate threat to your children has passed. However, considering what your husband has endured today I am prepared to leave a two or three-man detail behind if you so desire."

Stella was torn between having the estate returned to a normal setting or being left with Tom in his almost helpless state in the event some other calamity should strike. Until he was his old self, would she better off relying on Felix and the dogs in case of emergency or retaining a small FBI presence? But really, was there anything she couldn't handle without them? Her mind was made up, and in her usual decisive manner she said, "We all want to thank you for protecting us all this time. It would have been most difficult attempting to cope with those threats alone but I'm sure your agency has many more important duties to attend to with national security being what it is with this war in Vietnam escalating." The supervisor looked relieved by her words and in parting said, "It has been one of our more pleasant assignments ma'am, and with those two dogs roaming the grounds 24/7 you should be perfectly secure. If anything else happens to change that security, we are only a phone call away." By 9:30 P.M., as darkness set in, the FBI, with all their sophisticated equipment, were gone and the first peaceful calm in weeks settled over the estates grounds. There was a pleasant off-shore breeze with just enough velocity to dispel the mosquito population, so with the dogs fed and the children asleep, Stella set up a pair of lawn chairs between the main house and garage, then led Tom outside where they could set and gaze up at the cloudless sky full of stars, contemplating the beauty of the vast universe in total silence or talk if he so desired. They held hands like teenage lovers, Stella looking toward her husband hoping he would say something, anything, thus proving he was capable of intelligent speech. "Do we have any cold beer, sweetheart?" She couldn't have asked for anything more.

"Sure, honey, cold beer coming right up." Leo had heard his main friends voice and was lying at his feet when Stella returned with a small cooler full of iced Budweiser. "I'm so glad you're back in the land of the living, honey; you really had me worried." They sat in silence as Tom drank, only releasing her hand when opening a fresh can. "To tell you the truth, Stell, I don't remember a whole lot after getting that horrific headache until just an hour or so ago. I don't know what caused it or where my time was spent until you woke me. It's like I was in a time warp like in those science-fiction shows. It's scary."

"Are you tired enough now to go back to bed, honey, or do you want to have a few more beers?"

Tom hesitated before answering. "That depends on you, Stell. You're the one who has been put through the wringer today. Aren't you pretty well whipped?"

"There is one thing I would like you to do before you go back to New Orleans, my adoring husband, to alter the subject somewhat, it's what has bothered me the most today. Twins seem to have like diseases, case in point: My twin and I had something similar in our genes that gave us all the childhood diseases at exactly the same time plus the stamina, endurance, and body strength of males of the same height, weight, and age. We were not the weaker sex by any means. What I'm trying to get at here, my dear, what makes you think you and your twin were any different? My belief is that Fred must have had blackouts the same as you suffered today. Since I'm not a doctor and don't have any medical knowledge other than what I've read, why couldn't it be a tumor that is operable without too much risk? Modern medicine has come a long way forward in the last thirty years."

"Is this a decision I have to make immediately? It's very possible what happened today won't re-occur, then the further procedure would be moot."

"Honey, stop and think a minute. Would you want a repeat of today's incident to happen while you were on the job? If it did, you could possibly be maimed for life or even killed on the spot and threaten the safety of those working with you, even Felix. You wouldn't want that to be your legacy, I'm certain. Regardless, just consult a reputable specialist to see what he thinks. Will you do that for me, honey?" Tom squeezed her hand in reply. A lot of what she had said made sense, and besides it wouldn't cost him anything but time and for a little while, and he had that to spare. The only question now was who? You didn't just pick a name out of the phone book at random like choosing a plumber.

The next morning after a peaceful, dreamless night's sleep Tom joined everyone for breakfast. The children were delighted daddy was well again after his "sun stroke" experience. Stella mentioned daddy had to see a doctor again that day as a follow-up for his sickness, giving Tom a knowing look to remember his promise of the preceding evening. "So let that be a lesson to you all. Never go into the pool without sun-screen lotion on or until two hours after you've last eaten. That way you won't get cramps and drown or sun stroke and have to go to a hospital like daddy did. Remember the buddy system I've explained to you so there are always two of you to watch over each other while playing in the water and also stay out of the deep end unless you are wearing an inflatable. All these rules are for your own safety in the water. Mommy is teaching each one of you how to swim, and you're all progressing nicely." Tom sat and listened to her discourse, all the while his mind was elsewhere. He knew he had other things to do besides enjoying time with his family and there was no point stalling any longer. But his thoughts were interrupted by the ringing of the phone. "I'll get it, honey; I'm expecting a call." She took the extension in the living area instead of the one right here in the kitchen, which made Tom wonder. Five long minutes passed before she called him to join her. Holding the receiver against her body she mumbled "It's Lance Nolte from Columbus, Ohio."

"You were expecting a call from him?" "In a way, yes."

"Whoa sweetheart, you're going too fast for me."

"I'll have to give you a full explanation later; right now he wants to talk to you."

"Lance, how are things up north? Are the Buckeyes going to be contenders in the Big Ten this year?" Tom listened for a few moments then laughed. "You haven't changed a bit, now what is the purpose of this call; you're not just lonesome for nostalgic conversation, I don't suppose. Right, yes, something like that but I didn't know she called you yesterday. Oh, sure, I remember him; I just lost track of him when I left the university. His brother is? I'll be darned. Give me his phone number, will you, so I can call him for an appointment? That will solve one of the things I had to do today. How much? Holy Toledo, $200,000, WOW! You just don't mess around do you. I don't care what your percentage is, you've certainly earned it old friend. It's been great talking to you, and by the way your godson is growing by leaps and bounds. Let me know when you're going to vacation down here so I can be sure to be here. Goodbye for now." When Tom hung up he just looked at his wife with a perplexed expression. "I'm sorry, honey, I should have told you right off this morning that I called Lance yesterday, but after last night that was so pleasurable I let it slide."

"That's all right, Stella. The amount of the cash settlement makes up for any small slips like that." Which was as close to a rebuke as Tom would ever make to her. Even so, his words stung and she vowed to herself never to make such a mistake again at least not willingly. In the future, she would keep her own counsel. Yet, Lance had given her that shoulder to lean on she needed at the time, the kind of support she usually got from Tom when it was needed.

The doctor could fit Tom in that afternoon at three-thirty since it was a favor for Lance Nolte but cautioned to be prompt as that time-slot could evaporate suddenly. The doctor was a very busy man with patients traveling from all over the South to partake of his specialties, that of a neurosurgeon. The next problem to solve was one of transportation. Tom couldn't continue to use Stella's station wagon and since his windfall that Lance had produced as his crash settlement he wasn't about to go used car, but rather a new car off the showroom floor was the ticket now. One with all the bells and whistles. He had always liked General Motors products so he intended to stay with them. Instead of a Chevy or Pontiac Tom thought a Buick would be his best choice. A Cadillac would be too ostentatious for a government employee, so he let his fingers do the walking in the Miami phone book. There were two dealers in the greater Miami area to choose from, one also handled GMAC trucks so he chose the other hoping they would have what he was looking for on hand. He didn't want to order a car and have to wait for delivery since he had to get back to New Orleans soon. That office couldn't continue to be run by a secretary, however efficient she was. He found Felix and told him his plan and his partner seemed more than willing to drive him where he was going. "Ya' mean yer' gonna' buy a new one? Where's all this money comin' from?" So Tom had to explain how his OSU lawyer friend had negotiated his pickup truck accident cash settlement, not revealing how much he had received. "If they have what I'm looking for on hand you'll only have to drive me one-way then you'll have the rest of the day to do as you please. I have a three-thirty doctor's appointment that hopefully won't take more than a half hour."

"Sounds reasonable. What kinda' car ya' gonna' buy?"

"I'm going to look at Buick station wagons. Black in color, something that'll be indistinct for our kind of work, unlike your Plymouth that stands out like a sore thumb."

"I thought ya' liked my car."

"I do partner, it's just not suitable for surveillance or other clandestine purposes." Tom got that blank stare from the little man he usually received while he was thinking up some sensible retort.

"OK. I gottcha' so as ya' use ta' say all the time. Let's get this show on the road, heh, heh, heh."

Tom remembered to take the packet of brain X-rays, kissed his wife telling her not to worry, he had his head on straight and would do everything she had set out for his schedule today. "Is there anything special you'd like for me to pick up while I'm out?"

"No, honey, you have enough on your plate as it is. Just get back here safely with nothing but good news."

This was the first time Tom had ever bought a car where he wasn't hassled by a salesman or had to haggle like a horse trader to find what he wanted at the price he could afford to pay. This experience was pleasurable to the point to where all he had to do was point at what he wanted and listen to all the modern features that were pointed out. The only problem that arose they wanted Tom to finance it through the General Motors Acceptance Corporation, where naturally the dealership would receive a kick-back, while Tom wanted to pay cash, so the manager had to be called to agree on this kind of transaction, as if cash was no longer an acceptable commodity. Then, of course, his bank had to be called verifying he had enough in his account to cover that large of a check. All this time Felix sat there with a silly smirk on his face but never saying a word though his presence had a sobering effect on the salesman and manager as if didn't transpire to his satisfaction he might erupt like a spewing volcano. Tom noticed the effect but let him run with it, the little man did have his intimidating uses.

After the title was signed and notarized, he was given an instruction booklet for the proper care of a new GM product, Tom drove it off the showroom floor out to the street where Felix had left his car. Parking behind the Plymouth, with the air conditioner going full blast throwing out enough cold air to offset the ninety degree temperature they sat a few minutes while Tom was fiddling with different switches and levers to see what operated which function, Felix said, "I gotta' admit ya' got yerself a real beaut here, amigo, but if that gauge is right, ya' bettr find a gas station pronto or you'll be pushin' it. I'll get your envelope a' X-rays, an' ya' better get goin'."

Tom found a gas station two blocks away, filled the tank, and rather than chance parking on the street at a meter where his new car could get dinged by a careless driver, pulled into a parking garage where if anything did happen it would be his own fault and his insurance would cover it. He was only four blocks away from the doctor's office and it was only five after three so a brisk walk would get him there with time to spare. He took the envelope of X-rays and hurried off, his mind thinking about those two crazy clowns attempting to make a time bomb. Certainly few people would mourn Dominic Greco or Baptiste Castro but they would grieve all the innocents that died because of their misguided sense of revenge. He even felt a sense of guilt on his shoulders that in a roundabout way he was responsible. Thinking along those lines could be detrimental to your health. Had the white sedan making a turn at the corner not honked his horn, Tom would have been rudely awakened from his reverie to find himself another careless pedestrian casualty. He raised his hand in apology to the driver as he stepped back up on the curb. You didn't dare lose concentration in today's bustling urban traffic and expect to survive. When he reached the office and handed his envelope to the receptionist, Tom sat, admonishing himself for being like those unsafe drivers and pedestrians he so often criticized. Despite the doctor's claim of being busy, Tom looked around the reception room to find himself the only occupant. Even the receptionist had disappeared into another room. What is this, he wondered. Am I in the wrong place? Am I losing it again? The close brush with the car had the wrong effect on him. Instead of alerting him of further dangerous situations it had dulled his mind to the point where he wasn't certain if he knew why he was here to begin with. Another twenty minutes passed before a white-uniformed nurse opened the door and beckoned for Tom to follow her. First he was weighed, then his blood pressure taken by the silent nurse before she left him alone. Now Tom was thoroughly disgusted, he'd give it ten more minutes then he was out of here. Wouldn't you know it? Eight and a half went by and Tom was about to leave, and they could keep the X-ray pictures when a harassed looking little man the size of Felix walked in. "Sorry to keep you waiting, Mr. Mueller, but it has just been one of those hectic days where I can't seem to catch up." Tom noticed the doctor's fingers were long and as thin as a concert violinist's but nicotine-stained, indicating he was a heavy smoker. Even such a learned man as Dr. Murphy had a habit that would probably end up killing him.

"I see by your chart you have rather high blood pressure. Are you taking any medication to control it?"

"No, sir. I had a harrowing escape walking here from the parking garage, which may have caused it. Have you had time to look at the X-rays I gave your receptionist?"

"Yes, I'll get to them shortly. What caused your parent's deaths, and do you have any brothers and sisters?" Tom explained when and how his parents had died and that he had a twin brother who was killed in a boating accident, but since his body was never recovered he didn't know the actual cause of death.

"I see. You have a small tumor in your cranium located near the nerve switches that control memory. I understand from Lance you are a federal agent with command decisions to make on a daily basis, so my opinion is that you take the medication I will prescribe every day and return here at least quarterly for further treatment and a possible operation if your condition worsens. Of course, that decision would be a last resort. Do you still play piano?" The switch of topics so rapidly caused Tom to hesitate. "I'm sorry to say, there is little time left for that with my job schedule but it's like riding a bicycle; you never forget. My present assignment is heading the office in New Orleans taking me away from my family in Key Largo more than I would like, so I hope the medication you will have me taking will control any further re-occurrences of those symptoms." Dr. Murphy scribbled out the prescription for him and wished him good luck. "I'll keep these X-rays if you don't mind, and they will be readily available if you need them elsewhere." He handed Tom his card. When Tom left the office heading back to the parking garage, he kept his full attention on traffic, which seemed to be increasing as it neared the evening rush hour, so as not to have a repeat of the close encounter he'd had earlier. He noticed the simple act of concentrating was becoming increasingly difficult,, which bothered him because something he had always taken as a natural inbred course of action was no longer such. Dr. Murphy saw something changing in him through his questions and having known of him in college that over the course of years since caused him some concern. Had his changing acts of libido over those years altered his personality thus his mental inclinations? This train of thought was getting him nowhere, because he wasn't erudite enough on the ways of the human mind to explain it to himself. Another thing that stuck to him out of their session was the mention of his piano prowess that he had let slide because of lack of time to practice plus not having the instrument. That, Tom would remedy in short order. If Stella could have the renovation to the garage apartment surely she wouldn't begrudge having at least a spinet in the main house, tit for tat. To remedy that situation while he was thinking about it when he arrived at the parking garage he asked the attendant if he could use his phone book. Looking in the yellow pages under musical instruments, he copied the addresses of three new and used piano dealers noting which was the closest. Before getting into his new wagon he stood and admired it. You've got to have a name he thought. What would be appropriate he wondered, female of course. New cars had a way about them resembling the varietal moods of the distaff sex.

Driving with extreme caution, Tom arrived at the strip mall containing a sizable piano store that was closest on his route back home. Entering he was faced with every variety of what he was looking for priced from the low hundreds to the high thousands with several electric organs spotted around like newcomers in this field of ancients. He saw what he was looking for two aisles over, made it to a cherry wood spinet ahead of a converging salesman and sat on the bench running his fingers lightly over the keys without producing any sound just to get the feel of the ivories. Their absence had been too long he noted.

"A good choice, sir. This model is on sale this week for $1,600, including delivery within fifty miles. Is this a gift or for your own use?" Tom liked the price but wasn't about to agree on it just yet. He ignored the questions beginning to softly chord the intro to "Misty," then swinging into it as if he was auditioning for a night club gig he wanted badly. The salesman backed away to listen to this obvious professional ply his talent, all thoughts of sales forgotten as he was caught up in the beautiful strains eloquently performed. Tom finished with a flurry, letting the closing bars speak for themselves. He stood satisfied he still had the touch and was ready for negotiations.

"That was beautiful, man. Never have I heard that song played with such zeal other than recordings by Oscar Peterson. You'll be quite happy with this little spinet, I'm sure. It has the quality sound of a baby grand without the price tag." Tom let him rattle on with his sales pitch, then started for the front door. "Wait, sir, you're not leaving are you? Is it something I said that has upset you?"

"Look, there's more than one piano store in this town, and I'm sure I can get the price that I can afford for an instrument to teach my five year old daughter on from any one of them." The salesman followed him right to his car parked directly in front of the store and saw the brand new Buick wagon and wasn't about to let this affluent prospect out of his grasp.

"I assumed that spinet was for your own use."

"I haven't played professionally for over ten years. I'm a federal employee with too many other responsibilities to take the time for my own personal enjoyment."

"You should have told me right off about your employment. Do you have ID that backs that up?"

Tom flashed his CIA pictured card making sure the salesman got a glimpse of his Cobra under his light jacket. The mans eyes widened when he saw Tom was armed. "If you'll come back into the store and sign some papers you can take delivery of the spinet for $1,200."

Tom followed him back in pleased with the bargaining outcome. It never hurt to haggle, retail prices were often inflated to make a better profit margin for the store.

42

Tom pulled into the parking area expecting to see the Plymouth there, but Felix was still gone. Stella saw him from the house and came out, not to admire his new wheels but to inquire about what the doctor had to say. So Tom gave her a step-by-step explanation of his session with Dr. Murphy, omitting the possible future operation. "This medication he prescribed will erase the symptoms of my relapse. He also wants to see me quarterly if possible. You should have seen Dr. Murphy. He's about the size of Felix but heavier. He smokes like a chimney which will probably end up killing him. Now don't get upset sweetheart; I spent some more money on something besides the Buick, which by the way you haven't said whether or not you like."

"Oh it's beautiful, honey. Let's hope you have better luck with it than the pickup. I couldn't bear to go through that ordeal again. Now if you're done beating around the bush, what else did you buy?" "It's all Dr. Murphys fault; he instilled it in my mind with a casual remark he made about my working days at Ohio State, the way I earned money as a musician."

"You can be obverse, honey, get to the punch line will you?"

"Sorry. It will be delivered tomorrow morning, a spinet piano where I can relax and even teach one or all of the kids to play. I haven't touched one for years until today. Your sister thought I played well. We used to ... well that's another story." There was the beginning of a tear in her eye at the mention of her twin. "Oh, honey, I can't wait to hear you play." She wrapped her arms around him giving him one of her five-alarm kisses with the body action to go with it. Naturally Felix picked that moment to show up, forestalling further retaliation on his part.

"Can you hold on to your news for a minute? There is something that has to be attended to while it's fresh in my mind. Are the kids all in bed for the night, Stell?"

"They better be, honey; they have been running me ragged most of the day. The boys don't think they have to take afternoon naps anymore since seeing on television that other boys their age are in school already and don't. It caused a minor revolution for a few minutes until I explained to them they were two grades ahead of most school children in knowledge and weren't being exposed to all of their childhood diseases the rest are susceptible to thus with the afternoon naps they have a twofold purpose solved. They are digesting all they have learned while sleeping and building up more energy to ward off future sicknesses that try to attack their small bodies. Felix, your son is as bad as my son Freddie. He seems to side with him on almost any issue. It's if they have a tacit agreement between them; it can be scary at times. I've watched them closely and there's no actual whispered or hand-signaled exchange between the two. Home schooling does have its drawbacks and there will come a time when what I'm teaching them will be beyond what I can get out of books. I'm not an accredited teacher you know; there's a limit to my capabilities. And then they all will be thrown in to the cauldron of regular schooling. I only hope that event doesn't occur until at least the sixth grade. Now why did you want to know to begin with?"

"With your studio over the garage about to be started on, and Cliffs agreement with the Connotis' nearly finalized for their house, now would be the ideal time for us to take a vacation of sorts before my partner and I return to New Orleans to resume our work there. We have our new car for a comfortable form of transportation where we can dawdle along at a leisurely pace whereas a train or plane would keep us on a formal schedule and we couldn't stop whenever we so wished. There are loads of places we could see that you and I will never have the chance to see together again until the children are in college, and who knows where the agency will post me after our present position. It will take me about a week or ten days to wind things up here with Cliff and to notify Mr. McHenry of our plans. Wouldn't it be nice to relax for two or three weeks then when we returned find everything here ready to resume our normal and sometimes hectic life waiting for us?"

"It sounds wonderful, honey, but do you have some ulterior motive behind this and do you feel up to this physically? You have just been through a couple of very taxing situations that most people would need months to recuperate from and I don't want you having a relapse while we're away from familiar surroundings."

"That's why we'll take it slow and easy, sweetheart; my medication from Dr. Murphy will keep that from happening. You have only to pack some clothes, get a couple thousand in traveler's checks, and get the wagon ready for the three of us."

"Three?"

"Of course, you don't think I would go without Leo do you? He's an important part of our family and he'll watch over us like always. I never have to worry about leaving you alone for a minute with him around."

Felix had listened while Tom and Stella worked out their vacation plans without saying one word but he couldn't stay quiet any longer. "I guess my news isn't as important now as your plans, but ya' are gonna' hear it anyway. Ya' remember your thinkin' 'bout bein' called on ta' bein' an advisor in Vietnam, well guess who was called on for the same job?" Tom just stood there waiting for his partner to get to the punch line in his roundabout manner. "Give up, huh? Rocky got shipped over there yesterday. How's that for news?"

"If ya' two love birds can come up for air I got news."

"Let's just hope he survives, he's a tall man among small people as I've seen on television."

"Whadda' ya' mean small people? What's wrong with them?"

"Partner do you have to take affront anytime anyone mentions your size? I thought you were past that stage by now. I'd match you against any sized opponent with your skills. I'm going to bed. It's been a long and tedious day and I have to be up early." Tom headed toward the bedroom, leaving Stella to explain to Felix, and he to pass it on to Gennie, what she expected of them in the care of the children and their routines. "Anytime they badger you to use the pool, put that floating line across between the shallow and deep sides, and one of you must always monitor that they follow the rules I have taught them and the penalties for not doing so. And Felix feel free to spank either of the boys as you would treat Tomas. Before we leave I'll explain to them the period while we are gone is like their summer vacation if they were in regular school so they won't have any daily studies but they still must take their afternoon naps." Stella turned to leave to make sure Tom took his medicine. Don't ya' worry, Stella. Uncle Felix will treat 'em like his own. Ya' guys just have a good time. I might even take 'em ta' see the Miami Pelicans play if they're good." Tom was feigning sleep, with the open vial of medicine on the night stand, when Stella hesitated just long enough to notice it before continuing on to the shower, discarding clothing in her wake. She had just lathered up when the curtain parted and Tom slid in behind her. There followed several moments of silence before choruses of giggling ensued with her deep throated laughter outmatching his feeble giggles as the more serious consequences silenced them both except for heavy breathing now in syncopation. His retaliation completed, Tom slid into bed under a sheet with his lovely wife fitted to him spoonlike.

Bright and early the next morning, Tom slipped out of bed, put on some shorts and headed for the main living area and the phone to call Cliff Ajax. Surprisingly, despite the activity of the previous day and evening he felt reinvigorated. He imagined the evenings exercises were the best remedy for what had been diagnosed by Dr. Murphy as a tumor in his brain, that and the medication. Whichever, it was a pleasurable antidote, one that he hoped Stella would dose him with often. What a women his wife was. She deserved the vacation more than he did and he was going to cater to her every whim no matter how frivolous it might seem.

Cliff answered his phone personally as if Tom had called him at his office at a normal business hour instead of at home at 7:15 A.M. Tom got right to the point: They would be gone two to three weeks out of state and out of touch, and he hoped the builder would have Stella's studio finished by the time they returned. If it was, there would be additional work for him on the property. He was thinking of a small but acoustically soundproofed music room for himself and to use for possibly teaching one or all of the children. Cliff said he would do his darnedest to get the order for the special glass needed rushed through but until it was delivered he would start on the framing and electrical changes necessary. "Without any doubt, I'll have everything finished and waiting for the glass arrival. I hope the next project you have in mind isn't too large, Mr. Mueller, because you're running out of property to build on and may be sorry you let the Connotis have all of your northern lot. You may have to buy some of it back. Yet nothing you dream up in the way of expansion would surprise me any longer. Have a nice trip, and when you get back your wife's studio will be as ready for her as local weather conditions will permit."

Tom had no sooner put the phone back into its cradle than a horn sounded from the parking area. He looked out to see a piano moving truck idling there and ever vigilant Leo crouched less than ten feet from the drivers door. Tom knew he had to go call the mastiff off before the truck backed out and left. "Come here, Leo. That truck was expected here. You can relax now." The dog was instantly by his side looking up at his main friend as if to say "how was I to know?" As usual, that made Tom laugh. Leo was the best non-human friend he'd ever had and he wondered if he'd ever see one of his offspring from his match-up with the bull mastiff of the Taj Mahal property to the north. "Stay here, big fellow." Tom approached the truck and the driver rolled his window down. "We didn't know it was legal to keep lions outside of a cage in this state, but we weren't going to stick around to find out."

"I understand, fellows, but that animal isn't a lion, he just looks like one. He's a pedigreed mastiff used mostly as a guard dog these days, but his lineage goes back to the years when they were trained to hunt them. This particular dog is as gentle around my young children as you could imagine and we treat him as one of our family. My partner also had a large dog, and between the two of them we are never in danger from trespassers who would want to cause us harm. But enough of this history lesson. How close to the main house you want to get to put the spinet inside?" After getting their input, the two men took no time at all to get the piano where Tom wished it to be as its temporary home an were gone shaking their heads at each other about the eccentricities of some people.

By this time, Stella and the children, awakened by the commotion of moving the piano inside, were going about their ritual of the first meal of the day while his wife was explaining to them the upcoming change in their usual routine. "So you all can treat this like a summer vacation from your usual studies while your father and I are gone. You will mind Uncle Felix and Aunt Gennie's orders the same as if they were ours or expect to get the same punishments." The boys looked crestfallen, already planning adventures they could pursue without Felix being able to catch them because they all knew his habits when at the estate. Most of the waking hours that matched theirs he spent either eating, playing with Brutus, or sitting in the kitchen drinking beer and Aunt Gennie very seldom went outside other than to go shopping.

Sounds of live piano music drifted into the kitchen, silencing all small talk. Stella was the first to leave the room followed closely by all the children. Tom was just limbering his fingers, running through scales and riffs but when he saw he suddenly had an audience he deftly swung into a medley of present-day hit songs that even the children recognized from listening to TV and listening to the radio. Sheila was the first to climb on to the bench next to her daddy. She watched his fingers with fixed fascination as they ran from one end of the keyboard to the other. Tom could see his daughter was the obvious candidate to teach. So he took her little fingers and showed her how to place them on two keys. "Here's what you do, honey. This next song is the beginning of your lessons. We'll see what your sense of tempo produces." With a flourish he started a rendition of "Three Blind Mice," nodding to her when her part was due. She was on time and her delivery was perfect. After three times through, Tom picked her up and placed her in his lap. "Now you just watch what your Daddy can do when he puts his mind to it. This is how you'll play someday when your fingers grow longer." Tom began the opening strains of "Misty," embellishing more than he had at the store the previous day. Stella was soon leaning on the piano watching his expression as he became more engrossed in the rendition. At the soft finale of the song tears were flowing down her cheeks. She could understand why her twin sister so loved this man. They were kindred souls. But he was hers now, and she would do anything in her power to nurture his talent and keep him from harm's way. As he tooled around on the keyboard, another idea struck her out of the blue. This one she would keep to herself. The upcoming vacation would be the perfect time. Romance would surely be part of their commitment toward each other and that would be the perfect opportunity. What sex would the next child be she wondered, surely not multiple births again. Stella wanted another daughter. Boys were fine to carry on the family name and she loved her two deeply but they were so apt to get killed in a war or some freak automobile accident. No, another girl is what she needed, she even had a name picked out. Let's not put the cart before the horse, she told herself; first she had to conceive, but where there was a will there was a way, and she intended to exploit it to the fullest.

The next day, they both had chores outside the estate to complete before they left on their trip. Tom took the Buick into a carryall station where all types of baggage carriers from car tops to all sizes of trailers were rented. He explained to the manager what he was looking for and was shown the perfect model which he had installed. When he returned to the estate, Stella had already arrived and was packing four suitcases with hers and his clothing, all lightweight befitting the season. As he loaded the roof top carrier the second time she followed him out carrying a box of miscellaneous non-clothing articles. She handed the box to Tom. "What's this?"

"Just items I didn't want to put in suitcases, honey, mostly things I picked up for Leo today. Here are the check you asked for. I separated them into bundles of five hundred each. Three for you and one I'll keep in reserve for when you might need them."

"You're more efficient than our secretary, sweetheart, and with everything else on your mind it's a wonder you can remember all this."

om pocketed his three plastic-snapped bundles of traveler's checks which he intended to disburse to different locations later; they were too cumbersome to have on his person full-time what with his Cobra, wallet , car keys, and spare ammo clips already there.

"Are you as tired as I am, Stell? There isn't another thing I can think of to do tonight. How about an early trip to dreamland so we can start first thing tomorrow. Maybe we can exit Florida before it gets dark again."

"Are we in that much of a hurry? I thought you said we were going to take a leisurely trip stopping at places we might never see again together."

"I did say that, didn't I? I don't know what it is but there is something driving me back to Ohio. It's like a magnet pulling me. It's almost supernatural in its intensity if you believe in those powers which I don't. And it's not necessarily to Toledo, my hometown, yet there's seemingly a distant goal there that has to be discovered. Kind of eerie, huh? Then there's also the possibility that the shock I just went through unleashed something in my memory previously hidden somewhere in those recesses. It could be that the medicine Dr. Murphy prescribed has a bearing on all this, I don't know. One thing I do know, a good nights sleep can't hurt me and when I wake up in the morning this puzzle might be solved, you following all this?"

"I'm not sure, honey, but I do agree on one thing, the nights sleep with no hanky- panky."

"That will be hard for me to accept; you're so beautiful, sweetheart, but I'll give it the old college try." Tom went to sleep without even realizing it and woke the next morning again before the sun was up. He was surprised how refreshed he felt, that medicine really worked wonders. It ought to, it cost an arm and a leg for a three month supply. He was sitting at the kitchen table waiting for the fresh pot of coffee to finish brewing, still trying to figure out why he was being drawn toward Ohio, when Stella entered the room. For someone as busy as she kept herself she looked radiant in her wholesome fresh as a daisy countenance. Tom marveled at her beauty which was enough to make any red-blooded virile man stop in his tracks for a second look. This was his mate and he best show more appreciation for her wants as a beautiful woman who had borne three healthy and smart children for him. Up to this point he had tried to surprise her with all types of gifts he thought she would like, a selfish attitude on his part when what she really wanted was his comradeship and devotion forever.

"You look bright-eyed this morning, honey; see what a good nights sleep will do for you? One or two cups of coffee is all you can have. How do you want your eggs? I'll fill a thermos with the rest. I don't want you to have too much acid in your stomach without some food in there to counteract it."

"You sure like to pamper me, and I love it. Scrambled will be fine." Stella got busy with her preparations and wasn't half way through when Felix appeared. Anytime he smelled something cooking he gravitated toward the smell as if at the end of a fishing line. "Smells great, gonna' have any extra?"

"Put some bread in the toaster, and I'll make a portion for you. I don't want you to wither away for lack of food." She looked over at Tom and winked. "Fat chance of that ever happening, sweetheart; that man could find food if he was marooned on a desert island " Tom added going along with her quip, "even if he had to unravel his clothing to make a fishing line to catch a shark."

"Don't even mention that kinda' critter aroun' me in jest amigo, ya' know my dislike for 'em."

There wasn't a morsel of food left on their plates when Gennie and the little ones trooped into the kitchen. Stella never missed a beat. She was up and cracking eggs for another shift of eaters. Tom gathered the dirty plates, silverware, and cups, loading them into the dishwasher. His twin had every modern kitchen device available to lessen using old fashioned elbow grease. If their mother had seen all these appliances when they were growing up she would have thrown her hands in the air and said, "What will they think of next?"

They stopped for gas in Orlando and then continued on north to just short of Atlanta, where they decided to find a decent restaurant near a good motel. Leo needed a pit stop by that time anyway. He had spent most of the trip so far either sleeping or gnawing on one of those meat flavored rubber bones Stella had thoughtfully provided. Tom could tell he was getting antsy by the way the dog kept moving from one side of the wagon to the other. "See anything promising yet sweetheart? Big guy back there needs some time out of the car and if he doesn't get it soon I'm going to have a mess to clean up."

43

Once back on the main route, Stella carefully blended into the traffic flow that was diminishing at this hour. She was an attentive driver for she had a good teacher and she had paid close observance to his driving skills. As it was, they hadn't gone more than five miles when they began noticing roadside signs advertising a travel lodge called The Peach Stone. As they neared it, the signs got larger until they spotted a huge flashing neon sign fixed atop a two-storied structure denoting vacancy and the Peachtree restaurant open for business twenty-four hours serving the best southern cooking in the state.

"How does that place look to you, sweetheart? I don't know about you, but my stomach is starting to talk to me, yelling for immediate nourishment a.s.a.p."

"It certainly looks prosperous with all those cars parked around it, honey. Just so it's clean. I refuse to stay in a place that isn't, regardless of their image of what is."

"I'll be able to tell just by the orderliness of the registration office. You stay in the wagon with Leo until I check." A middle- aged man wearing a flamboyant colored shirt looking like he should be in Hawaii rather than Georgia – as it was covered with pineapples – looked up from behind the counter and flashed a toothy smile that practically lit up the office. "Good evening sir, welcome to the Peach Stone. How may I help you?"

"I'd like a first-floor room for the night for my wife and our pet, and are reservations necessary for dinner?"

"We have several first-floor openings and so allow small pets as long as they remain in their cages and no reservations are needed in the Peach Tree room. If you will fill out this registration form, I'll point out the room on our map. Will this be cash or check?"

"Make that room as far from the highway as possible, and payment will be made with traveler's checks." There was no point in explaining that Leo was not small or would be housed in a cage. Tom knew that if they even caught a glimpse of the dog he and his wife would be sent packing.

Tom backed the Buick to the walk in front of their room, which was one from the end of the building. He opened the door, turned on the lights, and took a good scan before returning for Stella. The room was neat and clean; that ought to satisfy her. For as little time waking time they would spend in it, it would be well worth the paltry amount it cost. "Is there anything you want out of the car-top carrier, Stell?"

"Just the one suitcase and I can get it. I know right where you put it, honey."

Tom let Leo out of the back with the room door open and the dog didn't hesitate; four quick paces and he was inside waiting patiently for his two main friends to follow.

"Well this is a surprise. How much did you say it cost?" she said as she dumped her suitcase on the bed readying herself and a change of clothes for dinner. "Is that all; it sounds like a bargain to me. Now you stay in here while I'm in the shower; any fooling around will have to wait for later. You best pay some attention to your non-human friend for awhile because there's no telling how long we'll be gone in the restaurant." Both Tom and Stella had learned when talking about Leo in his presence to use language that omitted key words and phrases he understood so as not to cause unwanted reactions.

"C'mon, big guy we'll take a short walk so you can get some fresh air and unload anything left in your system. Nobody will see you if you stick close to me and we'll see what's in the surrounding vicinity. You need exercise as much as I do." They were about fifty feet beyond the macadam parking area when they came to a body of water probably made by removal of dirt to level some other low spots nearby. "Stay away from that, Leo; there's no telling what germs that contains and I don't want you soaked when we return to the room." Leo showed his disdain for the pool by moving to it's edge, lifting his rear leg and adding his urine to the mass like he'd understood every word his main friend had said.

Stella was wearing her black cocktail dress that she had cleverly altered, making it more alluring than when she bought the original design. She made him look like a pauper, so he returned to the wagon to retrieve his own suitcase, which had his dark suit and a couple of white shirts in it. When he emerged from his shower and dressed he felt like a new man. Stella had taken a travel iron to the suit trousers to sharpen the crease in them and as he transferred all his pocket contents from one pair to the other, she stood making a pirouette on her toes. "Do I pass your inspection, my true love?":

"You look scrumptious, sweetheart."

"Now, now, that's an adjective to describe fine food." Tom held out his arm, "Would you do me the honor of escorting you to the ball? Guard, Leo and we'll bring you a treat." The dog raised his large front paw as if waving them a bon voyage. Tom laughed as he locked the door behind them causing him to explain what was so funny. "So either he is picking up on out voice patterns or the nuances of our speech. What do you think?"

"He is a smart dog, honey, but you've known him longer than I have. In my opinion nothing he does or will do would surprise me." By then they had reached the Peachtree room and found it three-quarters full so they stood at the entrance while Tom scanned the room looking for an empty table for two or four preferably against a wall. There was no hostess to seat patrons, so it looked like everyone had to seat themselves, and since the bar was only a five or six-seater there wasn't room to wait there for a table. Tom was about ready to take Stella back to the wagon and drive somewhere else when a party of four stood ready to leave. He watched their route and then noticed there was a cashier tucked away on the other side of the tiny bar he hadn't seen before. He steered Stell directly for the now vacated table while everyone in their path stopped eating or talking to stare at this beautiful woman at his side. Tom had grown used to the attention she caused in public places but he was still thrilled to see how others appreciated his choice of life partners. The food and service were excellent, and when Tom had ordered two steaks, one medium and one rare, their male waiter never blinked an eye. All the waiters were middle-aged men, all the busboys teenage girls. It was as if when hired they were all picked from the same mold, all within an inch in height and between five and ten pounds identical weight and all very efficient. Every employee that they saw wore the same outlandish tropical shirts and long pants. The busgirls wore toothy smiles, as though pasted on their pert faces. Both Tom and Stella agreed they were an interesting and fascinating combination of people they had never seen before in all the restaurants they ate at. If by some chance they returned by this route they would make it a point to come back.

Tom wrapped the rare steak for Leo in a paper napkin, waiting for it to cool enough so he could carry it inserted in one of the suit jackets side pockets so he would have both hands free to handle Stella, who had just finished her second mai tai cocktail, a rum concoction with enough power in it to floor the unwary drinker, which she was. "Just stay put, sweetheart, while I pay the check, then we'll go back to the room." Now, he could understand how this place could have such a genteel ambience with all the embellishments. When he looked at the size of the check, any thoughts of returning here vanished. The Peachtree could do without his patronage in the future. At this rate, the amount of traveler's checks they had with them wouldn't last more than a period of ten days. He returned to the table to collect Stella and found her starry-eyed with that look of reluctance to quit the lounge, where most imbibers had who wanted to continue partying. "Come on, sweetheart, time for bed." To her credit, when he gave her a hand up she deported herself like the princess she was. Holding tightly to his arm, she walked ramrod straight while they made for the exit. Once outside in the warm night air, she started to wilt, subconsciously realizing her man would get her safely to their room. There she could collapse for a while before putting the second part of her plan into action. Maybe another shower would be a good idea then when Tom came back from airing Leo and he was given his treat she could have her way with her husband.

Leo headed in the opposite direction of the polluted pond. "Hey Leo, where are you going?" The dog stopped in his tracks looking back to his main friend before resuming his ever-slower pace in the same direction toward the front of the motel nearing the registration office. Tom didn't like the route the mastiff was pursuing but short of yelling at him to stop which would only cause attention to be directed toward him, he followed. When Leo was within twenty feet of the office he crouched into his attack position, his massive head pointing right at the office door which was ajar. That was when Tom un-holstered his Cobra, holding it down by his right leg. Either Leo heard or smelled something that a human could not detect or he saw some quick movement when Tom let him out of their room, whatever, Tom knew from previous experience to trust those unwavering instincts of his which were never to be disregarded. He pulled the door slowly fully open enough to pass through. There was no one there, but Tom could smell the unmistakable odor of a gunpowder discharge. He advanced to the counter cautiously bringing the .38 up to where he could get off a fast shot if needed. Tom looked over the counter and found the clerk with the Hawaiian shirt and the bright smile lying on the floor near an open safe. He would smile no more, for there was part of his skull torn away which could only have been done by a shotgun at close range. The telephone cord had been yanked out of the wall so Tom had no choice but to return to the restaurant to call for assistance. He put the Cobra away and went outside. "Good boy, Leo, you're never mistaken are you? Now, stay by this door and guard until I get back. No one goes in there, you understand?"

When Tom reentered the lounge he went directly to the cashier, removing his picture ID before telling her he wanted the manager of the place here at once. He showed her his ID. This was a no-nonsense type of woman who picked up the phone realizing from the serious expression on his face something troublesome was afoot. A dapper little man of middle age appeared in minutes. Tom took him aside away from the cashier and told him what he had found. "You'd better call the nearest lawmen in this jurisdiction for assistance. There is no need for an ambulance. They'll notify the coroner." Tom gave him his room number and told him he could contact him there and left. He wanted to get Leo back to their room unnoticed.

Stella had taken her shower to sober up and was fighting to stay awake, but drowsiness finally got the best of her. As she fell into dreamland, covered only by a sheet, she never heard Tom and Leo come in. She would have slept the night through had it not been for the constant knocking on the door by over-zealous sheriff deputies who were given the room number by the motel manager. They needed a statement from the person who discovered the murdered motel employee. Tom was in the head using the facilities, and it was either soaking his suit trousers in his haste to answer the persistent knocking or allowing the racket to wake Stella, so Stella lost. She was sitting up in bed bare-breasted as Tom passed her. "I'll try to keep them outside, sweetheart, but sheriff deputies are unpredictable, so you better either roll over and cover up or join Leo in the bathroom."

Stella didn't question his directions; he would explain fully when the time was right. For now she hot-footed it into the bathroom to join Leo. At least there were bath towels in there to partially cover her nakedness.

"We were told by the manager that you discovered the murder victim, Mr. Mueller. How did that come about?"

"First, let's go outside. Your knocking woke my wife before I could answer the door; I was in the bathroom." Tom just walked through them, slamming the door behind him . That should tell Stella they were outside. "First, let me show you my credentials." As Tom removed his picture ID from his wallet, he made sure the deputies saw his holstered weapon. While one held his flashlight

183

on his ID, the other leaned back against the Buick, which caused Tom to say, "I'd appreciate it if you wouldn't lean on my wagon; your equipment may cause scratches on the finish." The deputy moved quickly away as though goosed by a cattle prod. Tom was tired of dealing with these two inept clowns, who it seemed were political appointees, always the most ill-trained and useless for anything other than giving out traffic tickets. "Pretty fancy car for a government employee, ain't it?" Tom wasn't about reveal his resources to these two, and he wanted to get inside, take his medicine, and play with his wife. "If there's nothing else, I'd like to get some sleep; it's been a long day and we've got a long drive ahead of us tomorrow. If your boss needs any further information, he can contact mine in Washington, D.C. He is the agency director, and I'll have to fill out a complete report on what happened here for him."

Stella was wide awake by the time Tom got back in the room, her curiosity keeping time with the beating of her heart. Tom took one look at that beautiful naked body and felt what he had gone through in the past few hours was all worth it. There was never a doubt in his mind that she would weather all that had happened previously ready for any event that would happen next. "You know what just seeing you like that is doing to me, I trust. My libido is demanding that it be satisfied."

"Well then, honey, get those clothes off and do something about it. This is a two-way street, and my juices are flowing. After they had both satisfied their needs and Tom had spent his seeds, he only hoped Stell wasn't at that period where she might get pregnant again. Three were all he could handle at the moment, even with the emerald for backup. He always let his desire for her get ahead of his better judgment. There was little point in worrying about it now; what was done was done. She was pressed to his back in her usual sleeping position, and by God what more could he ask for? Leo had come out of the bathroom, having finished his steak, and lay next to his main friend in his guard position. Tom felt his body there more by instinct than touch, and again he hoped the liaison with the bull mastiff at the Taj Mahal on the property to the north of his bore fruit. What a wonderful addition to his estate that would be. He could get him properly trained and use him in New Orleans to guard the office/warehouse, get him acquainted with Chris to keep her company when other agents came there, and eventually use him on raids where a ferocious looking, large dog could bring down drug smugglers. Even though he could be as docile as his sire, his lineage would do the rest. Hopefully he'd top out between 150 and 175 pounds.

The next day when Tom went in the now tidied up office to settle up on any extra charges, he was pleased to hear that the night manager had left a message that no extra costs would be levied and a cashier's check had been left covering his total disbursements. There was also a package containing a large steak bone for his dog so Tom hadn't done a very good job of hiding Leo's presence. When he got back to the Buick, he told Stella of their actions and handed her the bone to give to the dog. "Just goes to show you how wrong it is to take a place on first impressions, Stell."

44

They drove from near Atlanta, Georgia, to Charleston, West Virginia, taking only two breaks for Leo to discharge before they started to get hungry, existing to that point on candy bars and chewing gum. Before they got to the downtown area of Charleston, Tom pulled off the highway. "With our luck in motels, I have a suggestion to make. Why don't I look for an all-purpose hardware store or a sporting goods store and pick up a double or two single sleeping bags and after we find some decent place to eat we could sleep right in the back of the wagon? The big guy can crawl under the Buick or wherever else he might want as long as he maintains his guard duties. Do you think you could rough it a couple of nights?" "Only if you get two air mattresses for cushioning, honey. We can also stop at a convenience store for snacks and to fill up the thermos with hot coffee for tomorrow morning; it might be fun."

"That's the spirit, sweetheart; we'll make it fun." It will be a pleasure not to have a crowd of people around us, and we can mess with each other to our hearts content." It will certainly beat a hole in the ground, he thought to himself, thinking back to many of the nights he spent alone that way in Korea. This would be like all the comforts of home minus the amenities.

A large sporting goods store appeared first, so Tom pulled into the parking lot. "You want to come in with me, Stell?"

"Sure, you never know what I might find to add to our adventure. Anything we buy will still be cheaper than a nights lodging." The place was almost empty, since it was getting close to closing time. Tom found a clerk that showed him just what he wanted. He had placed everything on the counter next to the cash register when Stella showed up with items she had found that Tom would never have thought of. That was the woman's touch. An insulated canteen, a Coleman lantern with fuel, a waterproof container with matches, and a small tent that could be attached to the rear of the wagon in case of rain. "Looks like you folks are gonna' do some serious campin'. You've thought of everything." Tom paid with travelers checks and had enough change in cash to pay for their dinner. "Can you point out a good restaurant nearby?"

"Sure, the next block north on the other side of the street. It's nothing fancy, but it serves good wholesome home cooking. I eat there every once in awhile. Let me help you with your purchases to your car."

The sporting goods store clerk was right about wholesome food. They had enough rib-sticking victuals to eliminate finding a convenience store for snacks. Stella had the forethought to bring the insulated canteen in and had it filled with coffee for the next morning. She used the restroom before leaving, since they didn't have a port-a-potty then asked the waitress if she could find their dog a big bone, always thinking of Leo. They left and started hunting for a secluded camping site. Tom didn't want to get too far off the main highway so they couldn't find the way back but to be hidden enough so they couldn't be observed. Stella pointed out a dirt track through high grass that curved away and disappeared. "Now if it isn't leading to someone's house tucked away back there we might be in business. Their luck was holding; the track ended in an open glade practically surrounded by trees. It looked as if someone had used this spot before. They could see the remains of campfires in the waning light of nightfall. Stella got to work on the Coleman lantern and when the pressure was up it glowed nicely while Tom started blowing up the air mattresses. He almost asphyxiated himself in the process, but in about a half hour the job was completed enough that the sleeping bags laid open on them were comfortable. Leo had been given his bone and was happily gnawing on it just outside the rear door. At least he wouldn't be gaining any weight from that, Tom thought. They would put him back on his regular food wherever they stopped next. When Tom turned around to take off his clothes there was Stella lying naked as a jaybird on top of the open sleeping bags, looking as enticing as ever. He knew what she had in mind and was all for it. There wasn't any giggling or foreplay tonight; she held out her arms and Tom lowered himself into her embrace. The Coleman sputtered a few times and went out, not that they noticed.

The night passed without rain, the rising sun waking the two lovers, who had spent an exhausting night in each others arms, no spoonlike sleeping position that they usually had when in a proper bed and Toms right arm went to sleep cradling her head. She was up first, dressed quickly, and had let herself out of a side door with the canteen of coffee. She was rummaging around in the car top carrier when Tom began dressing. Finding what she wanted, she gathered some kindling and started a small fire on one of the former campfire sites. By the time, Tom was dressed and out of the car the pleasant aroma of brewing coffee greeted him. "Didn't your insulated canteen work, Stell?"

"Not like I thought it would, honey; it was just lukewarm, so it had to be reheated. Live and learn. Did you take your medicine last night?"

"I swallowed it dry as I was undressing. You were too interested in something else to notice. Did you enjoy your first night of camping out in the bush?"

"It had its good points, but I wouldn't want to make a steady diet of it, thank you very much. Do you want to take the first driving stint or should I?"

"You go ahead, sweetheart. I want to check our road atlas for a few things. Something is still drawing me toward a little town in Ohio. I can't explain it, but Shelby, which is mainly a railroad town, is beckoning to me."

"How far is it from here, honey?"

"I'll let you know once we get on the road and I can get my bearings, but offhand I'd estimate not much more than three hundred or three hundred and fifty miles but the atlas is in a side pocket of the passenger door. I'll help stow everything away so Leo will have room to stretch out. He's probably tired after his night of guard duty." That tended to Stella made sure her small campfire was completely out before getting behind the wheel to begin her shift of driving but being careful to retrace her exact track so as not to scratch the paint or damage the tires, then pulled out on to the highway blending carefully into heavy traffic. Tom was going through the atlas, checking mileage and not paying any attention to her driving, knowing how capable she was. "I think I have it; of course, I'm doing the math in my mind, and arithmetic has never been one of my strong suits. I was way off when I gave you that estimate. Two hundred and seventy five is more exact." When they crossed the Ohio River at Marietta, Ohio, Tom told Stella to change routes heading more northwesterly.

"It's kind of a rolling hill country, very scenic but sparsely populated, mostly farm land. We'll skirt Zanesville and pass through quite a few small farm towns until we get to Mansfield. If at any time you want to switch places so you can enjoy the scenery just give a holler."

"What quaint names those towns you've rattled off have. It's like a history lesson of the whole United States that I'm teaching the children which reminds me, I'd like to stop somewhere to call Felix to hear how they're behaving. Maybe he can enlighten us on any progress Cliff is making. How far is it from Mansfield to the little town you're looking for?"

"About twenty miles, we can either stop there to eat or stay in a motel overnight, your choice. I want to get to Shelby in broad daylight so I have plenty of time to nose around."

"After last night, a nice bed sounds wonderful where I can work my magic on you, honey. How's our passenger doing back there?" Tom took a quick glance over his shoulder. "Still out cold; I figured he would be. Riding in cars does that to him unless he's given a direct command which registers with him to keep him awake and alert. He doesn't give a hoot about scenery." They rode along several miles in companionable silence, content with just being together. Tom leaned in and turned on the radio, keeping the volume down just scanning the dial looking for some music but every time he thought he had something listenable it would fade out, obviously small stations with very short wave bands. Only one station didn't fluctuate. He couldn't get a call sign or location and it seemed more of a talk show than one of musical selections and he was about to turn it off for a lost cause when a song began playing, featuring some clown who thought he could sing. The ditty was "Winchester Cathedral." The song was repetitious and then the shows host had the nerve to play it again, stating the song would be the nations number one hit by the end of the week. To Tom, that had the smell of payola, and without John Q. Public realizing it, radio, television, and the sheet-music publishers could ram the song down their throats disguising it as a real hit. Thus music lovers all over the nation would scramble to buy the records, sheet music, and all groups still on the road would have to have arrangements written in their style to further the making of a fiasco into a number one song on the hit parade. Tom had seen and heard it happen before, and it was one of the reasons why he had taken a hiatus from the business he so loved to pursue other spheres of interest. He turned the car radio off in disgust. "You didn't care much for that song I take it, honey, can't say as I blame you. Martinsburg just ahead. Are you ready for some food? I could use a breather myself and I want to call home before it gets much later."

"Sounds good to me sweetheart plus I want to get our friend back there a meal from his regular food. I can sweeten it a bit with a couple of raw eggs from wherever we eat. He'll go through that like a buzz saw and it's good for his coat. I'll watch for a restaurant that looks hospitable." The town was only four blocks of business district in length. Stella was keeping the Buick crawling at about fifteen m.p.h. so that each of them could scan their side of the street. There wasn't much to see. Cars and trucks were angle parked toward the curb, what few of them there were and two blocks through was the towns lone traffic signal blinking yellow. The four businesses clockwise from Stella's position behind the wheel were a bank, a two pump gas station, a hardware, an a bar. They hadn't seen a restaurant yet, so Stella kept going straight. At the end of the last block sat the only building that even resembled a restaurant, and it looked more like an ice cream parlor, drug store combination and adding to its peculiarity outside the front door stood a wooden Indian, something Stella had never seen in person before, painted in bright colors including the headdress. "That looks like the only place to grab a bite in this whole town. Do you want to chance it or try for somewhere else further along?"

"What have we got to lose, Stella; it can't be any worse than some of the other places we've been in, and you can't hold your water forever. If the place sells ice cream for in-house consumption, they'll have to have restrooms. All right, big boy, it's time for you to wake up and guard the car. We won't be too long then you can eat your dinner and I'll try to get a couple of eggs to stir into your dog food." The dog's massive head rose off the floor and he looked directly at his main friend, his tongue hanging almost down to the floor. The inside of the ice cream store looked like a tintype photograph out of the 1920s. There were only two other people in the store, one customer and a mustachioed counterman wiping an old fashioned sundae glass with a towel. The place was spotless, in fact so clean Stella wondered how they could possibly keep it that way. Didn't it ever rain here? Then mud would be tracked in from outside. When she was directed to the restroom it was also as clean as her own. Joining Tom, back at the counter she heard just the end of the conversation with the counterman, he would receive two eggs free after they decided what they would purchase. "You must have a strange dog that likes eggs."

"Not really, they're good for his coat." The more Stella listened the funnier it got.

"What kind of dog is it?"

"I'd show you by bringing him in here but you'd probably be afraid of him and call the police on us."

"What kind of dog would scare a big fellow like me?"

"You'd be surprised . Leo is a three-hundred-plus-pound mastiff. Our children ride him like he's a pony, and he loves it and watches over them like the guard dog he is. No one would ever get on our property to harm them. It's already been tried. He never barks but when he sees possible harm coming toward me, my wife, or anyone he cares for they are lucky if they live to tell about it."

By this time the counterman's eyes looked resembled those of Eddie Cantor.

After looking over the abbreviated menu they both decided on BLT sandwiches, one with mayonnaise one without, and two milk shakes, one chocolate, one vanilla. The counterman went behind a partition and got busy. Soon the savory aroma of frying bacon drifted their way. The only other customer got up and left the shop after laying a couple of bills on the counter. "They must operate on an honor system here, honey, no bill, no asking for change. I wonder how they can continue to stay in business on that kind of basis? They must have one or two rush hours when extra help comes in and we're in between them. What a wonderful way to operate. It's a shame more businesses can't work that way. Martinsburg could be a role model for the entire country." The sandwiches and milk shakes consumed, the Muellers paid their bill and were presented with a foam box containing two eggs that would make Leo very happy. Tom removed the bag containing the dogs regular food from the car top carrier, putting it on the passenger side floor with the dish , handed the egg box to Stella in exchange for the keys and drove them away from Martinsburg to just short of Mount Vernon where he pulled off the road near a roadside telephone. While Stella placed her call to the estate, Tom went about fixing the mastiff's dinner using an ample amount of dry food before cracking the eggs and stirring the mixture up. Now after filling his water bowl, he sat them side by side and let Leo out of the rear door. The dog attacked the food as if he was starving.

"There's good news from the home front, honey. All the children with the exception of Freddie have been minding Felix and Gennie. It seems that little rascal has a penchant for getting into trouble. I'll have to crack down on him a little harder when we get home before he gets into something really serious that might endanger one of the others."

"Sounds just like my twin, sweetheart; he had the same values when we were young growing up in Toledo. Fortunately I joined the service before anything like that had a chance to occur. Thinking back, if I'd have talked Fred out of some of his shenanigans at the time he might not have followed the path he did but as the old proverb stated: 'No man is his brothers keeper.' "

Stella had one piece of news she was going to hold back. Gennie had missed her period for the second month in a row, which meant she was most likely pregnant. But the last time that happened, the baby was stillborn and her doctor told her she would never b able to birth a child again, the reason why they adopted Tomas. "Also, Cliff called and told Felix the special glass for the garage studio would be delivered in two days, which would be tomorrow. He already has glaziers lined up to help him with the installation weather permitting and when that job is completed to his satisfaction he'll tackle the music room addition so it sounds like he is going to be quite busy between now and when we return from our vacation. Since we don't really know when that's going to be there wasn't too much I could tell him."

They were nearing Mansfield in the late afternoon with bright sunshine on their left, causing Tom to turn the visor down, swinging it to the left to cut down the glare. Stella had moved across the seat and was fondling Tom's leg in a manner she knew would arouse him; it had worked often enough before but she got a reaction she hadn't expected.

"I can't very well concentrate on driving while you're playing games, Stell. If you hold that mood until we're in a proper bed tonight, I'll be more than happy to accommodate you. Stella knew better than to continue her pursuit of passion at the present. Besides, Tom was right. Traffic was thickening as they neared the larger town. Mansfield was no Miami, Florida, by any means yet it was much larger than the farm towns they had passed through since crossing the Ohio River. As they entered the outskirts, she was surprised it how big it actually was. Here business seemed to be booming even at this late hour when banks and most department stores were closed. Night life was just beginning with theater marquees lighting up and pedestrians milling about as they were deciding where to eat and what movie they wanted to see.

They ended up checking into the Waldorf Hotel, one block off the main business section they'd passed through, that contained the theatres and restaurants. It was rather an auspicious name for a hotel in a town this size but it had one amenity Tom couldn't resist, a sizable parking garage connected to it with a sheltered walkway to the main lobby which in the event of inclement weather was a nice feature. The room was good-sized and on the third floor, which would allow him to check on Leo during the night and let him out of the wagon if an emergency trip for watering purposes was necessary without being seen by other guests. There was also a Chinese restaurant directly across the street that looked promising. After cleaning up and changing clothes, they decided to investigate the nearby vicinity with no intention of seeing a movie but to get a breath of fresh air before retiring. Stella had her arm hooked to Tom's as they promenaded up and down the streets close to the hotel. There was just the slightest trace of cooler air that evening a harbinger of the winter weather the Midwestern states were known for, one of the reasons Stella so loved the Florida Keys and Key Largo in particular. She would never leave there if she had any say in the matter, an occasional vacation was fine but until the children were grown and were leaving the nest for college or career pursuits she was content despite some hurricanes that were few and far between. They decided to forego anything to eat after their walk so they both could get a good night's sleep before making the trip to Shelby in the morning. Of course, Stella had an ulterior motive, she was determined to have her way with Tom in another attempt to impregnate herself. She still wanted another girl.

While Tom went down to check on Leo Stella put on a dash of the perfume he liked so well then she oiled her body, arms, legs, and finally donned a thin see-through net wrap and propped the bed pillows up on the headboard. Nature should do the rest. The only light in the room was a table lamp which back lit her voluptuous figure. If this overall picture didn't excite her man, nothing would.

Tom entered the room not knowing what to expect. Stella had been in a strange mood the last two days acting as if she was sex-starved. Their night time antics had been on and off since the birth of the triplets then his recuperative period had curtailed any steady sex. But when he saw the effect her preparations produced Tom knew this night was going to be like old times with serious love making in the offing. He couldn't get his clothes off fast enough, and Stella didn't move to help him like she often did. Any further thoughts on the whys or wherefores were forgotten as he delved into the depths of his beautiful goddess. Stella awoke first, as she usually did, and began picking up the disheveled room. Bedding in a tangled mess, Tom's clothes and her own enticing costume of the night's love making were strewn about the room, so she started the tedious job of putting things in order. No wonder she kept her shape, with all the bending, straightening, bending she did. No love handles on her or need to take an exercise course at some spa. By the time she was finished and showered, Tom began to stir. "I'm afraid your suit needs professional cleaning this time, honey; it's beyond my travel iron's use. So do you want to order some kind of breakfast before we leave?"

"Coffee and orange juice will be enough for me, how about you?"

"I'll have the same."

As they approached the wagon they could see Leo up and moving from side to side in an agitated manner as if he could sense something amiss nearby. Tom stopped in his tracks, holding Stella with one hand and setting their bag down reaching for his Cobra. Stella saw the urgency in his manner so she stayed quiet and moved just enough to be at the side of another parked car to stay out of his way and not hinder his movements. Tom crouched down, moving stealthily in an oblique direction toward the Buick to be able to open the rear door and see how Leo reacted. With the grace of a charging elephant Leo exited and took off for the front of the wagon. What followed five seconds later was a God-awful howl as Leo's maw clamped down on a hand which held a weapon that clattered away on the cement flooring. Tom reached the mastiff's side and commanded, 'Hold,' which wasn't really necessary, for the perpetrator wasn't going anywhere. "Stell, go into the lobby and tell the desk clerk to call the police."

The would-be bandit was holding his eyes tightly shut, probably hoping this apparition from hell would disappear so he could make his getaway from the botched robbery attempt. Tom looked down at the baby-faced robber who he was certain was not yet twenty-one. They're starting on the path of crime at younger ages these days, he thought; he only hoped this youngster wasn't doing this to feed a cocaine habit. If so the authorities would put him in a detox program where he'd come off it the hard way. Stella returned with the hotel's house detective who looked like he'd just rolled out of bed with a dandy hangover. The man was enormous, most likely a retired lawman.

"You again, huh, Frankie. You're a habitual loser, an' this time the judge will throw the book at you. Your habit must be getting expensive." That statement proved Tom's worst thoughts, he was a user of narcotics.

By the time a Mansfield patrol car with one patrolman had taken the witness statement from the Muellers and Tom had explained Leos presence, over two hours had elapsed, making their departure for Shelby later than Tom had hoped for. Leo sat patiently by Tom's side.

When they arrived in Shelby, the first thing that attracted Tom was the sounds of music being played by a marching band. The familiar strains of Sousa's "Washington Post March" drifted through the autumn air, competing with traffic noises and occasional locomotive whistles. He followed his ears toward the source, which brought them to a sunken football stadium of the high school. There the music resumed with stops and starts as the band director found fault with certain passages and when he was satisfied the band started over. He couldn't see the players from where the wagon was parked, so he got out to get a more advantageous position. That was when he spotted a man raking leaves in a small front yard of a white-shingled house above him. Tom moved away from the wagon toward the man, and as the man turned toward him, Tom blanched. There stood Fred, rake stopped in mid-motion staring directly at him. Tom felt dizzy but there was nothing to hold on to. How could it be? Fred was dead, wasn't he? If not, this doppelganger had to be his reincarnation. As they stood motionless staring at each other, Tom was having flashbacks of his life from growing up in Toledo together to his time in Korea where he lost track of him altogether as they each went their separate ways, Tom to Ohio State, Fred to Harvard. The other man spoke first. "Do we know each other?"

"We should, My name is Tom Mueller. What's yours?"

"Ray Urich. Why don't you come up on the porch and sit a spell so we can get better acquainted."

"I'd like to, Ray but my wife is in the wagon, and she'll worry if I'm gone too long."

"Go get her while I put some coffee on."

45

Tom went to get Stella and let Leo out too. "You're not going to believe this until you see it, so I won't elaborate. C'mon, Leo, I want to see your reaction, or if you have one at all." When they climbed to the porch of Ray's house, he was still inside. When he came out carrying a tray with all the fixings, Stella turned as white as Tom had when he first saw his look-alike. Ray calmly put the tray on a side table before looking down at the mastiff. "What's his name?"

"Leo, get up and let Ray get a good look at you." The dog obeyed Tom and rose to his feet but then sat at his side his tongue hanging down as he looked first at his main friend then Ray and back again, the classic double-take. "He senses something, Ray, but he hasn't quite figured it out. What do you say, Stella?" It took Stella several tries to get enough saliva in her mouth to articulate clearly. "This is incredible, honey." Ray sat back, pouring coffee out for each of them. "Let me give you some facts as I know them." He gave his birth date, month, and year, which matched Tom's exactly. "I was born in Toledo at Flower Hospital", Tom added. "The birth certificate was lost in a fire at Mom's house but I'm sure the records department there has it on file along with Fred my twin brother, now deceased. What do you do for a living, Ray?"

"I'm an inventor and sculptor, and you?"

For an answer, Tom handed over his picture ID. "Now, honey, that may be your present vocation but you have another talent you've shelved. He is a talented pianist, Mr. Urich, and he could make a less dangerous living by pursuing that field."

"Ray, please. I know we've just met, but to further our friendship we should be on a first name basis."

"OK. Ray, and I'm Stella. I'd like to see some of your work. Do you have any nearby?" Tom had sat back during their discourse but felt his wife was side-stepping her artistic talent so he broke in. "I'd like to see your work also, Ray, but my wife is being modest to the extreme here. She is a painter in oils, water colors, and charcoal, and when we return home from this vacation to Key Largo, an employee of mine should have the special studio I commissioned ready for her. All that, plus she's home-schooling our triplets, so you see she is an extraordinary woman. You ever been married, Ray?"

"Never had time for it, Tom. I guess I've never met the right one yet. Oh, I've dated around a bit, but it seems once the initial attraction passes, we had nothing in common to talk about," and he winked. "The close neighbors are forever trying to fix me up. It seems they can't stand to see a single male in their midst. Over all, they treat me like an eccentric recluse, which is fine with me. Come out back, and I'll show you where I work, and bring Leo; there's something that should interest him. They followed Ray to the backyard that was ten times bigger than the front. It ran a hundred feet back to a graveled alley. Along the left side from the rear of the house to the alley were two rows of wires supporting grape vines that were loaded with the fruit, huge purple grapes which looked ready to pick. Leo took off down the outside of the inner row and disappeared. Ray laughed. "I thought he'd catch her scent pretty soon." Tom was going to call him back but then thought he'd wait to see what developed. "Grandpa Urich made some very good wine from these vines, something he learned in the old country when he was young. He died when I was seventeen, but up until his death he was employed as a night watchman at several local factories. He rode an old locally manufactured Whippet bicycle to and from work. I can still remember him taking me along when I was about seven or eight into one of his plants. It scared the pants off me, that huge machinery looking like monsters ready to gobble me up."

Stella had stopped behind us and was sampling some of the grapes. She caught up with a small bunch. "Try some of these, honey; they're wonderful."

They are rather sweet, aren't they? I'll harvest them in a couple more weeks before we have a deep frost that will injure them." They were nearing the huge workshop that was fifty feet deep extending to the alley and about thirty feet wide. There, they found Leo lying next to a two-hundred-plus-pound female mastiff. They looked like they had known each other for quite sometime instead of fifteen minutes. Both dogs were lying with their massive heads on their front paws, bodies touching.

"Her name is Leonarda, I call her Lee. She's AKC pedigree and a lot of comfort to me, plus I never have to worry about anyone breaking in here to steal any of my tools or other expensive equipment stored here. I haven't bred her yet for the reason I didn't want to leave her at the kennel during the process of finding a suitable mate." Ray looked at Tom in a suggestive manner as if waiting for him to make an offer to lend Leo for breeding purposes with Lee to keep it all in the family so to speak. Tom caught the inference but stalled while mulling it over in his mind. Stella, having heard the exchange and as usual reading his mind by the look on his face, said, "It makes good sense, honey; she and Leo would make a perfect match and you could get the choice of offspring. You've often said it would be good to have another Leo in your office in New Orleans so to quote you, 'Let's get this show on the road'." "Sound all right to you, Ray?"

"Let's get it done. We can leave these two love birds alone while I show you what I'm working on at present. I'd like your wife's opinion before I tell her what it represents. The only hint I'll give is it's a Korean War Memorial. The rest she'll have to figure out for herself. Stella stood looking up at the eight-foot-high creation from first the front then slowly started circling so she could see it from all angles.

"It's either a hill battle scene – I can make out three riflemen – or if you painted some of it white, that reservoir, what was it called? where so many men suffered frostbite, Closen – something like that. I remember reading about it."

"You are referring to Chosen Reservoir, and you have hit on it exactly, Stella. I knew you would see the nuances of the theme; you have quite an eye. I would like to see some of your work because there is an idea fermenting in my mind part of which has been just waiting for the opportunity and the right combination to present itself. We'll talk more about it after dinner tonight and a good night's sleep. You'll all stay here, as I have a perfectly comfortable guest room upstairs, and a restroom is also available up there. It's much better than a hotel or motel stay and you can stay here as long as you care to. Leo is quite content outside with Lee, but if you would rather have him inside with you, so be it. You can also get your wagon off the street and into the backyard by coming in off the alley. I'll go with you, Tom, to show you how and where. I noticed you have a car-top carrier which probably contains your clothes, and you'll have it closer at hand that way. Agreed?"

Tom was independent, too, and although Ray owned this house and they were his guests, he wanted a little more say in how they would spend their time here. He needed time alone with Stella to discuss the matter.

"What did you have in mind for dinner, Ray?"

"For a small railroad town, Shelby has several fine restaurants, nothing high class mind you, but adequate and clean. Most are family owned and operated where they are passed down from generation to generation, or we can eat in. I keep my larder well stocked, not that I eat in that much, but with Stella's help we likely could put a wholesome meal together. You think so, Stella?"

Stella just nodded. She could see Tom was getting edgy and could sense he wanted to get her alone to discuss something that was bothering him, so she side-stepped the dinner preparation question by saying, "Why don't you two bring the wagon around back so Tom can bring my suitcases in and join me upstairs in the guest room. What's the location, Ray?" When she was told where, the two men left on their errand, and she climbed to the second floor. She entered a room with furniture right out of the 1890s. Antiques probably worth a fortune at today's market values, to a collector of such things, anyway. The four-poster bed looked inviting, and when she pressed on the mattress her finger marks were left on the coverlet. Feather stuffing, she wondered? Stella didn't have much longer to think about it before she heard two car doors slam in the rear yard and within minutes Tom joined her carrying three suitcases, his, and her small overnight case, plus her garment bag. "These should be all we need for our stay here, sweetheart."

"What did you and Ray decide about dinner, honey. I hope it wasn't to prepare dinner here."

"No, he's determined to take us out for it, and he said to dress down, whatever that means. I would imagine it means not to gussy up."

"There's a word I haven't heard in a long time, honey; you can come up with some doozies. Have you taken your medicine yet?"

"I'll wait until after dinner for that, Stell."

After Ray helped Tom remove the last of the contents of the car-top carrier, stowing them in the workshop. Tom pulled the second tier of rear seats up while waiting for Stella to come downstairs to join them. Ray was giving instructions to the two dogs, who were still lying cheek by jowl together perfectly content. Lee raised her head watching her main friend during his discourse then settled back to her former position. Leo hadn't moved until he saw Stella crossing the rear yard toward his main friend, which caused him to raise his head and watch her progress. The dog's inbred intelligence and past experiences with his main friend made him wonder what was afoot.

Tom and Stella talked for a few moments before he went over to Leo who raised himself to a sitting position awaiting his arrival. "We're going out to eat, big guy, so you and Lee guard the property until we get back. Then if you decide to stay outside with her or come into the house with us, it'll be your choice." The dog's maw opened, releasing his tongue, and Tom would have sworn he nodded his head. It was easy to let your imagination get the better of you when it came to Leo.

They ended up at a steak house that a stranger to town would never know was there. No flashing neon sign or even a painted nameplate over the front door. "This is Sebastion's, the oldest restaurant in Shelby. They don't believe in flashy advertisement, and it's tucked away under the Masonic Lodge. It will surprise you how large it is. They serve some marinated steaks that will practically melt in your mouth. I've known the owner for years since I went to school with him from grade school through high school, where he was a pretty decent football player for such a small school. Jimmy was offered a full four-year scholarship at Ashland College but turned it down to take over this business because his father had a fatal heart attack and his mother couldn't run it alone, and he's never regretted it."

They were introduced to Jimmy Sebastion when they entered the place. He was sitting behind a counter checking a list of produce to be ordered, and when he stood Tom could see why he was offered the scholarship; he was built like a bull. It made him think of his high school playing days at DeVilbiss High in Toledo. "A brother, you say, and you never knew he existed until today. What a terrific surprise." He ushered them to a table for four in a prime location next to a raised platform holding a spinet.

"His wife tells me he's an accomplished pianist, so maybe after we eat you can get him to play. I know I'd like to hear him too."

"Is it in tune?"

"Sure, we have entertainment two nights a week; it's picked up our business dramatically on those two formerly slow nights. I hadn't realized there were so many folks who liked to sing-along with a piano player. We even printed up a song book we have on each table so that patrons who didn't know all the words for the songs wouldn't feel excluded."

Tom and Ray both ordered ribeye steaks that Ray recommended, while Stella said she would prefer the stuffed pork chop dinner. Large salads preceded the entrees that were loaded with sliced tomatoes and hard-boiled eggs topped off with a zesty house dressing. Stella only picked at it while the men devoured theirs. The steaks arrived that were on metal platters that were inserts and they were cautioned not to touch as the meat was broiled on them. Those were accompanied by baked potatoes with sour cream and onion rings, garnished by sliced baked apple halves. The men waded right in, attesting to their healthy appetites. This restaurant qualified for a five-star rating in Tom's estimation, another surprise tucked away in an obscure site in a small railroad town the size of Shelby. The meals consumed, they sat back to take a breather over coffee, skipping desserts. This was when Ray brought up his ideas for a future combination of artistic talents in a business venture where they could expand beyond his present geographical limits. Ray was talking directly to Stella, but Tom was listening intently, and he could see the wisdom in Ray's ideas. "Your coming into my life today has brought forward the end-game culminations of my plans, Stella, and your being in the family, so to speak, is simply the icing on the cake. A family operation, as you can see by where we, are has many merits." Further discussion was interrupted by Jimmy Sebastion when he asked how they enjoyed their meals or if they had any complaints. Hearing none of the latter, he asked if Tom would play a couple of songs before they left. Stella was in rapture when Tom agreed. "Give me a few moments with my wife before introducing me, please," and he turned his back on the remaining patrons and Ray while he slipped the Cobra out of its holster and handed it to her. "Hold on to this for me, sweetheart; it puts me off balance when I'm playing. Just put it in your purse until I'm done." Tom turned around and stepped up to Jimmy's side. Folks' most of you know Ray Urich;, well, this is his twin brother who has kindly agreed to play a few songs for us. Tom."

Tom sat down and doodled with the keys, his way of warming up, then swung right into an upbeat rendition of "Malaguena" like the professional entertainer he used to be, then slowed the tempo down to a heartfelt "Misty," glancing occasionally toward Stella with a twinkle in his eye, embellishing the song's refrain to its utmost, then to close out his act a rousing rendition of the Ohio State fight song usually played by the full brass marching band. For his set, which only lasted ten minutes or so, he got a standing ovation by the patrons and employees, who even came out of the kitchen to hear him. It was gratifying to his artistic soul as he stepped down to rejoin Ray and Stella, who had tears running down her cheeks. "You are very talented, brother; your wife was right when she said you could make a good living playing the piano."

"I could hear Sheila playing through your interpretations as if it were her at the keyboard when I closed my eyes, honey. I don't think there was a dry eye in the place."

Jimmy Sebastion came back to their table at that point. "I sure could use you here full time, Tom. After the way everyone here accepted your playing tonight, I could double my business and then some."

"Thanks, Jimmy, but I already have a full-time job that prevents my accepting your offer.

When Ray takes some time to come down to my home in Key Largo, he'll be able to explain the reasons why. I hate to eat and run but its been a long and hectic day, and frankly I'm bushed."

"Well, you'll have to accept this" and he took the check from the table and put it in his shirt pocket. "Bring him back anytime you can, Ray. Have a safe rip home folks."

Once outside, Tom said to his brother, "What a nice fellow to have for a friend. You're lucky. When you meet Felix, my friend and partner, you'll see what I mean."

"Tom, you've made the statement twice tonight, once to Jimmy and again just now, that you expect me to pay a visit to your home in Key Largo in the near future. How do you think I can just drop my work and drive down there? What would I do with Lee? You have already explained that after your vacation is over you are supposed to return to your post in New Orleans."

"I've given that some thought, Ray. It depends on two things happening. First, that we cut our vacation short to return home early and, of course that depends on Stella, because this trip was more for her benefit than mine, and I'm afraid it hasn't worked out that way. Secondly, I've been meaning to get Leo checked out at a veterinarian for a complete physical since he is getting older and seems to me slowing down. You said there was a very capable vet here in Shelby, so I propose since he and Lee have become attached that we put them both in the care of that doctor for both purposes, checkup and possible breeding, which would give you time to finish your memorial sculpture before catching a plane from Cleveland to Miami where I would have a rental car reserved in your name waiting, so you could drive the short distance to our home. Do you think all of these arrangements could be made in the next couple of days?"

"You can afford all of this, brother?"

"What are families for, Ray, if they can't help each other. If I couldn't afford it, I wouldn't have suggested it to begin with. I'm not wealthy, but I see a future business involving you and Stella that will keep you both content and working that I'll invest in. That should pay back handsome dividends. So what's your take on my ideas, sweetheart?"

"If there's nothing else I've learned during our marriage, it's to give you your lead when it comes to innovative ideas that are above the norm; they usually prove successful, so I say go for it. Other than our camp out night, this vacation hasn't been so relaxing as we thought it would be, and, besides, I miss the kids more every day. My life revolves around them so much that more than a week away from them makes me feel guilty for leaving them in the first place. If we leave for the trip back within two or three days we could stop at that new theme park in Orlando on the way home to check it out for a possible vacation spot in the future for the children. Disney World I believe it's called. I don't know what age they cater to there but anything connected to Walt Disney and his cartoon characters should be pre-teen age, you'd think."

"While we're on that subject there is another park just outside of Tampa sponsored by Anheuser-Busch, the maker of Budweiser beer, that is more adult orientated. They are supposed to have a monorail circling the plain where all types of wild animals roam. All that can survive in their temperatures which are tropical anyway. I wouldn't mind seeing something like that myself, and as an added bonus they have a pavilion where the history of how Budweiser is brewed that provides attendees all the Bud they can drink in twenty minutes free. Felix would love that feature. Knowing that bottomless pit as I do he'd figure some way to beat that time period."

"I could just see you two chug-a-lugging copious amounts of the brew trying to outdo each other. I can remember a Yankee-Red Sox game where both of you did the same thing. No thanks to seeing a repeat of that performance, honey. I didn't drive then, and as I remember it the cab fare back to your building was horrendous."

Ray had been listening to their banter and was wondering how many of the stories were factual or if they were exaggerating them for his benefit. He didn't know anyone in Shelby who could consume alcohol like that. Oh, he liked his wine and had invented a small mechanical press that took all the labor out of squeezing the grapes for it, but he had been brought up drinking the wine with meals instead of milk, tea, or coffee.

When Tom pulled into the backyard, the first thing he did was go over to where Leo and Lee were lying. "We're home for the night now, boy. Do you want to stay here or come into the house with us?" Leo more or less ignored his main friend, which Tom took for an answer. "See you in the morning then. Don't do anything I wouldn't." And he laughed as he joined Stella to go upstairs. His wife was going to make one more attempt to become impregnated even though she was reasonably certain the night in the Mansfield hotel had accomplished the deed. She certainly hoped so. While he was disrobing for bed, she decided a quick trip to the bathroom was in order. "Don't forget your medicine, honey. I'll be right back." As she was about to return, naked as a jay bird, she heard a noise behind her in the hall. She spun around and there stood Ray. "I, I, didn't know you were in there, Stella. I was just bringing some fresh towels up for you and Tom to use tomorrow. Please forgive me." There was no point in trying to cover her nakedness, he had already seen everything she had.

"Take a good look, Ray, because it'll have to last you for a lifetime. I'll never mention this scene to Tom unless you do or say something to cause me further embarrassment. Good night." She turned, heading for the bedroom trying to slow her racing heart so Tom wouldn't notice anything was amiss. He took one look at his naked goddess, and she could tell he was captivated enough not to know or care.

The next morning, they both slept in late so by the time they went downstairs for coffee it was almost noon. Ray must have been in his workshop, but there was hot coffee in the pot. "I don't know what's gotten into you lately, Stell, not that I'm complaining mind you, but your amorous frenzies in bed compare to just before and the early days of our marriage when we were younger and didn't have the responsibilities of the triplets. You're behaving like you want more. What gives?"

"It must be that we're away from home with all of those people coming and going there, the Connotis, Santanas, FBI personnel, and your attack has ceased and suddenly being alone together has released something in my psyche that has laid dormant for so long. That's all I can tell you, honey. It might continue this way until we get back home; then again my urges could take a U-turn and cease altogether. I'm not being facetious when I ask which would you prefer?"

Tom sat there looking at his wife while his mind was a thousand miles away. He didn't hear anything she said beyond her last question. His trance was so deep that Stella began to worry that his former ailment was returning. Was he telling her he was taking his medicine but really wasn't? It was not like him to lie to her about on anything so serious as that. Tom used her as a sounding board to further his plans and ideas so what could be causing this stupor? He came back to reality as quickly as he had slipped away. "I wonder what caused my parents to split the family up at our birth. I can't believe they were that strapped monetarily that the presence of a third baby would cause an extreme hardship and then to keep it a secret all of those years like one child had an ugly deformity such as two heads or three eyes. Ray looks as normal in every aspect as Fred and me. So what was the necessity of their action? This is going to bother me for the rest of my life because there is no way to discover the truth; no one who is still alive today who holds the key to unlock the truth of the mystery. As close as we were in our formative years in Toledo, there was never a hint or clue that something so mysterious lay just beneath the surface of our everyday life. Do you see what I'm getting at, Stell?" Stella was so pleased that her husband had returned to normalcy that it took a few moments for her to catch the drift of his thinking, but when it dawned on her consciousness, she could follow and understand his dilemma. "I get it, honey, but you simply have to put it out of your mind for now because there are more important matters to consider and act upon now such as Lee and Leo and our return trip home."

"You're right as usual, sweetheart; there I go again, putting the cart before the horse. I better go see how Ray is doing."

Ray was polishing his Korean War Memorial to a high sheen, the luster too bright to look at in direct sunlight, so Tom quickly closed the door. "You're going to have that done within the time allotted, I see" he practically shouted over the high whine of the sander/polisher. When you're finished there, we'll take the dogs to the vet." Ray removed the earmuffs he was using for sound protection, turned off the machine, and said, " Repeat that will you, brother; I didn't get all of it just reading your lips." Tom did. The stillness after the shriek of the machine was enough to make Tom wonder how his twin could stand it without going deaf altogether. What he didn't know was Ray had wads of cotton in his ears under the ear muffs. Ray, an old hand at working under adverse conditions, was very resourceful. He turned everything in the workshop off just leaving the overhead fans on to pull out the accumulated dust. "Let me wash up a bit and I'll be ready to go."

Stella would remain at the house to act as the watchdog while the men and dogs were gone. With her sense of ceaseless activity she would spend most of that time in the kitchen where she decided to put a meal together that they could have for a late lunch, taking time to look out the rear windows on occasion to check the yard. As she worked her thoughts were of the estate wondering if Cliff Ajax was progressing on her studio and Tom's music room. Rather than calling to allay her wonders, she continued searching Ray's larder for ingredients for her makeshift meal. A tin of Spam caught her eye, so she carefully opened it with the attached key, then sliced the meat into one-inch cubes to fry later with scrambled eggs. These actions took her mind off her previous thoughts of the estate, so by the time the men returned the meal she was putting together was more sumptuous than she originally intended. However, Stella had unconsciously timed it perfectly, for the wagon was just entering the backyard when she was putting it on the kitchen table.

"Wow, when you decide to make a little repast you don't spare the horses, do you?", as he went to the sink to wash his hands.

"That's what I meant when I said she was an extraordinary woman, Ray. Her creativity spills over into everything she tackles."

"All right, you two, let's skip the kudos and start eating before the hot dishes get cold and visa-versa. You can tell me about Lee and Leo over dessert."

"I'm afraid to ask but what did you conjure up for that?"

"Apple pie ala mode or with melted cheddar cheese topping."

"Where, pray tell, did you find fresh apples in my house? I know for a fact there aren't any."

"You asked, so I'll explain. They're canned slices. I have no idea how long they've been on the shelf because there was no date on the can."

Both men wolfed the food down without conversation for the next ten minutes, hardly pausing long enough between bites to ask for other portions. Stella continued dishing out segments of stew and eggs until nothing was left. They then sat back holding out cups, which she filled with coffee and tea, before taking the apple pie out of the oven, where it had been keeping warm. There was no discussion about its ingredients as half the pie disappeared into satisfied stomachs.

"If you're both full, who is going to explain what happened at the vet?" Ray deferred to Tom as he was finishing his portion of pie.

"The preliminary check made on Leo showed he had a deficiency of certain vitamins needed for strength in his hips, without out which he would seem sluggish. This condition could be remedied with shots of the necessary vitamin, a B-12 derivative, to the affected area, nothing too painful for the dog. Along with that treatment, a reduction of his overall weight could be achieved by a change in his food and elimination of meaty snacks, which I promised to stop. Leo might be disappointed and get his nose out of joint, but if it would improve his health and his indolence, so be it. Concerning the possible breeding with Lee, the vet said she would keep a close eye on Leo's health progress in the next few days while her night employees will be instructed to watch their behavior together when they are working. Miss Yanez seemed to have terrific rapport with her charges. Leo was the perfect gentleman while she examined him, he responded to her prodding and grasping without the slightest revulsion. I was proud of his behavior with a perfect stranger but her voice had a command to it while still soothing. It's hard to explain. Before we left, while Ray was spending time with Lee, I had a talk with the big guy out of the way of anyone else there. I explained to him I was going to leave him here with the lady doctor, and Lee and I wanted him to know it was only for a short while. "You are an important part of the Mueller family, big boy, so you hurry up and get well so you can return to the estate and your duties there. I'll expect you within a month." Leo looked up at his main friend with his multi-colored eyes watering slightly, the closest thing to human tears that Tom had ever seen the mastiff show, as if he felt he was being deserted by the only true human friend he had ever known in his life. I tried to jolly him up by squatting down to scratch behind his ears, but even that didn't get the usual response of the bath from the slavering tongue. Leo was acting in a way he knew something I didn't, something about our future relationship like a reversal of our roles. It was eerie, unlike anything I'd ever known the dog to do before. As I backed out of the room watching him sitting there he raised his right front paw and I swear to you, Stell, it appeared like he was waving goodbye as I closed the door."

Ray was visually upset when he rejoined Tom in the wagon. "I hope she will be reasonably content there while I'm gone, brother. I've never left her alone more than a few hours at a time before. Even though she knows Miss Yanez she will expect me to return sometime tomorrow for her and when I don't come back, it's hard to imagine what she'll think. Dogs become so attached to their owners, as I'm sure you know, they can almost read their minds. She's another reason I never married, most women I've met don't understand how a man can care so much about a dog and prefer its company to theirs after the sexual attraction is over. Well, it's water over the dam now. A week away from he won't alter how much we care for each other. It's too bad they don't live longer to grow old together. I can't imagine having children like you do and having to divide my attention between them, a wife, and Lee. I don't know how you do it Tom."

46

They stopped in Orlando to check out Disney World, and it was everything Stella had read about. She could bring the children here and they would have a great time. While they were there, they were going to have lunch at the German Pavilion. It was a replica of a Bavarian castle on the inside with a brass band plus accordion and kettle drum as the rhythm section on a small stage in what looked like a pit. Waiters dressed in lederhosen served lunches with authentic steins of beer and all German foods on red and white checkered plastic tablecloths, reminiscent of an old German beer hall. Coats of arms on shields adorned the walls all around the inside. There were so many things to look at, it was difficult to concentrate on the food, and the beer slid down their throats like water. Spaetzels, knockwurst, wiener schnitzel, lanjagers, and other of the old country foods filled them both to the bursting point. They both started looking for the restroom. A passing waiter pointed them out. Tom waited outside hers until she came out looking a little peaked around her beautiful face. "You feel all right, Stell?"

"Something I just ate didn't agree with me, honey. I think what I need is some fresh air outside without the din of noise and the continued swallowing of that delicious beer. Why don't you pay the bill and take me out. I'll wait by the door until you're done."

The fresh air that Stella craved had the opposite effect of what she expected. Tom found her sitting doubled up on a bench holding her stomach as if she were experiencing cramps. Stella realized the symptoms for what they really were, a form of morning sickness later in the day because her body clock was messed up by the irregular hours they had been keeping. This was proof she was pregnant, but at this moment she hoped these problems would cease when they got home. Her mother had explained to Sheila and her what to expect after they found a husband and bore him children. She had a taste of it when she was bearing the triplets but blamed it more on the suffocating confines of the truck they all were riding in when they were fleeing the wrath of Hurricane Betsy. Little did either of them know, a similar storm was lurking in their immediate future, another hurricane which would disrupt all of their plans which included the visit of Ray Urich.

While Tom drove, Stella lay down on the front seat using his right thigh as a pillow. There was no hanky-panky involved; she just needed the warmth of his body to lull her into dreamland, and dream she did. Stella was a practical woman, even though she had used her sexual prowess to gain her intent again instead of waiting for nature to take its course. She could actually see her next painting in her mind, even though it would be a difficult task to render the composite of the diagram in its entirety. No pain, no gain, she dreamt. The colors flashed in order like soldiers in a parade while the warmth of their progression blanketed her imagination like a child's building blocks. Her dream was interrupted by the gentle shaking of her shoulder. Her husband was trying to bring her back to reality without startling her unnecessarily. Her eyes opened to a repeat of the Hurricane Betsy nightmare. The Buick was under assault by the elements of another hurricane forming over Florida, and Tom had his hands fully occupied trying to keep the wagon on the road.

"Looks like we're in for another blow, Stell. I hope it doesn't cause too much damage at our estate. The kids and the Connotis will be scared out of their wits if it does. Are you feeling any better?"

"Some. I guess the bit of sleep I got was badly needed and I had a delicious dream. Has the radio given any weather reports?"

"Trying to hold the wagon on the road has taken both hands, why don't you see what you can find out." Stella turned on the set slowly turning the selection knob to find any station broadcasting weather but got mostly static and an occasional talk show, no weather.

"Push the far right button; it will raise the antenna, maybe that will help." Stella did and had to quickly turn the volume down from the blast of music that issued forth. Looking out the windshield she saw the antenna gyrating from wind blasts and pushed another button to lower it somewhat before it was damaged. Finally a weather report from a station in West Palm Beach was warning listeners to move inland if possible, as Hurricane Dora with winds of 100 to 125 miles per hour was pounding the costal areas raising high surf. Visibility was poor due to blowing sand, so smaller communities were using school and Greyhound buses to evacuate many of their citizens who otherwise would be stranded. Since they were just approaching Fort Lauderdale Tom looked over at Stella. "Do you want to chance continuing or hole up someplace? If it gets no worse than this, I'm for going on, but I don't want to endanger you if I'm wrong. From what I can see from the hood, this baby is going to need a new paint job either way."

"I'll rely on your judgment, honey, whichever you think is best. I always feel safe when you're nearby. Besides the sooner we get home we can be close to the children in case they need us to bolster up their spirits. Their summer vacation is over and it's back to their studies."

"They'll be a little upset at that, it was supposed to last longer if you remember."

"That's too bad; they will have to get over it. We hadn't planned on meeting their Uncle Ray when we started the trip. That changed the whole complexion of the vacation. After we have the chance to check the damage from Dora and I find out from Gennie and Felix how they behaved while we were gone it will be back to the books. I'll be particularly interested in Freddie's deportment, he's who seems to find the most mischief to get into and what he doesn't think of Tomas does. Those two rascals need a heavy hand to guide them, and mine is just heavy enough to do the job."

As Tom had thought, the most damage had slammed Key West with high winds and seas. The naval air station took a beating, but luckily suffered no loss of life. Dora then swung out to sea before veering back to landfall a half mile north of their estate. The winds of eighty-five miles per hour knocked two palms down and sand-blasted one side of the main house but did no more than that. The partially finished Connoti chalet took a skipping blow that would give Cliff Ajax and his crew a lot more work, then did the worst nearest destruction to the Taj Mahal property to their north tearing trees all over the property up to be used as battering rams against the building. One spire completely tore away, taking part of the dome with it, exposing the entire upper floor to wind and rain. Vehicles in the collapsed garages were tossed around like toys from an unruly child. The bull mastiff that Leo had courted somehow sensed the oncoming disaster and took shelter away from the main building, thus saving her life. The caretaker who Tom and Leo had the run-in with was not as fortunate. He was impaled by a shard of wood when the dome collapsed, to become one of the two deaths in Florida at the wiles of Dora. He wasn't found for more than three weeks after the storm, and by that time was quite ripe. By then, the nameless half-starved bull mastiff showed up at the Mueller estate, drawn there by both hunger and the remaining scent of Leo, her past illicit lover. Stella, being the kind-hearted soul that she was toward any abandoned child or animal was the first to notice the demented dog lurking near the studio/garage, first alerted by the fuss Brutus was making. After scolding the wolfhound half-heartedly – for she was secretly pleased by the dog's vigilance – she coaxed the animal toward the main house by placing Leo's full food dish near the pool. The grateful dog swallowed the food almost without chewing, then lay down by the empty bowl, indicating she was ready for seconds, which Stella promptly provided. She ate the second helping at a more leisurely pace, watching her benefactor during the course. Deciding that this human meant her no harm as her former feeder had at his whim, when she had finished she sat by the empty bowl allowing the kind human to approach and scratch behind her ears then pet her brindled coat. "You could use a bath, Missy, your coat is filthy. You stay right there while I get a brush and bucket. Stay." That was a word the dog understood so she waited while the human went into the house. She followed the human to a nearby hose and sat patiently during her bath and grooming. "If I'm not mistaken, you're going to have puppies, Missy. Did our Leo have anything to do with your pregnancy?" The dog's maw dropped in what looked like a contented grin, as though she understood and agreed with what the kind human was saying. She decided right then never to return to her former home.

Tom woke up feeling like he'd been drugged. He groped his way to the kitchen looking for Stella and coffee, there were neither. He made a cup of instant coffee and walked outside with it in search of Stella and found her just finishing up rinsing a bull mastiff an talking to it like she did with Leo.

"That dog looks familiar, sweetheart; I'd say it was the female from the Taj Mahal that I saw Leo courting, and if it is it should be about ready to spring with some pups. Are you certain you want to be responsible for raising and weaning a brood of them with everything else you have to do?"

"Now, there you go again doubting my capabilities, Tom. I wouldn't want you to miss out on seeing two or three cute pups grow up around here, plus you won't have to wait for Lee and Leo to breed before having one to take back to New Orleans with you."

"That's all I'd need taking a puppy on the drive back there. And as if I won't have enough to do when I get there but train it. You're assuming it will be potty trained on birth. C'mon, Stell, get real."

"Well the alternative is you won't have any guard dog at all to assist you in your raids on suspected drug locations unless Felix would agree to take Brutus for the same purpose and that would leave us unprotected here until Leo gets back. We would be in the proverbial position of between a rock and a hard place, so pay your money and take your choice."

Felix chose that moment to come out of the main house coffee in hand. "There wasn't no coffee so I brewed a pot. Somebody's fallin' down on the job and since Gennie isn't feelin' so good she decided to stay in bed. Where'd that mutt come from?"

"It's one of Leo's paramours, partner. My wife has adopted her since Leo had his way with her. We were just discussing what to do with the offspring. Maybe your input would help" and Tom explained Stella's ideas. Felix almost dropped his cup when he heard what she had in mind. "Ya' mean ya' want us ta' take one of the pups this hound is gonna' have ta' New Orleans with us ta' raise as a guard dog ta' take on raids? Yer' kiddin' ain't ya', Stella? Whatta' ya' mean that or Brutus? Muy Dios" and he broke into some undecipherable Spanish before sputtering to a stop looking at Tom . "I thought my amigo came up with all the hair-brained ideas but yer' gettin' worse than him."

"All right, Felix, don't blow a gasket over this; it was just a thought spoken out loud on her part, nothing more, I'm sure if she thinks it over, she'll realize our circumstances in New Orleans are just to fragile as it is without introducing any new characters whether they are human or animal. It's hard telling what condition the office is in since we were last there. Over a month has passed since we left. I'll call Chris later today for a recap. It's most likely since she hasn't called you here Chris is handling matters in her usual efficient manner and we should be grateful for that."

Stella had lost patience with the two men, and called the bull mastiff who she had named Missy to follow her into the house. It was time for the children to be up and clamoring for their breakfasts. They could be introduced to Missy while she was preparing it and it would be interesting to see how they would interact. She would warn them Missy was soon to have puppies so to be gentle with her, no roughhousing as they were used to with Leo. It was just like Freddie to ask where Leo was. Is this dog to take Leo's place?"

"No, honey. Leo is in Ohio with your Uncle Ray and will be back home soon. He had to stay in a dog hospital for awhile to receive treatment for his hips." That was all they needed to know for now, she thought, as she started frying bacon and eggs. The inevitable question came from Tom, Jr. "Who is Uncle Ray, mommy? I didn't know we had an Uncle."

"I'll let your father explain about that, young man; you just pour milk for your sister and brother while I finish cooking your meal, then it's back to the books. Your vacation is over."

"Aw, Mom," they chorused.

Tomas entered the kitchen at that point stopping dead in his tracks when he spotted Missy, a confused expression on his face, so Stella had to explain the entire story again for his benefit. "How is your mother feeling today?"

"Not so good, that's why I'm late for breakfast. She didn't wake me up at the usual time and I'm starved."

"Were you children frightened by the last storm?"

"No, Uncle Felix made sure we were safe. He just wouldn't let us go outside" spoken in bravado by her oldest son. "There would have been so much to see and he even kept us away from any windows" Freddie added. "What a spoilsport," and he laughed.

"You can thank your lucky stars that he was here to watch over you otherwise you might not be sitting here making sport of it. Now eat your breakfasts so we can get back to your lessons. We'll see how much you have retained from before our trip." Stella had put aside five strips of bacon to cool for Missy remembering how much Leo liked the treat. She had to admit she missed the big guy almost as much as Tom did, he was such a reassurance and comfort to rely on and nobody, friend or foe, had better threaten the children here at the estate or she or Tom anywhere for that matter.

Tom and Felix must have agreed on some stratagem concerning their trip back to New Orleans because when the came into the kitchen they were smiling, partners again. "I would imagine you're both hungry now that you have come to some kind of an agreement. I'll start what the children are eating but you'll have to finish because it's back to the books for them."

Cracking a dozen eggs and adding a pound of bacon, Stella took the now cooled strips of bacon she had put aside and hand fed Missy her treats. The bull mastiff took them daintily from her extended fingers much the way Leo had, not snapping at them so as to injure her new benefactor. "That's a good girl, Missy. We're going to get along just fine. Honey, before I take the children away, would you explain about their Uncle Ray to them? I told them I would defer that duty to you." While he did that in somewhat of a roundabout manner, she toasted the remainder of the loaf of bread half-listening while she worked a smile creasing her lips at his hesitancy, another chore she put on his broad shoulders. In reality she wouldn't have known how to explain it. "All right any further questions will have to wait for another time, let's get into the classroom. She winked at Tom, patting him on the head as she passed the table Missy following dutifully behind her.

"What was that all about, amigo?"

"You've got me, Felix. She has been acting very strange lately more so since we left Disney World. It all started shortly after we met Ray Urich in Shelby, Ohio, and it's been more mysterious as time has passed. Stella is a strong-willed person, as I'm sure you know, but she must be under so much pressure with the home schooling of the children and not being able to release her artistic talents, and now adopting that bull mastiff she could be heading for a nervous breakdown. Wouldn't that be a fine kettle of fish with us in New Orleans With your wife feeling poorly who would even be here to notify me if something like that happened?"

Ten days later, two things happened that had a calming effect on both Stella's condition and Toms worries. Cliff Ajax showed up with the glass for Stella's studio, and she announced she was pregnant. To top off events, Missy had a litter of three, two males and one female of the most God-awful coloring anyone could imagine. The birthing took place on a blanket Stella had folded up for her bed near the stove in the kitchen right in the mainstream of traffic where every person using the room would almost stumble over her. Stella heard her pitiful whining when she was about to prepare the children's breakfasts and stopped everything to act as midwife. By the time she had finished and cleaned up the puppies' placing them near their mother's teats where they could scramble for their first blind-eyed meal, the children were trooping in ready for their first meal also. After they oohed and aahed over the newborns, the adults were stomping into the now overcrowded room, even Gennie, putting an extra burden on Stella who had started making pancakes but quickly switched the scrambled eggs and sausages, creating quite a mess that Gennie adroitly stepped in to assist in rectifying. Between the two women, the meal went off without a further hitch, no thanks to the men who sat drinking their coffee like this hubbub was an everyday occurrence not worth interfering with. If it wouldn't have made a scene Stella would have thrown something at them but instead whispered to Gennie she would accompany her to her rooms for a private chat then said out loud, "You two can clean up and do the dishes if you expect another meal anytime soon."

When the women entered, Felix and Gennie's rooms, Stella couldn't believe Gennie had let them deteriorate into such squalor but kept her peace for the moment until Gennie explained her physical condition. "Why do you think you're pregnant?"

Her reasoning seemed quite valid to Stella when she compared them to her own symptoms when she was pregnant with the triplets and even now. "What I can't understand is why your doctor said you would be unable to conceive again after your first attempt ended the way it did. That's mainly the reason you followed my advice to adopt. What does she say now? If it were me I'd certainly change doctors."

Gennie looked nonplussed by Stella's logic; she had never considered that option before. Could her pediatrician be that inept? After all she was quite young and childless.

"Now let's get busy and clean up this mess. Pregnant or not, you can't continue to live like this with the possibility of incurring a disease." Forty-five minutes later, the rooms looked neater, and they had collected two garbage bags full of trash. "After these are gone, bring in the sweeper and vacuum the carpeting; that will have to do until Felix and Tom return to New Orleans and with them out from underfoot we can do a more thorough job."

Stella knew she had been neglecting the children for too long; there was no telling what mischief they were up to while she had been otherwise occupied. She also understood the men couldn't be in two places at once to clean the kitchen and supervise their conduct but she was pleasantly surprised when she passed through the kitchen to find Felix finishing up.

"Where's Tom?"

"He gathered up alla' kids an' took 'em in ta' the music room. That should keep 'em busy 'til ya' take over."

Bless my man, she thought. Again his keyboard ability came in handy to avoid any pranks being pulled by Freddie or Tomas the main two culprits to instigate shenanigans. She stood just outside of the music room out of sight of all the children except Sheila who could just barely see over the top of the spinet from her position on the bench next to her daddy. It didn't make much difference anyway because her total attention was focused on Tom's fingers as they raced over the keys. She listened as he switched from kiddie songs that they heard on television to show tunes. He'd stop for three or four bars to say something to his daughter that Stella couldn't hear, then resume playing so as to show Sheila what he'd just explained. His professionalism was so erudite Stella hated to interrupt so she backed silently away to rejoin Felix in the kitchen.

The little man did have his uses; the room was spotless. That's why she couldn't understand how he could allow his living quarters to fall in such disarray. Of course, three people sharing such a small area had to accumulate some clutter and since his wife had to be prodded to do any cleaning and to avoid an argument which would upset her further that was the result. Their bathroom though was as spotless as the job he'd done in the kitchen. Then again, he must have been doing all the laundry while they were gone, a time consuming job by itself. All of the children's clothes were neatly folded, and even Sheila's dresses were hung on hangers in their shared closet. So he had been a very busy man plus shopping and feeding and caring for Brutus. "My amigo still playin' for the kids, huh? He sure can keep 'em in a trance, heh, heh, heh."

"Yes he can. Now Felix, I know you have been quite busy assuming all of my duties with Gennie feeling so poorly but I hope you understand the reason for it. She is as pregnant as I am."

"Ya' too, what is it catchin'? This place is gonna' get so crowded with 'em yer' gonna' have ta' build another floor up ta' house this growin' brood or else my family is gonna' have ta' move someplace else."

"I don't think that will be necessary. With you and Tom gone most of the time, we should be able to get back into our regular routine quite handily and as our present children grow older they will be able to take care of the new arrivals taking some of the burden off of us. I know Gennie will feel better by then so ..."

"What's that got ta' do with livin' space?"

Tom sauntered in all smiles rubbing his hands together. "I'm ready for some coffee too."

"What are ya' so happy 'bout?"

"Yes, honey, you look like the cat who swallowed the canary, what gives?"

"I've found a way to keep the children occupied without forcing them to study the three R's. Right now they're writing scales on some blank musical scores used for composing I found in the bench led by Sheila. She grasped the idea immediately and of course none of the boys want a girl to best them so they are hard at work trying to keep up. They'll be at it for at least a half hour and then I'll go back in to correct them and then start them on a different key. It's sort of a contest that should keep them busy with a minimum of supervision. That will give you some respite in your home schooling sweetheart. Nothing like sharing the load." He poured himself a mug of java and sat at the table. "Another thing. I've been thinking about your Missy's pups and decided to take one of the males back to New Orleans with me. We won't be leaving for a few more days and by then the little bugger should have his eyes open. Chris will have to put up with him at the office for awhile but she's resourceful enough to figure a way to do it. That will break up the boredom of her everyday routine, but I digress. Stella, now that your studio is ready, you are going to want to start using it. I'm sure you are bubbling over with ideas of what your next project will be and since you are with child you're not going to have much more time to work on them. Remember, I'm as close as the telephone so when your time nears I expect you to call and let me know so I can hotfoot it back here to give you support. Now it's time for me to go back and check on my budding composers so you can relax for awhile longer."

Felix sat staring at Stella. "Man, he kinda' gets worked up on ideas don't he. I never know whatta' expect of him next. It's like I know him but don' know him."

As the time to head back to New Orleans neared, Tom was caught up in a flurry of activity. He took the wagon in for a fresh paint job that took two days to complete and was given a loaner when he told them he couldn't be without a car that long. It wasn't much of a car. It burned oil badly, leaving a trail of smoke and knocked so badly he hoped he wouldn't throw a rod before he got the Buick back. He supposed he could have rented a car or used Stella's but he was stuck with this monstrosity so he had to make the most of it. The fickle weather of the season was enough to make him glad the main house had air conditioning and true to her prognostications Stella had turned off in bed. It was just as well; she had worn him to a frazzle in the last two weeks.

—

Parris Island just a few miles southeast of Beaufort South Carolina is the east coast USMC training facility or "Boot Camp" as it is known by its graduates. It is the equivalent of the San Diego west coast facility. After ninety days of intense mental and physical training to the point of exhaustion the Parris Island grads call the Diego grads "candy-ass Marines" or "pogey-baiters," depending on whichever new Marine you listen to.

A section of Parris Island known only to the base commander and specified as top secret at the pentagon in Washington, D.C., has another use, a camp within a camp per se. There specialists of every nature recruited into the CIA from every branch of the military plus those of dubious character yet totally necessary not only to teach but to take part in future operations. These men and a few women were chosen mostly from senior classes of colleges and universities across the country, no dummies allowed, from varied academic fields most of whom had no prior military experience and were put through rigorous physical workouts over the four month course.

It was inevitable that some of them would be assigned to the New Orleans office. Among them was one of the few women who had graduated the course with flying colors. She was built like a pro football linebacker, and if you saw her from the rear you'd swear she was a man because she was wearing a pantsuit and she had a crew hair cut, but as soon as she spoke her falsetto tones gave her away, definitely a female. When Chris introduced her as the newest member of the New Orleans team, Tom didn't know whether to shake her hand or simply take her resume dossier with a nod, so he did the latter. Betty Ogilvie was a 1963 graduate of Ohio State and a member of the conference track team that had won its division title her senior year. She was the only girl in a family of six children from Akron, Ohio, and all her brothers were sports oriented – football and baseball. One sibling had been drafted by the Detroit Tigers and was presently playing in Erie, Pennsylvania, in an AA league. Betty held a conference record for shot put and could have been training for the upcoming Olympics when she decided to follow in her father's footsteps to enter law enforcement. Her dad was a sheriff's deputy in Summit County. When she saw the pup lying on a rug by Chris' desk, she quickly exclaimed, "What a cute puppy; whose is it?" bending down to pet the dog tenderly. Chris explained what the breed was and how it would eventually be used when it grew older and larger. Betty had a pensive expression as she straightened up. "I love all dogs. We always had two or three at home in Akron and they were always large breeds. As soon as I find a suitable place to live, I'd love to raise this one there." Her offer didn't take long to register on Tom's mind; there was the perfect solution, if Chris who had been treating the pup as her personal property wouldn't mind. Tom certainly didn't want to tick her off. "Well, Betty, I hope you understand this dog should top out at between a hundred and one seventy-five pounds and should spend most of his hours outside. He isn't a house dog by any means. His sire is my own personal friend and weighs in in the high two hundreds. His dam is my wife's protector at home. What do you think, Chris?"

"It's up to you' boss; he has been a great diversion from my routine here but whatever you say goes."

"Then' let's wait to see what kind of accommodations Miss Ogilvie comes up with before we make the final decision. That should be fair." As usual, Felix sat back listening but not adding any opinions. He had a beer in his hand from the fridge Chris kept stocked out of office petty cash. He never looked directly at Betty, and she avoided him like the plague.

The weather had taken an unprecedented turn for the better. The fall months saw the occasional hurricane or tornados spun off from them but this year seemed to be the exception, the weather was actually pleasant, reminiscent of northern Ohio minus the blazing colors of the changing leaves of oak, elm, beech, and poplars. Few states could compete with that showcase other than Michigan and western Pennsylvania. Tom had the feeling it wouldn't last, though; pleasantries never did. About the time you thought you lived in the Garden of Eden, you realized Mother Nature was just toying with you.

One of the trainees who was left over after Mr. Rowens moved to Washington, D.C., at the main headquarters of the agency had developed into somewhat of a marksman with pistols, any caliber or type. He had also purchased a number of weapons out of his own salary and always carried two or three on his person in different types of holsters, ankle, small of back at the waistline, and shoulder, without being obvious about it. Don Schultz was an impeccable dresser never showing up at the office-warehouse in less than a sport coat and slacks, more often in suits and never the same one twice in a row. Tom had never seen him arrive in a car. He would just suddenly appear as if in a magical act. Tom supposed that as a bachelor he had little else to spend his money on than clothing and weapons. Don was always cheerful and exceptionally polite to Chris, but Tom would notice when the young man was off guard the steely stone eyes of a hatchet man. He would make it a point to get to know him better and would ask Felix away from the shop what he thought of Don. His partner was a good judge of character if somewhat reticent to express an opinion being an unfathomable character himself but Tom had known the little man long enough to extract what he needed without being too obvious about it.

47

The Club Bayou was a huge building on the shore of Lake Ponchartrain with a parking lot that would hold over five hundred vehicles. The owners had found that customers who were high on booze and the illegal substances that were so prevalent could wander around looking for their cars and trucks until they dropped from fatigue and lay sprawled until they were run over by drivers who were in slightly better condition or had a designated driver so they hired people to patrol the lot looking for those lost souls where they herded them to an area where they could come down off their highs enough to negotiate an exit, thus saving several costly lawsuits. How the owners got away with these maneuvers under the noses of the parish trustees was a mystery to many, but the culpable law enforcement officers were handling it for a price. The club was so profitable there was enough money to handle all those payoffs. By rights, all of the owners should be serving long prison terms for a multitude of felony charges, the most serious of which would deny any possibility of parole.

The dress code of the Club Bayou was non-existent, so Tom didn't stick out like a sore thumb with his light OSU jacket, which he needed to cover his waist holster containing the .38 snub nose. Don Schultz was in one of his suits, which was no surprise. It was hard telling how many weapons he had on him. They were sitting at one of the bars scattered throughout the barn-like room. Women wore as little as possible while they mingled and danced. They were nursing two beers at the exorbitant price of $2.50 each. Don pointed out one of the owners sitting at a table against a wall. He looked like an ad for a jewelry store. A stunning blonde sat next to him, and a huge man stood next to the wall, obviously a bodyguard. Tom could smell marijuana smoke drifting throughout the room, despite the ceiling fans turning in competition with the spinning glass globes reflecting light from adjacent spot lights. The overall scene was enough to give any sober person an instant headache. Tom didn't intend to stay long. He just wanted to get an idea of the layout. Two scantily dressed girls approached them. "Do you want to dance, handsome?" Neither of the two looked over sixteen, but Don was ready to jump in, regardless, with one or both of them. "I'm ready to go, and since I'm driving I suggest you follow unless you want to walk." Tom put his arm over the smaller man's shoulder and bent down to speak softly into his ear. "These two girls are just kids, Don, and it could be a setup. What you do on your own time is your business, but you are actually working now, so it's mine. Let's go, I'd hate to see you charged with a felony for statutory rape; that would be the end of your career in the agency." Don had a dejected expression as he followed the boss out to the parking lot. "Why is it that everything that's fun in life is against the law?"

"It's all according to what you call fun, young man. I'm only six years older than you chronologically but fifteen experience-wise. I've seen and done things you haven't even thought of yet and despite your proficiency with pistols an small arms, there is world of weaponry out there for you to discover and conquer before you can be well-rounded." As they were driving away from the club, another thought came into Tom's mind. "How well do you know my partner, Felix?"

"You mean that ugly dwarf that's always drinking a beer at the office who doesn't say much?"

Tom felt like reaching over and back-handing the impudent pup but instead controlled his temper and said, "A few words to make you wiser and to prolong your life without serious injury: Never, I repeat never, say or do anything to rile that little man whether I'm near enough to save your bacon or not. Regardless of what you think of him, heed my warning. He's Colombian and a martial arts expert. I've seen him hospitalize a three hundred pound Mafia enforcer for simply insulting a girl who later became his wife. My children call them Aunt and Uncle even though there's no blood relationship and we go back a long way. I'm going to drop you off at the next corner, since I don't know where you're staying. Use your wiles to get there, which will give you time to think over what I've just told you. I'll see you in the office tomorrow with, I hope, a better attitude. Out you go."

Tom was still mumbling to himself when he got back to the apartment he and Felix were renting instead of the motel rooms they previously had. He grabbed a beer from the fridge and slammed the door so hard it brought Felix on the run, thinking someone was breaking in. When he saw Tom sitting at the kitchen table he asked, "What's happenin'?"

"I didn't mean to disturb you partner. It's just that Don Schultz ticks me off so much I'm thinking seriously of transferring him out regardless of how good a shot he is with small arms. The boy simply doesn't seem to fit in here. He's got these wild ideas of a good time. I had to practically drag him out of the Club Bayou tonight. He was about to become involved with two girls that didn't look to be over sixteen. I ended up dropping him off at a street corner to find his own way home before I did something that I'd later regret."

"What makes ya' think he won't change if I have a talk with him? I can be kinda' persuasive ya' know. Ya' keep droppin' agents off an' pretty soon it'll jus' be the two of us an' that 'butch' that jus' came in. I'd rather work wit' Chris than that one."

Tom got a phone call from Stella. Leo was at the estate along with Ray Urich, who brought him. The mastiff had slimmed down considerably, and the children were delighted to see him. He sniffed out Missy, but no one could figure out what he was thinking. After their original meeting, Leo completely ignored her, despite her trying to cozy up to him. Stella told Tom she was completely at a loss to explain it. If he had any suggestions she would welcome them. With everything that was going on in New Orleans, Tom didn't know what to say about that. "How are you feeling, sweetheart? Is your pregnancy bothering you at all? With all the other things you have to cope with, trying to entertain Ray is the last thing you need. I wish I could be there now, but there are problems here that can't be ignored, strictly personnel. I can't very well take more vacation time as yet without upsetting the apple cart here by leaving Felix in charge. How long is Ray planning on staying there? Has he said?"

"I've shown him some of my work and he's all enthused about combining our works if you still intend to back us as you said in Shelby. Are you?"

Miss Ogilvie picked that moment to breeze into the office, interrupting Tom's train of thought with a ribald tone of voice, very uncharacteristic of her normal demeanor. "I've found the perfect place to raise a growing dog; it'll be available tomorrow when all the utilities are turned on."

Now another problem, Tom concluded, separating the pup from Chris at a time she was so used to having it near her desk, where she could keep an eye on it and clean up its messes, which were becoming less frequent as the dog would nuzzle her legs when an emergency arose. Chris on her own had gone to a local pet store for special treats and what looked like a baby diaper she strapped on his rear if she was on the phone or otherwise occupied and couldn't take him out for a release. So how was she going to feel about losing him now?"

Whatever method Felix had used on Schultz, it seemed to be working. The agent didn't seem to have any marks from a physical altercation during the following days after Tom had mentioned to his partner that something had to be done to straighten out his attitude. Don had even asked Felix for advice on the purchase of a car, not knowing that the little man wouldn't have a clue about how or where to but one, not having any experience along that line. Regardless, Don showed up one day with a two-year-old Ford Mustang that he wanted everyone in the office to look at and admire. It was a dark green two-door with very little body damage or rust showing. Not only the car was new but his attitude had taken an abrupt turn for the better. Tom thought he could probably learn some lessons from Felix's methodology to get those same results in his dealings with people even if the psychology was learned second-hand from such an unlikely source. It was something else to think about. He would never ask Felix directly, yet he knew he had some shortcomings in that area. He would even use it with Stella because he realized she used it on him. That would be a reversal.

For some unknown reason, Miss Ogilvie had never parked her car inside the warehouse. Whether she didn't know she was allowed to or not, she chose to use one of the three spaces out front of the building where her flashy Ford convertible stuck out like a sunflower in a bed of roses. It didn't do much good to lock up the canvas-topped vehicle as anyone wanting to steal it only had to slit the top to gain entry by reaching through and pulling up the locking mechanism.

Since she was unfamiliar with New Orleans and the surrounding environs, Tom had her studying map and overlays, some hanging on walls others in local directories in book form where

Chris could point out locations where agents and their informants had found drug trafficking prevalent. Tom and Felix having longer experience in those trouble spots, had flagged them with colored pushpins keeping an update as they were reported.

Two long-time undercover agents, Sam Price and Tim Brewer, holdovers from Rowens' regime furnished most of the information hat Tom and Felix didn't know about, before their time here. One or the other of those two would only show up at the office to pick up both checks and expense money, and always at night after calling ahead of time so one of the principals could be there to accommodate them. They were very careful men. They had to be to avoid unwanted recognition, thus possible serious injury. Whoever came always parked their car several blocks away in different spots and took roundabout routes walking to the office. It was Tim who saw someone lurking around Betty's convertible and frightened them off upon suddenly appearing nearby. Since it was just dusk when that happened, it was enough to report inside, even though he didn't know who the car belonged to. The full crew were still hard at work studying maps when Tim Brewer entered and reported. Tom understood at once there was a leak somewhere within, maybe not a quisling per se, yet a hole which had to be plugged before some serious incident occurred where the would lose an agent through no direct fault of their own.

"Betty, from now on when you come to work, park on the inside. It shouldn't be hard for you to open the overhead door for ingress and that way it won't be stolen or worse – a bomb planted in it. Chris already has the knack of it so you shouldn't have any trouble at all. Come to think of it, I'd better have an automatic door opener installed so no one will have to get out of their cars to get inside or out. I don't know why I haven't thought of that before now."

"Now concerning the dog, Betty, he's getting big enough to roam the premises so I've decided to train him for watch dog use. Even though he doesn't bark any more than his sire, anyone thinking about breaking in who doesn't have a scent he recognizes will be pounced on. Since burglars don't usually carry weapons in their nefarious pursuits, the shock value of a silent marauder clamping his jaws on an arm or leg will have the advantage of both surprise and restraint in warding off even the most experienced bad guy. In the meantime, feel free to pet or play with Shank. Chris had named him that after the colloquialism of a dagger, so he gets used to you by sight and smell. He has a favorite hard-rubber ball he noses around when not sleeping or eating, but of course it's covered with his slobber, so be sure to wash your hands if you are allergic to that, as some people are, before touching your eyes or face. I'll have your automatic door selectors in two days, so make certain you keep those attached to your sun visor or handy somewhere in your car because if you lose it you will have to pay for all of them when a new coded selector is installed. Since I have nothing else to say why don't we call it a day."

When Tom, Felix, and Chris were the only ones left, Chris said, "I do believe you handled the Shank circumstance with the right amount of finesse. I'm not trying to be catty, but Betty-O did come on a little strong about assuming she would take Shank as her own to raise. I do understand she is an agent while I'm simply a hired secretary and I do appreciate the position and trust you have afforded me." Tom looked to Felix a moment and saw him nod slightly before he spoke. "Chris, you are more than just an employee. Felix and I both feel fortunate to have you here. Your wisdom and downright enthusiasm are greatly appreciated by both of us, and as far as we're concerned you are a vital member of the New Orleans CIA team. You have never missed a days work and take on burdens without prompting that no long-tenured secretary would ever consider so let's not delve into it any further. Enough said."

Tom wondered if now would be a good time to take Shank to an obedience school to begin his watch dog training to get him out from underfoot while all the work was in progress. He would have to be re-indoctrinated to all the new empty space in the building so he would feel at ease here. If he was going to be effective he would have to sniff out the place to decide where to spend most of his time while everyone was absent. Tom started going through the phone book to choose a nearby school so he could check on Shank's progress and see that he was being treated right. In all fairness he had to admit he was becoming attached to the dog. He was no Leo by any means; no dog could ever replace that animal in his eyes, yet in the absence of Leo, Shank would be a reasonable substitute.

48

Back at the Club Bayou, a meeting was being held by two of the owners, men who had no scruples whatsoever. They had called in one of their henchmen, a deputy sheriff on their payroll who was supposed to carry out what they figured was a simple task. "What do you mean you were scared off before you could finish the job? We don't pay you to hear that kind of nonsense. If you were stupid enough to be seen before you could set up the explosive device, it sounds to me like we are throwing our money away."

"But Boss Harvey told me nobody would be around during those hours. With bad information how was I supposed to finish attaching the device unseen? That's a very intricate apparatus, which has to be handled carefully to avoid blowing up in your face. One false move and bang it's all over; I've got a family to think of. Given another chance with someone to stand guard while I'm working will do the trick. With another person available and the remoteness of the building, if a repeat of an unexpected straggler should happen a mugging would go unnoticed for some time, nobody the wiser."

The two owners exchanged glances before the spokesman said, "One more try. If something goes wrong this time, family or no, you will lose the greater part of your income." His steely black eyes bored into the henchman. "I don't care how you do it, just get it done. Comprende? Now get out of here; we don't want to see your puss again before we read about the misfortune." The deputy couldn't leave fast enough, sweat rolling down his face before he made it to the parking lot, where the heat struck him like a sledge hammer. By the time he made it to his car he was soaked. You didn't disappoint those guys twice or you wouldn't be around to talk about it. Why did I get mixed up with these guys to begin with, he wondered. Oh, the money was good, and a certain amount of prestige among his peers made him feel like a big man, but he was in so deep there wasn't any way to get his head above water.

Four months passed so quickly that Tom Mueller completely lost track of time. It was so fast-paced with the inclusion of three new agents, two experienced transfers plus one novice out of the academy from Langley, that there were days he had to be reminded to break off to eat. There were continuous briefings and introductions to new field weaponry to be tested. Plus, it didn't help that both Chris and Felix came down with some sort of virus that incapacitated them. Shank was back from obedience school thirty pounds heavier and a year smarter. Tom was included in several sessions where the dog was put through paces he'd learned but needed someone he recognized to complete the handling. The procedure was explained to Tom inside the huge building before they went outside to apply what he'd been told in reality. Those periods were always at dusk or later to show what he had been taught in more life-like conditions. The hand signals were similar to those Tom was accustomed to using with Leo,, but voice commands had evolved to a greater degree,

210

making constant rehearsals necessary, very time consuming. There were nights Tom fell into bed physically exhausted, yet his mind wouldn't stop going over what he had learned and applied earlier in the evening. He would snap awake wondering if he had forgotten something before drifting off again. Those constant bouts with mental insecurities were sapping his ability to awaken fresh in the morning to begin another hectic series of problems. Each morning after wakeup coffee, he would check to see how Felix was feeling, hoping he would be able to share the load that seemed to be growing higher and heavier. One day he would look and feel better only to relapse the next.

Tom handed Chris the dossiers on the three new agents who had just recently arrived. "You might want to familiarize yourself with these before filing them. It seems this office has become popular for some reason lately. Two new transfers from the northeastern seaboard states, it must be the climate down here."

"Or else top management here. Don't sell yourself short, Mr. Mueller. The word gets around quickly how you handle your personnel." That was a nice compliment to hear from his secretary but Tom couldn't let that go to his head. Since taking over this district from Mr. Rowens after his promotion to headquarters, he had taken over a district decimated personnel-wise with very low morale, having to practically start from scratch rebuilding at a costly expense not only money-wise but health-wise, and looking back, Tom couldn't see where they had accomplished a great deal as of yet. He also understood if he was to have a Chinaman's chance of living up to some of the expectations of his agents, a full assault on Club Bayou would be necessary without injuries to any of his agents and to do that successfully was beyond his present grasp. What with the Club's apparent protection, of which Tom didn't completely understand how far up the ladder it went politically, it would seem the old adage "You can't fight City Hall" was an insurmountable barrier to overcome. Could it be done without the assistance another federal agency? Again the theory too many cooks spoiled the broth might be true in this case. That's where Mr. Rowens had found a leak, info being released just before a planned action was to be undertaken. Tom didn't want a reoccurrence of that misfortune. Was he being to considerate with his agents? Or maybe without the backup of his partner Felix there were too many decisions he had to make alone without his sounding board. Then again, he might have bit off more than he could chew in his promises to his new found brother Ray concerning backing of the extended business Ray intended to co-op with Stella. He wasn't made of money what with all the improvements he had financed at the estate, even though his backing of Cliff Ajax was paying off handsomely. Not only was Tom getting a cut rate for the work done for him but a good percentage of all Cliff's outside work. Still there were times when he felt over-extended. Also another child to be born didn't ease his anxiety any. He only hoped it wasn't another multiple birth. As much as he loved his children he would need another emerald to support more than four. Tom figured he'd better snap out of this reverie and get back to the business at hand. Even with the new agents, Tom was thinking about calling in the DEA for additional help since he understood most of the local law enforcement people were not to be trusted. It only took one or two bad apples to spoil everything around them, so an outside force unadulterated with local spoilage would be the ticket. He would check with Mr. McHenry first to make certain, now that he had his private phone number, to circumvent Mr. Rowens. His mentor wouldn't steer him wrong. Tom also knew he had most of these same thoughts earlier. Redundancy was idiotic.

Alf McHenry listened as Tom laid out his situation here. Knowing the problems Mr. Rowens had with leakage of plans for drug raids before they could be implemented, he understood why

Tom was calling for advice. "Do you feel there is a chance you may have the same problems Mr. Rowens had or is it you just don't trust the local authorities?"

"The latter, sir. The sheriff's department here seems to have many of their deputies in the employ of the club, where most of the serious drugs are being sold and even openly used on the premises. I've personally seen female minors used as attractions for the sale and use of more than just marijuana. They are used to entice the customers, mostly men who then may be mugged or worse. The operation seems to have full cooperation of the parish supervisors, who have to be on the take also. There's no other excuse for this large of an operation to be tolerated without already being closed down. With the personnel I now have there's no question of their loyalty, there's just not enough of them."

"How soon are you planning on making your move?"

"I can delay it until I have more troops that I can count on."

"I have an idea that may solve your problem but it will take two or three days to set it up properly. I'll get back to you soonest." Click, and he hung up. Some things never change, Tom thought, and Mr. McHenry's telephone etiquette was one of them. Despite that one failing, Tom knew Mr. McHenry would follow through on his idea so it was just his duty to get his own house in order so to speak. Tomorrow being Friday and an expense money and semi-monthly payday, all his people should be present. He would lay out his plan open to suggestions of course mainly from older agents who had been around the agency longer than him.

49

The night of the planned Club Bayou raid happened to fall on Halloween.

Tom unpacked a large crate filled with masks and reversible three-quarter-length lightweight jackets, one side garishly colored in stripes and polka dots, the other with POLICE in six-inch letters front and back, Tom didn't need to be hit in the head to understand McHenry's thinking. The masks were all the same, likenesses of LBJ, so all segments of the raiding party would recognize each other, thus avoiding any mistaken-identity mishaps. Three National Guard buses were to be used to transport each branch of raiders and then used to take plastic-handcuffed prisoners back to the armory, where they would be guarded before being separated by the seriousness of their charges, misdemeanors or felonies. Tom especially wanted the four head honchos and any of their lieutenants and bodyguards present that night, a form of payback for their attempt to demolish his district office building. Once they were incarcerated, that should shut down the club permanently and send the four owners to federal prisons for years to come. At least that was his intention and hope if nothing went awry from start to finish to hinder it. However the best laid plans of mice and men sometimes fell by the wayside.

Wearing the mask resembling the former president, Tom Mueller was wearing a business suit over a folded reversible jacket that made him look overly stout. He circulated throughout the cavernous interior of Club Bayou in the company of Frank Jimenez, who was unrecognizable to anyone who might know him from his position as senior detective with the New Orleans Police Department. His costume represented the picture of Father Time complete with a long gray beard, pointed-star-covered dunce cap, and walking stave to support the old age-wizened man who had seen it all, done it all during his tenure. He walked slowly, stooped over carrying the burden of the world's problems, but his eyes, hidden behind his wrinkled-skin facial mask, were darting continuously around the interior searching for any of the big bosses. Tom, looking toward the main entrance of the club, noticed through the milling crowd the unmistakable sight of his partner along with two other LBJ masks not moving from that spot, just casually holding the position to eliminate unwanted departure of main targets.

Many of the young women cavorting throughout the interior were as skimpily attired as possible, showing disgraceful parts of their bodies bordering on lewd. It seemed most males either hadn't drunk enough or ingested enough of the prevalent drugs which were openly being bought in all corners of the room so they hadn't as yet began to fondle any of the overexposed body parts, but Tom imagined if his teams didn't start their functions here before long the men young or old would be grabbing for everything in sight.

Tom sauntered toward the main entrance to confer with Felix to see if all the teams were in position while Father Time shuffled off in another direction, despite telling Tom he would be sticking close to him to point out the bosses and lieutenants Tom didn't know by sight.

Tom expected Frank to be right behind him, but when he turned around to include him in the conversation with Felix and the other two agents he was gone. Tom just shook his head but instead of voicing his displeasure to his partner, he said, "Where's the Schultz boy?"

"He's on one a' the outside teams don'tcha remember? Ya' said he was too recognizable inside 'cause of all the time he used ta' spend here until I had my little talk with him. How soon ya' gonna' start this shindig? Those two outside teams are gonna' start bein' suspicious lookin' pretty soon."

Tom knew Felix was right in his summation of the perils of delaying the starting action, but he simply had the feeling inside another fifteen minutes wouldn't be dangerous to any of the teams. "You stay here, Felix, and watch for Frank while I go outside for a final examination of our setup. I'll be back shortly; it's my intuition calling for this short pause, and I've learned over time not to doubt my inner feelings." Felix had that nonplussed expression covered by his mask. Sometimes he just didn't understand some of his amigo's ways of thinking, and since the planning for this raid had been gone over and over by everyone involved, this sudden change in tactics had him completely confused. The building heat in the huge room was stifling, and the masks certainly didn't help. The longer they wore them, the better chance arose that one or more of the agents would keel over from heat exhaustion. There wasn't a hint of a breeze inside or out.

Tom suddenly appeared without mask and with his police jacket showing. A portable bull horn hung by a strap over his left shoulder, and he was now all business. Somehow Frank Jimenez was right behind him sans Father Time costume, showing that there was some other exit which could be used in emergencies. Tom spoke through the bull horn: "May I have your attention, and I mean right now! Do not try to leave the building, all exits are covered inside and out. No one will be hurt if you follow my instructions to the letter." All agents inside were changing from costume and mask to police jackets and as surprised customers looked around nervously, they could pick out any number of them scattered about the room. An anxious hush spread slowly around the customers, many of whom were dropping small packages on the floor and sidling away from the damning evidence that could incriminate them on serious charges. The many agents present we no fools; they weren't about to nab anyone who did that, thus causing a sudden stampede that could overpower the agents present and cause serious injury to the fairly innocent party-goers, if you could call any of them completely innocent.

In an aside, Frank said to Tom: "There's two of the owners trying to escape out the rear exit. I'm going out the front main doors to circle around to intercept them. Is it all right if I take Felix along?" Tom nodded his approval, giving his partner the sign they used when oral commands were impractical. Right now he wished Leo was here; he would be the perfect assistant to corral those owners. Even the Irish wolfhound, although somewhat temperamental, would do. Any sane person would cease eluding when faced by a large dog. Tom didn't have the time to dwell on those ruminations. He had to start separating the herd by classifications, misdemeanor or felony, to load on the buses for the trip to the National Guard Armory, using the plastic handcuffs on any possible trouble makers. Three buses at first seemed enough, and they certainly couldn't make multiple trips. They would simply have to pack them in like sardines. It wasn't ten minutes before Frank and Felix returned with the two owners and a very young female. The two men were complaining in loud voices they couldn't be treated this way. They were going to sue for false arrest, et cetera, et cetera. Tom just said, "Get them on a bus before I say something they'll be sorry to hear." Frank prodded them aboard and stayed right with them. The young girl was crying copiously, her nose running like a leaky faucet.

So far, so good, Tom thought, with the exception of the other two bosses, so far absent. He wondered if there might not be some sort of hidden room up on the roof. Now was when a helicopter would come in handy but since one of them had not been figured into the plan his only recourse was to make an effort to scour the upper reaches of the building to make certain. "Well, partner, one more job before we leave," and he explained what he had in mind. "You're armed, I trust."

"Ya' shouldn't have ta' ask that of me, amigo. Lead on."

They found a stairway hidden behind the raised stage where the occasional live band played. It was reminiscent of Fred's New York City place above the cleaners that had all those hidden passageways between floors with plain paneled spring-opening entrances. Upon slowly climbing the squeaky wooden steps, Tom cautioned his partner to watch for hidden booby traps as the steps switched back in a different direction, still rising. While Tom climbed slowly his head swiveling from side to side, up and down, searching for hidden traps, Felix was counting the steps. After the switchback, he had just reached fifty when they were stopped by a solid metal door blocking further passage. Fifty steps meant at least fifty feet up Felix figured, while he paused to see how Tom was going to handle this blockage. Tom put his ear to the metal, listening intently while feeling the edges for hinge depression which would indicate what side the door was weakest since there was no knob or handle on this side. Then he began feeling along the walls on both sides of it before being rewarded by a loose six inch panel, which when depressed caused the door to swing outward a few inches. Tom pushed it slightly, unholstering his Cobra at the same time. They were on the roof in shadowy dimness, the only illumination resulting from the overhead parking lot lights to one side, just enough to reveal four square-shaped housings that could be air conditioning units or maybe something else. Tom scuffled one foot on the roof top, which felt smooth to him, not the normal tar-and-stone composition normally found on large roofs in the New Orleans area, which were subjected to heavy rains. Tom pointed to the closest housing and whispered: "That could be what we're looking for, partner. My guess is that may be a heavily fortified pillbox that the bosses use as a hideaway. That would explain the hidden stairs and cemented roof top walkway." Cautiously, they approached their objective, spreading apart the closer they got. They circled it looking for an entrance. When they met again they, both shook their heads, which puzzled Tom. How did they get inside? Did this mean they gained entry from underneath? Then why go to all the expense of building the stairway they just used? Tom searched his memory for something similar. There had to be an answer here. Tom's dilemma was solved when a hidden panel slid open and four men came out all most in his lap.

"Hold it right there. You're all under arrest. March right down that stairway ahead to the ground floor with no funny business. My cohort has an itchy trigger finger and won't hesitate to blow a hole in you."

"What's the charge?" a suited must-have-been-owner blurted out."

"Where do you want me to start? There are so many it'll take a Philadelphia lawyer two or three weeks to assemble them all. So I suggest you keep your trap shut until you know what the score is."

The Philadelphia lawyer statement wasn't too much of a bluff. Tom didn't play poker that way nor would it be an expression to be taken lightly. Mr. McHenry had seen the significance of alerting the Louisiana State Prosecutor's Office in Baton Rouge, run by a man who received his law degree from Temple University in Philadelphia, Pennsylvania, but was a native-born Louisianian. He had made arrangements to be present in New Orleans to supervise the overall results of the Club Bayou raid. The Club had been a thorn in his hide for quite some time, and a complete shake-up in local law enforcement was indicated, starting with the parish sheriff and a good number of his deputies. Sufficient evidence of parish supervisors accepting bribes had also been disclosed, but the hub of the whole rotten mess was the Bayou and its intrepid owners.

Tom picked three agents, two who looked big enough to eat hay and another Frank Jimenez's size and said: "Follow me up to the roof, there's a special job I want you to do." He grabbed a six-cell flashlight, taking it for them to use to clean out the pillbox where the other two bosses were apprehended. He showed them the sliding-panel entrance. "There must be some sort of an inside latch, so look around carefully. I want every bit of paper you find, and if there's a small safe bring that out too. Any and all property in there will be confiscated. I'm hoping a hoard of drugs will be in there, because I can't imagine where else the bosses would think them safer to be stored pre-sale. Be very thorough in your search, especially for spare keys. You could find your transportation out of here by limousine; that would be a welcome addition to our fleet of vehicles otherwise you will have to call a cab to return to our office." The three agents exchanged glances of extreme satisfaction in anticipation of the unsupervised mayhem they could wreak inside the hidden room.

When they arrived at the armory, the place was a literal mad house. The prisoners' buses stood empty near the motor pool where several guardsmen were cleaning them out under the supervision of a tech sergeant. At one bus they were actually using a high-velocity hose with a combination of steam and chemicals to sanitize the interior, where one or more of the prisoners couldn't hold their water or stomach contents, which showed what alcohol and drugs in tandem with a certain amount of fear could do to the human internal system.

That night temperatures were hovering in the middle eighties, a harbinger of another scorcher when the sun came up in the morning. Tom hoped there wouldn't be too many heat-stroke casualties requiring immediate hospitalization before this night was over, not only the prisoners but the heavily uniformed guardsmen cooped up in here as well.

While Tom was watching, several non-commissioned officers throughout the main room retrieved live ammunition from the guardsmen surrounding the detainees in an atmosphere that seemed to grow tenser by the minute, he spotted a short man in immaculate khakis leaning on a cane by the slightly raised overhead door. As he moved toward the familiar figure dodging in and out of the milling throng to keep the man in sight, he couldn't believe his eyes that it was old Master Sergeant George Maddox, the armorer who had aligned the sniper scope on his Springfield '03 rifle after watching Tom fire at the floating targets he'd set out in the bayous so many years ago before -when Tom and Felix had gone on the drug raid in Colombia by submarine. The man had to be over retirement age, way over, Tom thought. As he closed on him the old sarge spotted Tom, his eyes lighting up with recognition. "You are a sight for my old eyes; it's the shooter" he stated in his Southern drawl. "What brings you back to this neck of the woods?"

"Aren't you getting a little long in the tooth to still be in harness" Tom countered. "I can't imagine your commanding officer just keeping you around for old times sake. And what's with the cane?"

"I've gone through more COs than you can shake a stick at, boy, an' you haven't answered my question yet."

"I guess you don't keep track of what's going on outside of the military. I'm the district Supervisor for the local CIA office. In fact, what's happening here tonight is of my doing. I set up the drug raid at the Club Bayou where all these people came from. Felix Santana is my partner and assistant supervisor. He's around here somewhere. I'm surprised you two haven't run into each other before now."

There was a scuffle in progress nearby that drew Master Sergeant Maddox's attention away from Tom before he could answer any more of Tom's queries, and quick as a flash he moved away from the wall he'd been leaning against belying the need for his cane as he moved toward it but he was still too late to prevent what happened or the dire calamity that resulted. When a buck sergeant squad leader was attempting to disarm one of his private's loaded rifle, the young man failed to press the safety in his confusion, and his index finger inside the trigger guard pulled the trigger, involuntarily firing the piece. The round flew between the squad leader's legs, also missing the onrushing Master Sergeant, but as it ricocheted off the cement floor it struck the person who had the forethought to have the weapons unloaded of live clips of ammunition, Tom Mueller. The round struck him unhindered in the left ankle, the force of it knocking Tom off his feet, and when he fell his head struck the concrete floor, rendering him immediately unconscious. That might have been a blessing in disguise, as the pain from the smashed ankle would have been excruciating.

The first person to reach Tom was Master Sergeant Maddox, who with one glance took in the horrendous wound and quickly applied a tourniquet with his own belt that at least slowed the loss of blood. He also bellowed for a corpsman. Surprisingly, one was close at hand with full field assortment of medical supplies in his kit. He took over the temporary care of the injured while Maddox rushed for one of the unit ambulances in the motor pool, which he backed into the now completely raised overhead door. He yanked a stretcher out of the rear, placing it on the floor next to Tom where a platoon leader lieutenant and the corpsman lifted the heavy stretcher into the rear of the vehicle. The corpsman insisted on going along with his patient to the nearest hospital emergency room.

By this time, Felix showed up, alerted by Frank Jimenez who now stood nearby looking like an old mother hen brooding over an injured chick, while Felix in his authoritative manner jumped into the driver's seat, designating his old friend Sergeant Maddox to the passenger seat to explain how this tragedy had happened, at the same time trying to figure out how and when he was going to tell Stella. Knowing that headstrong woman as he did, it might be best not to call Key Largo until he notified Mr. McHenry to let him handle it. Felix wouldn't know the full extent of his amigo's injuries until he reached the hospital and talked to the doctors. While Maddox was explaining his take on how the shooting had occurred, Felix held the pedal to the metal, siren screaming, and with the directions given by the old Master Sergeant, did his best to wrestle the aging GMC ambulance through the fairly heavy evening traffic without causing any collisions that would slow his progress to the Methodist Hospital, which was the closest hospital to the armory, about five miles.

The corpsman in the rear of the ambulance with Mueller opened the sliding panel forward to be able to talk with the driver. "How much farther?" he had to shout over the wailing of the siren. "I don't like the looks of my patient back here. His pulse rate has increased dramatically like he's having some sort of seizure. Is he taking some kind of medication which would cause a reaction like this that you know of?"

In the frenzied preparation for the Bayou raid Tom did indeed forget to take the daily dose the physician had prescribed for his blackout spells simply because of an oversight and without Stella to remind him. That lapse was drawing him into the bottomless void that his brother Fred had experienced so often and that had ultimately and irreversibly contributed to his death at so young an age.

As Tom slipped deeper into his coma-like void the assisting corpsman became more anxious. This man's condition was completely beyond his limited field of expertise. He could handle the serious ankle wound until a competent physician became available if too long a period didn't elapse, like an hour or less, yet this trance the man had fallen into?

When Felix pulled into the emergency room bay, backed in actually, and the doors were pulled open, a whole squad of nurses and interns were johnny-on-the-spot to assist with a rolling cart where they transferred Tom with haste. Felix quickly explained what happened and told them government insurance would cover all expenses and he wanted to talk to the head surgeon on duty before any diagnosis was made. "Ya' can't do anythin' but stop the bleedin' until I talk ta' the doctor."

Showing his CIA picture identification seemed to mollify their doubts as they rolled Tom into the operating theater to prep him for further procedures once Felix gave the go ahead. A doctor Gerhardt, an orthopedic specialist was notified to wash up to be readily available while X-rays were taken of the damaged ankle and foot. For the busy second shift the mechanics of the hospital were rapidly meshing into gear.

Felix meanwhile was in communication with one of the night operators at headquarters in D.C., who after being apprised of the seriousness of the situation, took his phone number to return a call to him as soon as Mr. McHenry was located and informed.

A phone rang, and Mr. McHenry was on the line. "What happened and how bad is it?"

Felix explained what he knew and what Master Sergeant Maddox had told him while McHenry listened without interruption. "So an orthopedic surgeon is going to be necessary, a top man. But the other thin', that which is mental needs someone else, also the best we can find. Stella should be called, she might know if their is some kinda' medicine he should be takin' that we don't know 'bout. I'd rather you made that call if ya' catch my drift; it'd sound better comin' from the highest boss an' ya' can stop her from makin' any rash decisions like tryin' ta' drive over here. She's pregnant, ya' know. At the moment he's havin' X-rays of his ankle taken an' until the results come in I won't know anythin' more."

"Well then let me make some calls to people I know in the medical profession for advice on the top men in the orthopedic field. Whoever they recommend that is closest to New Orleans for quick response will be the man I get there. I'm sure they have adequate men connected to that hospital who are on call but I want the best available on short notice even if it's more than one. You hang in there, Felix, until I get some answers an get back to you. Don't let anyone perform surgery on Tom until you hear from me. This may be a long night for you after all your exertions of the club raid but we'll make it up to you."

Tom had been brought back from the X-ray department where specialists were discussing the photos. She should have a copy of their diagnosis shortly. She gave him the number to call in Washington, D.C., and suggested he wait for the forthcoming information before returning the call. 'That way that way you won't have to make a second call."

"Is he conscious now?" She shook her head no.

A copy of the X-rays arrived fifteen minutes later and the head nurse, finished with her other duties, scanned them quickly. "This is not good, Mr. Santana. When you return your call I'm afraid you'll have bad news to report. I won't get into the technical aspects of the injury that you wouldn't understand but I will say his ankle is so smashed Mr. Mueller will be lucky if the foot isn't amputated. Of course, if it is there are some wonderful false limbs in use these days that after extensive physical therapy he will be able to walk with only a slight limp with the use of a cane for support. That's better than having to depend on crutches."

Felix was appalled to think of his amigo going through the rest of his life so handicapped when he had always been so robust and vigorous. It would mean a total desk job for the rest of his career with the agency or else to be pensioned out, which would practically kill his spirit. Now he dreaded to make the call to Mr. McHenry and relay such bad news knowing what high esteem he held for Tom. Felix stood there wondering how he could phrase this news so it wouldn't sound so bad but he couldn't see any way to change the lousy facts. Not one to put off necessary duties, he trudged toward the phone feeling like he was walking the last steps to the gallows. Just as he was about to pick up the receiver it rang startling him. He hesitated before picking it up. Could this be McHenry with some good news that would alleviate his bad?

"Hello." It was McHenry. Felix held his breath. "I've got good news for you, Felix. I talked to Stella and there is medicine he's supposed to be taking daily, and you were right, she is a headstrong woman; she insisted on going to New Orleans. So you'll have to put her up where Tom lives until this crisis is over. We are going to fly here there as soon as she arranges for care for the children. She said she would call here when she knows. Tom's car should be there somewhere, which she can use for transportation while she's there so you won't have to worry about taking her around. As independent as she is, I'm certain she'll be no bother to you at all while you run the district office. The only thing you should do is introduce her to Chris so she can put a face to the name of your secretary; that would be a nice gesture when she gets there. I've contacted the top bone specialist near you, Doctor Steinhauer, based in Atlanta and he's already en route as a personal favor to the agency."

"Maybe now is the time ta' tell ya' the X-rays have shown the ankle has been smashed beyond repair, the head nurse tol' me. The doc's here are already talkin' amputation.?

"Don't allow that to happen until Steinhauer gets there; in fact, I'll call the head administrator to confirm that. I can pull heavy weight when necessary even if we have to transfer him to another facility, which they wouldn't like at all. That isn't the only hospital in New Orleans. Keep in touch with me regardless, Felix." And he hung up.

50

Stella Mueller arrived at the New Orleans airport the day after Felix's conversation with McHenry, carrying only one suitcase and a large over-the-shoulder purse which contained much more than the normal woman's handbag. She was noticeably with child by this time and was handled with kid gloves by everyone around her, other passengers, and even Felix, who was told what flight she would come in on. He had taxied into the National Guard armory where Tom's station wagon was parked, and after three hours sleep plus straightening up the premises a bit so Stella wouldn't complain about its messiness, he gave her the directions to the Methodist Hospital and volunteered to go along with her to introduce her to all those he had talked to about Tom's condition, so she wouldn't be going in cold having to find out everything by herself. But she turned him down flat, saying: "I'm perfectly capable of finding my way around there and talking to whomever is in charge after I see my husband. Since you haven't asked, Gennie is doing fine, other than a little morning sickness and is showing her pregnancy, more than I am. You might call her a little more often than you have; we womenfolk need assurance from our husbands, too, when we're home alone."

"I plead guilty an' will follow yer' advice to do just that." Felix thought to himself, the sooner he got her out of his hair where she could browbeat those at the hospital the sooner he could relax and have a couple of beers before going back to the office to clue Chris in on the latest developments. He was sure there would be questions from her about the other agents need to know that she needed his say on.

Pulling into the warehouse-office, he was overwhelmed by the number of vehicles scattered around the spacious floor. He could only identify three or four by their color and model tagging those by known agents who usually parked here plus Chris' that he had seen so often. Shank wandered over to sniff Felix's feet, always in hope of some sort of snack just like his sire Leo. "Go 'bout yer' bizness; I ain't got nuthin' fer' ya' ."

Felix headed for the office proper to find out from Chris who owned all the cars.

"Five of them were confiscated from the Bayou raid. You could drive around in the limo if you wanted to throw a party; it's big enough. I'll bet that beauty cost a bundle. How is Mr. Mueller?"

"I jus' gave his wife the keys to his station wagon. She flew in earlier an' is headed for the hospital ta' check his condition. Mr. McHenry called in a specialist from Atlanta ta' take over his case, an' I hate ta' be the bearer of bad news but jus' before I left the head nurse tol' me the present doctors were talkin' amputation 'cause the ankle was so smashed up. That could be the end a' his career in the agency 'cause knowin' Tom so well he won't be satisfied with a desk job, he's more of a' action in the field agent. Keep all a' this under yer' hat for now from the other agents 'til the word comes down from a higher authority, namely Mr. McHenry. That'll squelch any false rumors gettin' passed 'round."

"That's just terrible news, but don't worry; I know how to keep my mouth shut among the other agents. If asked, I'll just say he's in the hospital recovering and that I don't have any of the particulars; mums the word. If that word got out there might be a mass exodus of transfers out of here just like all the new agents that came here recently, then where would you be?"

Felix was thinking that statement over when her phone rang just as he was heading for the fridge and a cold Bud. Chris answered with the phone number in reverse which was the standard procedure used to eliminate crank calls or wrong numbers. Anyone with normal business knew this, but on occasion someone unfamiliar with the code would hang up frustrated and re-dial. Just then, Shank started raising a fuss with Chris, indicating he wanted to go outside, so she excused herself to take him out. Felix took that opportunity to get his cold Bud and had just taken his first swallow when the phone rang again. After four rings he picked up not using the code just listening. He recognized the caller's voice immediately. It was a panicky Gennie. "I'm so glad you answered, dear."

"Did ya' jus' call before?"

"Yes, I forgot that silly system in my haste to reach you. I just can't find Tomas anywhere."

"Four hours, I've looked in all his usual haunts, and since Freddie is still in the house under the watchful eyes of that woman friend of Stella's, those two can't be up to their usual mischief."

Now Felix was between the proverbial rock and a hard place. He couldn't leave New Orleans to hunt for a precocious eight year old. "How are ya' feelin', babe? Stella said you were still havin' some mornin' sickness." His mind was still trying to come up with a solution for finding Tomas. The only thing that came to mind was to notify the Florida state troopers giving them the authorization to guard the Key Largo Mueller compound where they could get a picture of Tomas from Gennie and make copies to distribute to the local law-enforcement officers in the hope of finding his son. He explained what he was going to do to his wife saying: "If in the meantime ya' find 'im call back her at once . Either Chris or I'll stay by the phone beyon' our regular hours."

Stella got right to Dr. Steinhauer within ten minutes of her arrival at the hospital. He was a smallish man similar in size to Felix with a definite German accent and long slender fingers like a concert pianist, and even though she towered over him she took an instant liking to the man being as humble to him as a novice to a seasoned professional. She figured she needed him on her side for any serious decisions that would affect her husband's condition and his future employment in or out of the agency. Stella could be a very devious woman to get what she wanted in life for herself and her family. She gave him a vial of the pills that Tom was supposed to take daily to avoid his blackout spells, and Dr. Steinhauer, after reading the ingredients, stated he could duplicate the pill for intravenous feeding, which would bring Tom to consciousness so he could explain what the procedure of the upcoming surgery would entail with the worst and best scenarios of the outcome. He would still be groggy but lucid enough to comprehend what lay ahead. Stella thought it over a few moments before agreeing to his plan. Tom had every right to know what to expect if the operation turned sour and he was left a cripple for the rest of his life. The agency would undoubtedly give him a reasonable pension if he decided against remaining as a desk jockey in any capacity especially if it were in Washington, D.C., over a thousand miles from his home in Key Largo and farther away than New Orleans. The decision would be his, of course, but it would break his spirit for the job, and that elan was what kept him going. All these thoughts ran through Stella's mind while she stood half listening to Dr. Steinhauer. After all, the diminutive specialist from Atlanta couldn't perform miracles despite his renown in his field. She wasn't about to allow amputation except as a life-saving recourse, and, despite the mangled ankle, she doubted it would be life threatening.

"When Mr. Mueller is awake I'll call you immediately from the waiting room where you should remain while I finish my diagnosis."

Forty-five minutes passed while Stella fidgeted, biting her nails in the waiting room before Dr. Steinhauer reappeared, fastidious as ever. "Your husband is awake and asking for you. I've completed my preliminaries and will begin surgery as soon as a competent surgical nurse becomes available. You will be glad to hear removal of the foot will not be necessary, but I will have to fuse the bones and tie off the arteries so he won't have any feeling down below the knee. It's a delicate operation which will take several hours, so I suggest you leave the hospital and get some rest rather than sit in the waiting room, where you will end up a nervous wreck. Trust me on that. Leave a phone number with the floor head nurse, and I'll contact you when he's taken into the recovery room and the anesthetic wears off. Go in to see him now and give him as much encouragement as you can to eliminate his anxiety." Stella didn't have to be told how to encourage her man; she'd had plenty of experience with his previous injuries. She would put on a false front, loving him as she always had from almost the first day she had met him. True love conquered all obstacles, Stella believed. Stella was not about to leave a phone number; she would sit in the station wagon under the nearest shade tree where she could stay fairly cool with the windows down so as not to run the air conditioner while in idle running the battery down.

Stella was still trying to figure all the angles out when the baby gave a ferocious kick that almost made her think she was ready to deliver. "Not yet, baby, there are other things to take care of before you can take your first breath of this world. We have to make sure your daddy is mentally whole to be able to welcome you to our growing family. You'll have two brothers and a sister to watch over and protect you as you grow up. Won't that be wonderful? Being the youngest has many advantages; you will benefit from their experiences both good and bad so you can decide which path to follow. There are so many treasures awaiting you to fulfill your dreams and aspirations. You will no doubt have pleasurable formative years. Plus, I'll always be there for you to guide your decisions and nurture your upbringing. Oh what a wonderful life you will have. So be patient, my little darling; everything in our world will be yours for the asking if only you will wait a few more days for me."

Meanwhile, the search was on for Tomas by first the Florida state troopers, who got several pictures of the boy which they all took a long look at before passing them on to a police artist. The artist made a remarkably life-like copy of one of the Polaroid snapshots which was duplicated along with all of the lads age, height and weight. Of course, Leo and the Irish wolfhound had to get into the act. Leo had already sensed something was wrong by the arrival of so many strange men but unlike his younger years when he would attack any stranger who trespassed on his main friends, he now simply sat and watched their comings and goings and the antics of the other dogs especially the wolfhound. Missy, the bull mastiff that Stella had adopted when the then-pregnant dog had wandered on to the compound, was completely devoted to the kind human who had fed, bathed, and groomed her then helped with the delivery of her brood, one of which Tom had taken back to New Orleans to be trained as a guard dog for that office/warehouse and had proven to be a valuable asset there. Chris, their secretary, had become the surrogate mother to Shank, similar to Stella's position with his.

The first indication of finding Tomas came from a deputy sheriff who spotted a boy that resembled the artist sketch he had been given. He reported this from his cruiser's radio. That sighting caused a flurry of activity at the Mueller compound, where five Florida State troopers were stationed around the perimeter. The most senior of the five drove to the deputy's location, his hopes high that a break in the case would culminate the outcome and ease the mother's worries. These aspirations were dashed when he saw the badly frightened lad sitting in the rear of the cruiser. He couldn't have been more than six, seven at tops and didn't resemble Tomas any more than his own nephew. After admonishing the deputy for his laxness in making unfounded reports, he scooped the youngster out of the rear seat calming him with soothing small talk until he settled down enough to tell the nice man where he lived. The trooper then drove him to his home, where his own distraught mother thanked him profusely for finding her son.

Stella couldn't stand the suspense any longer. She had to return to the waiting room to await the results of Tom's operation, regardless of the results she had to know. The floor head nurse informed her Dr. Steinhauer was in the physician's lounge having coffee, and pointed the way. The

221

dapper little man was surprised to see her, he was sitting talking to an obvious surgical nurse sans operating greens. She was his size, and with some instinct, stood and excused herself when she saw Stella approach. "I thought you were going home for some rest, but since you're here, will you join me for some liquid refreshment?" Stella eased herself into the chair vacated by the nurse, just sitting quietly waiting for the doctor to explain further. He understood her anxiety and began. "First this was a delicate procedure, as I told you before, and it couldn't have been done without the capable assistance of the nurse who just left. She could foretell what instrument I needed next before I asked for it. Second, he won't have any feeling in his leg below the knee, but after therapy he won't need crutches, just a cane. However, he will have to use that the rest of his life. I'm certain he'll get used to that. He's in the recovery room if you want to sit with him. He won't wake up for another hour or so, and he won't be in much pain while he takes the medicine I prescribed. By the way, how close to delivery are you?"

"Not to worry, doctor, I have no intention of having my baby here. It will be born in Key Largo where all the others were. I've had quite enough of this hospital, even with your expert guidance, and I can't thank you enough."

Gennie Santana could be just as strong-willed as Stella Mueller when she was feeling well, but at this moment, with the disappearance of Tomas along with her own pregnancy in its final weeks before delivery, and with her husband hundreds of miles away, she was feeling anything but. Several false alarms in finding Tomas didn't help. She was cried-out, and only her faith that the boy would be found alive and safe with all of he trained lawmen searching kept her from going off he deep end. She couldn't force herself to eat anything, even toast and coffee. Even the thought of solid food nauseated her, so all she did was sit in front of the TV without audio, not comprehending what she was seeing, looking from it to the nearby phone hoping for the best.

The best was not in the cards for Gennie. The next report was called in by a home owner farther down the Keys who was out fishing about a hundred yards from shore. He snagged what he thought was a grouper, an important food fish of the south Atlantic coast, only to reel in a fifty pound boy quite mangled as though chewed on by an alligator, an arm missing and a gouge out of his chest. It almost made him sick to see a youngster his age in such a condition. He couldn't get back to his slip fast enough to report his findings to the proper authorities. Within ten minutes, his property was swarming with state troopers, photographers, and a coroners truck. He had to tell his story several times before it was finally recorded by a hand-held tape recorder. Only then did everyone start to clear out, warning him not to talk to the media until the next of kin was notified and then to refer them to the Florida State Police local office. The lousy job of telling Mrs. Santana of the tragedy was left to the big trooper in charge of the perimeter detail. He had the foresight to have an ambulance standing by near enough in case Mrs. Santana needed immediate emergency treatment. It was a good thing the trooper thought to do that, for there was no easy way to break the news of the death of Tomas. First Gennie couldn't accept the facts, saying it must be some other unfortunate youngster, but when the trooper told her it was indeed her son and he was in the hands of the coroner to determine the exact time and cause of death, she fainted right where she sat. He called in the ambulance before carefully laying her full length on the floor with a cushion under her head and his own shirt to cover her, basic first aid. The ambulance crew had brought a stretcher into the house when they got the call, and all three men lifted her on to it. The paramedics, trained in the service, wasted no time rushing he to the closest hospital where trained doctors could take over to avoid the woman having a miscarriage. The original state trooper who broke the news rummaged through her purse, she had left behind, until he found the phone number of her husband's office in New Orleans. He made the call identifying himself and his position as one of the Florida state troopers Felix had called in to lead the search for his son. "I'm sorry to be the bearer of such bad news, Mr. Santana," and he went on to bring him up to date. Felix sat in shock after the trooper hung up. Chris asked him what was wrong, but he was too numb to give her a coherent answer.

51

When Stella Mueller awoke in the recovery room, she knew instantly her boast to Dr. Steinhauer of not delivering her baby until she got back home was just ostentatious bravado. She had several spasms within three minutes that told her otherwise. Tom was awake and he also knew by the sheen of sweat on her face and the white-knuckled grip on the wooden handles of her chair, she was about to go into final labor indicating delivery of childbirth was imminent. He pressed his call button repeatedly, bringing a nurse on the run. He pointed to his wife when the nurse arrived and she knew immediately what he meant, having borne children of her own.

Stella delivered a single child, a girl, instead of multiple births, delivered by Dr. Steinhauer. The able specialist wasn't a pediatrician by any means but was assisted by the nurse who called on him. It was just like riding a bicycle he thought. Once you learned how, you never forgot.

Had Stella heard about Tomas' fate, her delivery might not have been so easy.

Unbeknown by anyone, law-enforcement authorities or the grief-stricken family members, there was a random killer on the loose in the southeastern portion of the United States. He chose his victims only for their vulnerability and when he had the urge. The fate of Tomas was just such a case. No one would ever suspect a former lawman of committing those acts; that's why he was so successful. He was so mentally deranged, yet cunning, that even his own wife never had a clue to his dark side. He had many excuses for his absences, usually having law-enforcement connotations where she thought it was normal for his old way of life. Yet, Tomas wasn't simply a random choice. The boy was playing along the shore when the killer was heading toward his chalet, returning from another killing further down the Keys at Islamorada Key. He had tried to wash most of the blood from his clothes and body so he could travel inconspicuously, but he had obviously missed some. Using his knife was always a messy form of execution. Tomas recognized his adjacent neighbor and was moving toward him when he stopped dead in his tracks, having some forewarning of danger to himself, thus the necessity to kill the boy before he could reveal his findings to others. After throwing the dead boy into the ocean, Terry Connoti cleansed himself completely, taking painstaking care to make certain his wife wouldn't notice any discrepancies from his normal appearance, then looked the killing ground over thoroughly to be sure no physical evidence was apparent that would connect him to the scene – a habit stemming from his investigative activities on the sheriff's department. Terry was a very careful man on matters this serious. It took him the better part of an hour before he was completely satisfied that within a hundred feet in all directions there was no sign of his being there. By that time, his body heat from the exertions of his search had dried his clothing, and all that was left was the uncomfortable salt-water itch that he could remedy by taking a cold shower when he got back to his chalet.

Three days later, with the help of Mr. McHenry, Dr. Steinhauer, and most of the staff at the Methodist Hospital, arrangements were made to transport Tom, Stella, and Prissy – short for Priscilla – that Stella had dubbed her newborn baby girl, to the airport where a private two-engine plane had been chartered to return them to an airport in Key West, where another ambulance was waiting to drive them all to Key Largo. The rest of the children were overjoyed to see both their parents and much to-do was made over their new baby sister. Gennie was still in the hospital but also under psychiatric care to cope with the loss of Tomas. Her unborn child seemed healthy, so she hadn't had a miscarriage but was still under care.

Leo finally sensed his closest human friend was back in residence, so he nosed his way back into the house using his own private entrance. Stella saw him out of the corner of her eye and beckoned him to follow her. Leo obeyed instantly. He followed her into the room where she had put the medicinal bed and walked right up to put his head lightly next to Tom where he couldn't help but notice him. Toms' leg was raised so there was no pressure on his ankle, but otherwise his hands and upper body were free. "Hello there, big fella. Here I am in a bed again," he said, as he scratched behind the mastiff's ear.

The dog, remembering old times, gave Tom a sloppy kiss, his usual reward for anyone who scratched his ears that way. Tom burst out laughing, his best laugh since he was home. Better tonic for recovery couldn't be had. The big dog had always affected him that way. "I've missed you too, big boy. You can stay in here as much as you want, it's OK with me." The dog seemed to understand and settled down next to the bed with his multi-colored eyes fixed on Tom. He was at ease again more than he'd been in quite some time.

Stella was in the kitchen preparing a meal for the children, Missy at her feet as usual, listening to a radio as she worked when she heard a news bulletin that interrupted the music reporting the body of a woman had been discovered in the brush at the side of the main road, murdered by multiple stab wounds all over her body, which must have caused her to bleed to death. That act coupled with the murder of a young boy identified as Tomas Santana of Key Largo had local authorities wondering if there was any connection or if there was a killer on the loose in the Keys. Stella finished setting the table for her children and calling them to eat before telling Missy to stay while she entered the room where Tom and Leo were. "What can I get you to eat, honey? How about a bowl of minestrone soup that I added sausage bits to. And, Leo, if I can tear you away from your guard position it's time for your dinner, too." It took some coaxing to get the mastiff to leave Tom's side, but he finally obeyed reluctantly. When she brought the soup in for Tom, she sat by the side of his bed and reported what she had heard on the radio." That makes me a little uneasy, honey, even with Leo and the other dogs on the property. My weapon is out in the studio and I still have to cross the yard to get there.

As the days passed and Tom was beginning to feel better, he was more mobile. Each day he was spending more time out of the hospital bed sitting in a chair across the room, making trips to the bathroom with the aid of his crutches, and occasionally joining the children at a meal. It was both reassuring to the children to see the whole family together and it was good for Stella's morale to see her husband joining the family circle in a more normal routine. Missy, the bull mastiff she'd adopted was always in attendance also a reminder a protector was near her. Since no more murders had been reported in the area lately her trips to the studio in the early morning hours were less stressful and she no longer packed the .45 caliber automatic with her. Several of her paintings were in the final stages, ready to be shipped to Ray in Shelby, Ohio.

Tom was even showing interest in playing the piano, usually accompanied by little Sheila who seemed mesmerized by his technique, never too far from his side, even though she could no longer sit in his lap while he played. Tom was not only playing, but had started composing, first little ditties then later complete songs. He wasn't trying to write the great American concerto, yet the more he wrote the better they began to sound to him. He was becoming more and more involved and would wake up in the middle of the night with another melody he had to score before he forgot it. Stella would listen, sometimes outside his door so as not to disturb his train of thought, and had to admit to herself her man had a talent that should be exploited commercially, playing right in to what she hoped would be a new career, a full time job that would take him away from the CIA and its distance from Key Largo, yet fulfill his creative talents.

As Tom's leg strength returned, he dispensed with the crutches he had depended on for mobility and just used the cane the therapist provided. He had a noticeable limp, but otherwise seemed almost normal for someone who'd had such a delicate bone-fusion operation of his ankle. There would never be any question of gaining any feeling below the knee in that leg, but the constant swimming in the pool gave him the needed release of energy built up by just sitting at the piano or lying in bed listening to the radio. For someone who had lived such an active physical life, he now felt somewhat restrained but that was only a mental attitude, nothing he couldn't overcome.

Even though Missy, the bull mastiff Stella had adopted, stayed close to her, following her around the house, it had never been proven she would come to Stella's assistance if she was attacked or put into a life threatening situation because nothing like that had arisen to date with the lull in Florida's unsolved murders. Stella had begun to relax, no longer carrying a weapon when she made he early-morning trips to the studio over the garages to finish or start anew her paintings and sketches. She was a stickler for maintaining that routine, so any outsider watching from afar with ulterior motives could make plans for an assault with no one the wiser. That damn dog could be taken care of easily enough.

Just such an outsider had been casing the Mueller property for quite some time, just biding his time for action. No able-bodied men had been see by the watcher in the early morning visits and another plus was the absence of law-enforcement officers who had previously been stationed around the perimeter. Therefore, it was an unpleasant surprise to see Tom Mueller with that brute of a dog accompanying his intended victim to the garages one morning, particularly since it was the morning he was primed to make his move. It was like an omen to cease and desist, a bolt of lightening from above warning him, so he faded away toward his chalet to reconnoiter or re-think his scheme. Terry was as sly as a fox when it came to self-preservation, and his instincts had so far kept him from being detected. His glib tongue however he had told so many lies to so many people it was harder and harder for him to remember what was the truth.

"That is one beautiful painting, sweetheart, and you say it was all done from memory?"

Stella nodded, looking at the finished painting from all angles to get a better perception of the interior of Ray Urich's workshop in Shelby, Ohio, where she had first seen his sculptures. "How else could I have done this, honey? There were no pictures available to look at."

"You continue to amaze me, Stella. Your mind is always working on art forms even with all your other responsibilities here." Tom just shook his head in wonderment. What a wonderful woman he had been blessed with, the mother of four beautiful children, and his goddess was still as beautiful and vibrant as the day they first met.

"You look a little peaked, honey; what's the matter?"

"It's just those stairs. It takes a lot out of me just climbing them even though there's the railing to hold on to."

"Maybe you should call Cliff Ajax, and he could hook something up to help you."

"That's a good idea, Stell. I'll do that today right after I call Mr. McHenry."

"Oh, what do you have to talk to him about?"

"It's simply an idea I've been thinking over. I want his advice on how to go about it. He has a lot of clout, you know, not only in agency business but throughout the law enforcement field."

Stella had a look of consternation on her face. "You're not thinking of remaining in that line of work are you, not with your disability, you shouldn't."

"Take it easy, Stell, it's just an idea."

"Don't you honey me, Tom Mueller. I know your way of thinking. You think you're going to wheedle your way with me, well you're wrong this time, mister. I won't stand for it, no sir." And she stamped her foot for emphasis.

"Is it at all possible that when you are angry you're more beautiful than you already are?" Tom grabbed his beautiful wife and kissed her tenderly. Stella melted in his arms as she always did. Who could resist a man like this? An expert lover when his mood was like this. It was all she could do to resist falling on the nearby sofa and tearing his clothes off for a fanciful frolic. Missy the bull mastiff lay across the room completely bewildered. Why couldn't he forget about this agency business, she thought. Tom had all this musical talent and he could make a better living in that field than he ever would in law enforcement. Stella still had the thought of his playing in local clubs, where during the tourist season he could make a fortune in tips alone then eventually opening his own place where he could expand into personalized recordings to spread his fame. She could envision his own club with not only seasonal snowbirds but all Floridians going to for food, drinks, and entertainment. There weren't that many places in the Keys with all those attractions.

Stella's dreams were interrupted by Missy, who was on her feet backing up to her mistress, her hair raised along her back her nose pointing toward the stairs. No sound came from her throat, but her whole demeanor indicated approaching danger of some sort. Stella prodded her husband with her finger over her lips and pointed to the dog. Tom was instantly alert. He knew peril of some sort was approaching.

A sudden high pitched scream resounded in the stairwell, followed by the thump-thump-thump of a body being dragged down the steps. By the time he reached the halfway point of the wall, he saw the reason for all those noises. Terry Connoti was sprawled with Leo's jaws clamped around one leg, blood seeping on the steps. Tom couldn't tell from his angle whose blood it was, but as he neared he almost fell when he stepped on a Jim Bowie knife a good foot long. "Let go of him, Leo. He's not going anywhere." The mastiff let go of the intruder but either wouldn't or couldn't get up off Terry. Upon closer inspection, Tom yelled for Stella. "Come down and help me, Stell. I think he hurt Leo. Maybe between the two of us we can lift him off Terry ,so I can determine how bad he's hurt." Tom knew his old friend was hurt because when he talked lovingly to him and scratched behind his ears he didn't get the usual sloppy kiss reward. It was all the two of them could do with their combined efforts to lever Leo off Terry.

"Stell, I'll take it from here while you go into the house to call the Florida State Police and the vet, the latter first please."

To her credit Stella took off without further question, at a fast lope, for she cared about the mastiff almost as much as her husband did. He was a part of her family as much as the triplets or the new baby.

As luck would have it, the veterinarian arrived first and since he was familiar with Leo, having supplied the Muellers with various medicines for him as he grew older. Leo knew his scent, and even though he was gravely wounded, was docile to his ministrations. Terry had taken a wild backhanded swipe with his large knife when the mastiff grabbed his leg from behind. It was a panicking blow that chopped deeply into Leo's flank, a cut that bled copiously but was non-life threatening. As the vet worked in the cramped stairway, Terry started to regain consciousness. Tom remedied that by delivering a sharp blow to his head with the heavy handle of his cane explaining his action to the vet afterward. "This man was sneaking up the stairs to do bodily harm to me or my wife and since the State Police haven't arrived as yet, I want to make certain he doesn't go anywhere." That explanation didn't even faze the vet he just kept working on Leo.

The vet said, "I've given Leo two shots, one an antiseptic to cleanse the wound, the other an anesthetic to knock him out while he is moved to my truck. I'll take him back to my office to watch over him for infection. I hope the Florida troopers show up soon, as I'll need some strong backs to get him to and into my truck. You're certainly in no shape to help, plus you have to watch over the assailant."

When the troopers showed up, there were three cars with a total of five men. Three of them looked like Japanese sumo wrestlers; they were huge. The sergeant who had called Felix in New Orleans to report back about the fate of his son was again in charge of the detail, and he had an axe to grind when he got to the studio stairway, where Tom, who he'd never met before, was hovering over Terry Connoti. Having already detailed two of the largest men to help transport the large guard dog to the vets truck, the sergeant stood over Tom and Terry with a five-cell flashlight lighting up the scene and listened to Tom's version of what had happened and who the assailant was. One look at the knife lying nearby was enough evidence as far as he was concerned.

"And you say you know this guy?"

"Yes, he's a former high-ranking sheriff's deputy I knew from up north. He and his wife moved down here and built a chalet on some property I owned not too far from here. Little did I realize how deranged he had become, and I have little doubt he could be responsible for the Santana boys murder and God only knows for how many others in this region."

The trooper sergeant was no dummy. He began totaling all the unsolved slayings that had occurred in all of Florida that had been reported. This perp could be responsible for a good number of them. So he took his handcuffs from behind his back and snapped them on the wrist of the suspect before he could regain consciousness, carefully picked up the knife just below the hilt and bagged it, and called in another trooper to collect the evidence and have a squad car standing by to transport the suspect when he woke up. The sergeant was finishing his notes when the suspect began to stir. Terry was groggy but understood they could press charges on any number of counts, so his best defense was to remain silent until he found out what they intended. The sergeant helped him to his feet and not too gently led him out to the waiting squad car, turning him around to frisk him for any other weapons, something that couldn't be done in the stairwell. He was clean except for a snapshot of Stella Mueller taken from some distance and through foliage, incriminating enough under the present circumstances. "What's this? I suppose you are a nature lover taking pictures of birds and Mrs. Mueller just happened to be in the background. You've got a lot to answer for, mister. Get in the rear seat of the car. You're going to be taken to headquarters for further interrogation. Get going, Charlie, and don't dawdle." Still no reply from the suspect, who had a smug expression on his face, which the trooper sergeant would have truly loved to knock off.

When they reached the district headquarters in Homestead, which included barracks for bachelor troopers with all the comforts of a triple-A motel, they put Terry in an isolation cell in the main building where they could watch him continuously through a one-way glass partition. Since Homestead was just north of the Everglades, the humidity outside was like standing under a hot shower when no winds were blowing from The Atlantic or Gulf sides, as was the case this day. However, the main building and barracks were air-conditioned, which made life bearable. A lieutenant was in charge of this district, but he had gone on vacation three days before to New York City, leaving Sergeant Davidson in charge, but with the arrest of this suspect, Davidson was in a dilemma whether to conduct the complete interrogation or to call New York City to summon the return of the lieutenant who was a stickler on proper protocol. Then, too, he would want the credit for cracking the case, so it was a no-brainer. He'd call.

Terry was interrogated for five days before he broke. The district attorney was notified and after listening to the recording of his confession, decided the case was solid enough to indict and to be taken to the grand jury. By this time, his wife was notified of his arrest and confession, but she declined to be present during his upcoming trial, feeling so hurt that she had been deceived for so long that she immediately filed for divorce. Florida's punishment for such a capital crime was death. It was one state among many that felt a long prison term with the high expenses of incarceration was not just punishment. This particular case soon drew national attention, and defense attorneys were clamoring to take the case to gain notoriety for themselves regardless of the outcome. The winner, if you could call him that, was an ambulance-chasing shyster from New York City who was so unscrupulous he couldn't get hired in his home state and was very close to being disbarred there. But Terry was grabbing for straws by this time, possibly seeing the handwriting on the wall.

Meanwhile Tom Mueller's health was improving steadily as he was following the therapists' instructions to the letter and swimming daily in the pool. Leo was home, completely healed and again never let his best human friend too far out of his sight. Their bond tightened all the more after the close call that could have snuffed out both of their lights. Leo was getting up there in doggie years and both Tom and Stella had warned the boys not to expect him to provide rides for them any longer as they grew older and heavier, but every once in awhile the mastiff could be coaxed into the pool where natural buoyancy provided enough resiliency to climb on his back as he dog-paddled across the shallow end. Leo seemed to enjoy that as much as the boys until Tom called a halt to the liveliness. "Let's not wear him out in one day. There'll be other days."

Mr. McHenry got back to Tom about his idea. Tom had to be very careful about what he said because Stella was always near enough to hear his end of the conversation, not that she was intentionally snooping but because a phone call for Tom was rare these days, so Tom had to talk around important points sort of like a code that Mr. McHenry picked up on right away. "I'll see what I can do, Tom. Call me the day after tomorrow at five P.M. sharp. It will take me that long to set it up, and take care of it he did. Instead of Tom taking a full disability pension, he would be given a flat one hundred thousand dollars and remain a sleeper agent to oversee other agencies which would include the FBI, ATF, CIA, and Secret Service. So Tom would have the best of all worlds. His next call was to Cliff Ajax but it wasn't concerning an assist in the studio stairway. He would tell Cliff what he had in mind and ask his advice on how to do it, time to complete, costs, etc. Cliff asked what the time frame was and where would it be. "I'm right in the middle of two other projects, Tom but, of course, you will have priority."

"Give me about three days, Cliff, time for you to finish your projects or farm them out. I still have to discuss this with my wife but I'm saving that for last because there are other facets which are included. I'll get back to you then." Cliff agreed.

When Tom finally got Stella to sit down for a heart to heart talk he didn't pull any punches. First he explained about the $100,000 flat retirement money that was coming to him, sort of paving the way for what she would object to most before she blew her stack when she heard what his new job would entail. So far she just listened, no interruptions. Then he told her what his conversation with Cliff Ajax had been about. "Are you familiar with that abandoned building right off the highway on the right side going South? I think at one time it was called Marathon Plumbing and Heating." Stella just shook her head.

"Well anyhow I'd have to go through it completely with Cliff but maybe it will be suitable for an entertainment night club, a place where I could play solo or with one or two backup men, good guitar and string bass violin say. From the looks outside it has plenty of parking and I saw it on my trips to Key West both on the ground and up in the air flying over it in a helicopter."

Now Stella's eyes were lit up, and she was having a difficult time sitting still. "Do you really mean it, honey? This isn't just another of your pipe dreams is it?"

"No pipe dream, Stella, of course there is a catch."

Stella froze, there was always a catch. "All right let's have it. I knew this was too good to be true." After hearing him out she asked, "You mean you'll still be involved with Mr. McHenry in the agency where you'll be carrying a weapon and be put in harm's way?"

"Not quite, Stella, it's more of an overseers position where agents from other agencies will report their findings to me to pass on, like a central clearing house.

Once everything had been explained to her, Stella did what any loving wife would do, she backed her man to the hilt. Then she began planning how she could best assist him on his venture. She knew he would need a vehicle with some sort of hand controls to assist him in driving since the one leg had no feeling below the knee.

The traffic down Route One seemed heavy for this time of day to Tom who was riding in the passenger seat of the truck owned by Cliff Ajax. It was only ten o'clock in the morning of a Thursday, four days after he first talked to Cliff about the Marathon project. Cliff was his usual taciturn self simply paying attention to his driving. Tom had plenty of time to ponder over how much they accomplish at the old plumbing and heating building on this their first look inside. He had brought a notebook of sketches he'd made, not really knowing the inside dimensions hoping they wouldn't run into a wall which would have to be moved thus endangering the solidity of the entire structure costing more in time and material. Cliff had already obtained the keys from the real-estate agent handling the property so Tom was about to find out first hand – he could only hope.

Tom was pleasantly surprised when they got inside. Other than cobwebs hanging from rafters and a few spider webs, spiders included, the place was in pristine condition, and very few major changes were necessary

"What do you think, Cliff? It doesn't look like you'll have a lot to do as far as varying from these sketches I've drawn. The bandstand will be over against that wall, where a door can be put in just to its left to allow the combos members to get outside on breaks for some fresh air. He didn't mention that couriers from different agencies would be able to drop off pertinent information after a discreet coded knock without having to enter the club, where they might be identified. What Cliff didn't know about wouldn't incriminate him at a later date. They spent three hours in the building while Cliff took every possible measurement he could think of corresponding to the drawings Tom had made without ever having seen the interior of the building and some other changes he wanted after he had. When everything either man could think of was finished, Tom asked his builder if he was hungry?

"I could eat something, I guess."

"If I remember correctly there's a good restaurant on Big Pine Key half way down to Key West from here that serves some great food of all types, not just seafood. If you can spare the time I'd like to try it again. I'm famished." "Sure, Mr. Mueller, if you want."

Seated in the Normandy and furnished with menus, Tom looked around at the seafaring decor of the place. Pictures of the ill-fated vessel the restaurant was named for adorned the walls, exterior and interior, before and after it was used as a troop carrier during the second World War. Any history buff could spend hours taking it all in. That gave Tom another idea for his newly acquired business. He was mulling that over while nautically dressed waitresses skittered among the tables and booths bringing food and refreshing beverages. If they were this busy during the daytime, what was it like in here at night?

Another thing Tom had noticed when they parked in the large lot was a Veterans of Foreign Wars Post across the road on the Atlantic side. Tom had never bothered to join a post when he came back from Korea, mostly because he was so busy playing gigs and womanizing at Ohio State University there weren't enough hours in a day, and night, for much else. However, now might be a good time to join one when he would be so close, not necessarily the one across the road but there had to be others in the Keys.

"How's your steak, Cliff? Tender enough?"

"Practically melts in my mouth."

"Mine too, you can't beat a good ribeye broiled right."

As they were leaving the Normandy, Tom had Cliff swing across the road long enough so he could write down their telephone number listed on their bulletin board near the front entrance. The post didn't seem to be open at this hour, or he would have gone in.

When Cliff dropped Tom off at his home, Leo was right there to greet him, happy that his main friend was back. When Tom entered the main house the children mobbed him immediately, but Stella was nowhere to be seen. "Is she out in the studio?" he asked. No one would volunteer an answer, as if they'd all been sworn to secrecy very unlike their usual gabbiness. "I'm going into the music room for awhile and I expect all of you to behave in my absence." He stared at the two boys. "Got it?" Tom and Freddie knew at once who he was talking about as their father moved away. As Tom settled himself at the spinet not even Sheila his daughter entered with him, another rarity.

Stella had an appointment with a dealer of automobile specialties for the handicapped driver. She took a taxi there so as not to alert Tom of her intentions. Her mission was accomplished in two hours, and she cabbed back to the estate to find ,Tom hard at work at the piano, his fingers flashing over the keys faster than the eyes could follow. Then he would stop to write several notes in the score sheet in front of him before resuming his fast pace. She watched and listened for awhile at an angle where he couldn't see her fascinated by his concentration and technique. His talent was so obvious she wondered why he hadn't pursued a career in the music business instead of going into law enforcement, where the danger of getting hurt or killed was so high. His looks, personality, and talent were a combination that would guarantee instant success coupled with the latest addition of composing new material. Another idea surfaced while she stood there. She wondered if Ray Urich, Tom's newfound brother in Shelby, Ohio, would have any contacts in the publishing business? He had already heard Tom play and understood his talent. If she could pilfer one of his new scores without his missing it for sometime until she could get a copy made and returned the original to his portfolio – she'd give it a try.

In the meantime, Tom had finished his playing and composing and just sat there hands in his lap staring at the keys. He looked exhausted like he'd swam twenty laps in the pool at full speed and had to hold on to the edge for support.

Stella made herself known by clearing her throat in a "ahem" manner. Tom looked up from the keys and smiled in a wolfish manner. "So there you are, none of the kids would tell me so you'd better fess up."

Stella explained where she had been and what she had done. "Since you'll be driving back and forth from your club on Marathon Key, I decided certain changes would have to be made on your wagon so I called a specialist who does that kind of work and took a cab to meet him and tell him what I had in mind. I took Prissy along, knowing none of the other children would know what to do if she started to make a fuss. But she slept both going and returning like the little sweetheart she is. Anyway the cost is minimal and can be completed in three days so I gave them a down payment and set up the appointment. That is my gift to you, honey." Tom had a nonplussed look on his face. It took him several seconds to come up with a reply. "After you feed the mob and bed them down after their lessons are completed and you're ready for bed, I'll express my gratitude for your thoughtfulness in the way we both like best."

"Oh, feeling frisky are you? Do we take a preliminary shower or get right down to business?"

"Your choice, sweetheart, but don't let me go to sleep waiting."

"Oh, I don't know. I do have certain ways to wake you if you think about it" and she gave him that low-pitched dirty laugh that she knew he enjoyed.

"I'm going to take a dip in the pool with Leo to wear him out a bit so he doesn't bother us later."

After he left the music room, Stella realized now was a good time to grab one of his new arrangements and to get it copied at a later date. She felt like a thief as she shuffled through his portfolio and pulled one out. It had no name as yet, but she could leave that up to Ray Urich.

When Ray received the package containing her latest painting of the interior of his workshop and the copy of one of his brothers musical compositions, he was at first amazed at the quality of her painting and then dumbfounded by the sheets of music. He couldn't read a note, yet he knew what to do with it. The club where Tom had played to such raves had expanded its entertainment from one or two nights to four or five, with up and coming vocalists guesting with the different types of groups playing jazz, country western, rock and roll or other combinations. The place was quickly gaining a name for its variety pulling customers in from as far away as Cleveland, Columbus, Toledo, and all points in between all by word of mouth from satisfied patrons who didn't mind driving long distances to hear and dance to what they enjoyed. Presently there was a four piece group from Massillon, Ohio, that played middle of the road songs – no rock and roll – and the singer with them was a knock out colored girl named Georgia Washington who even the local Shelbyites enjoyed. The girl kept the place packed, so it was soon evident she would be retained with whatever group was playing. She told the manager she had no aversion to rock and roll as long as it wasn't a steady diet. The club was so enthralled with her work they paid for a nearby motel room and allowed her two meals daily from their kitchen.

When Ray handed her Tom's sheet music she handed it to her piano player and then hummed along. It was such a lilting melody she put her agile mind to work and within a week she had the finished product. Ray was present when the song now named "Dream Time" was first played for the public. It was a Saturday night, and the club was packed to the rafters. His special invite placed him less than three feet from the stage, and Georgia named him as the brother of the composer of the next selection. As she swung into the heartfelt lyrics of "Dream Time" a sudden hush fell over the crowded club. Georgia was expressing her whole body and soul into this performance, and the patrons and employees were captivated by both her conception and execution of the lovely airs. When she'd finished, complete silence prevailed for about thirty seconds before a tumultuous explosion of applause rocked the building so loudly it could be heard three blocks away, alerting the small police department who thought some sort of riot was taking place in the downtown area.

A publicity promoter happened to be in the small Ohio town that night on his way to Cleveland to hear a new sensation. His company, Decca Recording Co., had given him full reign to sign possible future stars to recording contracts and by coincidence happened to be staying at the same motel which housed Miss Washington. The manager mentioned that fact when he checked in, giving him directions to the popular night club, so he was in attendance when Georgia introduced "Dream Time." He knew an up and comer when he heard one, so after the applause finally died down he made his way to the bandstand to discuss his business with the entertainer. During the course of that he was overheard by Ray Urich. That was the impetus the sculptor needed to promote Tom's song. What did you think of the song itself?"

Georgia introduced the two men to each other saying, "Mr. Urich is a prominent sculptor who lives here in town. He has pieces all over the country and he gave me "Dream Time" that his brother composed. He, by the way lives in southern Florida and is an accomplished pianist", downplaying her part in naming the song and providing the lyrics. He played here once while visiting Ray and I understand he has an open invitation to repeat his performance whenever he makes a return visit."

His gorgeous wife is quite the artist herself" Ray added. "She paints mostly in oils and has a magnificent eye for detail and shading."

"That's all well and good, Mr. Urich, but you must understand I promote artists for recording contracts for Decca Records in New York City, and they don't care about composers or painters."

"I understand, sir but you must have contact with people who do. Wouldn't it be a feather in your cap if say you discovered another Gershwin?"

That gave the promoter pause, and Ray could almost see the wheels turning in his head as he thought what a boon that would be. "Do you have a business card where I can reach you?"

"Sure." And he handed him one, turning to wink at Georgia. Ray was as persuasive as he was creative. Georgia almost laughed aloud at his wit.

52

The Gotcha club was an instant success after Tom Mueller put an advertisement in three newspapers for side men. The response was overwhelming. He had his pick of bass violin players, and guitar players. Several auditions later, he gleaned what he had in mind. The guitar man was an absolute gem, only twenty-five years old, and he also had a beautiful singing voice. Joel Varga was a wonder to behold. Whereas most guitar players used a plastic pick, Joel's fingertips were so conditioned he didn't need one. He'd turned down a scholarship to Juilliard Academy to continue working with a local group in Miami where he could experiment further. Then the stand-up double bass player, Mel Podansky, had a style reminiscent of Eddie Safranski of the Stan Kenton Orchestra. Joel and Mel became permanent fixtures at the club, working five nights a week, Tom soloing the other dates. There was seldom a night when the Gotcha wasn't packed to overflowing and Tom had little time for composing at home. When a new idea struck him, he'd try it out after closing with Joel and Mel. Many nights he never went home but slept on a cot in the   back room office, jerking awake in the middle of he wee hours with a new idea and scoring it before being able to return to sleep. Cliff had installed a shower in the room, where he could sit while bathing.

The Gotcha hadn't been open four months when Stella came down to Marathon with Leo, the mastiff Tom so loved. Since Tom was spending so much time away from home the dog had become a nuisance looking for his main friend. She also had a letter from a Decca Records promoter stating a song Tom had written and performed by Georgia Washington had become a hit nationally – see check enclosed – and he would like to come down to Key Largo to discuss future songs. When would it be convenient?

"What song was that and how did she get it?"

"Oh, honey, give me a little credit; you know how devious I can be. I swiped one of your scores and had it copied then sent it up to Ray in Shelby along with my painting of his workshop and he took it from there. I'm quite concerned about the length of time it took for that Decca Record representative to act on it. That song is just the tip of the iceberg, honey. As long as it's played on jukeboxes and radio, those checks will continue to roll in to you, a nice return for your creativity."

He had composed a total of five new ones his combo was playing, and Joel was singing with lyrics he had dreamt up, so he told his wife to contact the Decca representative and set up a date for him to come down.

Tom decided it was time to tell Stella of his latest idea. "The time is ripe for an expansion," he said. "There won't be any competition. We'll have the ground floor to ourselves. I feel as well physically as just before the armory shooting accident, so health isn't a factor. The start-up cost will be minimal and can be covered by our present club net. My main concern is: am I putting too much of a burden on you? I don't want to interfere with your painting and child-raising responsibilities. I've been thinking about this since we first opened this club. It will be an innovation that can't miss."

"All right, honey, if you feel that strongly about it and can handle the strain, take a stab at it; your ideas usually pan out and we can always pull in our horns if it begins to look shaky. I see by the books the business is on the upswing at Gotcha, so your original idea is bearing fruit and the tourist season hasn't even started yet. By this time next year you'll be free and clear anyway without composing another song."

"I've got three in the works now, and with Joel's help should be completed soon. That promoter from Decca Records should be down here by then and I can spring them on him for his use."

Once the Gotcha's remodeling was finished and the new equipment installed, Tom was more than satisfied with the results but still had other ideas to make the exterior of the building more attractive to the passer-by.

Tom spotted an old upright piano sitting where his spinet had been. It was anything but new. "Where did this antique come from?"

"Mommy bought it for me to practice on," Sheila said. "Isn't it neat?" Tom withheld a laugh and said "Show me how you're doing." She lifted the seat, took several pieces of sheet music out, and hopped up before wiggling her fingers like her daddy did before he started, then swung into a lento passage of "Moonglow." She never missed a note but her fingers weren't long enough yet to get all the left hand chords, so Tom told her to move over so he could take that part. Their playing attracted Stella, who had heard the washer going, then started looking for her husband. She stayed out of sight listening to the duo. When they finished and Tom hugged his daughter, Stella broke into applause. Sheila jumped off the seat and bowed making both her parents wonder if they had another virtuoso in the making.

Tom called home this time to see if the record company promoter had contacted Stella yet, but who should answer the phone but his former long time partner who had been put in charge of the

New Orleans office after Tom's injury. "What are you doing there, Felix? I thought you would still be in New Orleans. Has something happened to Gennie?"

"Naw, she jus' had a baby girl an' McHenry gave me convalescen' leave ta' be with her until she's settled back here. Ya' wanna' talk ta' yer wife?"

It took some time for Tom to get used to Felix Santana's broken English after so long away.

"Well, yes, if she's nearby."

"Hi, honey, isn't that something about Gennie and her new baby? Now Prissy will have a playmate her own age as they grow up together."

"How about Gennie's mental health? That isn't hereditary, I hope; we don't want Prissy subjected to that kind of atmosphere."

"Don't be such an old fuddy-duddy, Tom; it's unlike you to be so. Now, what is the purpose of this call. I'm sure you have one."

"I just wondered if you'd heard from that record company promoter yet? Now that the new sign has been installed I was thinking of having a grand opening, and I'd like him to be present for it, and not just him but you and the children if you could get a competent babysitter for Prissy. You could bring Felix along too if he wanted to come."

"I can call Ray to stir him up, and that's sweet of you, honey, to think of us; I take back what I said about you being trivial. I love you just the way you are. I know Sheila will be thrilled too. I'll let you go so I can call Shelby. I'll get back to you soonest."

"It took four tries before Stella could raise Ray. She'd almost given up when he finally answered. After she had explained what Tom had in mind for his grand opening she then sweet-talked him into using his best effort to get fast results. Ray reacted as she'd hoped. I'll get in touch with him tomorrow first thing. I know how to track him down."

It just so happened Mr. Barry was in New Orleans listening to a new eight piece Dixieland sensation and called the New York City office to set up a recording date an after he finished that business the secretary gave him the message to contact Ray Urich in Shelby, Ohio, before he went anywhere else. "He said it was quite important, Mr. Barry." Barry knew Georgia was already under contract so it had to be that artist-composer down in the Florida Keys. He called Ray when he hung up from the main office and Ray passed on the message from Stella concerning the grand opening of the newly improved and expanded night club that Tom owned on Marathon Key and that featured his trio with vocals by Joel Varga on many of he new songs he had composed. The time and date were passed on an he was urged not to miss it if it were at all possible. He could either stop at Key Largo and be directed from there or go directly to Marathon Key.

Even Stella didn't know about the flyers Tom had had printed and paid people to distribute from South Miami to Key West at businesses, social clubs, pasted on poles and trees, and even on military bases. There were fifteen hundred printed and he expected them all to be posted.

The day of the grand opening found Tom fast asleep, exhausted by all the ballyhooed preliminaries. By three o'clock, Leo who was resting by his cot knew his main friend should be stirring by this time of day, so he put his massive head on Tom's pillow breathing in his face. That brought Tom out of his stupor. For a change, everything seemed to be working out in his favor. The flyers were paying off handsomely. Even before the trio was on stage there wasn't a vacant seat in the building. His children were seated on the side of the stage and Stella had been acting as hostess. Felix was in the kitchen familiarizing with the oven and seeing how many pizzas would be available for him to eat. Mr. Barry arrived on his own, not needing any help in finding the place. Not knowing who the hostess was, he couldn't keep his eyes off her and decided he would chat her up at the first opportunity being a bachelor on the loose. She was a beauty he couldn't resist.

The trio swung into one of Tom's new songs with Joel singing. Tom could tell by the applause it was destined to be a hit and he was all smiles as he winked at Stella who had joined the children. Mr. Barry looked at the children, then the hostess again and could see the resemblance at once. Then he looked at the pianist. He didn't have to be clairvoyant to recognize they were all related, which dashed his hopes for making a play for her, so he concentrated on the music and the individuals playing and singing it. The guitar-vocalist was a winner and the original songs by Mr. Mueller were terrific so his first thought was to team them up with Georgia Washington. She could sing harmony with the guitar man an he thought he'd better sign this group up before any other record company discovered them. At the first intermission, he made his way toward the bandstand confident he could sign them up. He had to dodge young waiters who were delivering drinks and portions of hot pizzas on the quick step so he took his eyes off of the main goal, and by the time he arrived at the stage only the bass man was still there and he was preparing to leave too. Mr. Barry looked around wondering how they disappeared. Where did they go?

Tom had planned to play three sets, each one an hour and fifteen minutes in duration but the crowd seemed to want more they were enjoying themselves so much. After the second set which ran an extra twenty minutes Tom could see both Tom and Mel were starting to wane, he himself was playing on pure adrenaline, yet he knew a crash was inevitable. He turned to his two side men. "Let's give them one more rouser then call it a night. Any suggestions?" "Your choice, Mr. Mueller, anything to get us out of here. I think your patrons got their money's worth tonight."

"Here's one that's always been a favorite of mine, if you don't know it just fake it", and he announced on the public address system, "I went to college at this following song, feel free to sing along if you know the words", and he started the Ohio State University fight song with a flourish.

Felix, the galloping gourmet, had wolfed down two whole pizzas with the works by his lonesome while he was serving the rest of the hungry crowd portions. He most likely would have gone for another, but the stock was depleted. Even with the building expansion, the so-called kitchen was overcrowded what with other appliances, and two bartenders serving drinks in great profusion. There ought to be a better system than this Felix thought to himself.

Stella told Tom she'd better drive the children home because they were all worn out from the excitement plus stuffing themselves with pizzas and soft drinks. "If you're coming home later you can bring Felix; otherwise; I'd better take him home now."

"I'm really tuckered out; sweetheart; and this Barry guy has to be dealt with yet."

"I forgot about him, honey. Don't let him sell you on anything you don't want to do. From what I can see, the Gotcha is about all you can handle for now and it looks profitable. I'll be able to tell you more when I go over the ledgers for the month. Your idea for the pizza oven has certainly panned out. Now what do you want to do about Felix tonight?"

He can stay here, I'll bring him home tomorrow. Hold on a minute, and I'll help you out with the kids. Tom, Jr., and Freddie can take charge of Sheila; you just be careful driving."

Mr. Barry was having an anxiety attack as he watched the Muellers packing up the children to leave, his hopes of signing the group up to a recording contract with Decca Records dwindling as he watched.

"I'll be right back, Mr. Barry, once my wife is on her way."

That statement seemed to assuage his misgivings.

When Tom returned he called to Felix, "You might want to sit in on this partner then I'll take you home tomorrow. He heard Felix talking to Leo. "Get away from me ya' beggar. I ain't got nuthin' fur ya' so don' be stickin' yer nose in where it don' belong."

When Mr. Barry heard him called partner he was puzzled again. He'd thought Mueller owned the club outright.

They finally sat down at a table where Barry could make his pitch. Then the object to whom Felix had been scolding wandered into the room sitting down next to Mueller. It was the biggest damn dog Mr. Barry ever had the displeasure of seeing up close. It just sat there like it was interested in what was to be discussed.

"Now let me explain what I can do for you. Decca Recording Studio in New York City will allow you to record two sides on 45 discs. All you have to do is sign this contract. I personally think Joel, your guitar man, and Georgia Washington the singing sensation from Shelby should sing a duet on one side."

"Who pays our air fare to New York?" Tom asked.

"That's your responsibility for the privilege of being recorded."

Tom told Mr. Barry he'd have to think about it after talking it over with his wife. "She's the bookkeeper and after we put our heads together we'll let you know."

Mr. Barry saw he wasn't going to get anywhere further tonight, this man was too shrewd so all he could do was retreat and lick his wounds.

Tom, Felix, and Leo got back to the estate about 2:45 A.M. and made straight for the kitchen, opening two beers each so they wouldn't have to get up so often.

They were interrupted by the ringing telephone. "Get that will you partner before it wakes up the whole household? Nothing bodes well from a call this time of the morning." And it didn't. It seems that Rocky Newbole who had been sent to Vietnam as a military advisor had been killed by a booby trap and left Tom his worldly goods as his main beneficiary. When Tom, who had been called to the phone, heard this he couldn't believe the man would do that for such a casual friendship.

When Tom hung up he had a dazed expression on his face.

"What, amigo? Ya' look like ya' just been beaned by a baseball."

So Tom explained all he'd been told.

"Can ya' 'magine that? Ya' seem ta' draw good fortune like a magnet. First the emerald, then yer' wife, now this. The rich get richer an' us poor workin' people get nuthin'."

A collection of pre-1900 pistols and rifles interested Tom. They could be invaluable if they were in good firing shape. He couldn't wait to see what the package would contain. Why had Rocky done this? It really wasn't a package but a three hundred plus pound wooden crate that was delivered by truck to the Mueller estate two weeks later. Tom wasn't in residence at the time and Felix had returned to New Orleans to resume his position as director of that office with the capable assistance of his secretary Chris.

Much to the chagrin of Mr. Barry, a lesser known recording company from Columbia, South Carolina had heard about the popular trio at a club on Marathon Key, Florida and sent a representative down to hear and report back her opinion. It was so favorable a follow-up deputy director made the trip to hear for himself and he was amazed that some larger company hadn't already subscribed the group which he did on the spot. He met all of Tom's specifications to make the recordings live at the Gotcha night club, to advertise in advance, and explain all the other sundry elements of the business without having to sign any contract. Mr. Guy also informed Tom of his portion of net profit on every record sold which raised Tom's eyebrows. The club itself was turning such a profit it would be completely paid off, including the Ajax remodeling, by the end of the tourist season and with what Mr. Guy had just told him everything was coming up a bed of roses.

Sometimes, usually Friday and Saturday nights, there was a quintet, including Johnny Stoner, who could play trumpet, trombone, and fleugel horn, and Lisa Toth on marimbas – with four-part harmony sung by Joel, Tom, Lisa, and Mel the bassist. They were an instant success, mostly because the numbers they sang were popular with young married couples who found the Gotcha romantic before they were tied down by children and had to stay closer to home.

A full-time cook was added as new items were added to the menu, another crowd pleaser.

Stella had sold four more paintings during this period and two more were hanging inside the Gotcha with price tags Tom thought were exorbitant, yet one of which had already been sold to a well-to-do tourist.

When the shipping crate from Rocky Newbole was pried open, Tom found more than just the antique weapons. How Rocky had ever accumulated all of it and where remained a mystery. Another priceless item, a jeweled Incan knife from Peru, a 16th century Spanish conquistador helmet, and a deed with perpetually paid taxes to eighty acres of farmland outside of Hispania, California. The diversity of the contents were mind-boggling to the extreme.

"You're going to need a pretty large safety deposit box for all that, honey," Stella said facetiously.

"Yes, the eighty acres alone will take up most of the space" Tom retorted. Two can play that game, he thought with a smirk on his face. "We'll have to find some time to go out to California to decide what we're going to do with that land. Sell it or develop it."

"I don't know when you're going to find that time with your present work schedule."

"I'll think of something sweetheart."

"You usually do. In the meantime let's go to bed."

"It's the middle of the day."

"So?" and she laughed with that deep throated pitch she knew excited her man.

The end - or just the beginning?

The year 1975 found the Tom Mueller family of Key Largo, Florida prospering beyond even the patriarchs vivid imagination. Tom and his painter wife had just returned from a fact finding trip to Hispania, California, where they had finalized plans for subdividing eighty acres of prime land into quarter-acre lots, costing according to location, upward of twenty-five thousand dollars. The land had lain dormant and fertile for ten years since the Mueller family had inherited it from Rocky Newbole who had been killed in Vietnam acting as an advisor for the CIA. Rocky and Tom went back twenty years when they were recruited into the Agency. Tom first, Rocky later.

Leo died a year earlier and they buried him four feet from the studio where the dog had saved their bacon from Terry Connoti's knife, putting an engraved marker saying "Rest in peace, old friend. You will be sorely missed by the whole Mueller family." There was no way to replace the mastiff in their hearts, so they hadn't bought another dog. Tom Mueller was the most heartbroken. The dog was almost human and they had been together for such a long time. When Felix Santana heard he was speechless for once. As much as he scolded Leo, he had a benevolent regard for him too.

The triplets were growing fast, home schooling was now out of the question for several reasons.

The main one was Stella no longer had the time to devote as her paintings were a hot commodity, their value increasing by the year, plus the fact her range of topics were no longer suitable for those three, so they took aptitude tests at the local high school where all three were enrolled as sophomores. They were not only smart but popular with their new classmates. Of course Freddie was still a cutup but he too had found his niche among his peers despite many trips to the deans office and notes of warnings of after regular school hour detentions. Those notes he always purposely lost and phone calls from the school he erased from the answering machine. He had a certain charm about him that was contagious to adults and was forgiven for many transgressions. Sheila, though diminutive compared to her brothers, had turned into a real beauty. Although she was much chased by good looking boys, she was mostly interested in her piano studies. She was usually followed home by a beau hopeful who would carry her books just to be seen with her and perhaps get a kiss. But she would only pat his face saying, "Later," then rush into the main house, do her homework, and have dinner before going into the music room and her upright. Even though she was small the constant work with her agile fingers grew to the point where she could reach full chords with both hands.

AUTHOR'S NOTE: *Many people helped in the writing and production of this book, especially members of VFW Post 2510, who offered advice, research, computer assistance, and other support. My heartfelt thanks go to Rocky Newbold, Bernard Andrews, Dan Cannode, Homer Brickey, Tom Gearhart, and others too numerous to mention here. Those who helped know who they are. Thanks again.*